FARLEY MOWAT was born in Belleville, Ontario, in 1921, and grew up in Belleville, Trenton, Windsor, Saskatoon, Toronto, and Richmond Hill. He served in World War II from 1940 until 1945, entering the army as a private and emerging with the rank of captain. He began writing for his living in 1949 after spending two years in the Arctic. Since 1949 he has lived in or visited almost every part of Canada and many other lands, including the distant regions of Siberia. He remains an inveterate traveller with a passion for remote places and peoples. He has twenty-five books to his name, which have been published in translations in over twenty languages in more than sixty countries. They include such internationally known works as *People of the Deer*, *The Dog Who Wouldn't Be*, *Never Cry Wolf*, *Westviking*, *The Boat Who Wouldn't Float*, *Sibir*, *A Whale for the Killing*, *The Snow Walker*, *And No Birds Sang*, and *Virunga: The Passion of Dian Fossey*. His short stories and articles have appeared in *The Saturday Evening Post*, *Maclean's*, *Atlantic Monthly* and other magazines.

P9-DFB-464

Books by Farley Mowat

People of the Deer (1952, revised edition 1975)
The Regiment (1955, new edition 1973)
Lost in the Barrens (1956)
The Dog Who Wouldn't Be (1957)
Grey Seas Under (1959)
The Desperate People (1959, revised edition 1975)
Owls in the Family (1961)
The Serpent's Coil (1961)
The Black Joke (1962)
Never Cry Wolf (1963, new edition 1973)
Westviking (1965)
The Curse of the Viking Grave (1966)
Canada North (illustrated edition 1967)
Canada North Now (revised paperback edition 1976)
This Rock Within the Sea (with John de Visser)
(1968, reissued 1976)
The Boat Who Wouldn't Float
(1969, illustrated edition 1974)
Sibir (1970, new edition 1973)
A Whale for the Killing (1972)
Wake of the Great Sealers
(with David Blackwood) (1973)
The Snow Walker (1975)
And No Birds Sang (1979)
The World of Farley Mowat, a selection
from his works (edited by Peter Davison) (1980)
Sea of Slaughter (1984)
My Discovery of America (1985)
Virunga: The Passion of Dian Fossey (1987)

Edited by Farley Mowat

Coppermine Journey (1958)

The Top of the World Trilogy

Ordeal by Ice (1960, revised edition 1973)
The Polar Passion (1967, revised edition 1973)
Tundra (1973)

FARLEY MOWAT
Tundra

Selections from the Great Accounts of Arctic Land Voyages

with illustrations and maps

This is Volume III of
The Top of the World trilogy

M&S

An M&S Paperback from
McClelland & Stewart Inc.
The Canadian Publishers

An M&S Paperback from McClelland & Stewart Inc.
First printing July 1989

Cloth edition printed 1973
Trade paperback (revised) edition printed 1977
Collector's edition printed 1980

Canadian Cataloguing in Publication Data

Main entry under title:

Tundra

(M&S paperback)
(The Top of the world ; 3)
Includes bibliographical references and index.
ISBN 0-7710-6688-0

1. Arctic regions — Discovery and exploration.
2. Northwest, Canadian — Discovery and exploration.
3. Voyages and travels. 4. Canada, Northern —
Discovery and exploration. I. Mowat, Farley, 1921–   .
II. Series: Mowat, Farley, 1921–   . The top of
the world ; 3.

G620.T86 1989   917.19'904   C88-094998-8

Cover design by Pronk & Associates
Interior maps by Catherine Farley

Typesetting by Compeer Typographic Services Ltd.
Printed and bound in Canada

I wish to thank Mr. Alan Cooke and Mrs. Lily Miller for the great help they gave me in preparing this volume.

McClelland & Stewart Inc.
The Canadian Publishers
481 University Avenue
Toronto, Ontario
M5G 2E9

For the People of the Deer Whose
Land It Was

Maps
Tracing Routes
of the Explorers

Illustrations

A 32-page section of illustrations
appears after page 216.

Contents

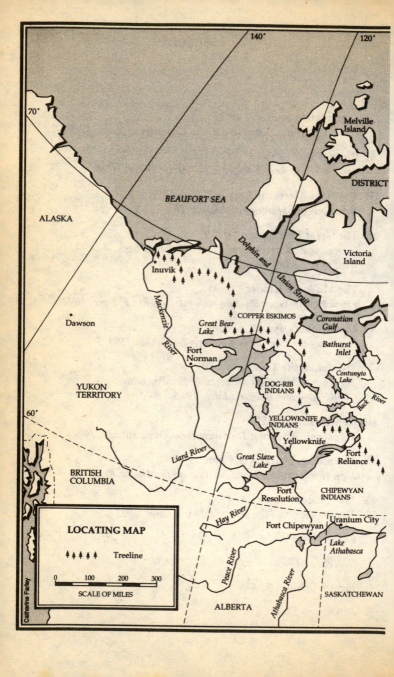

FOREWORD

In recent times North Americans have tended to ignore the almost limitless expanse of sea and land which comprises the northern reaches of their continent except to think of it as a frozen treasure house of natural resources.

It has not always been so. Until fifty or sixty years ago the Arctic was a living reality to North Americans of every walk of life. It had become real, and it stayed real for them because men of their own kind were daring its remote fastnesses in search of pure adventure, unprotected by the elaborate mechnical shields that we now demand whenever we step out of our air-conditioned sanctuaries. Press and magazines followed the fortunes of these men with a good deal more honest enthusiasm than that with which they now follow the exploits of space travellers. Personal accounts of arctic voyages and journeys lined the shelves of book shops. Those who stayed at home identi- fied themselves with arctic travellers, as they can no longer truly identify themselves with the mechanical heroes of modern times.

Most of those great tales of human venturing into the Arctic (and they are legion) are no longer current or avail- able. The majority of the original books are out of print and a good many of them are so rare they are not even to be found on public library shelves but are kept in special rooms where they are available only to the eyes of scholars.

It has long been my belief that these chronicles of high endeavour retain a powerful and essential validity for modern man. In the late 1950's I set myself the task of shaking the dust from some of them and of finding a way to restore them to the mainstream of human experience. The answer seemed to lie in gathering, editing and publishing a coherent collection of the most meaningful accounts of exploration and travel in the North American arctic regions. This collection — which now comprises the trilogy, *The Top of the World* — was designed to provide us with an insight into the true nature of the northern world, while at the same time demonstrating the magnitude and grandeur of human endeavour in that hard environment. It was not, and is not, intended to be a history of the exploration of the North American Arctic. Rather it is the varied tale of how many individual men grappled with and came to terms with the great polar adversary. It brings the quality of these men into sharp focus so that we recognize them as superb animals, imbued with that innate strength derived from struggle with physical adversity, to which we owe ascendancy over all other forms of life.

This is an ascendancy we may be throwing away. Almost insensibly we appear to be drifting toward a biological condition which can make of us a species of unshelled blobs of protoplasm relying wholly for our survival on the mechanical maintenance of a grossly artificial, and fearfully vulnerable, environment. Witness one of our new supermen — an astronaut, the hero of our times — wombed in his gleaming layers of machinery and about as essential to the success of the electronically controlled robot that carries him as was the chimpanzee that so recently preceded him. If he is not yet completely superfluous to the machine, he is nearly so; and in the near future will be totally so. This is a matter of the flesh, but it is also becoming very much a matter of the spirit. When, and if, man comes to regard himself as being in effect an alien entity in the ancient world that formed him, then he will have become the ultimate egomaniac, imprisoned in an infinitely fragile bubble-world of his own contriving — and unquestionably doomed.

Although the selections in my trilogy are not intended to persuade modern man that he must completely divest himself of his technical proficiency and crawl back into a neolithic cave, they *are* designed to remind him, through the lips, eyes and ears of his fellows of a few short decades ago (fellows who are already beginning to have a strangely foreign look about them), that he dare not put all his future into the keeping of the machine. I hope they will suggest to him that he would be wise to retain the primal virtues of a tough, unflinching, physically competent, durable and daring animal in his own right, and *of* the world that spawned him. It is certain that we need a recognition of this truth if we are not to go over the evolutionary peak and down the sharp decline leading to the immense graveyard of other species that armoured themselves too heavily against the physical danger and challenges, and the reality, of the world around them.

In *Ordeal by Ice* (1960) I dealt with man's efforts, between 1576 and 1906, to force a sea passage through the ice barriers blocking the water routes to the north of the continent, and to find a way to link Europe with Cathay and the East. This ancient dream was one of surprising strength and viability. It gripped the imaginations of Europeans through at least four centuries and it impelled innumerable men and ships into the north-western reaches to endure the trials posed by a frozen ocean.

The Polar Passion (1967) begins shortly before *Ordeal by Ice* leaves off. By about 1850 the dream of finding a usable Northwest Passage was almost dead. Interest in the

Arctic had shifted to the pursuit of a new chimera — the North Pole. This also was a development from a much older dream — that of being able to sail direct to China across the very top of the world. The search for the North-west Passage had been rooted in commercial motives; the struggle to reach the Pole was fuelled by national pride — chauvinism, really — coupled with a burning sense of mission on the part of a handful of almost unbelievably intrepid seekers after fame.

Tundra (1973) deals with the European penetration of the gigantic arctic land mass stretching north from timber line and occupying the top of the continent west of Hudson Bay. This vast expanse of frozen wastes posed almost as great a challenge to the passage of European man as did the polar seas, or the ice-clogged channels between the arctic islands.

These stories are linked by many common elements, but one of them in particular deserves special mention. The European explorers were never the first arrivals on the scene. Ages before their coming the Arctic had become an abiding home to men — to the Eskimos and the high latitude Indians, and to their forbears who, as early as six thousand years ago, had mastered the arctic environment despite (or it may have been because of) the limitations imposed by a stone-age technology. Their story remains unwritten, for they had no written language; but elements of it are reflected in the accounts of all European venturers into our northern regions. Their story is integral to the other accounts since, without the physical assistance of the native peoples, and without the object lessons in adaptation provided by them, most European accomplishments in the Arctic would have been impossible. This is by no means a minor theme. The Eskimo and the Indian were, and are, a living symbol of the tremendous flexibility and the enduring qualities which are man's birthright, and which any species, whether man or mouse, must nurture if it is to maintain its place on the implacable and unforgiving evolutionary treadmill.

The problems involved in assembling the materials for this project have been formidable. One was the fact that we have been so careless with the stuff of history that we have allowed many of the original accounts of arctic venturing prior to the sixteenth century to vanish utterly. I have therefore had the choice of ignoring this vast section of the story or of overtly intruding myself into it by writing my own account of the events of that obscure period. I chose the second solution. By gathering the facts that do exist, and by filling in the gaps, I have provided at least a shadow picture of the achievements of many long-forgotten men.

Another problem was that some of the older chroniclers wrote in a style that is hard for a modern reader to follow. I have therefore presented such accounts using modern spelling, phraseology and punctuation, wherever there was the possibility that the style or idiom would make easy comradeship between the original author and the modern reader difficult, if not impossible.

Still another difficulty lay in the fact that there was a good deal of repetition in the chronicles. If I had reprinted each account in full, the sheer bulk of the material would have required scores of volumes, and many of the stories would have differed, one from the other, only in detail. So I have selected those parts of each chosen voyage which are particularly revealing, and have condensed or eliminated repetitive material, sometimes substituting brief bridging paragraphs to maintain the narrative flow.

Then there was the primary problem of deciding which of the many accounts I was to include. My decision in every case is arbitrary. I have never hesitated to ignore famous voyagers in favour of little-known ones who I felt were particularly deserving of recognition.

The foregoing is in no sense an apology for the liberties I have taken with other men's works. It is merely a warning that these selections are to be read for what they are — the moving, sometimes humorous, often tragic accounts of enduring men in conflict. Scholars, and those who are interested in the minutiae of history, should go to the original sources.

PROLOGUE

Sprawled across the upper mainland of Canada lies a tremendous tract of treeless tundra plains that, for centuries, has been known to people of European stock as the Barren Grounds, the Barren Lands, or simply the Barrens. West of Hudson Bay the Barrens form an immense triangle whose apex touches the Alaska-Yukon border at the Beaufort Sea. The long, northern arm of this triangle stretches east and west some fourteen hundred miles along the arctic coast between the Beaufort Sea and Hudson Bay. The southern arm runs fourteen hundred miles diagonally south-east, north-west, between the mouth of the Mackenzie River and Churchill, Manitoba. The base of the triangle runs north and south along the west coast of Hudson Bay between Churchill and Repulse Bay.

The mainland tundra of Canada embraces better than *half a million square miles* of naked, rolling, lake-dotted plains broken here and there by ranges of worn-down hills and vast regions of frost-shattered grey rock and gravel. To an observer in a small aircraft droning for endless hours over this seemingly illimitable space, the tundra seems to be almost as much a world of water as of land. Its lakes, ponds and rivers are beyond counting. Seen from the air the land between appears to be dun-coloured, monochromatic, apparently featureless, reaching to the horizon on all sides with an illusion of terrible monotony.

This is strictly an illusion. Look closer and the void of land and water becomes an intricate and living mosaic, varied and colourful. The multitudes of tundra ponds are shallow and reflect the pale northern skies in every shade of blue and violet or, discoloured by the organic stains of muskeg water, they become sepia, burnished copper, burning red or shimmering green. The numberless rivers run no straight courses but twist tortuously through chocolate-brown muskegs or between silver-grey ridges of stone and gravel (the moraines of the vanished glaciers) or compete in pattern-making with the meandering embankments of sandy eskers (the casts of dead rivers that once flowed under the melting ice sheet). Some eskers roam for hundreds of miles and bear a disconcerting appearance of being the constructions of a long-forgotten race of manic giants.

Viewed by a summer traveller on the ground, the tundra gives the feeling of limitless space, intensified until one wonders if there can be any end to this terrestrial ocean whose waves are the rolling ridges. Perhaps nowhere else in the world, except far out at sea, does a man feel so exposed. On this northern prairie it is as if the ceiling of the world no longer exists and no walls remain to close one in.

In winter this sea-simile gains even greater weight, for then both land and water vanish, blending into one impassive sweep of frozen undulations that seems to have no shore.

The climate of the northern prairies is not so very different from that of their southern counterparts. Winter is longer on the tundra but not a great deal colder than on the Saskatchewan plains. Summer is shorter, but the sun shines throughout most of every 24-hour period and during summer days the northern plains can become uncomfortably hot. Soil is scanty, but the long summer day helps make up for that and growth is fast and lush. As on the southern prairies, precipitation, both rain and snow, is light; but in the tundra where the soil is shallow, permafrost ever-present and evaporation slow, this hardly matters.

Why these mighty plains should have been called "barren" is hard to understand. Even if the word is only intended to mean treeless, it is not entirely valid. Along the entire southern fringe there are trees, small and stunted it is true, but trees. And scattered over the southern half of the northern prairies are islands of timber. One of these, on the Thelon River and almost dead centre in the plains, forms a timbered oasis forty or fifty miles in length, with some single trees growing thirty feet in height. If "barren" is meant to mean barren of life it is a gross misnomer. True, in winter there is not much life to be seen, but in summer the tundra is vividly alive.

For the most part the land is covered with a rich carpet of mosses, lichens, grasses, sedges, and dwarf shrubbery. The flowers are small, many of them minute, but they grow in fantastic abundance. Even on the naked ridges and on the frost-riven graveyards of broken stone that lie between some of the muskeg valleys, there is brilliant life; the rocks glow with the splashed kaleidoscope of lichens in a hundred shades.

Animate life is just as abundant. The ponds, muskegs and lakes are the breeding grounds for innumerable ducks, geese and wading birds. The dry tundra and the rock tundra are the habitat of the northern grouse called ptarmigan, and of innumerable other birds. Snowy owls nest on the grassy flats and rough-legged hawks and falcons share the pale sky with the uncompromising raven which, almost alone among arctic animals, refuses to change his colour when winter whiteness obliterates the world. The waters of the larger lakes (those that do not freeze to the bottom in winter) and, in summer, the rivers too are full of white fish, lake trout (forty-pounders are not uncommon), suckers and a flamboyant and peculiar fish — a distant relative of the trout — called grayling.

Insects there are in quantity — a mixed blessing, for although it is pleasant to see butterflies and bumblebees it is not so pleasant to cope with the hordes of mosquitoes and black flies that, particularly in the more southerly regions, can make life hell on windless days. Fortunately, there are few totally windless days in the tundra and, in any case, the flies are not a great deal worse than they are in parts of the southern forest regions where Canadians delight to spend their summer holidays.

It is the mammals that dominate the land. During the peak periods of their cycles, short-tailed, mouse-like lemmings are so abundant that one can hardly walk across the sedge and moss without sending them scuttling clumsily from underfoot. They provide the chief food of the white fox whose cycle of abundance is keyed to theirs. Lemmings know nothing about birth control. They breed so prolifically that every four or five years they literally eat and crowd themselves out of house and home and then must either die or migrate elsewhere — and such migrations are fatal for most of them.

Even squirrels live on the tundra — gaudy, orange-coloured ground squirrels that den in the sandy eskers or on dry gravel ridges, where the perpetual frost does not deny them entry to the ground.

The great white wolves, once abundant, display an amiable curiosity, visiting human campsites to sit with cocked ears as they watch the inscrutable activities of men.

One of the most impressive of all the tundra beasts is the great brown bear called the Barren-Land grizzly. Only a few decades ago this shambling giant roamed over most of the mainland tundra west of Hudson Bay, but now, like so many other species that have roused our murderous appetites, he has become so rare as almost to be just a memory.

Equally strange is the musk-ox — a black, stolid beast

20

that looks like a cross between a bull and a huge shaggy goat (actually it is related, distantly, to both). Slow and placid but armed with sweeping horns, the musk-oxen have evolved the tactic of forming a hollow square when threatened. Because of their fine underlying wool, the wildest winter weather cannot affect them. They have no real enemies save man, and in other times they called almost the entire tundra, both on the mainland and on the islands, home. But by the mid-twenties they had been exterminated from most of their range.

By far the most impressive of all the tundra beasts is the caribou. Caribou have literally provided the lifeblood of the human residents of the northern plains and of the taiga since time immemorial. These cousins of the reindeer formerly existed in such huge herds that they approached in numbers the buffalo of the southern prairies and probably outnumbered any of the great herd beasts of Africa. When Europeans first arrived on the edge of the northern prairie there may have been as many as five million caribou. Caribou and their predators, chiefly wolves, and the native peoples, had lived together in balance for uncounted ages. We changed all that. In 1949, after Ottawa had finally taken notice of the terrible destruction of these northern deer, an aerial survey showed that only about 650,000 remained alive. By 1955 there were estimated to be about 280,000. By 1960 there were estimated to be fewer than 200,000, most of them west of Hudson Bay.

Men came early to the tundra plains. Along the ancient gravel beaches that now cling crazily to hillsides three hundred feet above the shrunken levels of existing lakes, quartz flakes lie in profusion, and the broken points made by clumsy or unlucky workmen keep them company. They are as fresh-appearing now as when men gave them their present form, for no leaves have fallen to bury them in detritus; and the long winters have covered them with nothing more permanent than snow.

Little is known about these first comers except that they were plains dwellers; probably reindeer hunters out of the Asian north who may have entered the Amerian continent along the narrow defile of tundra lying between the Brooks Range in Alaska and the polar sea. Reaching the mouth of the Mackenzie River, these plainsmen found a new world waiting to be occupied, a world which was almost identical in character to what they must have known in Asia.

Over the centuries new waves of nomads entered these arctic prairies until, by about 1700, the tundra seems to have been mainly held by Eskimos of an ancient inland culture, while to the south of them, in the thin border forests of the taiga, people of the Athapascan race (notably the Chipewyan, Copper and Dog-Rib Indians) lived apart, for the two peoples were hostile to one another. Nevertheless, the inland Eskimos and the taiga Indians were closely linked in that caribou was the mainstay of their lives.

Early in the eighteenth century all this began to change. White traders had appeared on the southern prairies, bringing guns which they traded to the southern plains Indians. These people, of Cree stock, began to wage modern war with their new weapons and they brought great pressure to bear on the taiga people who were then armed only with bows, spears and slings. Within a very few years this pressure drove the Athabascan Indians right out onto the open tundra and into bitter conflict with the inland Eskimos. Then the Chipewyans, in their turn, made contact with the white men and got guns, and soon they drove the tundra Eskimos into the most northerly reaches of the land.

This was how things stood when Europeans first approached the borders of the Barren Grounds. Most of the early visitors were not interested in exploring the formidable wastelands, but were concerned, rather, with trying to find a way around, or through, the plains in order to open a route to Asia — a Northwest Passage. In 1719, James Knight, an ageing Governor of the Hudson's Bay

Company which, in that period, had no establishments north of timber line, sailed out of James Bay north up the west coast of Hudson Bay as far as Marble Island. But here his ships were wrecked, and he and his whole party perished.

In 1741–42, Captain Middleton, R.N., extended the probing and discovered Wager Bay, one of two great inlets thrusting westward into the tundra from Hudson Bay. Then, in 1761 and 1762, Captain Christopher of the Hudson's Bay Company discovered and explored the second, Chesterfield Inlet, and followed it two hundred miles westward to the extremity of Baker Lake. However, neither of these voyages was directed at exploring the land itself.

The first European to attempt to penetrate the western tundra by land was a young man named Henry Kelsey, who had assisted in the establishment of the first Hudson's Bay Company post at the mouth of the Churchill River. In 1688, accompanied by a "Northern Indian" (a Chipewyan, as opposed to the "Southern Indians" who were the Crees with whom the Company had dealt in James Bay for many years), Kelsey walked perhaps 150 miles north-west from the mouth of the Churchill. He met no other human beings, but his guide became terrified of encountering the inland Eskimos and so Kelsey turned back.

The first attempt to build a post at Churchill proved abortive and the site was abandoned in 1689. However, in 1715 the Company dispatched one of its apprentices, William Stewart, in company with a strong party of Southern Indians guided by a Northern Indian woman, to go north from York Factory in James Bay, and make contact with the tundra people.

Winter overtook the party on the Barrens and these strangers from the forested lands found it hard to hold on to life. On one occasion they starved for eight days and were finally forced to eat their dogs. Eventually they stumbled on a camp of the Northern Indians. It contained only dead men, who had been slaughtered by a band of raiding

Crees. The Northern Indian woman insisted on pressing on alone, and after some days she returned to the death camp accompanied by over a hundred of her people, so that a firm contact was at last established between the traders and the tundra dwellers. Stewart's party regained York Factory in May of the following year.

Lured by the prospects of a new fur trade, the Hudson's Bay Company returned to the mouth of the Churchill River in 1717. It was not fur alone that drew the Company north. It was also attracted by reports (from the Northern Indians) of fabulous mines of copper, and perhaps of gold, lying no great distance to the north-west of Churchill River. It was the rumoured existence of these mines that was to lead European man into the heart of the tundra wilderness.

There were three possible approaches to the great plains. The eastern one was from the coast of Hudson Bay. It was the first to be attempted. The second was a north-easterly approach from Great Slave Lake and the Mackenzie River. The third was due north through the forests of what is now northern Saskatchewan.

The forcing of all three approaches requires more than a hundred years, and during that long period many changes took place within the tundra world. These changes, and the nature of the struggle to conquer the tundra, are reflected in the ten accounts contained in this book.

Throughout this volume the passages set in italics are those of Farley Mowat.

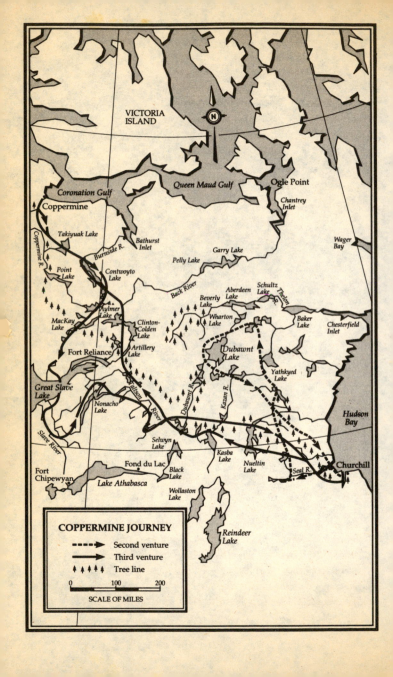

VICTORIA
ISLAND

N

Coronation Gulf

Queen Maud Gulf

Ogle Point

Coppermine

Chantrey
Inlet

Takiyuak Lake

Bathurst
Inlet

Wager
Bay

Coppermine R.

Burnside R.

Garry Lake

Point
Lake

Contwoyto
Lake

Pelly Lake

Back River

MacKay
Lake

Aylmer
Lake

Clinton-
Colden
Lake

Beverly
Lake

Aberdeen
Lake

Schultz
Lake

Thelon R.

Baker
Lake

Chesterfield
Inlet

Wharton
Lake

Fort Reliance

Artillery
Lake

Dubawnt
Lake

Yathkyed
Lake

Great Slave
Lake

Nonacho
Lake

Hanbury River

Dubawnt R.

Kazan R.

Hudson
Bay

Slave River

Selwyn
Lake

Kasba
Lake

Nueltin
Lake

Churchill

Fort
Chipewyan

Fond du Lac

Black
Lake

Lake Athabasca

Wollaston
Lake

Seal R.

Reindeer
Lake

COPPERMINE JOURNEY

- - - → Second venture
———→ Third venture
🌲🌲🌲🌲 Tree line

0   100   200
SCALE OF MILES

I

Coppermine Journey

SAMUEL HEARNE'S EXPEDITION TO THE COPPERMINE RIVER, 1769–72

On a summer day in 1947, with two companions, I was crossing the arm of a great lake called Angikuni which lies in the heart of the Keewatin Barren Lands. The sun beat down upon us with the furious intensity it reserves for summer in high northern latitudes, and there was no escape from it, for the surrounding lands were as naked as a flayed carcass. We paddled slowly across a windless reach and the uninhabited shores faded behind us into a void of pallid waters from which the massive sun had sucked all colour and vitality.

Straining my eyes under the sun's glare I saw an island ahead of us upon whose crest a low pyramid rose like a beacon from a waste of frost-shattered and malignant rocks. We paddled toward it, and when we reached the shore we saw that others had landed here before us. Through the millennia the herds of caribou which are the life-blood of this land had used this island (which lies in

*the middle of a narrow strait) as a stepping-stone during
their passages to and from the distant forests to the south.
They had not always passed unscathed. Across the crest
ran a line of up-ended granite slabs placed in such a
manner as to turn the herds toward rock-built ambuscades
intended to conceal Eskimo archers. Nor had the Eskimos
been the only ones to take advantage of this hunting site.
Wedged in a crevice of the rocks we found a roll of brittle
birch bark, doubtless intended for canoe repairs, which
must have been carried north more than three hundred
miles from the edge of the forests by nomadic Chipewyan
hunters.*

*We climbed from the shore to the crest and reached
the pyramid. It was a cairn standing about six feet tall
which, in its careful regularity, dominated the chaotic
world about us. It bore no kinship to the scanty traces of
themselves which the native peoples had left upon these
empty plains. Beyond doubt, it was the work of a white
man — and the proof was there. Under a flat rock at the
base of the cairn we found the rotted fragments of a small
oak casket.*

*In that moment I had a sudden vision of a European
trudging eastward over an endless plain, like a pariah, in
the wake of a band of nomad Indians who had cast him off.
I saw him at this island, waiting while the Indians feasted,
and putting in the hours raising this symbol of his indomitable spirit. In my mind's eye I watched him write a laconic
description of his plight before he once again took up the
hard uncertainty of his survival in this tundra world.*

*Some months earlier I had read this man's name where
he had engraved it with his own hands upon the grey rocks
at the mouth of the Churchill River, on Hudson Bay. Unlike
the now-vanished words in the cairn at Angikuni Lake, the
rock-carved words have remained exactly as they were
inscribed during an idle summer's day two years before his
great adventure was begun.*

S*ʳ* Hearne
July ye 1, 1767

It was indeed a great adventure. Between 1769 and 1772 Samuel Hearne explored more than a quarter of a million square miles of the tundra plains that cap this continent. He was the first European to see the mighty sweep of arctic coast stretching westward from Hudson Bay to the Siberian seas. With no company other than that of often reluctant, and sometimes hostile, Indians, he walked close upon five thousand miles through a land so difficult that some of Hearne's major areas of discovery were not revisited by white men until the 1920's.

His accomplishments as an explorer are spectacular enough, but they do not properly display the full stature of the man. The living features of an unknown country—those aspects that ebb and flow with the impermanence of life itself—are the true revelations of the nature of new worlds; but it takes genius to capture them and to preserve them for future eyes and minds to wonder at. Hearne had this genius. He was able to defeat the years and to bequeath to us a living moment out of a vanished time. Hearne was the Marco Polo of the Barren Lands.

Samuel Hearne was born in London, England, in 1745. When he was three his father died and his mother took him to Dorset where she did her best to give him a gentleman's education. But not even the heavy-handed school masters of the day could make the boy take an interest in scholastic studies, and the only thing he showed real aptitude for was drawing. His mother tried to interest him in the world of business, but the grubby stink of money had no appeal to young Hearne. He wanted to go to sea; and he had his way.

He was eleven years old when he boarded the flagship of Captain (later Lord) Hood as Hood's servant boy. Within

*the year he had taken part in a brisk battle with the French
and had been awarded prize money. When peace brought
an end to opportunities for excitement and promotion in
the Royal Navy, Hearne left the Service and, in 1766, at
the age of twenty-one, he joined the Hudson's Bay Company. In August of that year he arrived at Prince of Wales
Fort at the mouth of the Churchill River, on the west coast
of Hudson Bay.*

*During the next two years he served as mate of the
sixty-ton sloop* Churchill *engaged in trading with the Eskimos up the west coast as far as Marble Island. Hearne
liked the work, and liked the land, but he grew restive in
the constricted atmosphere of the Fort and began to agitate
for a commission which would give him greater scope for
adventure and achievement.*

*The grey-eyed, fair-haired, lightly built young Eng-
lishman, who had already seen more adventure than is
most men's lot in a long lifetime, was to find what he was
seeking, in full measure.*

*The selections from Hearne's book begin as he sets out on
the second of his attempts to reach the Coppermine River.
The first had been doomed by the stupidities of the Governor of Prince of Wales Fort, Moses Norton, and had
achieved very little. The second journey began under better
auspices but in ferocious weather. February is* not *a pleasant month for arctic travel. The Southern Indians accompanying Hearne were Crees from the vicinity of York
Factory. The Northern Indians were Chipewyans. "Deer"
were, of course, caribou.*

A JOURNEY TO THE NORTHERN OCEAN

The Northern Indians, who range over the immense tract
of land lying north and west of the Churchill River, very
often brought samples of copper ore to the Hudson's Bay

Company's factory at Prince of Wales Fort. Many of the Company people there conjectured that this ore was found not far from the settlement, and the Indians informed them that the mines were not very far distant from a large river.

Some Northern Indians who came to trade at Prince of Wales Fort brought further accounts of the grand river in the spring of 1768, together with several pieces of copper.

In consequence, the Company resolved to send an intelligent person by land to observe the longitude and latitude of the river's mouth, and to make a chart of the country he might walk through, with such remarks as occurred to him during the journey. I was pitched on as a proper person to conduct the expedition.

Several Northern Indians had arrived at the Factory in great distress from hunger. One of these, named Conneequese, said that he had once been very near the river that I sought, and accordingly Mr. Norton engaged him with two other Northern Indians to accompany me.

On the 23rd of February, 1770, I began my journey accompanied by three Northern and two Southern Indians.[1] The winter weather was so remarkably boisterous and changeable that we were frequently obliged to stay two or three nights in the same camp. To make up for this inconvenience the deer [caribou] were so plentiful, for the first eight or ten days, that the Indians killed all we needed; but we were so heavily laden that we could not possibly take much of the meat with us. This I soon perceived to be a great evil which exposed us — in the event of not killing anything for three or four days — to a severe want of provisions. However, we seldom went to bed entirely supperless until the 8th of March, when we could not produce a single thing to eat, not even a partridge. This being the case, we prepared some hooks and lines with which to

[1] The first part of the journey, until May, was through the taiga, the sparse spruce forests just to the south of the true tundra.

angle for fish through the ice of Sheethanee Lake, near which we had encamped.

For the succeeding ten days we caught fish enough to survive, but on the 19th, catching nothing, we moved our camp eight miles farther to the westward on this same lake, and that night caught several fine pike. The following day we set four nets and, in the course of the day, caught many fine fish, particularly pike, trout and tittymeg or whitefish.

Now as this place where we were camped seemed likely to afford us a constant supply of fish, my guide proposed to stay here till the geese began to fly.

The remaining part of March passed without occurrence worth relating. Our nets provided us with sufficient food and our Indians had too much philosophy about them to give themselves such additional trouble as even to look for a partridge with which to vary their diet.

On the 1st of April, to our great surprise, the nets did not yield a single fish. We then went out to angle, but could not procure a fish the whole day. This sudden change of circumstance alarmed one of my companions so much that he even began to think of resuming the use of his gun, after having laid it by for near a month.

My guide, who was a steady man, closely pursued the hunting, seldom returning to the tent till after dark, but without success for several days. On the 10th he continued away longer than usual. We lay down to sleep, having had but little refreshment for three days except a pipe of tobacco and a draught of water. About midnight, to our great joy, our hunter arrived home bringing the blood and fragments of two deer that he had killed. In an instant we were busy cooking a large kettle of broth made with the blood and some scraps of fat and meat shreds boiled with it. This might be reckoned a dainty dish at any time, but was particularly so in our present famished state.

On the 24th of April a great body of Indians was seen

approaching from the south-west. On their arrival we discovered them to be the wives and families of Northern Indian men who were gone to Prince of Wales Fort. These people were bound toward the barren ground to await the return of their husbands and relations.

My guide now determined to move out to the barren ground also, so we took down our tent on the morning of the 27th and proceeded in company with some of the newcomers. It was the 13th of May before we could procure any of the birds we saw flying north. On that day the Indians killed two swans and three geese. These somewhat alleviated our distress, which was very great, for we had found no subsistence for five or six days other than a few old cranberries gathered from the dry ridges where the snow had melted. The Northern Indians who had joined us had stocks of dried meat with them, but though they secretly provided for our Northern guides, they gave me and my Southern Indians not the least supply.

We proceeded on toward the barren ground, with my crew augmented to twelve persons by the addition of one of my guide's wives, and five others whom I engaged to assist in carrying our luggage when the [sledge] hauling season ended.

Game of all kinds was plentiful as we walked northward on the ice, until the 1st of June when we arrived at a place called Baralzon. On the way one of my companions had the misfortune to shatter his hand by the bursting of his gun, but I bound up the wound and, with the assistance of some Turlington's Drops, yellow basilicon, etc., I soon restored the use of his hand so that in a very short time he seemed to be out of danger.

By the 6th, the thaws were so general and the snows so melted that our snowshoes were attended by more trouble than service, so we cast them away. The sledges still proved useful, particularly in crossing lakes and ponds on the ice; but on the 10th, that mode of travel growing dangerous, we determined to throw away the sledges and everyone had to take a load on his back.[2]

This I found to be hard work, since my luggage consisted of the following articles: the quadrant and its stand, a trunk containing books and papers, a land compass, and a large bag containing all my wearing apparel; also a hatchet, knives, and files, besides several small articles intended for presents to the natives. The awkwardness of my load, and its weight, combined with the excessive heat during the day, rendered walking the most laborious task I had ever encountered. The badness of the road and the coarseness of our lodging—on account of the want of tents — exposed us to the utmost severity of the weather and greatly increased our hardships.

We also experienced real distress for want of victuals. What little we got we were forced to consume raw, for lack of fuel; and raw fish, particularly, was little relished by either my Southern companions or myself. Notwithstanding these complicated hardships, we continued in perfect health and in good spirits.

From the 20th to the 23rd of June, we walked nearly twenty miles a day without any subsistence other than a pipe of tobacco and a drink of water when we pleased. Early on the 23rd we saw three musk-oxen, and the Indians soon killed them. But to our great mortification it rained before we got them skinned, and the moss could not be made to burn to make a fire. This was poor comfort for people who had not broken their fast for three or four days. Necessity, however, has no law, even though the raw flesh of musk-oxen is not only coarse and tough, but smells and tastes most disagreeably of musk.

The weather remained so bad, with rain, snow, and sleet, that by the time we were again able to make a fire of moss, we had eaten the amount of one musk-ox quite raw.

---

[2]They were now north of tree line and on the tundra.

I must confess that now my spirits began to fail me a little. Indeed our other misfortunes were greatly aggravated by the weather, which was cold and so very wet that for three days and nights I had not one dry thread on me. But when the fine weather returned, and we had dried our clothing by a fire of moss, I endeavoured, like a sailor after a storm, to forget past misfortunes.

Another disagreeable circumstance of long fasting is the extreme difficulty and pain attending the natural evacuation for the first time after eating; it is so dreadful that none but those who have experienced it can have an adequate idea of its effect.

Our journey to this point had been either feast or famine. Sometimes we had too much, seldom just enough, frequently too little, and often none at all. We often fasted two days and nights; twice, three days, and once, upward of seven days, during which we tasted not a mouthful of anything except a few cranberries, scraps of old leather, and burnt bones. On these pressing occasions I have often seen the Indians examining their wardrobes and considering what part could best be spared; sometimes a piece of an old, half-rotten deerskin, and at others a pair of old moccasins were sacrificed to alleviate extreme hunger. However, these are no more than common occurrences in the Indians' life, in which they are sometimes even driven to the necessity of eating one another.

On the 26th of June we again proceeded northward and on the 30th arrived at a river called Cathawhachaga,[3] which empties itself into a very large lake called Yathkyed Whoie, or White Snow Lake.

Here we found several tents of Indians who were employed spearing deer from their canoes, as the animals crossed the river on their journey to the north. Here also we met a Northern Indian leader or "Captain" called Keel-

---

[3] The Kazan River at its entry into Yathkyed Lake.

shies who, with a small band, was bound to Prince of Wales Fort with furs.

When Keelshies was made acquainted with the intent of my journey he volunteered to bring me anything from the Fort that we were likely to need, and he promised to join us again, at a place appointed by my guide, when winter set in. As we were somewhat short of tobacco, powder, shot, and other articles for trade, I determined to send a letter to the Governor, and although we were more than three hundred miles north-west of the Fort, I asked for the articles I needed to be sent on to me by the hand of Captain Keelshies.

On preparing to leave, my guide informed me that a canoe would be absolutely necessary to cross some unfordable rivers ahead of us, and this induced me to purchase one from the strange Indians at the easy rate of a knife, the full value of which did not exceed a penny.

The canoes made by these people were extremely small and scarce able to carry two men, one of whom had to lie full length on the bottom. Nevertheless, this additional piece of luggage obliged me to engage another Indian; and we were lucky enough to get a poor, forlorn fellow who was used to the office, never having been in a much better state than that of a beast of burthen.

Thus provided, we left Cathawhachaga and continued our course over open rocky plains toward the north and west. On the 17th we saw many musk-oxen, seven of which the Indians killed, and we halted a day or two to dry and pound some of the meat. Nevertheless, when we proceeded we left behind us a great quantity of meat which we could neither eat nor carry.

We had by now reached a great watery plain lying about 450 miles to the north-west of Prince of Wales Fort, and my guide seemed to hestiate about proceeding farther. Instead he kept pitching our camp back and forth in company with the strange Indians who were only engaged in following the roving deer, wherever these might choose to lead. On my asking him the reason for his action, he answered that the year was too far advanced to admit of reaching the Coppermine River that summer, and we would be better served to winter with the Indians we had met, in their country to the south, and to proceed the following summer. As I could not pretend to contradict him, I was reconciled to his proposal. Accordingly, we kept moving with the other Indians, who became daily more numerous until by the 30th of July we had in all about seventy tents, which contained at least six hundred persons. Indeed our encampment at night had the appearance of a small town, and in the morning, when we began to move, the whole country seemed to be alive with men, women, children, and dogs which carried packs upon their backs.

I may not be amiss to give some description of the people with whom I was now living. These Northern Indians are, in general, above middle size, being well-proportioned, strong and robust. Their complexion is somewhat of a copper cast, and their hair is black and straight. Few of the men have any beard, and those who do have no other method of eradicating it than of pulling it out between their fingers and the edge of a blunt knife. Neither sex have any hair under their armpits, and very little on any other part of their body, particularly the women; but on the place where Nature plants the hair I have never known them attempt to eradicate it.

Their features are peculiar, and different from any other tribe in those parts; for they have low foreheads, small eyes, high cheekbones, Roman noses and, in general, long broad chins. Their skins are soft, smooth and polished, and when they are dressed in clean clothing they are as free from an offensive smell as any of the human race.

They differ so much from the rest of mankind that harsh, uncourteous usage seems to agree better with the generality of them, particularly the lower class, than mild treatment. If the least respect is shown them it makes them insolent, and though some of their leaders may be exempt from this characteristic, there are few even of them who have sense enough to set a proper value on favours and indulgences.

Though the ground over which we were now travelling was entirely barren and destitute of every kind of herbage except dwarf shrubs and moss, the deer were so numerous that the Indians not only killed as many as were sufficient for our large numbers, but often killed merely for the skins, the marrow, etc., and left the carcasses to rot or to be devoured by the wolves and foxes.

We moved westward until we crossed the Dubawnt River which, with its immense lake, was fresh, proving that we had not yet come near the northern coast.

On the 12th of August, when I had set the quadrant on its stand and was eating my dinner, to my great mortification a sudden gust of wind blew the quadrant down. The ground was stony, and the bubble, vernier and sight-vane were broken to pieces, rendering the instrument of no further use.

In consequence of this bitter misfortune, which made it impossible for me to obtain any further latitudes, I was forced to the hard resolve of returning once again to the Fort, even though I was then almost five hundred miles west-north-west of Churchill River, and had thought myself to be well advanced toward the goal I sought.

On the day after I had the misfortune to break my quadrant, several Indians joined us from the northward, and some of them plundered me and my companions of every useful article we had, among which was my gun; but it not being in my power to recover what had been taken, we were obliged to rest contented.

Early in the morning of the 19th of August we set out on our return journey, accompanied by some Northern Indians who were bound to the Fort with furs. I had fortunately recovered my gun, since the Indian who took it had no powder or shot and it was therefore of no value to him. Since everything else was taken from me, I found that my load was now so light that this part of the journey was the easiest and most pleasant of any I had experienced; particularly as the deer were plentiful, and the weather fine.

We rounded the bottom of Dubawnt Lake, which is vast enough to be an inland sea, and then proceeded in a south-easterly direction. Frequently we met other Indians, so that scarcely a day passed without our seeing several smokes made by strangers. Many of these joined our party, having furs to trade which they had gathered to the westward during the previous winter.

As the fall advanced we began to feel the cold very severely, for want of proper clothing. My guide was exempted from this inconvenience, having procured a good warm suit of furs and, as one of his wives was with him, he was provided with a tent and every other necessity. But the old fellow was so far from interesting himself in our behalf that he had, for some time past, entirely withdrawn from our company and did not contribute at all to our support. The deer, however, remained in great plenty and we did not suffer from his neglect in this respect.

Provisions still continued plentiful well into September, which was a singular piece of good fortune, and the only happy circumstance of that part of the journey, for the weather was remarkably bad, and severely cold. We were in a forlorn state as we continued to the south-east until, on the 20th of September, we encountered the famous Captain Matonabbee.

Matonabbee was the son of a Northern Indian, by a slave woman bought from the Southern Indians by Mr. Richard Norton, the father of the present Governor. Mr. Norton himself brought about the match between Matonabbee's father and the slave woman, probably in 1736, and Matonabbee was born soon afterwards.

His father dying while the boy was still young, Mr. Norton then took Matonabbee and, according to Indian custom, adopted him as a son. However, Mr. Norton went to England soon afterwards, and the boy did not experience the same regard from the new Governor. He was therefore taken from the Factory by some of his Northern relations and continued with them until Mr. Ferdinand Jacobs succeeded to the command of Prince of Wales Fort in 1752. Out of regard to old Mr. Norton, who by that time was dead, Mr. Jacobs detained Matonabbee at the Factory for several years.

During the course of his long stay in and near the Fort, he mastered the Southern Indian language perfectly and made some progress in English. He also gained some knowledge of the Christian faith; but he always declared that it was too intricate for his comprehension, and he could by no means be induced to believe in any part of our religion. However, he had so much natural good sense and liberality of sentiment that he would not ridicule any particular sect on account of their religious opinion. He held them all in equal esteem, but was determined that as he came into this world, so he would go out of it — without professing any religion at all. Notwithstanding, I have met few Christians who possessed more good qualities, or fewer bad ones.

It is impossible for any man to have been more punctual in the performance of a promise than he was. His scrupulous adherence to truth and honesty would have done honour to the most enlightened and devout Christian, while his benevolence and universal humanity to all the human race — with but one exception, of which I will speak later — could not have been exceeded by the most illustrious person now on record.

He was remarkably fond of Spanish wines, though he never drank to excess; and as he would not take spirits, however good they were, he always remained master of himself.

Now, as no man is totally exempt from frailties, it must be imagined that Matonabbee had his share; yet the greatest with which I can charge him is jealousy, and that sometimes carried him beyond the bounds of humanity.

In his early youth he displayed such talents that Mr. Jacobs engaged him as an ambassador and mediator between the Northern and the Athapuscow Indians[4] who, till then, had always been at war with one another. In the pursuit of this task Matonabbee displayed the most brilliant and solid parts, and demonstrated such personal courage and magnanimity as are rarely to be found amongst persons of superior condition and rank.

He had not penetrated far into the country of the Athapuscow Indians (which lies seven or eight hundred miles to the west of Churchill River) before he came to several tents and found, to his great surprise, Captain Keelshies, with all his family, held prisoner. Though Matonabbee was young enough to be Keelshies's son, he nevertheless contrived to obtain the release of Keelshies, though that worthy lost all his effects, and his six wives.

After Keelshies and his small party had been permitted to depart, Matonabbee not only held his ground but penetrated into the very heart of the Athapuscow country in order to have a personal conference with all the principal inhabitants.

The farther he advanced, the more occasion he had for bravery. At one Athapuscow camp he and his wife, with a servant boy, were alone amongst sixteen families of the enemy. These Southern Indians, who were always treacherous, seemed to give him a hearty welcome and invited him to each tent in turn for a feast and entertainment, having planned to kill him at the last tent. But he was so perfect a master of their language that he discovered their design and told them that, though he had come without enmity, he would sell his life dear enough.

On hearing this some of them ordered that his gun, snowshoes, and servant should be seized and secured; but

---

[4]The Slave Indians around Great Slave Lake.

Matonabbee sprang from his seat, grasped his gun and leapt outside the tent, telling them that this was the proper place to try and murder him, for then he could see his enemy, and not be shot cowardly through the back.

"I am sure," he said, "of taking two or three of you with me, but if you choose to purchase my life at that price, now is the time. Otherwise let me depart."

They told him he was at liberty, but that he must leave his servant. On hearing this he rushed into the tent and took his servant by force from two men who held him, and only then did he set out on his return to the frontiers of his own country, and from thence to the Factory.

After performing this great work he was prevailed upon to visit the Coppermine River in company with another famous leader called Idotleaza; and it was from the report of these two men that Governor Moses Norton was encouraged to obtain permission for an expedition to be sent overland to the Coppermine.

Matonabbee's courteous behaviour, upon our meeting, struck me greatly. As soon as he was acquainted with our distress he got such skins as we had with us dressed for my Southern Indians, and furnished me with a good warm suit of otter and other skins.

During our conversation Matonabbee asked me very seriously if I would attempt another journey to the Coppermine River. On my answering in the affirmative, providing I could get better guides than I had hitherto possessed, he said that he would readily engage in this service himself. I assured him that his offer would be very gladly accepted; and as I had already experienced every hardship that was likely to accompany a future trial, I was now determined to complete the discovery even at the risk of life itself.

Matonabbee attributed our present misfortunes partly to the misconduct of our guides, but mainly to the insistence of the Governor that we should take no women.

"For," said he, "when all the men are heavy laden,

they can neither hunt nor travel any distance
they should meet with some success in hunting,
carry the produce of their labour? Women were made
labour. One of them can carry or haul as much as two men.
They also pitch our tents, make and mend our clothes,
keep us warm at night—and in fact there is no such thing
as travelling any considerable distance without their assistance. More than this, women can be maintained at trifling
expense, for, as they always cook, the very licking of their
fingers in scarce times is sufficient for their sustenance.''

On the 22nd of November, after parting again from
Matonabbee's party in order to speed our way to the Fort,
we were caught in a mighty blizzard on the barren plains
near the coast. The snow drifted so excessively thick that
we could not see our way, and between seven and eight in
the evening it grew so bitter cold that my dog, a valuable
brute, froze to death.

The following day proving fine and clear we were able
to continue, and on the 25th we reached Prince of Wales
Fort, having been absent from it for eight months and
twenty-two days upon a fruitless or at least an unsuccessful
journey.

On the 28th Matonabbee and his party arrived, and I
promptly offered my services to Governor Norton for a
new excursion. The offer was readily accepted, as my
abilities and approved courage in persevering under difficulties were thought adequate to the task. I immediately
engaged Matonabbee as my guide.

This Governor Moses Norton was the son of Mr. Richard Norton, a former Governor, and of a Southern Indian
woman. He was born at Prince of Wales Fort, though he
subsequently spent nine years in school in England. At his
return to Hudson Bay he entered into all the abominable
vices of his countrymen. He kept for his own use five or
six of the finest Indian girls which he could select, but
notwithstanding his own uncommon propensity to the fair
sex, he took every means in his power to prevent the other

Europeans from having intercourse with the women of the country.

His apartments were elegant, but always crowded with his favourite Indians. At night he kept them with him, but locked the door and put the keys under his pillow so that in the morning, for want of necessary conveniences, his rooms were worse than a pig sty.

As he advanced in years his jealousy increased, and he actually poisoned two of his women because he thought them partial to other men more suitable to their ages. He was also a notorious smuggler, but strangely, though he put many thousands into the pockets of his Indian Captains, he seldom put a shilling in his own.

An inflammation of the bowels occasioned his death some time after the completion of my Coppermine adventures; and though he died in the most excruciating pain, he retained his jealousy to the last. A few minutes before he expired, happening to see an officer lay hold of the hand of one of his women who was standing by, he bellowed in as loud a voice as his situation would admit:

"God damn you for a bitch! If I live, I'll knock your brains out!"

A few minutes after this elegant apostrophe he expired in the greatest agonies that can possibly be conceived.

The Third Attempt

On the 7th of December in the year 1770, I set out on my third journey.

On the 16th we arrived at Egg River, where Maton-abbee and the rest of his crew had laid up some provisions. On reaching this place we found, to our great mortification, that some of the Indians, whom the Governor had first traded with and then dispatched from the Fort, had robbed the cache of every article.

Nevertheless, this loss was borne with the greatest fortitude, and I did not hear one of them breathe the least hint of revenge in case they ever found the offenders. The only effect was to make them put their best foot forward, and for some time we walked every day from morning to night. However, the days being short, the sledges heavy, and the road very bad, we seldom exceeded sixteen or eighteen miles a day.

From the 19th of December we traversed nothing but barren ground, with our bellies empty, until the 27th when we arrived at some small woods, and some deer were killed. The Indians never ceased eating the whole day, and indeed we had been in great want, having had no morsel of food for three days past.

I must admit that I have never spent so dull a Christmas. My Indians, however, kept in good spirits, and as we began to see the fresh tracks of many deer, they thought that the worst of the road was over for that winter.

After leaving Island Lake we continued our course between the west and north at the easy pace of eight or nine miles a day. Provisions were scarce until January 16th, when twelve deer were killed, and we thereupon decided to remain a few days to dry some of the meat. On the 22nd we met the first stranger we had seen since leaving the Fort, though we had travelled several hundred miles, which shows how thinly this part of the country is inhabited.

It is a truth well known to the natives that there are many very extensive tracts of ground in these parts which are incapable of affording support to members of the human race even when these are in the capacity of migrants. Few of the lakes and rivers are completely destitute of fish, but the uncertainty of meeting with a sufficient supply makes the natives very cautious about how they put their whole dependence on this article, as such dependence has too frequently been the means of many hundreds being starved to death.

Having got across the Cathawhachaga River we came to Cossed Whoie, or Partridge Lake, and began to cross it on the 7th of February. It is impossible to describe the intenseness of the cold we experienced that day, but the dispatch we made in crossing fourteen miles was almost incredible, for the greatest part of the men performed it in two hours; though the women, being heavier laden, took much longer.

Several of the Indians were frozen, but none of them more disagreeably than one of Matonabbee's wives, whose thighs and buttocks were encrusted with ice so that, when they thawed, several blisters arose which were as large as sheep's bladders. The pain the poor woman suffered was greatly aggravated by the laughter and jeering of her companions, who said that she was rightly served for belting her clothes so high. I must admit that I was not of the number who pitied her, as I thought she took too much pains to show a clean heel and a good leg; her garters always being in sight which, though not considered indecent here, is by far too airy for the rigorous cold of the severe winter in a high northern latitude.

So we continued but slowly until we came to Whold-yah'd, or Pike Lake, which is drained by the Dubawnt River. Here we met some Northern Indians who had been living there since the beginning of winter and had found a plentiful subsistence in catching deer in a pound.

When the Indians wish to build such a pound they first find a main deer path, preferably where it crosses a lake or other opening. The pound is then constructed by enclosing a circular space with a strong fence made of brushy trees. I have seen some that were a mile round, and am informed that others are even bigger. The door is no larger than a common gate, and the inside of the pound is so crowded with small counterhedges as to resemble a maze. In every opening of these is set a snare made with thongs of deerskin, and each snare is usually made fast to a living tree or, if these are not plentiful, to a log of such a size that the deer cannot drag it far.

The pound having been prepared, a row of small

brushwood is stuck up in the snow on each side of the door and continued out on the open space, where neither stick nor stump besides is to be seen; which makes the brushwood yet more distinctly observed. These pieces of brushwood are placed at fifteen or twenty yards apart, and in such a manner as to form two sides of a long acute angle growing gradually wider as the distance from the pound increases. Sometimes the arms of the angle extend as far as two or three miles.

The Indians pitch their tents near an eminence so that they can observe the approach of the deer which, when they are seen, are driven toward the pound by the women and children. The poor, timorous deer, finding themselves thus pursued, and taking the two rows of brushwood to be rows of men, run straight down the path into the pound. The Indians then close in and block the door with brushy trees that have been cut for the purpose. Then, while the women and children walk around the pound to prevent any of the deer escaping, the men spear those animals which are ensnared, and shoot with bows and arrows any that remain loose.

This method of hunting is so successful that many families of Northern Indians subsist by it all the winter. When the spring advances, both the deer and the Indians draw out into the barren ground, and remain on the move until the following winter.

What, then, do the industrious gatherers of fur gain for their trouble? The real wants of these people are few and easily supplied. A hatchet, ice-chisel, file and knife are all that is required to enable them to procure a comfortable livelihood. Those of them who endeavour to possess more are always the most unhappy and may, in fact, be said to be only slaves and carriers to the rest, whose ambition does not lead them beyond the need of procuring food and clothing for themselves.

It is undoubtedly the duty of every one of the Company's servants to encourage a spirit of industry among the natives and to use every means in their power to induce them to procure furs; and I can truly say that this has ever been the grand object of my attention. But at the same time I must confess that such conduct is by no means for the real benefit of the poor Indians, it being well known that those who have the least intercourse with the Factories are by far the happiest.

We pursued our way on the 23rd of March and during the following days saw many Northern Indians employed with pounds. Some of them joined our crew and proceeded with us to the westward until, on April 8th, we arrived at a small lake called Theleweyaza Yeth, or Lake of the Little Fish Hill.

Our numbers had now increased to not less than seventy people, who, during our ten-day stay at Theleweyaza Yeth, were employed in preparing meat, and in making small staves of birchwood about one and a quarter inches square and seven or eight feet long. These were to serve as tent poles all the summer on the barren ground, and would then be converted into snowshoe frames. Birch bark, together with wood for building canoes, was also gathered at this place.

On the 18th of April we set out northward, but had gone only ten miles when we came to the tent of some Northern Indians from whom Matonabbee purchased another wife, so that he now had no less than seven, most of whom, for size, would have made good grenadiers.

He prided himself much on the height and strength of his wives, and would frequently say that few women could carry or haul heavier loads. Though they had a most masculine appearance, he preferred them to those of a more delicate form. Indeed, in a country like this, where a partner in excessive hard labour is the chief motive for the union, and where the softer endearments of a conjugal life are only considered as a secondary object, there seemed to be great propriety in such a choice.

But if all the men were of this way of thinking, what

would become of the greater part of the women, who in general are but of low stature, and many of them of the most delicate make? However, taken in a body, the women of these Indians are as destitute of real beauty as any nation I ever saw, although there are some few of them who, when young, are tolerable enough.

Ask a Northern Indian what is beauty, and he will answer: a broad, flat face, small eyes, high cheekbones, three or four black lines across each cheek, a tawny hide — and breasts hanging down to the belt.

From the age of eight or nine years, the girls are prohibited from joining in the most innocent amusements with male children. When sitting in their tents, or even when travelling, they are watched and guarded with an unremitting vigilance that cannot be exceeded by the most rigid discipline of an English boarding-school. Fortunately, custom makes such restraints sit lightly on them.

Divorces are pretty common; sometimes for incontinency, but more frequently for want of what they deem the necessary accomplishments, or for bad behaviour. The ceremony of divorce consists of nothing more nor less than a good drubbing and then turning the woman out of doors, telling her to go to her paramour or her relations, according to the nature of the crime.

There are certain periods when the women are not permitted to abide in the same tent with the men. At such times they must make a small hovel for themselves some distance from the tents. This universal custom is also a favoured policy with the women who, after a difference with their husbands, make it an excuse for a temporary separation. The use of this custom is so prevalent that I have known some sulky dames to leave their husbands and their tents for four or five days at a time, and repeat the farce twice or thrice a month, while the poor men have never suspected the deceit — or, if they have, delicacy has not permitted them to inquire into the matter. I once knew Matonabbee's handsome wife to live apart from him for several weeks, under this pretence. He, however, had some suspicions, for she was carefully watched to prevent her giving company to another man.

The 21st was the day appointed for moving this camp, but one of the women having been taken in labour, and it being rather an extraordinary case, we were detained two days. However, the instant the poor woman was delivered, after having suffered the birth pangs for fifty-two hours, the signal was made for moving. The poor creature then took her infant on her back and set out with the rest of our company.

On the 23rd of April, as I have said, we had begun to move north. The weather had now begun to grow so hot, and so much snow melted, that it made bad walking in snowshoes, and such exceedingly heavy hauling that it was the 3rd of May before we reached the Lake Clowey.

This lake is only about twelve miles broad in its widest part and is said to drain westward into Lake Athapuscow. It is a famous collecting-place for Indians proceeding to the barren ground, for it is the last place with good woods about it, and it is here that they halt to build their canoes. The same day that we arrived, several other Indians joined us from various quarters and, before we left, upwards of two hundred Indians had come.

Their canoes are very singular, being so small and light, and so simple in their construction, as to somewhat resemble the kayaks used by the Eskimos. Their chief use is to ferry over rivers, although they are sometimes used in the spearing of deer as these swim across a narrow place, and they are also useful for killing swans and geese in the moulting season. This kind of canoe is only built to use upon the barren grounds in summer, and not for river travel.

All the tools used by the Indians in building their sledges and canoes, as well as in making snowshoes and all other kinds of woodwork, consist of a hatchet, a knife, a file and an awl. Yet they are so dexterous that everything they make is executed with a neatness not to be excelled by the most expert mechanic assisted with every tool he could wish.

The tents made use of by the Northern Indians, for both summer and winter, are generally composed of deer-skin with the hair attached and, for convenience of carriage, are always made in small pieces. These tents, as also their pots and some other light lumber, are carried by pack dogs which are trained to that service.

In the fall of the year, with the advance of winter, the people sew the skins of deer's legs together in the shape of a long portmanteau, which is as slippery as an otter when hauled over the snow, and which serves as a temporary sledge while in the barren ground.

On the 20th of May we had left Clowey and were proceeding northward when a gang of strangers joined us with the information that Captain Keelshies was within a day's walk to the southward. I had not seen nor heard of Keelshies since I had sent a letter for supplies by him to the Fort the previous year, so Matonabbee dispatched two young men to bring him after us, with the goods which he might have for us.

On the 28th we were on the ice of the large lake called Peshew, and here the Indians proposed to rest until Captain Keelshies caught up to us. During the night one of Maton-abbee's wives, and another woman, eloped. It was supposed that they went off eastward in order to meet their former husbands, from whom they had been taken by force.

The affair made more noise and bustle than I could have supposed, and Matonabbee seemed entirely discon-certed and was quite inconsolable. In truth the wife he had lost seemed to have every good quality that could render her an agreeable companion in this part of the world. She had, however, chosen to return to a sprightly young fellow of no note who had been her former husband, rather than to have the seventh share of the affection of the greatest man in the country.

Early on the morning of the 29th of May, Captain Keelshies joined us. He delivered a two-quart keg of French brandy and a packet of letters to me, which he had carried with him for many months.

On this same day an Indian man, who had been some time in our company, insisted on taking one of Matonabbee's wives by force, unless Matonabbee should give him a certain quantity of ammunition, some ironwork, a kettle, and other objects. All these Mattonabbee was obliged to deliver or lose the woman, for he could not hope to out-wrestle the other man, who far excelled him in strength.[5] Matonabbee was the more exasperated as the man had sold him this same woman no longer ago than the preceding month.

This dispute was likely to prove fatal to my expedition, for Matonabbee, who had thought himself as great a man as ever lived, took this affront so much to heart (especially as it was offered in my presence) that he was on the point of striking off to the westward to join the Athapuscow Indians who, he said, would treat him with more civility than his countrymen ever did.

After a good deal of entreaty he at last consented to proceed. Though it was then late afternoon, he gave orders for moving, and accordingly we walked seven miles before putting up at an island in Peshew Lake. That day we saw our first deer since leaving the vicinity of Theleweyaza Yeth; we had been subsisting meanwhile on dried meat.

On the last day of May we reached the north end of Peshew Lake, and now Matonabbee made all the arrangements to speed our design to reach the copper mines. He

---

[5]It was customary for the men to wrestle with one another for the possession of a woman, whether she was unattached or already married.

selected two of his young wives, who had no children, to accompany us forward, while the rest of the women and children of the party were to proceed northward at their leisure and, at a particular place in the barren grounds, await our return from the Coppermine River. We then made all our loads as light as possible, taking no more ammunition than was needed for our support, and by the next evening were ready to proceed toward our goal.

I must now return to another event which occurred at Lake Clowey, for during our stay at that place a great number of Indians had entered into combination with my party to accompany us to the Coppermine River, with no other intent than to murder the Eskimos who are understood to frequent that river in numbers.

When I first heard of these plans I endeavoured to persuade the Indians against putting their inhuman design into execution; but it was concluded by them that I was only actuated by cowardice, and they told me, with great derision, that I was afraid of the Eskimos. As I knew that my personal safety depended on the favourable opinion they entertained of me, I was obliged to change my tone. I replied that I did not care if they rendered the Eskimos extinct, and, though I did not see the necessity of attacking them without cause, yet, so far from being afraid of a poor Eskimo, whom I despised more than feared, nothing should be wanting on my part to protect all those who were with me.

This declaration was received with great satisfaction, and I never afterwards ventured to interfere with their war plans, for to have done so would have been the height of folly for a man in my position.

Without the encumbrance of the women and children, we travelled northward at great speed, but the weather was so precarious, and the snow, sleet and rain so frequent, that it was the 16th of June before we arrived at Cogead Lake.

On the 22nd we arrived at the banks of Congecathawhachaga River where we met some Copper Indians who were assembled, according to their annual custom, to kill the deer which cross the river here.

The ice now being broken we were obliged to make use of our canoes for the first time, to ferry across this river; which would have proved very tedious had it not been for the kindness of the Copper Indians who sent their own canoes to our assistance.

No sooner had the Copper Indians been made acquainted with the warlike nature of our journey than they expressed complete approbation. They even offered to lend us several canoes which, they assured us, would prove useful in the remaining part of our journey.

As I was the first white man they had ever seen, and would in all probability be the last, it was curious how they flocked around me, expressing as much desire to examine me from top to toe as a European naturalist would a nondescript animal.

They found and pronounced me to be a perfect human being, except in the colour of my hair and eyes. The former, they said, was like the stained hair of a buffalo's tail; the latter, being light, were like those of a gull. The whiteness of my skin was, in their opinion, no ornament, as they said it resembled meat which had been sodden in water till all the blood was extracted.

We had not been many days at Congecathawhachaga before I had reason to be greatly concerned at the behaviour of certain of my crew toward the Copper Indians. They not only took many of their young women, furs, and ready-dressed skins, but also several of their bows and arrows, which were the only implements they had to procure food and clothing.

To do Matonabbee justice, he endeavoured to make his countrymen give a satisfactory return for the material things they took but he did not hinder them from taking as many women as they pleased. Indeed the Copper Indian women seem to be much esteemed by our Northern Indians, for what reason I know not, as they are in reality the same people in every respect.

On the 3rd of July the weather was again very bad, but we made shift to walk ten or eleven miles until we were obliged to put up because of not being able to see, due to the drifting snow. By putting up, no more is to be understood than that we got to leeward of a great stone, or into the crevices of the rocks, where we smoked our pipes or went to sleep until the weather permitted us to proceed.

Although there was a constant light snow on the 4th, which made it very disagreeable underfoot, we nevertheless managed to walk twenty-seven miles to the north-west, fourteen of which were over the Stony Mountains.

Surely no part of the world better deserves this name. When we first approached these mountains they appeared to be a vast and confused heap of rocks, utterly inaccessible to the foot of man. But having some Copper Indians with us, who knew the road, we made a tolerable shift to get on, though not without being frequently obliged to crawl on our hands and knees. Despite the intricacy of the road, there is a visible path the whole way across these mountains, even in the most difficult parts. In places it is as clear as an English foot-path, by reason of the great stretch of ages during which parties of Indians have gone over the mountains to reach the copper mines. By the side of the path there are several flat table-stones which are covered with thousands of small pebbles. The Copper Indians say these have resulted from a universal custom which requires everyone who passes this way to add a pebble to the heap. Each of us added a small stone in order to increase the number, for luck.

At the foot of the Stony Mountains, three of our Indians turned back after observing that, from every appearance, the remainder of the journey seemed likely to be attended by more trouble than would be counterbalanced by going to war with the Eskimos.

On the 5th, the weather was so bad, with constant

sleet, snow and rain, that we could not see our way and so did not attempt to move. The next day we made about eleven miles to the northwest, and again had to look for shelter among the rocks. The morning after that fifteen more Indians deserted us, being quite sick of the road and the uncommon badness of the weather.

Indeed, though these people are inured to any hardship, their complaint upon this occasion was not without reason. From our leaving Congecathawhachaga we scarcely had a dry garment of any kind, nor anything to screen us from the inclemency of the weather, except rocks and caves. The best of these were but damp and unwholesome lodging, and we had not been able to make one spark of fire except what was sufficient to light a pipe.

This night we had no sooner entered our retreats amongst the rocks, to eat our supper of raw venison, than a very sudden and heavy gale of wind came upon us, attended by a great fall of snow. The flakes were so large as to surpass all credibility, and they fell in such vast quantities for nine hours that we were in danger of being smothered in our caves.

On the 7th, a fresh breeze and some showers of rain, with some warm sunshine, dissolved the greatest part of the snow and we crawled out of our holes and walked about twenty miles to the north-west by west. On our way we crossed on the ice over part of a large lake, which was still far from being thawed. This lake I distinguished as Buffalo or Musk-Ox Lake, from the number of these animals that we found grazing on its margin. The Indians killed many of them but, finding them lean, took only some of the bulls' hides for moccasin soles. At night the bad weather returned, with a gale of wind and very cold rain and sleet.

This was the first time we had seen any of the musk-oxen since we had left the Factory, although I saw a great many during my first and second journeys. They are also found at times in considerable numbers near the coast of

Hudson Bay, all the way from Knapp's Bay to Wager Water; but they are most plentiful within the Arctic Circle.

When full grown the musk-oxen are as large as the middling size of English black cattle, but their legs are not so long; nor is their tail longer than a bear's, and it is entirely hid by the long hair of the rump and hindquarters. Their hair is, in many parts, very long; but the longest hair about them, particularly the bulls, is under the throat, extending from the chin to the lower part of the chest. It hangs down like a horse's mane inverted, and is fully as long, which gives the animal a most formidable appearance.

On the 8th of July the weather was more moderate, though still with rain showers, and we walked eighteen miles to the north, when the Indians killed some deer and put up by the side of a small creek which provided some willows. These were the first we had seen since leaving Congecathawhachaga, and so it was here we had our first cooked meal for a whole week. This was well relished by all parties and, as the sun had dried our clothing, we felt more comfortable than at any time since leaving the women.

The place where we lay that night is not far from Grizzled Bear Hill, which takes its name from the numbers of those animals which are known to resort thither to bear their young in a cave.[6] The wonderful description given of this place by the Copper Indians so excited the curiosity of my companions and myself that we went to view it. On our arrival we found a high lump of earth, of loamy quality, which with several others of its kind stands in the middle of a large marsh, like so many islands in a lake. The sides of these islands are quite perpendicular and the largest is about twenty feet high. They are excellent places of refuge

---

[6]The Barren-Land grizzly was once widely distributed over the tundra region.

for birds, which nest upon their level tops in perfect safety from every beast except the wolverine or quickhatch.

We saw a cave that had evidently been occupied by the bears, but it did not interest me half so much as the sight of the many hills and dry ridges to the east which had been turned over like ploughed land by these animals in their search for ground-squirrels, which constitute a favourite part of their food. At first I thought these long and deep furrows, out of which some enormous stones had been rolled, were the work of lightning; but the Indians assured me it was entirely the work of the Grizzled Bears.

During the next two days we walked sixty miles, in weather that was sometimes cold and wet, and at other times very hot and sultry; but the mosquitoes were always uncommonly numerous, and their stings almost insufferable. On the 10th, Matonabbee sent several Indians ahead with orders to proceed as fast as possible to the Coppermine River to acquaint any Indians they might meet of our approach.

On the 11th we met a Northern Indian called Oule-eye, in company with some Copper Indians, killing deer with bows and arrows and spears as the animals crossed a little river. I smoked my calumet with them but found them a different set of people from those at Congecathawhachaga, for though they had plenty of provisions they did not offer us a mouthful. They would certainly have robbed me of the last garment from my back had I not been protected.

Bows and arrows, though the original weapons of these Northern Indians, are, since the introduction of fire-arms, becoming less used except in killing deer at crossing-places, or as they walk or run through a narrow pass prepared for their reception. This latter method of hunting is only practicable on the barren ground, where there is an extensive prospect enabling the hunters to see the herds at a distance, as well as to discover the nature of the country.

When the Indians prepare to hunt in this manner they first observe the direction of the wind and then go down to leeward of the herd. They then search out a convenient place where those who are to do the shooting may hide. This done, a large bundle of sticks, like ramrods (which they carry with them the whole summer for this purpose) are ranged in two ranks to form the sides of a very acute angle; the sticks being placed at a distance of fifteen or twenty yards apart, rather in the same manner that the fences are constructed for deer pounds in the winter. The women and boys then separate into two parties and make a great circuit to get behind the deer, when they form a crescent and drive the animals towards the arms of the angle. As each of the sticks has a pennant fastened to it, which is easily moved by the wind, and a lump of moss stuck on top, the poor timorous deer probably take them for lines of people, and run straight between the two ranks. As they approach the point of the angle, the Indians in hiding rise up and begin to shoot, but as the deer generally pass at full speed they seldom have time to fire more than one or two arrows unless the herd is very large.

The next day my companions took what provisions they wanted from the unsociable strangers, and we walked fifteen miles, in expectation of finally reaching the Coppermine River that day. But when we had reached the top of a long chain of hills through which the river was said to run, we found it to be no more than a branch which emptied into the main stream about forty miles from its influx into the sea.

At that time all our Copper Indians were dispatched on various tasks in different directions, and there was no one left who knew the shortest cut to the river; but seeing some woods to the westward, we directed our course toward them. The Indians now destroyed several fine bucks and we enjoyed the luxury of cooking them over abundant fires, for these were the first woods we had seen since shortly after leaving Clowey Lake.

As such favourable opportunities for indulging the appetite happen but seldom, we did not neglect any art, in dressing our food, which the most refined skill of Indian cookery has been able to invent. These consist chiefly of boiling, broiling and roasting, but also of a dish called beeatee, which is most delicious. It is made with the blood, a good quantity of fat (shredded small), some of the tenderest flesh, and the heart and lungs torn into small slivers. All of this is put in the deer's stomach and roasted by being suspended before the fire. When it is sufficiently done it will emit steam, which is as much as to say "Come and eat me now!"

This preparation is somewhat related to the most remarkable dish known to both the Northern and Southern Indians, which is made of blood mixed with the half-digested foods found in the deer's stomach, and which is then boiled to the consistency of pease-porridge. Some fat and scraps of tender flesh are also boiled with it. To render this dish more palatable, they have a method of mixing the blood with the stomach contents in the paunch itself, and then hanging it up in the heat and smoke of the fire for several days. This puts the whole mass into a state of fermentation, and gives it such an agreeably acid taste that, were it not for prejudice, it might be eaten by those who have the nicest palates.

It is true that some people with delicate stomachs would not be persuaded to partake of this dish if they saw it being prepared, for most of the fat is first chewed by the men and boys in order to break the globules, so that it will all boil out and mingle with the broth. To do justice, however, to their cleanliness in this particular, I must observe that neither old people with bad teeth, nor young children, have any hand in preparing this dish.

At first, I must admit that I was rather shy of partaking of this mess; but when I was sufficiently convinced of the truth of the above statement, I no longer made any scruple, but always thought it exceedingly good.

The stomach of no other large animal, except the deer, is eaten by the Indians bordering Hudson Bay. In the winter, when the deer feed on fine white moss, the contents are so much esteemed that I have often seen them sit around a fresh-killed deer and eat the contents warm out of its stomach. In summer the deer feed more coarsely, and therefore this dish, if it deserves the appellation, is not then so much in favour.

Young calves, fawns, and beaver, taken from the bellies of their mothers, are all reckoned most delicate food, and I am not the only European who heartily joins in pronouncing them the greatest dainties that can be eaten. The same may be said of young geese and ducks in the shell. In fact, it has become almost a proverb in the northern settlements that whoever wishes to know what is good must live with the Indians.

The parts of generation belonging to any beast they kill, both male and female, are always eaten by the men and boys. Although those parts, particularly in the males, are generally very tough, they must not on any account be cut with an edge-tool, but must be torn to pieces with the teeth. When any part proves too tough to be masticated, it is thrown into the fire and burnt, for the Indians believe that if a dog should eat any of the generative parts, it would have an adverse effect upon their hunting.

They are also remarkably fond of the womb of the buffalo, elk, deer, etc., which are eagerly devoured without washing, or any other process but barely stroking out the contents. This, in some of the larger animals, and especially when they are some time gone with young, needs no description to make it sufficiently disgusting. Yet I have known some men in the Company's service who were remarkably fond of the dish; though I am not of their number. The womb of the beaver and deer is well enough, but that of moose and buffalo is very rank.

I was surprised to find the Coppermine River so different from the description of it which the Indians had given at the Factory. Instead of being so large as to be navigable for shipping, as it had been represented by them, it was at this part scarcely navigable for an Indian canoe, being no more than 180 yards wide, full of shoals, and with three falls in sight at the first view.

Soon after our arrival three Indians were sent off as spies in order to see if any Eskimos were inhabiting the river-side between us and the sea. We followed more slowly, and after three-quarters of a mile we put up while most of the Indians went hunting and killed several musk-oxen and some deer. They were employed the rest of the day and night in splitting and drying the meat by the fire.

As we were not then in want of provisions, and as deer and other animals were plentiful, I was at a loss to account for this unusual economy on the part of my companions. However, I was soon informed that these precautions were made with a view to having ready-cooked victuals to serve us to the river's mouth, without being obliged to fire guns, or make the smoke of fires, and so alarm the natives if any should be at hand.

We set out again on the morning of the 15th of July, and I began a survey of the river, which I continued for about ten miles, until a heavy rain obliged us to put up. We lay that night at the northern extremity of the woods, the space before us to the sea being entirely barren hills and wide open marshes. In the course of the day I found the river full of shoals, and in places so diminished in width that it formed two more capital falls.

The weather being more pleasant the next day, I proceeded with my survey for another ten miles, but still found the river the same as before, being everywhere full of shoals and rapids.

About noon the three spies returned, and reported that five tents of Eskimos were on the west side of the river. They said also that the situation was very convenient for surprising them, and that they were only twelve miles from us.

The Indians would now pay no further attention to my

survey, but were immediately engaged in planning how they might steal up on the poor Eskimos in the night, and kill them all while they slept. To accomplish this bloody design more effectively, the Indians thought it necessary to cross the river as soon as possible. Accordingly, after they had put their guns, spears and shields into good order, we made the crossing.

Upon our arrival on the west side, each man painted the front of his shield; some with the image of the sun, others with the moon, others with different kinds of birds and beasts of prey, and still others with the images of imaginary beings which, according to their silly notions, are the inhabitants of the different elements of Earth, Sea and Air.

When I inquired their reasons for doing this, I was told that each man painted his shield with the image of the being on which he most relied for success in the intended battle. Some were content with a single representation, while others, doubtful I suppose of the power of any single one, covered their shields, to the very margins, with groups of hieroglyphics which were quite unintelligible to everyone except the painter.

When this piece of superstition was completed we began to advance toward the Eskimo camp. Since we were carful to avoid crossing any hills, the distance was made much greater and for the sake of keeping to the low ground, we were forced to walk through entire swamps of stiff, marly clay, sometimes up to the knees. However, our course, though very serpentine, was not so remote from the river as to exclude me from a view of it, and I was able to convince myself that it was just as unnavigable as the parts I had surveyed.

It is worth remarking that my crew, though an undisciplined rabble, and by no means accustomed to war or to command, seemingly acted, on this horrid occasion, with the utmost uniformity of sentiment. All were united in the general cause and ready to follow Matonabbee, who had taken the lead, in accord with the advice of an old Copper Indian who had joined us on our first arrival at the river.

For once, reciprocity of interest was in general high regard amongst these people and no one was in want of anything that another could spare. Property of every kind that could be of use now ceased to be private, and those with more than they needed seemed proud to lend or give the surplus to those who were most in need.

The number of my crew was so much greater than what the five tents could contain, and the warlike manner in which the Indians were equipped was so superior to what could be expected of the poor Eskimos, that no less than a total massacre seemed likely to be the result, unless Providence should work a miracle for their deliverance.

The land was so situated that we walked under cover of hills and rocks till we were two hundred yards from the tents. There we lay in ambush for some time, watching the movements of the Eskimos; and here the Indians would have advised me to stay until the fight was over. To this plan I could by no means consent for I considered that, when the Eskimos came to be surprised, they would try every way to escape and, if they found me alone, not knowing me from an enemy, they would probably proceed to violence against me when no person was near me to assist.

For this reason I determined to accompany the Indians, telling them at the same time that I would not have any hand in the murder they were about to commit, unless I found it necessary for my own safety.

The Indians were not displeased with this proposal. One of them immediately fixed me a spear. Another lent me a broad bayonet for my protection, but it was too late to provide me with a shield, nor did I want to be encumbered with such an unnecessary piece of lumber.

While we lay in ambush, the Indians performed the last-minute ceremonies which were thought necessary before the engagement. These consisted chiefly of painting their faces; some all black, some all red, and some with a mixture of the two. To prevent their hair blowing in their eyes it was either tied before and behind on both sides, or else cut off short all around. The next thing they considered was to make themselves as light as possible for running, which they did by pulling off their stockings, and either cutting off the sleeves of their jackets or rolling them up close to their armpits. Though the mosquitoes were so numerous as to surpass all credibility, some of the Indians actually pulled off their jackets and prepared to enter the lists quite naked, except for their breech-clouts and moccasins.

Fearing that I might have occasion to run with the rest, I also thought it advisable to pull off my stockings and cap, and to tie my hair as close as possible.

By the time the Indians had made themselves thus completely frightful, it was near one o'clock in the morning of the 17th. Finding all the Eskimos now quiet in their tents, the Indians chose this moment to attack. They rushed forth from their ambuscade, unperceived by the poor unsuspecting creatures until they were close to the very eaves of the tents. And so began the bloody slaughter, while I stood neuter in the rear.

The horrible scene was shocking beyond description. The unhappy victims had been surprised in the midst of their sleep, and had neither time nor power to make any resistance. Men, women and children, numbering upwards of twenty, ran stark naked from the tents and endeavoured to make good their escape; but the Indians having possession of all the landside, there was no place they could fly for shelter. The only alternative was to leap into the river; but, as none of them attempted it, they all fell victim to Indian barbarity.

The shrieks and groans of the poor expiring victims were truly dreadful. My horror was much increased at seeing a young girl of about eighteen years attacked so near me that, when the first spear was thrust into her side, she fell at my feet and twisted herself around my legs, so that it was with difficulty I could disengage myself from her dying grasp. Two Indian men were pursuing this unfortunate victim, and I solicited very hard for her life. The murderers made no reply until they had stuck both their spears through her body and transfixed her to the ground. They then looked me sternly in the face and began to ridicule me by asking if I desired an Eskimo wife; meanwhile paying not the slightest heed to the shrieks and agony of the poor wretch who was still twining around their spears like an eel.

Indeed, after receiving much abuse from them, I was at length obliged to desire only that they would be more expeditious in dispatching their victim out of her misery; otherwise I should be obliged, out of pity, to assist in the friendly office of putting an end to a fellow creature who had been so cruelly wounded.

On this request being made, one of the Indians hastily drew his spear from the place where it was first lodged, and pierced it through her breast near the heart. The love of life, however, even in this most miserable state, was so predominant that though this might justly be called the most merciful act that could be done for the poor creature, it still seemed to be unwelcome. Though much exhausted by pain and loss of blood, she made several efforts to ward off this friendly blow.

My situation, and the terror of my mind at beholding this butchery, cannot easily be conceived, much less described; and though I summed up all the fortitude which I was master of on the occasion, it was with difficulty that I could refrain from tears. I am confident that my features must have feelingly expressed how sincerely I was affected by this barbarous scene. Even at this hour I cannot reflect on the transactions of that horrid day without shedding tears.

The brutish manner in which these savages used the

bodies that had been so cruelly bereaved of life was so shocking that it would be indecent to describe it, particularly their curiosity in examining, and the remarks they made on, the formation of the women; which, they pretended to say, differed materially from their own. For my own part I must acknowledge that however favourable the opportunity for determining that point might have been, my thoughts at the time were too much agitated to admit of any such remarks, and I firmly believed that had there actually been as much difference between them as there is said to be between the Hottentots and those of Europe, it would not have been in my power to have marked the distinction. I have reason to think, however, that there is no ground for the assertion, and I really believe that the declaration of the Indians on this occasion was utterly devoid of truth and proceeded only from the implacable hatred they bore to the whole tribe of people of whom I am speaking.

After the Indians had completed the murder of the poor Eskimos, seven other tents on the east side of the river immediately engaged their attention. Luckily for their inhabitants, our canoes and baggage had been left at some distance up the river, so that there was no means of getting across. However, the river was little more than eighty yards wide at this point, and the Indians began firing at the Eskimos. The poor Eskimos, though all up in arms, did not attempt to abandon their tents. In fact they were so unacquainted with firearms that, when the bullets struck the ground, they ran in crowds to see what was sent to them. At length one of the Eskimo men was shot in the calf of the leg, which put them in great confusion. They all immediately embarked in their kayaks and paddled to a shoal in he middle of the river which, being more than a gunshot from any part of the shore, put them out of the reach of our barbarians.

The Indians now began to plunder the tents of the deceased of all the copper utensils they could find, such as hatchets, bayonets, and knives. Afterwards they assembled on top of an adjacent high hill and, standing all in a cluster so as to form a solid circle, with their spears erect, gave many shouts of victory, while constantly clashing their spears against each other and calling out "Tima! Tima!" (which is to say, Friend, Friend!) by way of derision to the surviving Eskimos who were standing on the shoal almost knee-deep in water.

After parading the hill for some time, it was agreed to return up the river to the place where we had left our canoes and baggage, and then to cross the river again and plunder the tents on the east side. This resolution was immediately put in force, but, as ferrying across with only three canoes took a considerable time, several of the poor surviving Eskimos, probably thinking we had gone about our business, had meanwhile returned from the shoal to their habitations.

When we approached their tents, which we did under the cover of the rocks, we found them busily employed tying up bundles. These the Indians seized upon with their usual ferocity, and the Eskimos immediately embarked. All of them got safe to the shoal except an old man who was so intent on collecting his things that the Indians came upon him before he could reach his kayak and he fell a sacrifice to their fury. I verily believe that not less than twenty had a hand in his death, as his whole body was like a sieve.

I ought to have mentioned in its proper place that, in returning for the canoes, we saw an old woman sitting by the side of the water killing salmon, which lay at the foot of the fall as thick as a shoal of herrings. Whether from the noise of the fall, or a natural defect in the old woman's hearing, she had no knowledge of the tragical scene which had so lately been transacted at the tents. When we first perceived her, she seemed perfectly at ease, and was entirely surrounded with the produce of her labour. From her behaviour, and from the appearance of her eyes, which were as red as blood, it is probable that her sight was not very good, for she scarcely discerned that the Indians were her enemies till they were within two spear-lengths of her.

It was then in vain that she attempted to fly, for the wretches of my crew transfixed her to the ground in a few seconds, and butchered her in the most savage manner. There was scarcely a man among them who had not a thrust at her with his spear. Many, in doing this, aimed at torture rather than immediate death, as they not only poked out her eyes, but stabbed her in many parts very remote from those which are vital.

When the Indians had plundered the seven tents of all the copper utensils (which seemed the only things worth their notice) they threw all the tents and tent poles into the river, destroyed a vast quantity of dried salmon, musk-oxen flesh and other provisions, broke all the stone kettles and, in fact, did all the mischief they possibly could to distress the poor creatures they could not murder, and who were still standing on the shoal aforementioned, obliged to be woeful spectators of their great and perhaps irreparable loss.

After the Indians had completed this piece of wantonness, we sat down and made a good meal of fresh salmon. When we had finished our meal, which was the first we had enjoyed in many hours, the Indians told me they were again ready to assist me in making an end to my survey.

It was then five o'clock in the morning of the 17th, and the sea was in sight about eight miles distant. I therefore instantly commenced my survey and pursued it to the mouth of the river, which I found all the way so full of shoals and rapids that it was not navigable even for a boat, and it emptied itself into the sea over a ridge or bar. The tide was out, but I judged from the marks I saw on the edge of the ice that it flowed about twelve or fourteen feet, which will only reach a little way into the river's mouth. Here the sea is full of islands and shoals, as far as I could see with the assistance of a good pocket telescope. The sea ice was not then broken up, but was melted away for a distance of three-quarters of a mile from the main shore, and to a little distance round the islands and shoals. Having completed my survey, I erected a mark and took possession of the coast, which I was the first white man ever to see, on behalf of the Hudson's Bay Company.

Having finished our business at the river, we set out to visit the copper mines themselves; but after walking about twelve miles south by east, we stopped and took a little sleep. This was the first time any of us had closed his eyes since the 15th, and it was now six o'clock in the morning of the 18th. The Indians killed a musk-ox, but as we had nothing but wet moss for fuel, and so could not have a fire, we were obliged to eat the meat raw, and found it intolerable, as it happened to be an old beast.

After a sleep of five or six hours we once more set out and walked eighteen miles to the south-south-east, when we arrived at one of the copper mines, which lies twenty-nine or thirty miles distant from the river mouth.

The mine, if it deserves that appellation, is no more than an entire jumble of rocks and gravel which has been rent many ways by an earthquake. Through the ruins there runs a small river. The Indians had represented this mine as so rich and valuable that, if a Factory were built at the river, a ship might be ballasted with the ore with the same ease and dispatch as is done with stones at Churchill River. By their account the hills were entirely composed of copper, all in handy lumps, like a heap of pebbles.

Their account differed so much from the truth that I, and all my companions, expended near four hours in search of some of the metal, with such poor success that only one piece of any size could be found. This, however, was remarkably good, and weighed above four pounds.

The Indians imagine that every bit of copper they find resembles some object in nature but, from what I saw, it requires a great share of invention to make this out. Different people had different ideas on the subject, for the large piece of copper had not been long found before it had twenty different names, although at last it was generally allowed to resemble an Alpine hare couchant. The Indians consider the largest pieces, with the least dross and the fewest branches, are best for their use; as by the help of fire and two stones they can beat it into any shape they wish.

Before Churchill River was settled by the Hudson's Bay Company some fifty years previously, the Northern Indians had no other metal but copper, except a small quantity of ironwork which a party who had visited York Factory about 1714 had purchased, and some pieces of old iron left at Churchill River by Captain Monk. This being the case, numbers of them from all quarters used to resort to these hills every summer in search of copper, from which they made hatchets, ice-chisels, bayonets, knives, awls, arrow-heads, etc. The many paths which had been beaten by the Indians on these occasions are yet perfect in many places, especially on the dry ridges and hills.

The Copper Indians set a great value on their native metal even to this day, and prefer it to iron for almost every use except that of hatchet, knife and awl. There is a strange tradition amongst them that the first person to discover these mines was a woman. For several years she conducted them to this place, but as she was the only woman in the company, some of the men took such liberties with her that she vowed revenge on them. She was a great conjurer [medicine-woman], and when the men loaded themselves with copper and were going to return to their homes, she refused to accompany them. She said that she would sit on the mine until she sank into the ground, and the copper would sink with her. The next year, when the men went for more copper, they found her sunk to the waist, though still alive; and the quantity of copper had much decreased. The year following, she had quite disappeared, and all the

71

principal parts of the mine with her. After that, nothing remained on the surface but a few small pieces scattered at a great distance from each other.

The Copper Indians no longer barter much copper to the Northern Indians, as they were wont to do, but now barter fur instead. The established rule is that everything brought from Churchill River shall be sold to them at ten times the price paid for it by the Northern Indians. Thus a hatchet, bought at the Factory for one beaver-skin, is sold to these people at the advanced price of one thousand per cent. For a small brass kettle they pay sixty marten, or [the value of] twenty beaver in other kinds of fur.

Though it is no part of the record of my journey, I must here carry forward in time and interject a tragic addition to the account of the ultimate results of the peace between the Northern and the Southern Indians.

Some years after my journey was concluded, the Northern Indians, by visiting their Southern friends, contracted the smallpox from them. In a few years this disease carried off nine-tenths of them; and particularly those who composed the trade at Churchill Factory. The few survivors afterwards followed the example of the Athapuscow tribe, and traded with the Canadians[7] who were then becoming established in the country of those Indians.

Thus it is that a very few years have proved our short-sightedness; for it would really have been much more to the advantage of the Company, as well as having prevented the depopulation of the Northern Indian country, if they had still remained at war with the Southern Indians. At the same time it is impossible now to say what increase in trade

---

[7]These were mainly Scots traders from Montreal who later formed the North West Company in opposition to the Hudson's Bay Company, and who reached the Arctic by travelling west through the Great Lakes, across the prairies, then north down the Athabasca, Slave and Mackenzie Rivers.

might not have risen in time from a constant and regular traffic with the Copper and Dog-Rib peoples. But these, having been cut off from our Factory by the decimation of the Northern Indians, soon sank into their original barbarism, and a war ensued between the two tribes for the sake of a few remnants of ironwork that was left amongst them; with the result that almost the whole Copper Indian race was destroyed.

The Homeward Journey

We now proceeded at a very great pace to the south-eastward to rejoin the people we had left, and after six days of travel, during one of which we walked forty-two miles, we arrived at Congecathawhachaga.

To our great disappointment we found that our women had departed, so that when we arrived not an Indian was to be found except an old man and his family who had arrived in our absence and was waiting at the crossing-place with some furs for Matonabbee. This old man, who was the Leader's father-in-law, had another of his daughters with him which he offered to the great man; but she was not accepted.

Our stay was of very short duration for, on seeing a smoke to the southward, we immediately crossed the river and walked toward it. We found it to be burning moss which had been fired by our women; but they had departed. Although the afternoon was far advanced, we pursued them. We had not gone far before we saw another smoke at a great distance, toward which we shaped our course; but notwithstanding that we redoubled our pace, it was eleven o'clock at night before we reached it. To our great mortification we found it to be the place where the women had slept the night before.

The Indians, finding that their wives were so near as to be within one ordinary day's walk, determined not to rest until they had joined them. Accordingly, we pursued our course and, about two o'clock in the morning of the 25th of July, we came up with some of the women who had pitched their tents by the side of Cogead Lake.

Since leaving Coppermine we had travelled so hard and had taken so little rest that my feet had swelled considerably and I had become quite stiff at the ankles. I had so little power to direct my feet, when walking, that I frequently knocked them against the stones with such force as not only to jar and disorder them, but my legs also. The nails of my toes were bruised to such a degree that several of them festered and dropped off. To add to this mishap, the skin was entirely chafed from the tops of both feet and from between every toe. The sand and gravel, which I could by no means exclude, irritated the raw parts so much that, for a day before we arrived at the women's tents, I left the print of my feet in blood with every step. Several of the Indians complained that their feet also were sore; but not one of them was in so bad a state as mine.

This being the first time I had seen anyone foot-foundered, I was in great apprehension for the consequences. Though I was but little fatigued in body, the excruciating pain suffered in walking had such an effect on my spirits that, if the Indians had continued to travel two or three days longer at that unmerciful rate, I must unavoidably have been left behind, for my feet were quite honeycombed by the dirt and gravel eating into the raw flesh.

As soon as we arrived at the tents, I washed and cleaned my feet in warm water, then bathed the swelled parts with spirits of wine and dressed the raw places with Turner's cerate. As we did not move on the following day, the swelling abated and the raw parts were not so much inflamed.

Rest, though essential to my recovery, could not be procured, for the Indians were desirous of joining the remainder of their wives and families as soon as possible. Consequently, they would not stop even a day, so that on the 27th we again began to move. Though they now travelled only eight or nine miles a day, it was with the utmost difficulty that I could follow them. Fortunately, the weather proved fine and pleasant and the ground was, in general, pretty dry and free from stones.

On July 31st we arrived at the place where the wives and children left behind at Peshew Lake were to have joined us on our return from the Coppermine River. Here we found several tents of Indians, but these belonged to Matonabbee and some few others, and the rest of the women had not yet arrived. However, we saw a large smoke to the eastward, which we guessed might be the missing people. Accordingly, the next morning Matonabbee dispatched some of his young men in quest of them, and on the 5th of August they joined us. Contrary to expectations, a great number of other Indians were with them, to the amount of more than forty tents.

Among these Indians was a man Matonabbee had stabbed when we were at Clowey.[8] Now, with the greatest submission, he led his wife to the Leader's tent, set her down by his side, and retired without saying a word.

Matonabbee took no notice of her, though she was bathed in tears. By degrees, after reclining herself on her elbow for a time, she lay down, sobbing, and said: "See'd dinne! See'd dinne!" which is "My husband! My husband!"

On hearing this, Matonabbee told her that if she had respected him as such she would not have run away from him, and that now she was at liberty to go where she pleased. On which she got up with seeming reluctance, though most assuredly with a light heart, and returned to her former husband's tent.

Several of the Indians at this camp being very ill, the conjurers, who are always the doctors, and who pretend to perform great cures, began to try their skill.

***

[8] He had formerly been the husband of the wife of Matonabbee who ran away at Peshew Lake.

The death of a near relation affects these people so much that they rend all their clothes from their backs and go naked until some person, less afflicted, relieves them. After the death of a close relative they mourn, as it may be called, for a whole year. These mournful periods are distinguished not by any particular dress but only by cutting off the hair; and the ceremony consists of almost perpetual crying. Even when walking they make an odd howling noise, often repeating the relationship of the deceased. When they reflect seriously on the loss of a good friend, it has such an effect upon them that they give uncommon loose to their grief.

They had a tradition among them that the first person upon earth was a woman who, after being some time alone, found an animal like a dog which followed her to her cave and soon grew fond and domestic. This dog, they said, had the art of transforming itself into the shape of a handsome young man, which it frequently did at night. With the approach of day, however, it resumed its former shape, so that the woman looked on all that happened in the nights as dreams and delusions. But the transformations were productive of the same consequences which at present generally follow such intimate connections between the two sexes; and so the mother of the world began to advance in her pregnancy.

Not long after this happened, a man of such surprising height that his head reached up to the clouds came to level the land, which at that time was a very rude mass. After he had done this, with the help of his walking-stick, he marked out the lakes, ponds and rivers, and immediately caused them to be filled with water.

He then took the dog, tore it to pieces, and threw the guts into the lakes and rivers, commanding them to become the different kinds of fish. The dog's flesh he dispersed over the land to become different kinds of beasts and land animals. He also tore the skin into small pieces and threw it into the air, commanding it to become all kinds of birds.

After this was done he gave the woman and her offspring full power to kill, eat, and never spare; for he had commanded the fish, birds, and beasts to multiply for her use, in abundance. After this injunction he returned to the place whence he came, and has not been heard of since.

On the 9th of August we once more pursued our way, continuing in the south-west quarter. All the Indians who had been in our company, except twelve tents, struck off in different ways. As to myself, having had several days' rest, my feet were completely healed, though the skin remained very tender for some time.

From the 19th to the 25th we walked by the side of Large White Stone Lake, which is about forty miles long but of very unequal breadth. The river coursing from this lake is said to run a long way westward, and then trend north to form the main branch of the Coppermine River.

Deer were very plentiful the whole way, and the Indians killed great numbers of them daily, for the sake of their skins; for at this time of the year their pelts were in good season, and the hair was of a proper length for clothing.

The great destruction which is made of the deer in those parts, at this season of the year, is almost incredible. As they are never known to have more than one young at a time, it is wonderful that they do not become scarce; but so far is this from being the case that the eldest Northern Indian in all their tribe will affirm that the deer are as plentiful now as they have ever been. The scarcity or abundance of these animals in different places at the same season is caused, in a great measure, by the winds which prevail for some time before. The deer are supposed by the natives to walk always in the direction from which the wind blows, except when they migrate in search of the opposite sex, for the purpose of propagating their species.

Skins that are taken after the rutting season are not only very thin, but also full of worms and warbles which render them of little value. Indeed the chief use of the hides taken in winter is for the purposes of food, and really, when the hair is properly taken off, and all the warbles are squeezed out, if they are then well boiled they are far from being disagreeable.

The Indians never could persuade me to eat the warble worms, of which some of them, and in particular the children, are remarkably fond. They are eaten raw and alive, and are said, by those who like them, to be as fine as gooseberries. But the idea of eating such things (many of which are as large as the first joint of the little finger) was sufficient to give me an unalterable disgust.

The type of clothing worn by these people makes them very subject to be lousy; but that is so far from being thought a disgrace that the best among them amuse themselves with catching and eating these vermin. They are so fond of this sport that the produce of a lousy head or garment affords them not only pleasing amusement, but a delicious repast. Matonabbee was so fond of these vermin that he frequently set five or six of his strapping wives to work to louse their hairy deerskin shifts; the produce of which being always very considerable, he eagerly received it with both hands and licked them up as fast, and with as good a grace, as any European epicure would eat the mites in cheese.

However, when I acknowledge that the warbles out of the deer's back, and the domestic human lice, were the only things I ever saw my companions eat of which I did not partake myself, I trust I shall not be reckoned over-delicate in my appetite.

After leaving White Stone Lake, we continued our travels until the 3rd of September, when we arrived at a small river belonging to Point Lake. Here we were forced to remain for several days because of the boisterous weather which, with much rain, snow and frost, prevented us from crossing the river in our small canoes.

On the 8th we came to a few small scrubby woods, which were the first we had seen from the 25th of May, except those we had perceived at the Coppermine River.

During our passage to this place, one of the Indians' wives, who for some time had been in a consumption, had become so weak as to be unable to travel. Amongst these people this is the most deplorable state to which a human being can possibly be brought. Whether she had been given over by the doctors, or whether it was from want of friends, no expedients were taken for her recovery so that, without much ceremony, she was left unassisted to perish above ground.

Though this was the first instance of its kind I had seen, it is the common practice of these Indians. When a grown person is so ill, especially in the summer, as not to be able to walk, they say it is better to leave one who is past recovery than for the whole family to sit down and starve to death, without being able to assist the afflicted one. On these occasions the relations of the sick generally leave them some victuals and water and, if the situation affords it, some fuel. The person being left is also acquainted with the road the rest will follow. After covering the sick persons with deerskin, the rest then take their leave and walk away crying.

Sometimes persons left thus will recover, and come up to their friends, or wander about till they meet with other Indians. Although instances of this kind are seldom known, the poor woman above-mentioned came up with us three times. At length, poor creature, she dropped back for the last time.

A custom apparently so unnatural is, perhaps, not to be found among any other of the human race. If properly considered, however, it may with justice be ascribed to necessity and self-preservation rather than to the want of humanity.

The weather had now become very cold, with much snow and sleet, which seemed to promise an early winter. Since the deer were very plentiful, and there were here sufficient woods for fuel and tent poles, the Indians proposed that we encamp in order to make winter clothing, snowshoes and temporary sledges, and to prepare a large quantity of dried meat and fat to carry us forward. This seemed particularly necessary from the accounts of the Indians that they had always experienced a scarcity of every kind of game in the direction we proposed to go after leaving Point Lake.

The weather grew worse until, by the 30th of September, all the ponds and lakes were frozen over so hard that we were enabled to cross them on the ice without danger. October came in very roughly, attended by heavy falls of snow and much drift. On the night of the 6th, a heavy gale of wind put us in great disorder, for the few woods about did not furnish us with the least shelter from it. It overset several of the tents, and mine shared in the disaster; which I cannot sufficiently lament, for the butt-ends of the poles fell on my quadrant and broke it so that it was rendered completely useless. As it was no longer even worth the carriage, I gave the brass-work to the Indians, who cut it into small lumps and made use of it for ammunition.

On the 23rd of October, some Copper and Dog-Rib Indians came to our tents to trade their furs. They made their purchases from us at a very extravagant price, for one of the Indians in my company got no less than forty beaver and sixty marten skins for one piece of iron which he had stolen when he was last at the Fort.

Another of the strangers had about forty beaver skins which he owed to Matonabbee because of an old debt; but one of the Northern Indians seized this fur, notwithstanding that he knew it to be Matonabbee's property. This treatment, together with the other insults he had received, so annoyed the Leader that he now renewed his earlier resolution of leaving his own country and going to reside with the Athapuscow Indians.

As the objective of my journey had now been achieved, I did not try to influence him, either one way or the other. Indeed, by his conversations with the other Indians of our party, I soon understood that they all intended to make an excursion into the Athapuscow country in order to kill beaver and moose.

While out hunting on January 11th, some of my companions saw the track of a strange snowshoe. They followed it, and at a considerable distance came to a little hut where they discovered a young woman sitting quite alone. As she understood their language, they brought her back to our camp.

On examination she proved to be one of the western Dog-Rib Indians who had been taken prisoner by the Athapuscows in the summer of 1770. The following summer, when the Indians who took her were near this part, she eloped from them with intent to return to her own country. However, the distance was so vast, and she had been carried such a great way by canoe along the twistings and turnings of the rivers and lakes, that she had forgotten the way to her home. She therefore built the hut in which we found her, and here she had resided from the first setting-in of fall.

From her account of the moons which had passed since her elopement, it appeared that she had been near seven months without seeing a human face. During this time she had supported herself very well by snaring partridge, rabbits and squirrels, and she had also killed two or three beaver and some porcupines. That she had not been in want was evident from the fact that she still had a small store of provisions by her when she was discovered. She was in good health and condition, and I think was one of the finest Indian women that I have seen in any part of North America.

The methods practised by this poor creature to procure a livelihood were truly admirable. When the few deer sinews that she had taken with her were all expended in making snares, and sewing her clothing, she had nothing with which to replace them but the sinews of rabbits' legs and feet. These she twisted together with great dexterity and success. The rabbits, and other things that she caught in her snares, not only furnished her with a comfortable subsistence but also with enough skins to make a warm and neat suit of winter clothing.

It is scarcely possible to think that a person in her forlorn situation could be so composed as to contrive, or execute, anything not absolutely essential to her existence. Nevertheless, all her clothing, besides being calculated for real service, showed great taste and no little variety of ornament. The materials, though rude, were very curiously wrought, and so judiciously placed as to make the whole of her garb have a very pleasing and rather romantic appearance.

Her leisure hours from hunting had been employed in twisting the inner rind or bark of willows into small-lines, like net-twine, of which she had some hundred fathoms. With this she intended to weave a fishing net as soon as the spring advanced. It is the custom of the Dog-Rib Indians to make their nets in this manner, and they are much preferable to the deer-thong nets of the Northern Indians which, although they appear very good when dry, grow so soft and slippery in the water that the hitches are apt to slip and let the fish escape. They are also liable to rot, unless frequently taken out of the water and dried.

Five or six inches of an iron hoop, made into a knife, and the shank of an arrow-head of iron, which served as an awl, were all the metals this poor woman had. However, with these simple implements she had made herself complete snowshoes and several other useful articles.

Her method of making a fire was equally singular, since she had no materials for the purpose other than two hard, sulphurous rocks. By long friction and hard knocking, she made these produce a few sparks which she communicated to some touch-wood. However, as this method was attended by great trouble, and was not always certain of success, she did not suffer her fire to go out all that winter. Hence we may conclude that she did not know how to produce fire by friction, as is done amongst the Eskimos and many other uncivilized nations.

The singularity of her circumstances, the comeliness of her person, and her proven accomplishments, occasioned a strong contest between several of the Indians of my party as to who should have her for a wife. The poor girl was actually won and lost at wrestling by half a score of different men that same evening.

On February 24th, we encountered a strange Northern Indian leader called Thlewsanellie who, with his band, joined us from the eastward.

Thlewsanellie and his party told us that all was well at the Fort when they left it, which must have been about the 5th of November in 1771. Most of them now proceeded north-westward, but some, who had procured furs in the early part of the winter, joined our party.

Setting off to the south-east on the 28th, we now proceeded at a much greater rate, since little or no time was lost in hunting. The next day we came on the tracks of strangers, and some of my companions were at pains to search them out. Finding them to be poor, inoffensive people, they plundered them of the few furs they had, together with one young woman.

Every additional act of violence, committed by my companions on the poor and the distressed, served to increase my indignation and dislike. This last act, however, displeased me more than all their former actions because it was committed on a set of harmless creatures whose general manner of life renders them the most secluded from society of any of the human race.

The people of this family, as it may be called, have for a generation past taken up their abode in some woods which are situated so far out on the barren grounds as to be quite out of the track of other Indians. This place is some hundreds of miles distant both from the main woods and from the sea. Few of the trading Northern Indians have ever visited it, but those who have give a most pleasing description of it. It is situated on the banks of a river which has communications with several fine lakes. As the current sets north-eastward, it empties itself, in all probability, into some part of Hudson Bay, probably into Baker Lake at the head of Chesterfield Inlet.[9]

The accounts given of this place, and of the manner of life of its inhabitants, would fill a volume. Let it suffice to observe that it is remarkably favourable for every kind of game that the barren ground produces. However, the seasonal continuance of game is somewhat uncertain, which being the case, the few people who compose this little commonwealth are, by long custom and the constant example of their forefathers, possessed of a provident turn of mind, together with a degree of frugality unknown to every other tribe in this country except the Eskimos.

Deer are said to visit their country in astonishing number both in spring and autumn. The inhabitants kill and dry as much deer flesh as possible, particularly in the fall, so they are seldom in want of a good winter's stock.

Geese, ducks and swans visit them in great plenty during their migrations, and are caught in considerable numbers in snares. It is also reported (though I doubt the truth of it) that a remarkable species of partridge, as big as English fowls, are found in that part of the country only. These, it is said, as well as common partridges, are killed in great numbers with snares as well as with bows and arrows.

The rivers and lakes near the little forest where the family has fixed its abode abound with fine fish that are easily caught with hooks and nets. In fact, I have not seen or heard of any part of this country which seems to possess half the advantages requisite for a constant residence that are ascribed to this little spot.

---

[9] This isolated wood was undoubtedly the "forest oasis" on the Thelon River.

The descendants of the present inhabitants, however, must in time evacuate it for want of wood, which is of so slow a growth in these regions. What is used in one year, exclusive of what is carried away by Eskimos who resort to this place for lumber, must cost many years to replace.

It may be thought strange that any part of such a happily situated community should be found so far away from their home. Indeed, nothing but necessity could possibly have urged them to undertake a journey of so many hundred miles as they had done. But no situation is without its inconvenience, and their woods containing few, if any, birch trees, they had come so far to procure birch bark for canoes, as well as some of the fungus that grows on the birch tree and is used for tinder.

Matonabbee, and the other Indians who were bound for the Fort, now decided to leave the elderly people and young children behind, in the care of some Indians who had orders to proceed to Cathawhachaga on the barren grounds. There they were to await the return of the trading party from the Factory.

We resumed our journey on the 11th of May, at a much brisker pace, and that night pitched our tents beside the Dubawnt River. This day most of us threw away our snowshoes, but our sledges were occasionally serviceable for some time to come, particularly when we walked on the ice of rivers and lakes.

On the 12th, we halted to build canoes. These were completed on the 18th, and we continued along the ice of the Dubawnt River. By the 21st we had crossed the northwest bay of Wholdyah'd Lake, and on this day several of the Indians were forced to turn back by a shortage of provisions. Indeed, game of all sorts was so scarce that, with the exception of a few geese, we had killed nothing from the time of our leaving the women and children.

On the 22nd we killed four deer, but our numbers were still so large that these scarcely afforded us a single meal. On the 25th we crossed Snowbird Lake and at night got clear of the woods, and lay on the barren ground. This day a number of Indians struck off on a different route, not being able to proceed further with us for want of ammunition.

As we had been making good journeys for some days past, and at the same time were heavy laden and in great distress for want of provisions, some of my companions were now so weak that they were obliged to leave their bundles of furs. Many others were so reduced as to be no longer capable of continuing with us. Being without guns or ammunition, they had become completely dependent on the fish they could catch; and though fish were pretty plentiful hereabouts, they were not always to be relied upon for such an immediate supply of food as these poor people needed.

Though I still had a sufficient stock of ammunition to serve me and all my own companions to the Fort, self-preservation is the first law of nature. I therefore thought it advisable to reserve the greater part of this ammunition for our own use, especially as geese and other smaller birds were the only game we met, and these bear hard on supplies of powder and shot. Most of the Indians who accompanied me the whole way had enough ammunition remaining to enable them to travel; but of the others, though we assisted many of them, several of their women died from want.

We continued our course eastward and crossed the Cathawhachaga River on the 30th of May. Soon after the last person had crossed it, the ice broke up. Then, perceiving the approach of bad weather, we made what preparations our situation would admit. The rain soon began to descend in torrents that made the river overflow to such a degree as to convert our first place of retreat into an open sea and oblige us—in the middle of the night—to assemble at the top of an adjacent hill. The violence of the wind would not allow us to pitch a tent, and the only shelter we could obtain was to take the tent-cloth over our shoulders and sit with our backs to the wind.

In this situation we were obliged to remain, without any refreshment, for three full days, until the weather moderated somewhat on the 3rd of June. Early that morning we continued our journey, but the wet and cold I had experienced in the preceding days had so benumbed my lower extremities as to render walking very troublesome for some time.

From the 3rd to the 8th we killed sufficient geese to preserve our lives, but on the 8th we at last perceived plenty of deer and the Indians shot five. This put us into good spirits again, and the number of deer we saw afforded us hopes of more plentiful times during the remainder of our journey.

We expended a little time in eating, and then in slicing some of the meat, but the drying of it occasioned no delay as it was fastened to the women's bundles where it dried in the sun and wind while we were walking. Strange as it may appear, meat thus prepared is not only very substantial food, but pleasant to the taste. It is much esteemed by the natives, and I have found that I could travel farther on a meal of it than upon any other kind of food.

On the 9th of June we spoke with many Northern Indians who were bound for Knapp's Bay to meet the trading sloop from Churchill. Having some time before taken up goods on trust from the Prince of Wales Fort, they were now taking their furs to Knapp's Bay to delay the payment of their debts. Frauds of this kind have been practised by many of these people with great success; by which means debts to a considerable amount are annually lost to the Company.

We did not lose much time in conversation with these Indians but proceeded to the south-east, and for many days afterwards we had the good fortune to meet with plenty of provisions and remarkably fine and pleasant weather. It was as if the country was desirous to make amends for the severe cold, hunger, and excessive hardships we had suffered, and which had reduced us to the greatest misery and want.

On the 18th, we arrived at Egg River and I sent a letter off post-haste to my chief at Prince of Wales Fort, advising him of my being so far advanced on my return. On the 26th we ferried over Seal River, and on the morning of the 29th of June, 1772, I arrived again at Prince of Wales Fort.

I had been absent eighteen months and twenty-three days on this, my third expedition; but it was two years and seven months since I had first set out to find the Coppermine River.

After his return from the Coppermine, Hearne served as mate of the Hudson's Bay Company brigantine Charlotte *before being sent inland from York Factory, in 1774, to establish Cumberland House in what is now east-central Saskatchewan.*

Two years later he was called back to salt water to take command of Prince of Wales Fort, and he was still Governor there when the Fort was attacked by a French naval force under La Pérouse in 1782. The French had four hundred men and Hearne had thirty-nine. The uncompleted fort was, as La Pérouse noted, indefensible, and Hearne had no choice but to surrender. He was taken prisoner, but as the French force was returning homeward through Hudson Strait, Hearne boldly asked La Pérouse to let him have one of the small freighting sloops which the French had seized. Hearne proposed to sail to England in this sloop with the other Hudson's Bay Company prisoners. This was such an audacious suggestion that it caught the chivalric fancy of the French commander and he agreed to it. In due course, Hearne and his tiny vessel made landfall at Gosport, England.

In the summer of 1783, Hearne sailed back to re-found the post at Churchill River. Abandoning the wreckage of Prince of Wales Fort, he chose a much more realistic site on the east side of the river (the present site of Churchill, Manitoba). He remained in command of this new post until 1787, when he returned to England for the last time. In 1792, at the age of forty-seven, he died of dropsy.

By his remarkable tour de force in reaching the Coppermine, Hearne not only forced the eastern door into the great tundra plains, he flung it wide open. But a combination of tragic events soon swung it shut again. The terrible epidemic (smallpox) mentioned by Hearne in his journal almost destroyed the Chipewyans, and communications between Fort Churchill and the Indians of the western plains were irretrievably broken. For well over a century no real attempt was made by Europeans to re-enter the Barren Grounds from the west coast of Hudson Bay. The Hudson's Bay Company confined itself to trading with the coastal Eskimos, and to the struggle for the Southern Indian trade with its great rivals, the Canadian traders, who were pushing up from the south.

Hearne's accomplishments as an explorer are unique. Not only did he visit and describe most of the major regions of the tundra plains east of the Coppermine, but he was able to describe, from Indian sources, many of the remaining areas, including the mysterious Thelon River valley. He met, studied, and accurately described all of the native peoples who occupied or made use of the interior plains. In the field of natural history he made a monumental contribution, and he was the first European to actually see and describe the musk-ox and wood buffalo. His discovery of the arctic coast at the mouth of the Coppermine had a tremendous effect in stimulating later attempts to find a Northwest Passage by sea.

If we are to give Hearne his due, we must credit him with being far and away the greatest traveller and explorer ever to enter those almost limitless arctic plains he called the Barren Grounds.

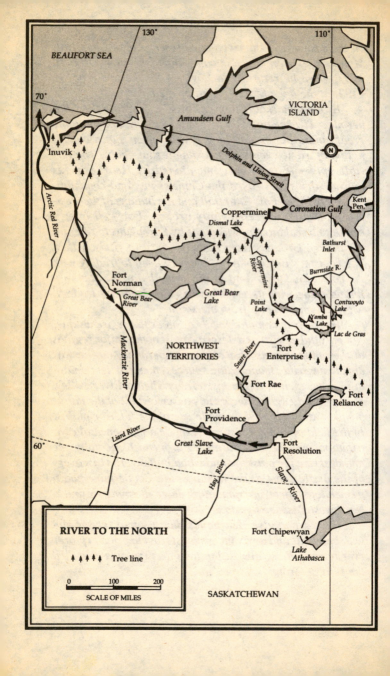

RIVER TO THE NORTH

♠♠♠♠♠ Tree line

0   100   200

SCALE OF MILES

II

River to the North

ALEXANDER MACKENZIE REACHES THE ARCTIC OCEAN, 1789

After Wolfe defeated Montcalm at Quebec in 1759, the new English owners of Canada were quick to take possession of the country, bringing in their train certain tough-minded entrepreneurs, camp followers, and ordinary desperadoes looking for a quick killing amongst the debris of the wrecked French colony. They found an easy source of wealth in the fur trade. Within three or four years after the conquest of Canada, these money-minded gentlemen had sniffed out the old French voyageur routes leading westward to Lake Superior. This only whetted their appetites. They knew about the fat trade monopoly the Hudson's Bay Company had developed with the tribes to the west of the Bay, and some of them determined to intercept this trade and choke it off.

In 1775 several "Canadian" traders struck out to the west and north from the Grand Portage on the western borders of the Lake Superior country. They included

Alexander Henry, born in New Jersey; Peter Pond, from Connecticut; Jean Baptiste Cadotte, a French-Canadian; two Yorkshiremen, Joseph and Thomas Frobisher; and a shadowy gentleman by the name of Paterson.

By chance these several traders met at the north end of Lake Winnipeg, where they seem to have devised a unified plan to cut the Hudson's Bay Company off from its source of western wealth. They decided to split their forces, which consisted of ten birch-bark canoes loaded with men and supplies, sending part far to the west along the Saskatchewan to intercept the Cree and Plains Indians before these people could reach the new Hudson's Bay Company post at Cumberland House, while another party was to strike north to the Churchill River in an attempt to intercept the north-western Indian tribes.

They were hard men — and hard to stop. When they were blocked near the mouth of the Saskatchewan by a band of hostile Indians, they bribed their way through, without any guarantee that they would be allowed to return. Brazenly by-passing Cumberland House, which had been established by Samuel Hearne from Churchill only a year previously, they headed west and north.

The northern group, consisting of Henry and the Frobishers, nearly starved to death the first winter but succeeded in locating the upper reaches of the Churchill River. Failing to find any trace of the Northern Indians, they set out to the north-west up the Churchill to look for them. Eight days later, they encountered a band of Chipewyans bound east for Prince of Wales Fort. This was the first time any "outsider" had contacted the Chipewyans, and it meant the end of the Hudson's Bay Company monopoly of trade with them, and with the other tribes of the north-west for whom the Chipewyans acted as middlemen.

Despite the fact that they were now more than three thousand miles by canoe from their home base at Montreal, the Frobishers and Henry pushed still farther west in an attempt to reach Lake Athabasca which, as yet, had not been seen by any white man. They failed, but they did build a post at Ile à la Crosse in north-western Saskatchewan, within easy canoeing distance of the Athabasca River. Here they learned, from the Indians, of several good water routes leading farther west and north. They had arrived at the door that led into the whole immense region now known as the District of Mackenzie.

However, the free traders were not able to open that door. Their energies were drained off by the most desperate internecine strife as scores of newcomers tried, not only to cut out the Hudson's Bay Company men, but to cut out — or cut up — each other as well. Pitched battles, murders, ambushes, thefts, intimidation, and incitement of the Indians to massacre rivals became commonplace in the north-west. It was frontier anarchy at its worst — and very bad for business.

In Montreal a number of Scottish merchants, who had become the dominant mercantile influence in that city, decided to take things in hand. Chaos was costing them money, and so in 1779 the North West Company was founded by nine of the main firms engaged in supplying the north-western trade. This first attempt to bring order into the business broke down a few years later; but the Company was re-formed in 1783.

The Hudson's Bay Company, in its pursuit of wealth in the form of copper and other minerals, had opened the eastern door into the Barren Grounds. Now the North West Company, in its pursuit of wealth in the form of furs, pried open the western door.

The man chosen to extend the dominion of the "Canadians" (as the Hudson's Bay Company men comtemptuously called the Nor'westers) was Alexander Mackenzie. Born in Inverness in 1763, he came to Canada as a lad of sixteen — penniless, of course — and was soon involved in the fur trade. He had a knack for it and by the time he was twenty-one he had become a wintering partner in charge of the whole Churchill River district. When he was twenty-five he sent his cousin, Roderick Mackenzie, to establish Fort Chipewyan on Lake Athabasca. The following year, using the new Fort as his base, he set out to make a voyage of discovery that he hoped would lead him to the coast of the Pacific Ocean.

From our vantage point in history, the general ignorance of those times as to what really lay to the west seems astounding; yet many men in the North West Company (men who knew the country better than anyone else) were quite convinced that the Pacific was only a few days' travel west of Great Slave Lake. When Mackenzie set out from Fort Chipewyan he had no real knowledge of where he was going. Once clear of Great Slave (which had first been reached by the Nor'westers only four years earlier) his was a journey into the blue.

Mackenzie's story of his journey is told in an austere style which is lean almost to the point of starvation. Only rarely does he allow himself to deviate from the stern purpose of his enterprise, and we have the feeling that he must have been irritated by the fluent, discursive style and wide-ranging curiosity displayed in Samuel Hearne's book. These two young men, both in their middle twenties when they made their great voyages, were leagues apart in their personalities. Mackenzie, the Highland Scot, seems to have had just as powerful a sense a purpose as Hearne, but it stemmed from another source. Mackenzie was primarily a businessman. He tended to be dour, practical and dogged —a no-nonsense sort of fellow who would be assured of a seat on the board of any modern corporation. His sense of humour, if he had one, was kept under firm control. Hearne pursued material goals only as an excuse to go exploring, whereas Mackenzie seems to have considered exploration as serving no useful purpose other than the discovery and exploitation of new sources of wealth. Or, at any rate, this was the guise he felt he had to wear. One can guess why, for he was undoubtedly a victim of the bleak Scots conscience which would have forbidden him to do anything for the sheer joy of it. Still there are moments when the reader of his book suspects that, underneath the careful restraint, there lurked the high, bold spirit of the true adventurer who savoured adventure for its own sake.

VOYAGE TO THE FROZEN OCEAN

June 3rd, 1789. We embarked at nine o'clock in the morning from Fort Chipewyan on Lake Athabasca in a canoe made of birch bark. The crew consisted of four Canadians [French-Canadian voyageurs], two of whom were attended by their wives, and a German; we were accompanied also by an Indian, who had acquired the title of English Chief, and his two wives, in a small canoe with two young Indians, his followers, in another small canoe. This Indian was one of the followers of the chief [Matonabbee] who conducted Mr. Hearne to the Coppermine River. He had since been a principal leader of his countrymen who were in the habit of carrying furs to Churchill Factory, Hudson Bay, and till of late very much attached to the interests of that company. This circumstance procured him the appellation of the English Chief.

We were also accompanied by a canoe I had equipped for the purpose of trade, and given the charge of to M. LeRoux, one of North West Company's clerks. In this I was obliged to ship part of our provisions which, with the clothing necessary for us on the voyage, a proper assortment of the articles of merchandise as presents to insure us a friendly reception among the Indians, and the ammunition and arms requisite for defence, as well as a supply for our hunters, were more than our own canoe could carry.

June 4th. We embarked at four this morning and proceeded to the Peace River which is upward of a mile broad at this spot. Here, indeed, it assumes the name of the Slave River. We now descended our first rapid and proceeded to the north-west. The following day we arrived at another carrying place where we found some difficulty in reloading because of the large quantity of ice which had not yet thawed. The next carrying place, called the Portage d'Embarras, is about six miles and is occasioned by the driftwood filling up the small channel. The whole of the party was employed in taking the baggage and the canoe up the hill. One of the Indian canoes went down the fall and was dashed to pieces. The woman who had the management of it, by quitting it in time, preserved her life, though she lost the little property it contained.

The course from the place we quitted in the morning is about north-west and comprehends a distance of fifteen miles. The carrying path at the next rapid is very bad. In the year 1786, five men were drowned, and two canoes and some packages lost in the rapids on the other side of the river, which occasioned this place to be called Portage des Noyés. The men and Indians were very much fatigued; but the hunters had procured seven geese, a beaver and four ducks. On June 6th we landed early in the evening and encamped. Nets were set in a small adjacent river. We had a head wind during the greater part of the day and the weather had become so cold that the Indians were obliged to make use of their mittens. In this day's progress we killed seven geese and six ducks.

June 9th. We embarked at half past two in the morning. Soon after, two of our young men, whom we had not seen for two days, rejoined us; but during their absence they had killed four beaver and ten geese. The course of this river is meandering, and tends to the north, and in about ten miles falls into the [Great] Slave Lake, where we arrived at nine in the morning, when we found a great change in the weather as it had become extremely cold. The lake was entirely covered with ice and did not seem in any degree to have given way, but near the shore. The gnats and mosquitoes, which were very troublesome during our passage along the river, did not venture to accompany us to this colder region.

The Indians informed me that at a very small distance from either bank of the river are very extensive plains, frequented by large herds of buffaloes; while the moose and reindeer keep in the woods that border on it. The beavers, which are in great numbers, build their habitations in the small lakes and rivers as, in the larger streams, the ice carries everything along with it during the spring. The mud banks in the river are covered with wild fowl and this morning we killed two swans, ten geese, and one beaver, without suffering the delay of an hour; so that we might have soon filled the canoe with them, if that had been our object.

We steered east along the inside of a long sand bank which stretches as far as the houses built by Messrs. Grant and LeRoux in 1785.[1] We often ran aground, as for five successive miles the depth of the water nowhere exceeds three feet. There we found some of our people who had arrived early in the morning and whom we had not seen since the preceding Sunday. We now unloaded the canoe and pitched our tents as there was every appearance that we should be obliged to remain here for some time. I ordered the nets to be set as it was absolutely necessary that the stores provided for our future voyage should remain untouched. The fish we now caught were carp, poisson, inconnu, whitefish and trout.

From the 10th until the 15th of June the party was held up waiting for the ice to break up near shore and make it possible for the canoes to proceed.

June 16th. We were prevented from embarking this morning by a very strong wind from the north and the vast quantity of floating ice. Some trout were caught with hook

---

[1] Now the site of Fort Resolution.

97

and line but the net was not successful. The wind becoming moderate we embarked, taking a north-west course through islands for ten miles. On the 18th our nets had an abundance of fish and we steered north-west until the ice again prevented our progress. Two of our hunters had killed a reindeer and its fawn. They had met with two Indian families and in the evening a man belonging to one of them paid me a visit. These people lived entirely on fish and were waiting to cross the lake as soon as it should become clear of ice.

We saw some reindeer on one of the islands and our hunters went in pursuit of them. They killed five large and two small ones, which was easily accomplished, as the animals had no shelter to which they could run for protection. They had, without doubt, crossed the ice to this spot, and the thaw coming on had detained them there and made them an easy prey to the pursuer. This island was accordingly named Isle de Carreboeuf.

Though the weather was far from being warm we were tormented, and our rest interrupted, by the host of mosquitoes that accompanied us.

June 23rd. The north-west side of the bay was covered with many small islands that were surrounded with ice; but the wind driving it a little off the land, we had a clear passage on the inside of them. At half past two we landed on the mainland at three lodges of Red Knife Indians,[2] so called from their copper knives. They informed us that there were many more lodges of their friends at no great distance; and one of the Indians set out to fetch them. They also said that we should see no more of them at present, as the Slave and Beaver Indians, as well as others of the tribe, would not be here till the time that the swans cast their feathers.

---

[2] Usually called Yellowknives. These were the Copper Indians of Hearne.

M. LeRoux purchased of these Indians upwards of eight packs of good beaver and marten skins although there were not above twelve of them qualified to kill beaver. The English Chief got upwards of an hundred skins [from these people] on the score of debts due to him, of which he has many outstanding in this country. Forty of them he gave [us] on account of debts due by him since the winter of 1786 and 1787 at the Slave Lake; the rest he exchanged [with us] for rum and other necessary articles; and I added a small quantity of that liquor as an encouraging present to him and his young men. I had several consultations with these Copper Indian people but could obtain no information that was material to our expedition; nor were they acquainted with any part of the river which was the object of my research, but the mouth of it. In order to save as much time as possible in circumnavigating the bays, I engaged one of the Indians to conduct us [to the mouth] and I accordingly equipped him with various articles of clothing, etc. I also purchased a large new canoe that he might embark with the two young Indians in my service.

In the afternoon I assembled the Indians in order to inform them that I should take my departure on the following day; that some of our people would remain on the spot till their countrymen, whom they had mentioned, should arrive; and that, if they brought a sufficient quantity of skins to make it answer, the Frenchman [LeRoux] would return for more goods, with a view to winter here and build a fort (fort is the name given to any establishment in this country) which would be continued as long as they should be found to deserve it. They assured me that it would be a great encouragement to them to have a settlement of ours in their country; and that they should exert themselves to the utmost to kill beaver, as they would then be certain of getting an adequate value for them. Hitherto, they said, the Chipewyans always pillaged them or, at most, gave little or nothing for the fruits of their labour, which had greatly discouraged them; and that, in consequence of this treatment, they had no motive to pursue the beaver, except to obtain a sufficient quantity of food and raiment.[3]

We left this place on Thursday, June 25th, our canoe being deeply laden. We were saluted on our departure by M. LeRoux with some volleys of small arms, which we returned, and steered south by west straight across the [western] bay [of Great Slave Lake].

We were very much interrupted by drifting ice and with some difficulty reached an island. I immediately proceeded to the farther part of it. It is about five miles in circumference and I was very much surprised to find that the greater part of the wood with which it was formerly covered had been cut down within twelve or fifteen years. On making inquiries concerning the cause of this extraordinary circumstance, the English Chief informed me that several winters ago many of the Slave Indians inhabited the islands that were scattered over the bay, as the surrounding waters abound with fish throughout the year, but that they had been driven away by the Knisteneaux [Cree Indians], who continually made war upon them. If an establishment is to be made in this country it must be in the neighbourhood of this place, on account of the wood and the fishery.

Friday, June 22nd. We continued at five o'clock steering south-east for ten miles across two deep bays. There was some floating ice in the lake and the Indians killed a couple of swans.

On June 28th we were again on the water at a quarter past three, and after another twenty-seven miles we steered

---

[3]The Indians were referring to time past. At this date the Barren-Land Chipewyans had almost been wiped out by the smallpox epidemic, and there was little or no direct trade between the Yellowknives and Churchill. This was the first time the North West Company had made direct contact with the Copper Indians of Hearne's account.

into a deep bay and though we had no land ahead in sight we indulged the hope of finding a passage which, according to the Indians, would conduct us to the entrance of the river.

Having a strong wind aft, we lost sight of our Indians, nor could we put on shore to wait for them, without risking damage to the canoe, till we ran to the bottom of the bay when we discovered there was no passage there. In two or three hours they joined us. The English Chief was very much irritated against the Red Knife Indian and even threatened to murder him for having undertaken to guide us in a course of which he was ignorant. In the blowing weather today we were obliged to [bail with] our large kettle to keep our canoe from filling, although we did not carry above three feet of sail. The Indians very narrowly escaped [swamping].

June 29th. At half past five we doubled the extremity of a point and found the river. The water appeared to abound in fish and was covered with fowl such as swans, geese, and several kinds of ducks. The current, though not very strong, set us south-west by west and we followed this course fourteen miles till we passed the point of a long island where the Slave Lake discharges itself and is ten miles in breadth. The river now turns to the westward becoming gradually narrow for twenty-four miles till it is not more than half a mile wide. Our Red Knife Indian had never explored beyond our present situation. He informed us that a river falls in from the north which takes its rise in the Horn Mountains, now in sight, which is the country of the Beaver Indians; and that he and his relations frequently meet on that river. He also added that there are very extensive plains on both sides of it which abound in buffaloes and moose deer.

At six in the afternoon there was an appearance of bad weather. We landed therefore for the night but before we could pitch our tents a violent tempest came on. The Indians were very much fatigued, having been employed in running after wild fowl which had lately cast their feathers;[4] they caught five swans and the same number of geese.

July 1st. We landed upon a small island where there were the poles of four lodges standing which we concluded to have belonged to Knisteneaux, on their war excursions six or seven years ago. As our canoes were deeply laden, and being also in daily expectation of coming to rapids or falls, which we had been taught to consider with apprehension, we here concealed two bags of pemmican in the hope they would be of future service to us. The Indians were of a different opinion, as they entertained no expectation of returning that season, by which time the hidden provisions would be spoiled. Near us were two Indian encampments of the last year. By the manner in which these people cut their wood it appears that they have no iron tools.

Our course had been west-south-west thirty miles, and we proceeded with great caution, as we continually expected to approach some great rapid or falls. This was such a prevalent idea that all of us were occasionally persuaded that we heard those sounds which betokened a fall of water. The Indians complained of the perseverance with which we pushed forward and that they were not accustomed to such severe fatigue as it occasioned.

July 3rd. According to my reckoning since my last observation we had run 217 miles west and 44 miles north. We encamped at eight in the evening at the foot of a high hill. I immediately ascended it accompanied by two men and some Indians, and I was much surprised to find it crowned by an encampment. The Indians informed me that it is the custom of those people who have no fire arms to choose these elevated spots for the places of their residence, as they can render them inaccessible to their enemies, particularly the Knisteneaux of whom they are in continual dread.

---

[4]The birds were moulting and could not fly.

We were obliged to shorten our stay here, from the swarms of mosquitoes which attacked us on all sides and were, indeed, the only inhabitants of the place. We saw several encampments of natives in the course of the day but none of these were of this year's establishment. Since four in the afternoon the current has been so strong that it was at length in an actual ebullition and produced a hissing sound like a kettle of water in a moderate state of boiling.

July 5th. The river increased in breadth and the current began to slacken. We perceived a ridge of high mountains before us covered with snow. At three-quarters past seven o'clock we saw several smokes on the north shore which we made every exertion to approach. As we drew nearer we discovered natives running about in apparent great confusion; some were making to the woods, and others hurrying to their canoes. Our hunters landed before us, and addressed a few that had not escaped, in the Chipewyan language, which, so great was their confusion and terror, they did not appear to understand. But when they perceived that it was impossible to avoid us, as we were all landed, they made a sign to keep at a distance, with which we complied, and we not only unloaded our canoes but pitched our tents before we made any attempt to approach them.

During this interval the English Chief and his young men were employed in reconciling them to our arrival and when they had recovered from the alarm of hostile intention it appeared that some of them comprehended the language of our Indians so that they were at length persuaded to come to us.

There were five families, consisting of twenty-five or thirty people of two different tribes, the Slave and the Dog-Rib Indians. We made them smoke, though it was evident they did not know the use of tobacco; we likewise supplied them with grog; but I am disposed to think that they accepted our civilities rather from fear than inclination. We acquired a more effectual influence over them by the distribution of knives, beads, rings, gartering, fire steels, flints and hatchets; so that they became more familiar even than we expected, for we could not keep them out of our tents; though I did not observe that they attempted to purloin anything.

The information they gave respecting the river had so much of the fabulous that I shall not detail it; it will be sufficient just to mention their attempts to persuade us that it would require several winters to get to the sea, and that old age would come upon us before the time of our return. We were also to encounter monsters of such horrid shapes and destructive powers as could not exist but in their wild imaginations. They added, besides, that there were two impassable falls in the river, the first of which was about thirty days' march from us.

Though I placed no faith in these strange relations, they had a very different effect upon our Indians, who were tiring of the voyage. It was their opinion and anxious wish that we should not hesitate to return. They said that according to the information, there were very few animals in the country beyond us, and that as we proceeded the scarcity would increase and we should absolutely perish from hunger, if no other accidents befell us. It was with no small trouble that they were convinced of the folly of these reasonings; and by my desire they induced one of these Indians to accompany us in consideration of a small kettle, an axe, a knife and some other articles.

Previous to this man's departure, a ceremony took place of which I could not learn the meaning; he cut off a lock of his hair and having divided it into three parts he fastened one of them to the hair on the upper part of his wife's head, blowing on it three times with the utmost violence, and uttering certain words. The other two he fastened with the same formalities on the heads of his two children.

They are a meagre, ugly, ill-made people, particularly about the legs which are very clumsy and covered with scabs. Many of them appeared to be in a very unhealthy state, which is owing, as I imagine, to their natural filthiness. They are of a moderate stature and, as far as could be discovered through the coat of dirt and grease that covered them, are of a fairer complexion than the generality of Indians who are natives of warmer climates.

Some have their hair of great lengths; while others suffer a long tress to fall behind, and the rest is cut so short as to expose their ears, but no other attention is paid to it. The beards of some of the old men were long, and the rest had them pulled out by the roots so that not a hair could be seen on their chins. Their clothing is made of the dressed skins of the rein or moose deer though more commonly of the former. These they prepare in the hair for winter, and make shirts of both, which reach the middle of their thighs. Their upper garments are sufficiently large as to cover the whole body, with a fringe around the bottom, and are used both sleeping and awake. The dress of the women is the same as that of the men. The former have no covering on their private parts, except a tassel of leather which dangles from a small cord, to keep off the flies which would otherwise be fairly troublesome. Whether circumcision be practiced among them I cannot pretend to say, but the appearance of it was general amongst those whom I saw.

Their lodges are a very simple structure; a few poles supported by a fork, and forming a semi-circle at the bottom with some branches or a piece of bark as a covering, constitutes the whole of their native architecture. They build two of these huts facing each other and make the fire between them. They have a few dishes of wood, bark, or horn; the vessels in which they cook their victuals are in the shape of a gourd, narrow at the top and wide at the bottom, and of *watape* (this is a name given to the divided roots of the spruce, which the natives weave into a degree of compactness that renders it capable of containing a fluid) which is made to boil by putting a succession of red hot stones into it. They always keep a large quantity of the fibres of willow bark, which they work into thread on their thighs. Their nets (of willow-bark thread) are from three to forty fathoms in length and from thirteen to thirty-six meshes in depth. They likewise make lines of the sinews of the reindeer and manufacture their hooks from wood, horn, or bone. Their arms and weapons for hunting are bows and arrows, spears, daggers and clubs. The bows are about five or six feet in length, and the strings are of sinews or raw skins. The arrows are two and a half feet long including the barb which is variously formed of bone, horn, flint, iron or copper, and are winged with three feathers. The daggers are flat and pointed, about twelve inches long, and made of horn or bone. The club is made of the horn of the reindeer, the branches being all cut off except those which form the extremities. This instrument is about two feet in length and is employed to dispatch their enemies in battle. The axes are manufactured of a piece of brown or grey stone from six to eight inches long and two inches thick. The inside is flat and the outside round and tapering to an edge an inch wide. They are fastened by the middle to a handle two feet long with a cord of green skin. From the adjoining tribes — the Red Knives and Chipewyans—they procure, in barter for marten skins and a few beaver, small pieces of iron of which they manufacture knives by fixing them at the end of a short stick and, with them and beaver teeth, they finish all their work.

Their canoes are small, pointed at both ends, flat-bottomed and covered in the forepart. They are made of the bark of the birch tree and fir wood, but of so light a construction that the man whom one of these light vessels bears on the water can, in return, carry it over land without any difficulty.

At four in the afternoon we embarked. Our course was west-north-west and we soon passed the river of the Great Bear Lake. We encamped beneath a rocky hill where, according to the information of our guide, it blew a storm every day throughout the year. He found himself very uncomfortable and pretended that he was very ill in order that he might be permitted to return to his relatives. To prevent his escape it became necessary to keep a strict watch over him during the night.

July 6th. We passed through numerous islands and had the ridge of snowy mountains always in sight. Our conductor informed us that great numbers of bears and small white buffaloes [mountain goats] frequent those mountains, which are also inhabited by Indians. We camped in a similar situation to that of the preceding evening beneath a high rocky hill which I attempted to ascend in company with one of the hunters, but before we got halfway to the summit we were almost suffocated by a cloud of mosquitoes and were obliged to return.

The following day we landed in an encampment of four fires, all the inhabitants of which ran off with the utmost speed except an old man and an old woman. He appeared too indifferent about the short time he had to remain in the world to be very anxious about escaping from any danger. He pulled his grey hairs from his head by handfuls to distribute amongst us and implored our favour for himself and his relations. Our guide at length removed his fears and persuaded him to recall the fugitives, consisting of eighteen people, whom I reconciled to me on their return with presents of beads, knives, awls, etc. They differed in no respect from those we had already seen nor were they deficient in hospitable attention; they provided us with fish, which was very well boiled and cheerfully accepted by us. Our guide still sickened after his home and was so anxious to return thither that we were under the necessity of forcing him to embark.

These people informed us that we were close to another great rapid and that there were several lodges of their relations in the vicinity. Four canoes with a man in each followed us to point out the particular channels we should follow for the secure passage of the rapids. They also abounded in discouraging stories concerning the dangers and difficulties which we were to encounter.

We then steered north three miles and landed at an encampment of three or more families which was situated on the bank of the river. They very much regretted that they had no goods or merchandise to exchange with us, as they had left them at a lake from which the river issued, in whose vicinity some of their people were employed setting snares for reindeer. There was a youth among them in the capacity of a slave whom our Indians understood much better than any of the natives of this country whom they had yet seen; he was invited to accompany us, but took the first opportunity to conceal himself and we saw him no more.

Our conductor renewed his complaints, not, as he assured us, from any apprehension of our ill-treatment, but of the Eskimo, whom he represented as a very wicked and malignant people who would put us all to death. He added, also, that it was but two summers since a large party of them had come up this river and killed many of his relations.

July 8th. At half past two we came ashore at two lodges of nine Indians. Several of them were clad in hare skins but in every other circumstance resembled those we had already seen. We were, however, informed that they were of a different tribe called the Hare Indians, as hares and fish are their principal support from the scarcity of reindeer and beaver which are the only animals of the larger kind that frequent this part of the country.

Here we made an exchange of our guide, who had been so troublesome that we were obliged to watch him night and day except when he was on the water. The man, however, who had agreed to go in his place soon repented of his engagement and endeavoured to persuade us that some of his relations further down the river would readily accompany us, and were much better acquainted with the river than he was. But as he had informed us ten minutes earlier that we should see no more of his tribe, we paid very little attention to his remonstrances, and compelled him to embark. In about three hours a man overtook us in a small canoe, and we suspected that his object was to facilitate in some way or other the escape of our conductor. About twelve we also observed an Indian walking along the north-east shore, when the small canoe paddled toward him. We followed and found three men, three women, and two children who had been on a hunting expedition. They had some flesh of the reindeer which was offered to us but it was so rotten, as well as offensive to the smell, that we excused ourselves.

July 9th. Thunder and rain prevailed during the night and during the course of it our guide deserted us; we therefore compelled another of these people, very much against his will, to supply the place of his fugitive countryman.

In a short time we saw smoke on the east shore. Our new guide began immediately to call to the people that belonged to it in a particular manner. He informed us that they were not of his tribe but were a very wicked people who would beat us cruelly, pull our hair with great violence from our heads, and maltreat us in various other ways. There were but four of these people and, previous to our landing, they all harangued us at the same moment and apparently with violent anger and resentment. Our hunters did not understand them, but no sooner had our guide addressed them than they were appeased. There were fifteen of them altogether with women and children when they returned from the woods, and of a more pleasing appearance than any which we had hitherto seen, as they were healthy, full of flesh and clean in their person. Their language was somewhat different.

The only iron they had was in small pieces which serve them for knives. Their arrows are made of light wood and are winged only with two feathers; their bows differed from any others we had seen and we understood they were furnished by the Eskimos who are their neighbours. They consist of two pieces with a very strong cord of sinews along the back, which is tied in several places to preserve its shape.

We prevailed on the native whose language was most intelligible to accompany us. He informed us that we should sleep ten nights more before we arrived at the sea; that several of his relations resided in the immediate vicinity of this part of the river; and that in three nights we should meet with the Eskimos with whom they had formerly made war, but were now in a state of peace.

As we pushed off, some of my men discharged their fowling pieces, that were only loaded with powder, at the report of which the Indians were very much alarmed as they had not before heard the discharge of a firearm.

Two of our guide's companions followed us in their canoes and they amused us not only with native songs but with others in imitation of the Eskimos; and our new guide was so enlivened that the antics he performed in keeping time to the singing alarmed us with continual apprehension that his boat might upset; but he was not long content with his confined situation, and paddling up alongside our canoe, requested us to receive him in it though but a short time before he had resolutely refused to accept our invitation. No sooner had he entered our canoe than he began to perform an Eskimo dance, to our no small alarm. He was, however, prevailed upon to be more tranquil, when he began to display various indecencies, according to the customs of the Eskimos, of which he boasted an intimate acquaintance. On our putting to shore to leave his canoe he informed us that, on the opposite hill, the Eskimos, three winters before, had killed his grandfather.

About four in the afternoon we perceived a smoke on the west shore and landed. The natives made a most terrible uproar, running about as if they were deprived of their senses, while the greater part of the women and children fled away. I have no doubt if we had been without people to introduce us that they would have attempted some violence against us. At length we pacified them and I gave them some small quantity of ornamental baubles. This party consisted of five families to the amount of, as I suppose, forty men, women and children; they are called Deguthee Denees or the Quarrellers.[5]

July 10th. So various had the channels of the river become at the present time that we were at a loss which to take. Our guide preferred the easternmost on account of the Eskimos, but I determined to take the middle channel, as it appeared to be a larger body of water. The snowy mountains lie west by south from us, and stretch to the northward as far as we could see. According to the information of the Indians, they are part of the chain of mountains which we approached on the third of this month. From hence it was evident that these waters emptied themselves into the Hyperborean [Arctic] Sea; and though it was probable that, from want of provisions, we could not return to Athabasca in the course of the season, I nevertheless determined to penetrate to the discharge of them.

My new guide, being very much discouraged and quite tired of his situation, used his influence to prevent our proceeding. In short, my hunters also became so disheartened from his accounts and other circumstances that I was confident they would have left me if it had been in their power. I, however, satisfied them in some degree by the assurance that I would proceed onwards but seven days more, and if I did not get to the sea, I would return. Indeed the low state of our provisions formed a very sufficient security for the maintenance of my statement.

At half past eight we landed and pitched our tents near to where there had been three encampments of the Eskimos since the breaking up of the ice.

July 11th. I sat up all night to observe the sun. At half

_____
[5]A branch of the Kutchin Indians of northeastern Alaska.

past twelve I called up one of the men to view the spectacle which he had never before seen. On seeing the sun so high, he thought it was a signal to embark and began to call the rest of his companions who would scarcely be persuaded by me that the sun had not descended nearer to the horizon and that it was now but a short time past midnight.

At four, we landed where there were three houses, or rather huts, belonging to natives [Eskimos]. Their ground plan is of an oval form about fifteen feet long, ten feet wide in the middle and eight feet at either end; the whole of it is dug about twelve inches below the surface of the ground. One-half of it is covered over with willow branches which probably serves as a bed for the whole family. In and about the house we found sledge runners and bones, pieces of whalebone, and poplar bark cut in circles which are used as corks to buoy the nets.

We continued our voyage and encamped at eight o'clock. On several of the islands we perceived the print of their feet in the sand as if they had been there but a few days previous.

The discontent of our hunters was now renewed by the accounts the guide had been giving of that part of our voyage now approaching. According to his information we were to see a larger lake on the morrow. The Eskimos alone, he added, inhabit the shores, and kill a large fish that is found in it which is the principal part of their food; this, we presume, must be the whale. He also mentioned white bears and another large animal which was seen in these parts, but our hunters could not understand the description which he gave of it. To reconcile the English Chief to the necessary continuance in my service, I now presented him with one of my capotes or travelling coats; at the same time, to satisfy the guide, and keep him if possible in good humour, I gave him a skin of the moose deer, which in his opinion was a valuable present.

July 12th. I took an observation which gave 69° 1′ N. latitude. We continued the same course for a high island

at a distance of fifteen miles. At five o'clock we arrived at
an island and landed at the boundary of our voyage in this
direction. As soon as the tents were pitched I proceeded
with the English Chief to the highest part of the island from
which we discovered the solid ice extending from the
north-west to the eastward. As far as the eye could reach
to the south-westward we could dimly perceive a chain of
mountains stretching farther to the north than the edge of
the ice. To the eastward we saw many islands, and in our
progress met with a considerable number of white partridges. The Indians informed me that they had landed on
a small island about four leagues from hence where they
had seen the tracks of two men that were quite fresh; they
had also found a secret store of train oil,[6] and several bones
of white bears were scattered about the place where it was
hidden.

My people could not, at this time, refrain from expressions of real concern that they were obliged to return without reaching the seas. For some time past, their spirits
were animated by the expectation that another day would
bring them to the western ocean; and even in our present
situation they declared their readiness to follow me wherever I should be pleased to lead them.

This afternoon I re-ascended the hill but could not
discover that the ice had been put in motion by the force
of the wind. I now thought it necessary to give a new net
to my men in order to obtain as much provisions as possible
from the water, our stores being reduced to about five
hundred-weight which, without any other supply, would
not have sufficed for fifteen people above twelve days.

July 14th. It blew very hard from the north-west. I
slept longer than usual; but about eight one of my men
saw a great many animals in the water, which he at first
supposed to be pieces of ice. I immediately perceived that
they were whales and having ordered the canoe to be

---

[6]Rendered seal or whale oil.

113

prepared we embarked in pursuit of them. It was, indeed, a very wild and unreflecting enterprise, and it was a very fortunate circumstance that we failed in our attempt to overtake them, as the stroke from the tail of one of these enormous fish would have dashed the canoe to pieces. Our guide informed us that they are the same kind of fish which are the principal food of the Eskimos and they were frequently seen as large as our canoe. The part of them which appeared above the water was altogether white, and they were much larger than the largest porpoise.[7]

At twelve the fog dispersed and being curious to take a view of the ice I gave orders for the canoe to be got in readiness. We had not, however, been an hour on the water when the wind rose on a sudden from the north-east. We were in a state of actual danger and felt every corresponding emotion of pleasure when we reached the land. As I did not propose to satisfy my curiosity at the risk of similar dangers, we continued our course along the islands which screened us from the wind. I was in the hope that I might be able to meet some parties of natives and obtain some interesting intelligence, though our guide discouraged my expectations by representing them as a very shy and inaccessible people. This morning I ordered a post to be erected close to our tent, on which I engraved the latitude of the place, my own name, the number of persons which I had with me, and the time we remained there.

Until July 21st Mackenzie and his party remained in the estuary of the great river which now bears his name, searching for the absent Eskimos and trying to reach the actual mouth of the river. Although they found many campsites and winter houses, they found none of the people

---

[7]These were beluga, or white whales, which often enter river estuaries.

themselves, nor were they able to reach the Arctic Ocean proper. With supplies running dangerously low, Mackenzie finally had to turn for home.

The Journey Back

July 21st. We embarked at half past one this morning when the weather was cold and unpleasant and the wind southwest. At ten we left the channels formed by the islands for the uninterrupted channel of the river, where we found a current so strong that it was absolutely necessary to tow the canoe with a line. The men in the canoe relieved two of those on shore every two hours, so that it was very hard and fatiguing duty, but it saved a great deal of that time which was so precious to us. At half past eight we landed at the same spot where we had already encamped on the 9th of July. In about an hour after our arrival we were joined by eleven of the Indians who were stationed farther up the river. I now saw the sun set for the first time since I had been here.

July 22nd. We began our march at half past three this morning, the men being employed to tow the canoes. I walked with the Indians to their huts. They had hid their effects and sent their young women into the woods as we saw but very few of the former and none of the latter. They had large huts built of driftwood on the declivity of the beach and in the inside the earth was dug away so as to form a level floor. At each end was a stout fork whereon was laid a strong ridgepole which formed a support to the whole structure, and a covering of spruce bark preserved it from the rain. There were rails on the outside of the building which were hung around with fish. The spawn is also carefully preserved and dried in the same manner. We obtained as many fish from them as the canoe could conveniently contain and some strings of beads were the price paid for them.

During the two hours I was here, I employed the English Chief in a continual state of inquiry concerning these people. The information that resulted was as follows:

This nation or tribe [the Deguthee Denees, or Quarrellers] is very numerous, with whom the Eskimos had been continually at variance, a people [i.e., the Eskimos] who take every advantage of attacking those who are not in a state to defend themselves; and though they had promised friendship, they had lately, in the most treacherous manner, butchered some of their people. They declared their determination to withdraw all confidence in future from the Eskimos, and to collect themselves in a formidable body that they might be enabled to revenge the death of their friends.

From their account, a strong party of Eskimos occasionally ascends the river in large canoes [umiaks] in search of flint stones which they employ to point their spears and arrows. They were now at their lake [the Eskimo Lakes] due east from the spot where we then were, which was at no great distance overland, where they kill the reindeer; and they would soon begin to catch big fish for the winter stock.

The Eskimos inform them that they saw large canoes full of white men to the westward, eight or ten winters ago, from whom they obtained iron in exchange for leather. The lake where they met these canoes is called by them Belhoullay Toe or White Man's Lake.[8] They also represented the Eskimos as dressing like themselves. They wear their hair short and have two holes perforated, one on each

---

[8]This part of White Man's Lake was probably the Chukchi Sea lying between Siberia and Alaska, north of Bering Strait. It seems certain that the ships filled with white men seen to the westward about eight or ten years earlier were Captain James Cook's two ships, *Discovery* and *Resolution*, which in the summer of 1778 penetrated into the Chukchi Sea as far to the north and west as Icy Cape and so were within a hundred miles of rounding Cape Barrow and entering the Beaufort Sea, into which the Mackenzie River drains.

side of the mouth in a line with the under lip, in which they place long beads that they find in the lake. Their bows are somewhat different from those used by the natives we had seen and they employ slings from whence they throw stones with such dexterity that they prove very formidable weapons in the day of battle.

We proceeded with the tracking line throughout the day, except two hours, when we employed the sail.

July 23rd. At five in the morning we proceeded but found it very difficult to travel along the beach. At five o'clock [that evening] our Indians put to shore in order to encamp, but we proceeded onward, which displeased them very much from the fatigue they suffered. At ten our hunters returned, sullen and dissatisfied. We had not touched any of our [preserved] provisions for six days, in which time we had consumed two reindeer, four swans, forty-five geese and a considerable quantity of fish. I have always observed that the north men possessed very hearty appetites but they were very much exceeded by those with me, since we entered this river. I should really have thought it absolute gluttony in my people if my appetite had not increased in a similar proportion.

July 24th. We passed a small river on each side of which the natives and Eskimos collect flint. Among them are found pieces of petroleum, which bears a resemblance to yellow wax but is more friable. The English Chief informed me that rock of a similar kind is scattered about the country at the back of Slave Lake where the Chipewyans collect copper.

At twelve we observed a lodge on the side of the river and its inhabitants running about in great confusion. The men awaited our arrival with their bows and arrows ready to be employed. The English Chief, whose language they in some degree understood, endeavoured to remove their distrust of us, but till I went to them with a present of beads they refused to have any communications with us.

When they first perceived our sail they took us for the

Eskimos, who employ a sail in their canoes. On seeing us in possession of the clothes, bows, etc. which must have belonged to some of the Deguthee Denees or Quarrellers, they imagined we had killed some of them and were bearing away the fruits of our victory.

They would not acknowledge that they had any women with them, though we had seen them running to the woods; but pretended they had been left a considerable distance from the river.

The English Chief was during the whole of this time in the woods, where some of the hidden property was discovered, but the women contrived to elude the search that was made after them. Our Chief expressed his displeasure at their running away to conceal themselves, their property, and their young women, in very bitter terms. He said his heart was set against those Slaves; and complained loudly of his disappointment in coming so far without getting something from them.

July 26th. At eight we landed at three Indian lodges. There were five or six persons whom we had not seen before and among them was a Dog-Rib Indian, whom some private quarrel had driven from his country. The English Chief understood him as well as one of his own nation and gave the following account of their conversation:

He had been informed by the people with whom he now lives, the Hare Indians, that there is another river on the other side of the mountain to the south-west which falls into the Belhoullay Toe or White Man's Lake; that the natives were very large and very wicked, and killed common men with their eyes; that they make canoes larger than ours; that those who inhabit the entrance of this river kill a kind of beaver, the skin of which is almost red; and that large canoes often frequent it. As there is no known communication by water with this river, the natives who saw it went over the mountains.

My Indians were very anxious to possess themselves of a woman who was with the natives but, as they were not willing to part with her, I interfered to prevent her being taken by force; indeed, I was obliged to exercise the utmost vigilance, as the Indians who accompanied me were ever ready to take what they could from the natives, without making them any return.

July 27th. At seven we landed where there were three families situated close to the rapids. During the time we remained with them I endeavoured to obtain additional intelligence respecting the river which had been mentioned on the preceding day; they had been informed that it was larger than that which washed the banks whereon they lived, and that its course was toward the midday sun. They added that there were people at a short distance up the river who inhabited the opposite mountains and had lately descended from them to obtain supplies of fish. These people, they suggested, must be well acquainted with the other river which was the object of my inquiry. I engaged one of them, by a bribe of some beads, to describe this country upon the sand. This singular map he immediately undertook to delineate and accordingly traced out a very long point of land between the rivers, though without paying the least attention to their courses, which he represented as running into the Great Lake, at the extremity of which, as he had been told by Indians of other nations, there was a Belhoullay Couin, or White Man's Fort. This I took to be Unalascha Fort, and consequently the river to the west to be Cook's River, and assumed that the body of water or sea into which this river discharges itself at Whale Island communicates with Norton Sound. I made an advantageous proposition to this man to accompany me across the mountains to the other river, but he refused it.

One of the small company of natives was grievously afflicted with ulcers in his back and the only attention which was paid to his miserable condition, as far as could be discovered, proceeded from a woman who carefully employed a bunch of feathers in preventing the flies from settling upon his sores.

119

I now found that it would be fruitless for me to expect any account of the country [to the west] or the other great river, till I got to the river of the Bear Lake where I expected to find some natives who had promised to wait for us there. These people had actually mentioned this river to me when we passed them, but I then paid no attention to that circumstance. I imagined it to be a misunderstanding.

We were plentifully supplied with fish by these people and I purchased a few beaver skins of them. They were alarmed for some of their young men, who were killing geese farther up the river, and entreated us to do them no harm. About sunset I was under the necessity of shooting one of their dogs, as we could not keep those animals from our baggage. When the people heard the report of the pistol and saw the dead dog, they were seized with a very general alarm and the women took their children on their backs and ran into the woods. The woman to whom the dog belonged was very much affected, and declared that the loss of five children during the preceding winter had not affected her as much as the death of this animal. When we arrived this morning we found the women in tears from an apprehension that we had come to take them away. To the eyes of an European they certainly were objects of disgust; but there were those among my party who observed some hidden charms in these females which rendered them objects of desire, and means were found, I believe, that very soon dissipated their alarms and subdued their coyness.

July 28th. At four this morning I ordered my people to prepare for our departure, and while they were loading the canoe I went with the English Chief to visit the lodges, but the greater part of their inhabitants had quitted them during the night and those that remained pretended sickness and refused to rise. When, however, they were convinced that we did not intend to take any of them with us, their sickness abandoned them, and when we embarked they came forth from their huts to desire that we would visit their nets and take all the fish we might find in them. We accordingly availed ourselves of this permission.

We landed shortly after where there were two more lodges which were full of fish but without any inhabitants. My Indians, in rummaging these places, found several articles which they proposed to take; I therefore gave beads and awls to be left as a purchase of them. I took up a net and left a large knife in its place. It was about four fathoms long and more convenient to set in the eddy current than our long ones. This is the place the Indians call a rapid, though we went up it all the way with the paddle.

At one in the afternoon we went onshore at a fire. The hunters found a canoe and fowl. Out of two hundred geese we picked thirty-six which were eatable; the rest were putrid and emitted a horrid stench. They had been killed for some time without having been gutted, and in this state of loathesome rottenness we have every reason to suppose they were eaten by the natives.

July 30th. We renewed our voyage at four this morning after a rainy night. The weather had moderated and the wind was north-west. We were enabled to employ the sail during part of the day. The English Chief was very much irritated against one of his young men: that jealousy occasioned this uneasiness, and that it was not without sufficient cause, was all I could discover. The next day we were much impeded in our way by shoals of sand and small stones. In other places the bank of the river is lofty: it is formed of black earth and sand and, as it is continually falling, displayed to us in some parts a face of solid ice to within a foot of the surface.

August 2nd. We set off at three this morning with the towing line. I walked with my Indians as they went faster than the canoe and as I suspected that they wanted to arrive at the huts of the natives before me. In our way I observed several small springs of mineral water running from the foot of the mountain, and along the beach saw several lumps of iron ore.

When we came to the river of the Great Bear Lake I ordered one of the young Indians to wait for my canoe and I took my place in their small canoe [which one of the Indians had presumably carried with him]. This river is about 250 yards broad. When I landed on the opposite shore I discovered that the natives had been there very lately from the print of their feet in the sand. We continued walking till five in the afternoon when we saw several smokes along the shore. As we naturally concluded that these were certain indications where we should meet the natives who were the object of our search, we quickened our pace; but in our progress experienced a very sulphurous smell, and at length discovered that the whole bank was on fire for a very considerable distance. It proved to be a coal mine to which the fire had communicated from an old Indian encampment. The beach was covered with coals and the English Chief gathered some of the softest he could find, as a black dye — it being the mineral, he informed me, with which the natives render their quills black.

August 7th. We embarked at half past three and soon after perceived two reindeer on the beach before us. We checked our course but our Indians, in contending who should be the first to get near these animals, alarmed and lost them. We, however, killed a female reindeer and from the wounds in her hind legs it was supposed that she had been pursued by wolves, who had devoured her young one; her udder was full of milk and one of the young Indians poured it amongst some boiled corn, which he ate with great delight.

At this juncture Mackenzie had become desperately anxious to communicate with any natives who could give him information about a river flowing westward to the Pacific Ocean; but all of his accompanying Indians were doing their level best to prevent him from obtaining such infor-

mation, since they were afraid it would mean the expedition would not proceed home to Lake Athabasca that autumn.

August 10th. The Indians were before us in pursuit of game. At ten we landed opposite to the mountains which we had passed on the 2nd of last month. One of the hunters joined us here, fatigued and unsuccessful. As these mountains are the last of any considerable magnitude on the south-west side of the river, I ordered my men to cross to that side that I might ascend one of them. It was near four in the afternoon when I landed and I lost no time in proceeding to the attainment of my object. I was accompanied only by a young Indian as the curiosity of my people was subdued by the fatigue they had undergone; and we soon had reason to believe we should pay dearly for the indulgence of our own. When we had walked upwards of an hour the underwood decreased. The ground began to rise and was covered with small pines, and at length we got the first view of the mountains since we had left the canoe. The Indian's shoes and leggings were torn to pieces and he was alarmed at the idea of passing through such bad roads during the night. I persisted, however, in proceeding, with the determination to pass the night on the mountains and return on the morrow. As we approached them, the ground was quite marshy and I found it impossible to proceed. I therefore determined to return to the canoe, and arrived there about midnight, very much fatigued with this fruitless journey.

August 11th. We embarked before three, and at five traversed the river when we saw two of our hunters coming down in search of us. They had seen several native encampments at no great distance from the river; and it was their opinion that they had discovered us in our passage down river and had taken care to avoid us—which accounted for the small numbers we had seen on our return.

I requested the English Chief to return with me to the

other side of the river in order that he might proceed to discover the natives whose tracks and habitations we had seen there; but he was backward in complying with my desire, and proposed to send the young men; but I could not trust them, and at the same time was becoming rather doubtful of him. They were still afraid lest I should obtain such accounts of the other river as would induce me to travel overland to it, and that they should be called upon to accompany me. I was informed by one of my own people that the English Chief, his wives and companions, had determined to leave me on this side of the Slave Lake in order to go to the country of the Beaver Indians.

August 13th. At seven we were opposite the island where our pemmican had been concealed: two of the Indians were accordingly dispatched in search of it, and it proved very acceptable as it rendered us independent of the provisions which were to be obtained by our fowling pieces, and qualified us to get out of the river without that delay which our hunters would otherwise have required.

In a short time we perceived a smoke on the shore to the south-west. The Indians, who were a little ahead of us, did not discover it, being engaged in the pursuit of a flock of geese. They fired several shots, whereupon the smoke immediately disappeared, and in a short time we saw several of the natives run along the shore, some of whom entered their canoes. Though we were almost opposite to them we could not cross the river without going farther up it, from the strength of the current. I therefore ordered our Indians to make every possible exertion to speak with them, and await our arrival. But as soon as our small canoe struck off, we could perceive the poor affrighted people hasten to the shore and, after drawing their canoes on the beach, hurry into the woods.

It was past ten when we landed at the place where they had deserted their canoes. They were so terrified that they had left several articles on the beach. I was very much displeased with my Indians, who instead of seeking the natives, were dividing their property. I rebuked the English Chief with some severity for his conduct. The English Chief was very much displeased with my reproaches and expressed himself to me in person to that effect. This was the very opportunity I wanted, to make him acquainted with my dissatisfaction for some time past. I stated to him that I had come a great way, and at a very considerable expense, without having completed the object of my wishes, and that I suspected he had concealed from me a principal part of what the natives had told him respecting the country, lest he should be obliged to follow me; that his reason for not killing game, etc. was his jealousy, which likewise prevented him from looking after the natives as he ought; and that we had never given him cause for any suspicions of us.

These suggestions irritated him to a very high degree. He concluded by informing me that he would not accompany me any farther; that though he was without ammunition he could live in the same manner as the Slaves and he would remain amongst them. His harangue was succeeded by a loud and bitter lamentation; and his relations assisted the vociferation of his grief. For two hours I did not interrupt their grief, but as I could not well do without them, I was at length obliged to soothe it, and induced the Chief to change his resolution.

We pitched our tents at half past eight. I sent for the English Chief to sup with me, and a dram or two dispelled all his heart-burning and discontent. He informed me that it was a custom with the Chipewyan chiefs to go to war after they had shed tears, in order to wipe away the disgrace attached to such a feminine weakness, and that in the ensuing spring he should not fail to execute his design. I took care that he should carry some liquid consolation to his lodge, to prevent the return of his chagrin.

The following day we went about two miles up the River of the Mountains [probably the Liard River]. Fire was in the ground on each side of it.

August 18th. At four this morning I equipped all the Indians for an hunting expedition and sent them onward, as our stock of provisions was nearly exhausted.

Near this place a river flowed in from the Horn Mountains which are at no great distance. We landed at five and the English Chief arrived with the tongue of a cow or female buffalo, which four men and Indians were dispatched for the flesh; but they did not return till it was dark.

August 20th. The current was very strong and we crossed over to an island opposite us; but here it was still more impetuous, assuming the fury of a rapid. We found an awl and a paddle on the side of the water, the former we knew to belong to the Knisteneaux: I supposed it to be the Chief Merde-d'ours and his party, who went to war last spring, and had taken this route on their return to Athabasca. Nor is it improbable that they may have been the cause that we saw so few of the natives on the banks of this river.

August 22nd. We renewed our voyage and in three hours reached the entrance of the Slave Lake under half sail; under paddle it would have taken us at least eight hours. The women gathered large quantities of the fruit called pathagomenan [cloud berries] and cranberries, crowberries, moose berries, etc.

The next day we hoisted sail and were driven on at a great rate. At twelve the wind and swell were augmented to such a degree that our underyard broke, but luckily the mast thwart resisted till we had time to fasten down the yard without lowering sail. We took in a large quantity of water and, had our mast given way, in all probability we should have filled and sunk. Two men were continually employed in bailing out the water. We fortunately doubled a point that screened us from the wind and swell, and we encamped for the night.

The next day at four in the afternoon we perceived a large canoe with a sail and two small ones ahead. We soon

126

came up with them when they proved to be Monsieur LeRoux and an Indian with his family who were on a hunting party and had been out twenty-five days. He had made a voyage to Lac La Martre, where he met eighteen small canoes of the Slave Indians from whom he obtained five packs of skins.

September 10th. There was rain and violent winds during the night. At six in the evening we landed at a lodge of the Knisteneaux, consisting of three men and five women and children. They were on their return from war, and one of them was very sick: they separated from the rest of their party in the enemy country, from absolute hunger. After the separation they met with a family of the hostile tribe, whom they destroyed. They were ignorant of the fate of their friends, but imagined they had returned to the Peace River or perished for want of food. They appeared to have been the greater sufferers by their expedition.

September 12th. At night we embarked with a northeast wind and entered the Lake of the Hills [Lake Athabasca]. About ten the wind veered to westward and was as strong as we could bear it with the high sail, so that we arrived at Fort Chipewyan at three o'clock in the afternoon, where we found Mr. MacLeod with five men busily employed building a new house. Here, then, we concluded this voyage, which had occupied the considerable space of 102 days.

Mackenzie's river had not carried him to the Pacific; instead it had taken him almost a thousand miles due north of Great Slave to the shores of the Arctic Ocean. The result was a sore disappointment to him—but not to anyone else. He had discovered one of the greatest natural highways in North America—a vast river system beginning in the headwaters of the Athabasca not far north of modern Edmonton, running into Lake Athabasca, then down the Slave to Great Slave Lake, then into the Mackenzie and so to the northern ocean. This discovery inevitably led to many others of almost equal importance. In 1792 he himself ascended the tributary Peace River to its headwaters, portaged across the divide, and finally reached the Pacific, becoming the first European to span the continent by land.

Innumerable other men later used Mackenzie's water highway, and some of them turned off to the east along the subsidiary waterways, all of which led into the Barren Grounds.

It is worth noting that again a member of the Chipewyan tribe played a prominent role in Mackenzie's expedition. What Matonabbee had been to Samuel Hearne, the English Chief, friend and follower of Matonabbee, was to Alexander Mackenzie. It is easy to forget that none of the great land explorations of this continent would have been possible without the assistance and guidance of the people whose land it was.

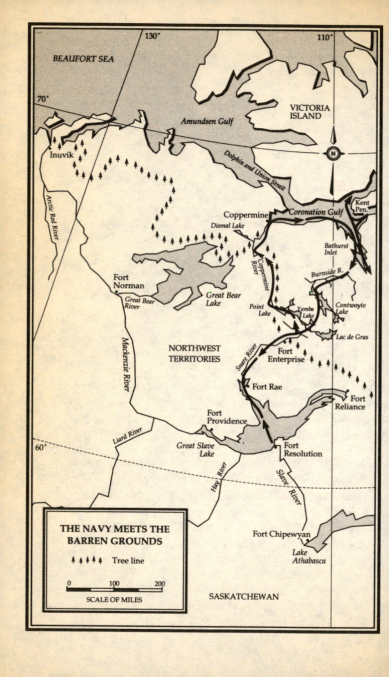

BEAUFORT SEA

Amundsen Gulf

VICTORIA ISLAND

70°

Inuvik

Arctic Red River

Dolphin and Union Strait

Coppermine

Dismal Lake

Coronation Gulf

Kent Pen.

Bathurst Inlet

Burnside R.

Fort Norman

Great Bear River

Great Bear Lake

Coppermine River

Point Lake

Yamba Lake

Contwoyto Lake

Lac de Gras

NORTHWEST TERRITORIES

Snare River

Fort Enterprise

Fort Rae

Fort Reliance

Mackenzie River

Fort Providence

Great Slave Lake

Fort Resolution

60°

Liard River

Hay River

Slave River

Fort Chipewyan

Lake Athabasca

THE NAVY MEETS THE BARREN GROUNDS

▲▲▲▲▲ Tree line

0   100   200

SCALE OF MILES

SASKATCHEWAN

III

The Navy Meets the Barren Grounds

JOHN FRANKLIN MARCHES TO THE SEA, 1819–22

Mackenzie's journey down the great river to the Frozen Ocean opened the way to the traders, but they were in no immediate hurry to follow him. "Let the Indians come to us," they said; and the Indians came. Consequently, many years passed before much more was learned through first-hand exploration about the immensity of the sub-arctic and arctic wilderness lying north, north-west and north-east from Great Slave Lake.

In 1819 the best maps of North America showed nothing of the arctic coast between Cook's Icy Cape in northern Alaska and Hudson Bay except two dots—one marking the point where Hearne had reached the northern sea; the other, the place where Mackenzie glimpsed the Frozen Ocean.

It was at this time that the British Navy decided to engage the Arctic in lieu of any other worthy antagonist— the Battle of Trafalgar having, for the moment, rid the seas of human challengers. The Navy's primary concern was to

131

force a Northwest Passage by sea; but, surprisingly enough, it also launched a subsidiary attack by land. Thus at the same time that the Admiralty sent Captain William Parry to lead a naval flotilla into Lancaster Sound in a bold bid to strike west to Bering Strait, the naval lords also dispatched an expedition to Hudson Bay, with orders to travel westward by the river routes to Great Slave Lake; then north to the mouth of the Coppermine; and, turning east, to explore and chart the coast of the continent as far as the eastern extremity of North America. This was a colossal undertaking and one that bore clear witness to the sublime belief of a victorious navy that nothing was impossible to British sailors, while displaying an equally sublime ignorance of the facts of life in the arctic regions.

The Admiralty's lack of touch with reality is underscored by its decision that this monumental assignment could be handled by one Captain, two midshipmen, a surgeon, and one naval rating, operating completely divorced from their native element.

Command of the expedition was given to Captain John Franklin, a career officer who had only just been promoted from lieutenant after a taste of arctic work when, in 1818, he had commanded one of two ships under orders to sail north by way of Spitsbergen right across the polar sea to the Pacific. Franklin's vessel and her consort got as far as Spitsbergen, and no farther; but this rebuff did nothing to discourage either the lords of Admiralty or Franklin himself.

His preparation for the overland venture included a chat with Alexander Mackenzie, a reading of Hearne's book, and some very casual arrangements with the Hudson's Bay Company and the North West Company. Franklin seems to have learned remarkably little about land operations in the Arctic from either Mackenzie or Hearne, and his arrangements with the trading companies turned out to be almost fatally inadequate.

Franklin was thirty-three years old in May of 1819 when he and his little party embarked from Britain on the

Hudson's Bay Company's ship Prince of Wales. *His account of his subsequent journey is so marvellously detailed that it needs no explanatory comment except on a single point. Like most explorers, he failed to give anything like sufficient credit to the people who actually did the work. In his case these people were "Canadians" (a mixture of French-Canadian voyageurs, French-Indian Métis, and Iroquois half-breeds), and members of the Athapascan tribe known as Copper Indians. The reader is invited to keep the essential presence of these people in mind, and to spare some of his interest and compassion for them, as he follows the mellifluous prose of Captain Franklin.*

JOURNEY TO THE SHORES OF THE POLAR SEAS

The Outbound Voyage

His Majesty's government having determined upon sending an expedition from the shores of Hudson Bay by land, to explore the northern coast of America from the mouth of the Coppermine River to the eastward, I had the honour to be appointed to this service. At the same time were appointed Dr. John Richardson, surgeon in the Royal Navy; Mr. George Back and Mr. Robert Hood, two Admiralty midshipmen. The main object of the expedition was that of determining the latitudes and longitudes of the northern coast of North America, and the trending of that coast from the mouth of the Coppermine to the eastern extremity of that continent. I was instructed, on my arrival at, or near, the mouth of the Coppermine River, to make every inquiry as to the situation of the spot from whence native copper had been brought down by the Indians to the Hudson's Bay establishment, and to visit and explore the place in question. Here I must be permitted to pay the tribute which is due the fidelity, exertion and uniform good conduct in the most trying situations, of John Hepburn, an

English seaman and our only attendant, to whom in the latter part of our journey we owe, under Divine Providence, the preservation of the lives of some of the party.

The party embarked on the ship Prince of Wales *on May 23, 1819, in company with a number of officers of the Hudson's Bay Company. The ship made a prolonged stop at the Orkney Islands, during which Franklin engaged four Orkney islanders as boatmen for the expedition. The westbound voyage commenced on June 16 with the* Prince of Wales *sailing in convoy with the* Eddystone, *the* Wear, *and the* Harmony. *The* Harmony, *belonging to the Moravian Missionary Society and bound for Nain on the Labrador coast, left the convoy on June 22. On July 25 the remaining ships opened the entrance of Davis Strait and spoke to the* Andrew Marvel, *a whaler, bound home to England with a cargo of fourteen whales. Her master reported that the ice had been extremely bad and that the ship, as well as several others, had suffered injury, and two ships had been entirely crushed. Because of ice, icebergs, fog and adverse weather, the convoy did not sight Resolution Island at the mouth of Hudson Strait until August 7. The ships* Eddystone *and* Wear, *incidentally, were filled to the hatches with Scottish colonists going out to join Lord Selkirk's settlement in the Red River region of Manitoba. Conditions on these two ships were dreadful, and were compounded by the conditions that were encountered from this point foreward.*

In the morning of the 7th, the island of Resolution was indistinctly seen through a dense fog. The favouring breeze subsided and left the ships surrounded by loose ice. At this time the *Eddystone* was perceived to be driving rapidly toward some of the larger ice masses, and the stern boats of this ship and the *Wear* were dispatched to assist in towing her clear. Our ship was quite unmanageable and was under the sole governance of the currents, which ran in small eddies between the masses of ice. We could see the *Wear* within hail, and the *Eddystone* within a short distance from us. The fog made it impossible to ascertain the direction in which we were driving until half past twelve when we had an alarming view of a barren rugged shore within a few yards, towering over the mastheads.

Almost instantly afterwards the ship struck violently on a point of rocks, and the side was brought so near to the shore that poles were prepared to push her off. This blow displaced the rudder. A swell freed the ship from this perilous situation but the current hurried us along in contact with the rocky shore, and the prospect was most alarming. Off the outward bow we perceived a rugged and precipitous cliff whose summit was hid in the fog, and the vessel's head was pointing toward the bottom of a small bay into which we were rapidly driving.

There now seemed to be no probability of escaping shipwreck, being without wind and having the rudder in a useless state. The only assistance available was that of a boat employed in towing which had been placed in the water between the ship and the shore, at the imminent risk of its being crushed.

The ship again struck over a ledge of rocks and, happily, the blow replaced the rudder, which enabled us to take advantage of a light breeze and to direct the ship's head outside the projecting cliff. But the breeze was only momentary and the ship was a third time driven onshore on the rocky termination of the cliff.

Once more we were extricated by the swell from this ledge and carried still farther along the shore. The coast became more rugged and our view of it was terminated by another high point on the starboard bow. Happily, before we had reached it, a light breeze enabled us to turn the ship's head to seaward and when the sails were trimmed she drew off the shore. She had made but little progress, however, when she was violently forced by the current against a large iceberg lying aground.

Our prospects were now even more alarming. It would be difficult for me to portray the anxiety and dismay of the female passengers and children who were rushing on deck in spite of endeavours of the officers to keep them below, out of danger. After the first concussion the ship was driven along the steep and rugged side of this iceberg with such amazing rapidity that the destruction of the mast seemed inevitable, and everyone expected we should again be forced on the rocks in the most disabled state. But we providentially escaped this perilous result.

The dense fog now cleared away for a short time and we discovered the *Eddystone* close to some rocks, having three boats employed in towing; but the *Wear* was not visible.

Our ship was making water very fast. The pumps were manned and kept in continual use and signals of distress were made to the *Eddystone* whose commander came on board and then ordered to our assistance his carpenter and all the men he could spare. As the wind was increasing it was determined the *Eddystone* should take our ship in tow, that the undivided attention of our passengers and crew might be directed to pumping and clearing the hold to see whether there was a possibility of stopping the leak.

We soon had reason to suppose the principal injury had been received from a blow near the stern and, after cutting away part of the sealing, the carpenters attempted to stop the rushing in of the water by forcing oakum between the timbers; but this had not the desired effect. In spite of our efforts at the pumps the leak increased so much that the parties of officers and passengers were stationed to bail out the water in buckets.

A heavy gale came on, blowing from the land, as the night advanced; the sails were split, the ship was encompassed by heavy ice and, in forcing through a stream of ice, the tow rope broke and obliged us to take a portion of the seamen from the pumps and appoint them to management of the ship.

Fatigue had caused us to relax in our exertions at the pumps during the night of the 8th, and on the following morning upward of five feet of water was found in the hold. Renewed exertions were now put forth by every person and before eight o'clock the water was much reduced, enabling the carpenters to get at other defective places. Our labours just sufficed to keep the ship in the same state until six p.m. when the strength of everyone began to fail. The carpenters now tried the expedient of thrusting in felt, as well as oakum, and a plank nailed over all. After this operation we put forth our utmost exertion and before night, to our infinite joy, the leak was so over-powered that the pumps were only required to be used at intervals of ten minutes. A sail covered with every sub-stance that could be carried into the leaks by the pressure of the water was drawn under the quarter of the ship and secured by ropes on each side.

As a precaution in the event of having to abandon ship the elderly women and children were removed to the *Eddy-stone*, but the young women remained to assist at the pumps, and their services were highly valuable both for their personal labour and for the encouragement their example and perseverance gave to the men.

After further hair-raising adventures, the ships finally reached an anchorage off York Factory in James Bay, and it can be assumed that the voyage ended none too soon as far as the Selkirk colonists were concerned. When Franklin went ashore he discovered that the North West Company and the Hudson's Bay Company were, for all practical purposes, in a state of war with each other. This greatly complicated his problems since he had to depend upon both organizations in order to forward his explorations.

For a while Franklin contemplated the idea of hiring a small boat and sailing north up the west coast of Hudson Bay and trying to reach the arctic coast from there. He gave this idea up when he discovered that no Eskimo inter-preters were available and in fact no boat was available. He then decided, on the advice of the Hudson's Bay Com-

*pany men and some North West Company traders, that his
best hope was to proceed via the canoe route to Cumberland House on the Saskatchewan and then through the
chain of trading posts to Great Slave Lake, from which
point he could attempt to reach the arctic coast.*

*Franklin's party left York Factory on September 9.
Laboriously ascending the Hayes River they crossed the
height of land to reach Lake Winnipeg. From the north end
of Lake Winnipeg they began to ascend the Saskatchewan
River and on October 22, with the weather so cold that
spray froze as it fell, and the oars had become so loaded
with ice as to be almost unmanageable, they reached Cumberland House. They were just in time. Within a few days
the rivers and lakes were frozen over. During this boat
journey they had travelled a distance of almost seven
hundred miles but they were still a very long way from
their jumping-off point at Great Slave Lake. Franklin and
his party remained here until January 18, during which
time they had a chance to meet the Cree Indians.*

The tribe of Indians who reside in the vicinity and frequent
these establishments is that of the Crees or Knisteneaux.
They were formerly a powerful and numerous nation ranging over a very extensive country, and were most successful in their excursions against their neighbours,
particularly the Northern Indians. But they have long
ceased to be held in any fear and are now, perhaps, the
most harmless and inoffensive of the whole Indian race.
This change is entirely to be attributed to their intercourse
with Europeans, and their vast reduction in numbers occasioned, I fear, in a considerable degree by the injudicious
introduction amongst them of ardent spirits.

They are so passionately fond of this poison that they
will make any sacrifice to obtain it. They are esteemed
good hunters and are generally assiduous. Having laid the
bow and arrow altogether aside, and also the use of snares

except for rabbits and partridge, they depend entirely on the Europeans for the means of gaining their subsistence, as they require guns and a constant supply of powder and shot; so that these Indians are probably more completely under the power of the traders than any other tribe. I saw only a few straggling parties of them during short intervals and unfavourable circumstances, since sickness and famine were rife through the land.

On January 18, 1820, the party set out to complete the journey to Fort Chipewyan on Lake Athabasca, travelling on snowshoes, and accompanied by a number of sleds and carioles supplies by the two competing fur-trading companies. Although this mode of travel was quite beyond the experience of English officers and gentlemen, they seem to have taken it in their stride with the usual British phlegm. The following brief excerpts from the account of the journey give the flavour of it.

Being accompanied by Mr. Mackenzie of the Hudson's Bay Company with four sledges under his charge, we formed quite a procession keeping in Indian file in the track of the man ahead. As the snow was deep we proceeded slowly on the surface of the [Saskatchewan] river. At the place of our night encampment we could scarce find sufficient pine branches to floor the "hut," as the Orkney men term the place where travellers rest. Its preparation consists simply of clearing away the snow to the ground and covering that space with pine branches, over which the party spread their blankets and coats, and sleep in warmth and comfort by keeping a good fire at their feet, without any other canopy than the heaven, even though the thermometer should be far below zero.

This evening we found the mercury of our thermometer had sunk into the bulb and was frozen. It rose into the tube on being held to the fire, but quickly redescended into the bulb on being removed into the air. We could not, therefore, ascertain by it the temperature of the atmosphere, either then or during the rest of our journey.[1]

The next day we pursued our course along the river, the dogs having the greatest difficulty in dragging their heavy burden through the snow. We encamped after walking about nine miles. The termination of the journey was a great relief to me, who had been suffering during the greater part of it in consequence of my feet being galled by the snowshoes. This, however, was an evil which few escape on their initiation in winter travelling. It excites no pity from the more experienced companions of the journey.

We passed the ruins of an establishment which the traders had been compelled to abandon, in consequence of the intractable conduct of the Assiniboine Indians, and learned that all the residents at a post to the south had been cut off by the same tribe some years ago. The wolves serenaded us through the night with a chorus of their agreeable howling, but none ventured near. Mr. Back's repose was disturbed by a more serious evil; his buffalo robe caught fire and the shoes on his feet, being contracted by the heat, gave him such a pain that he jumped up in the cold and ran into the snow as the only means of obtaining relief.

On the 28th we had a strong and piercing wind from the north-west and much snowdrift and were compelled to walk as quickly as we could and keep rubbing the exposed parts of skin to prevent their being frozen. The night was miserably cold; our tea froze in the tin pots before we could drink it, and even a mixture of spirits and water became quite thick by congelation.

On January 30th we reached Carlton House [also on the Saskatchewan] and had the gratification of changing our travelling dresses which we had worn for fourteen days. Carlton House is a provision post. The provisions are procured in the winter season from the Indians, in the

---

[1] Mercury solidifies, or freezes, at $-38°$ F.

form of dried [buffalo] meat and fat and when converted by a mixture into pemmican, furnishes the principal support of the voyageurs in their passages to and from the various depots in the summer. The mode of making pemmican is very simple — the meat is dried by the Indians in the sun or over a fire, and pounded by beating it with stones when spread on a skin. In this state it is brought to the forts where the admixture of hair is partially sifted out, and a third part of melted fat incorporated with it, partly by turning them over with a wooden shovel, partly by kneading them together with the hands. The pemmican is now firmly pressed into leathern bags each capable of containing eighty-five pounds and, being placed in an airy place to cool, is fit for use. It keeps in this state, if not allowed to get wet, very well for one year, and with great care may be preserved for two. Between three and four hundred bags were made here by each of the companies this year.[2]

On March 25th with the guidance of an old [French] Canadian we went forward toward Lake Athabasca. We had not advanced far before we came up with two men we had dispatched ahead of us that morning. Stormy weather had compelled them to camp as there was too much drifting of snow for any attempt to cross the lake. We were obliged to follow their example but we comforted ourselves with the reflection that this was the first time we had been stopped by the weather during our long journey, which was so nearly at an end.

The following day the boisterous weather continued but two of the Canadians were sent off with letters to the gentlemen at Fort Chipewyan. After breakfast we also started, but our Indian friends, having a great indisposition to move in such weather, remained by the fire. When we quitted the land we found our error as to the strength of

---

[2]This represents about five hundred thousand pounds, live weight, of meat. It was no wonder that the vast herds of buffalo disappeared so rapidly!

the wind, which still blew violently, and there was so much drifting of snow as to cover all distant objects. Our Indian guide conducted us between islands over a small lake and by a swampy river into Lake Athabasca. At four p.m. we had the pleasure of arriving at Fort Chipewyan and of being received by Messrs. Keith and Black, the partners of the North West Company in charge, in the most kind and hospitable manner. Thus has terminated a winter journey of 857 miles, in the progress of which there has been a great intermixture of agreeable and disagreeable circumstances. Amongst these latter the initiation into the practice of walking in snowshoes must be considered as prominent. The suffering it occasions can be but faintly imagined by a person who thinks upon the inconvenience of marching with a weight of between two or three pounds constantly attached to galled feet and swelled ankles.

There are other inconveniences which, though keenly felt during the day's journey, are speedily forgotten when, stretched out in the encampment before a large fire, you enjoy the social mirth of your companions, who usually pass the evening in recounting their former feats in travelling. At this time the Canadians [voyageurs] are always cheerful and merry, and the only bar to comfort arises from the frequent interruptions occasioned by the dogs, who are constantly prowling the circle snatching at every kind of food that happens to be within reach. These useful animals are a comfort afterwards, by the warmth they impart when lying down by one's side or feet, as they usually do. But the greatest gratification a traveller in these regions enjoys is derived from the hospitable welcome he receives at every trading post, however poor the means of the host may be; and from being disrobed even for a short time of the trappings of a voyager, and experiencing the pleasures of cleanliness.

Our next object was to obtain some certain information respecting our future route and accordingly we received from one of the North West Company's interpreters, named Beaulieu, a half-breed who had been brought up amongst the Dog-Rib and Copper Indians, some information respecting the way of reaching the Coppermine River. The Copper Indians, however, he said, would be able to give us more accurate information as to the later part of its course as they occasionally pursue it to the sea. He sketched on the floor a representation of the river and a line of coast according to his idea of it. Just as he finished, an old Chipewyan Indian named Black Meat unexpectedly came in, and instantly recognized the plan. He then took the charcoal from Beaulieu and inserted a track along the sea coast, which he had followed in returning from a war excursion made by his tribe against the Eskimos. He described two other rivers to the eastward of the Coppermine which also fall into the northern ocean. One issues from Contwoyto Lake and the Thloueeatessy or Fish River,[3] which rises near the eastern boundary of the Great Slave Lake. During our conversation an old Chipewyan Indian, named the Rabbit's Head, entered the room. He was the step-son of the late Chief Matonabbee, who had accompanied Mr. Hearne on his journey to the sea, and had himself been of the party, but being a mere boy had forgotten many of the circumstances. As he was esteemed as a good Indian, I presented him with a medal which he received gratefully.

A curious incident was related to us here. A young Chipewyan had separated from the rest of his band when his wife, who was in her first pregnancy, was seized with

---

[3]This is another example of the fantastic range of geographic knowledge possessed by the Chipewyans, but not, apparently, by any other Northern Indian tribe. The river issuing from Contwoyto Lake is the Burnside, emptying into Bathurst Inlet. The Thloueeatessy empties into Chantrey Inlet, five hundred miles to the north-east of Great Slave Lake. In 1835 it was explored by the same Lieut. Back who was with Franklin, and it is now named after him. The story of his voyage is told later in this book.

the labour pains. She died on the third day after giving birth. The husband was inconsolable but his grief was absorbed in his anxiety for the fate of his infant son. To preserve its life he descended to the office of nurse, so degrading in the eyes of a Chipewyan as partaking of the duties of a woman. He swaddled it in soft moss, fed it with broth made from the flesh of deer and, to still its cries, applied it to his breast. The force of the powerful passion by which he was actuated produced the same effect in his case as it has done in some others which are recorded. A flow of milk actually took place from his breast. He succeeded in rearing his child, taught him to be a hunter, and when he attained the age of manhood chose him a wife from the tribe.

Franklin and Back remained in the vicinity of Fort Chipewyan through the spring and into the summer, making preparations for the next stage of their journey north, and waiting for Hood and Dr. Richardson, who were bringing forward their supplies from the south. Franklin had a new birch-bark canoe made for the voyage north. Its length was thirty-two feet and its greatest breadth four foot ten inches. It was designed to carry twenty-five pieces of luggage, each weighing ninety pounds, plus five or six men and their personal gear, the whole weighing about 3,300 pounds. There was a shortage of supplies at Lake Athabasca due to the rivalry between the North West Company and the Hudson's Bay Company. Franklin had therefore sent word to Richardson telling him to bring forward a new supply from Cumberland and Ile à la Crosse.

When Richardson and Hood arrived on July 13 they had to report almost total lack of success in obtaining supplies. They had also had a serious accident when the upsetting of a canoe resulted in the drowning of one of their bowmen. With typical understatement Franklin notes: "The prospect of having to commence our journey from hence, almost destitute of provisions, and scantily supplied with stores, was distressing to us.'' In truth it was an exceedingly scanty outfit that was assembled when the expedition was ready to depart from Lake Athabasca.

We then made final arrangements respecting the voyageurs who were to accompany the party. The Canadians whom Dr. Richardson and Mr. Hood had brought were most desirous of being continued, and we felt pleasure in being able to keep men who were so zealous in the cause. When the numbers were completed which we had been recommended to take by the traders as a precaution against the Eskimos, we had sixteen Canadian voyageurs, and our worthy and only English attendant, John Hepburn, besides two interpreters which we were to receive at the Great Slave Lake. We were also accompanied by a Chipewyan woman.

Early on the morning of July 18th, 1820, the stores were distributed to the three canoes. Our stock of provisions did not amount to more than was sufficient for one day's consumption, exclusive of two barrels of flour, three cases of preserved meats, some chocolate, arrowroot, and portable soup which we had brought from England and intended to preserve for our journey to the coast next season. Seventy pounds of moose meat and a little barley were all that the traders at Lake Athabasca had been able to give us. This scarcity of food did not depress the spirits of our Canadian companions who cheerfully loaded their canoes and embarked in high glee after they had received the customary dram. We soon reached the western boundary of the lake and entered the Slave River.

Passing the entrance of Dog River we halted to set the fishing nets. These were examined in the evening but we obtained only four small trout and were compelled to issue part of our preserved meat for supper. In the morning the nets furnished only a solitary pike. We lost no time in embarking but, while crossing the crooked channel, two of the canoes came in violent contact and the sternmost had its bow broken off. We were fortunately near shore or the disabled canoe would have sunk. The injury being repaired in two hours, we again embarked but later in the day another accident happened to one of the canoes, by the bowman slipping and letting it fall upon a rock during a portage, and breaking it in two. Two hours were occupied in sewing the detached pieces together and covering the seam with pitch, but this being done it was as good as new.

Near the mouth of the Salt River several salt springs issue from the foot of a ridge. After filling some casks with salt for our use during the winter we again began to descend the river when, turning a point, we perceived a buffalo plunge into the river before us. We instantly opened fire upon him from four muskets and in a few minutes he fell, but not before he had received fourteen balls. The carcass was towed to the bank and the canoes speedily laden with meat. After this piece of good fortune we descended the stream merrily, our voyageurs chanting their liveliest songs.

On the 27th of July we entered a deep bay of Great Slave Lake, close to the eastern side of the bay, and at eight the next morning arrived at Fort Providence. This post is exclusively occupied by the North West Company, the Hudson's Bay Company having no settlement to the northward of Great Slave Lake. Here we acquired Mr. Wentzel of the North West Company who was to be responsible for the management of the Indians, the superintendence of the Canadian voyageurs, the obtaining and general distribution of provisions, etc. He was a great acquisition to our party, being one of the few traders who speak the Chipewyan language.

Mr. Wentzel now prepared our first conference with the Chipewyan Indians. The chief, whose name is Akaitcho or Big Foot, assured us that he and his party would attend us to the end of our journey and they would do their utmost to provide us with the means of subsistence. He admitted that his tribe had made war upon the Eskimos but said they were now desirous of peace. He added, however, that the Eskimos were very treacherous and therefore recommended we should advance toward them with caution.

As the water was unusually high this season, the Indian guides recommended our going by a short route to the Coppermine River. As a reason for the change they said the reindeer would be sooner found upon this track. They drew a chart of the proposed route on the floor with charcoal, exhibiting a chain of twenty-five small lakes extending toward the north from a small river which flows into Slave Lake near Fort Providence. They pointed to another lake to the southward of the Coppermine River and about three days' journey from it, on which the chief proposed the winter establishment should be formed, as the reindeer would pass there in autumn and spring. Its waters contained fish and there was a sufficiency of wood for building.

It had been my original plan to descend the Mackenzie River and to cross the Great Bear Lake, from the eastern side of which, Beaulieu had informed me, there is communication with the Coppermine by four small lakes. But under our present circumstances, this course could not be followed because it would remove us too far from the establishments at Great Slave Lake to receive the supplies of ammunition and other stores in the winter which were absolutely necessary, or for us to get an Eskimo interpreter, who was being forwarded to us from Churchill.

Akaitcho and the guides having communicated all the information they had, I placed a medal around the neck of the chief, and the officers presented theirs to an elder brother of his and the two guides, telling them that these marks of distinction were tokens of our friendship. Their acquisition was highly gratifying to them but they studiously avoided any great expression of joy because such an exposure would have been unbecoming to the dignity which the senior Indians assume. We presented to the chief, the two guides, and the seven hunters who had been engaged to accompany us cloth, blankets, tobacco, knives, daggers, and a gun to each; also a keg of very weak spirits and water which they kept until the evening, as they had to try their guns before dark.

On August 1st the Indians set out, intending to wait for us at the mouth of the Yellowknife River. We remained behind to pack our stores in bales of eighty pounds each, an operation which could not be done in the presence of these Indians as they are in the habit of begging for everything they see. Our stores consisted of two barrels of gunpowder, 140 pounds of ball and small shot, four fowling pieces, a few old trade guns, eight pistols, twenty-four Indian daggers, some packages of knives, chisels, axes, nails, etc. etc. etc. Our provisions were only two casks of flour, two hundred dried reindeer tongues, some dried moose meat, portable soup and arrowroot, sufficient in the whole for ten days' consumption. The expedition now consisted of twenty-eight persons including the officers, and the wives of three of our voyageurs. There were also three children belonging to two of these women.

On the afternoon of the 2nd of August we commenced our journey having, in addition to our three canoes, a smaller one to convey the women. We were all in high spirits being heartily glad that the time had at length arrived when our course was to be directed toward the Coppermine River and through a line of country which had not previously been visited by any European. At the entrance of the Yellowknife River we found Akaitcho and the hunters with their families encamped. This party was quickly in motion and we were soon surrounded by a fleet of seventeen Indian canoes. We began paddling up this small river. Akaitcho caused himself to be paddled by his slave, a young man of the Dog-Rib nation whom he had taken by force. Several of the canoes were managed by women, who proved to be noisy companions, for they quarrelled frequently. The lamentations of one were not diminished when her husband attempted to settle a difference by a few blows with his paddle.

Leaving the first lake we ascended a strong rapid to three steep cascades where a portage of thirteen hundred yards over a rocky hill was required. We found the Indians had greatly the advantage over us in this operation. The men carried their small canoes, the women and children carried the clothes and provisions and at the end of the portage they were ready to embark, while it was necessary for our people to return four times before they could transport the weighty cargo with which we were burdened.

As soon as the tents were pitched that night the officers and men were divided into watches, a precaution intended to be taken throughout the journey, not merely to prevent our being surprised by strangers, but also to show our companions that we were constantly on our guard.

Rations ran out almost immediately and the back-breaking labour of portaging the heavy loads over a steady succession of ponds and lakelets soon began to tell upon the voyageurs. The nets produced almost no fish and by August 8 starvation was already staring the expedition in the face.

On August 8th we crossed five portages, passing over a very bad road. The men were exhausted with fatigue by five p.m. when we were obliged to encamp. We commenced our labours the next day in a very uncomfortable state as it had rained through the night. The fifth lake was crossed, and four others, with their intervening portages, when we returned to the river and had to twice carry the cargoes along its banks to avoid stony rapids. We encamped that night on Lower Carp Lake. The chief having told us that this was a good lake for fishing, we determined on halting to recruit our men, of whom three were lame and several others had swelled legs. The chief himself went forward to look after the hunters and he promised to make a fire if they killed any reindeer. All the Indians had left us in the course of yesterday and today to seek these animals.

The nets furnished only four carp and we embarked

for purposes of searching for a better spot the next morning. The men were gratified by finding an abundance of blueberries which made an agreeable and substantial addition to their scanty fare. Here we caught sufficient fish to afford the party two hearty meals, and being recovered from their fatigue the men proceeded on. The next day an Indian met us to say the hunters had made several fires which were certain indication of their having killed reindeer. This inspired our companions with fresh energy and they traversed the next portage and paddled through Reindeer Lake. At the far side we found the canoes of our hunters and learned from our guide that the Indians usually leave their canoes here, as the water communication on the hunting grounds is bad. Akaitcho was here and pointed out to us the smoke of distant fires. The country in general is destitute of almost every vegetable and has a very barren aspect.

On the 13th our Canadian voyageurs, who had been for some days murmuring at their meagre diet and striving to get at the whole of our little reserve provisions, broke out into open discontent and several of them threatened they would not proceed unless more food was given to them. This conduct was the more unpardonable as they saw we were rapidly approaching the fires of the hunters. I therefore addressed them in the strongest manner on the danger of insubordination and assured them of my determination to inflict the heaviest punishment on any who should persist in their refusal to go on. In the course of the day we crossed seven lakes and seven portages. Just as we encamped we were delighted to see four hunters arrive with the flesh of two reindeer.

The Indians were now able to keep the party supplied with meat, and on August 19 the expedition reached the lake where Akaitcho had suggested they pass the winter. It had been a gruelling trip. According to Franklin, "The united length of the portages we had crossed since leaving Fort

*Providence is twenty-one statute miles, and as our men
had to traverse each portage four times with a load of 180
pounds, and return three times light, they walked in the
whole upwards of 150 miles. The total length of our actual
voyage from Fort Chipewyan to the north was 553 miles."
Despite the fatigue of the men, the lateness of the season
and the shortage of supplies, the insatiable Franklin now
hoped to continue on to the Coppermine River and perhaps
to the arctic coast while leaving some of his men to build
a winter house on the shores of Winter Lake.*

Fort Enterprise

When Mr. Wentzel communicated to Akaitcho my intention of proceeding at once to the Coppermine River, he
desired a conference with me. He stated that the very
attempt would be rash and dangerous as the weather was
cold, the leaves were falling, and the geese were passing
to the south, and winter would shortly set in. He considered
the lives of all who went on such a journey would be
forfeited. He said there was no wood within eleven days'
march, during which time we could not have any fires. He
said we would be forty days descending the Coppermine
River and that during the whole journey the party would
experience great suffering from want of food as the reindeer had already left the river. We informed him that we
were provided with instruments by which we could tell the
state of air and water, and we did not imagine the winter
to be so near as he supposed. Akaitcho appeared to feel
hurt that we should continue to press the matter and
answered with warmth: "Well, I have said everything I
can to dissuade you from going on. It seems you wish to
sacrifice your own lives as well as the Indians who might
attend you. However, if after all I have said you are determined, some of my young men shall join the party, because
it shall not be said that we allowed you to die alone having
brought you hither. But from the moment they embark in

the canoes I and my relatives will lament them as dead.'' Afterward he told Mr. Wentzel that, as his advice was neglected, his presence was useless, and he would therefore return to Fort Providence with his hunters. I therefore came reluctantly to the determination of relinquishing my intention of going any distance down the river this season. However, I determined on dispatching Messrs. Back and Hood in a light canoe to ascertain the distance and size of the Coppermine River.[4]

Having received a supply of dried meat from the Indian lodges, on the 29th Mr. Back and Mr. Hood embarked in a light canoe with St. Germain, eight other Canadians, and one Indian. We could not furnish them with more than eight days' provisions. As soon as the canoes had started, Akaitcho and the Indians took their departure also, except two of the hunters who stayed behind to kill deer in our neighbourhood.

The month of September commenced with very disagreeable weather. Temperatures ranged between 39° and 31° during the first three days. These circumstances led us to fear for the comfort, if not for the safety, of our absent friends. On the 4th we commenced building our dwelling house, having cut sufficient wood for the frame of it. Leaving Mr. Wentzel in charge of the men, to superintend the building [of Fort Enterprise], Dr. Richardson and I determined on taking a pedestrian excursion to the Coppermine River, accompanied by John Hepburn.

Our guide led us from the top of one hill to another making a straight course to the northward. From the time

---

[4]Franklin's bull-headed conviction, that an officer of the Royal Navy knew more about local conditions than any inhabitant, would undoubtedly have led to the destruction of his party — as Akaitcho prophesied — had the Chipewyan chief not forced him to give up the attempt to go on to the coast that autumn. But Franklin did not learn anything from this lesson, as the tragic course of the famous Franklin Expedition of 1845 demonstrated all too clearly.

we quitted the banks of Winter Lake we saw only a few detached clumps of trees and after we passed Dog-Rib Rock even these disappeared and we travelled through a naked country. Our guide, Keskarrah, killed a reindeer and offered us as a great treat the raw marrow from the hind legs of the animal, of which all the party except myself ate and thought it good. I was also of the same opinion when I subsequently conquered my then too fastidious taste.

Where we camped for the night there were four ancient pine trees which did not exceed six or seven feet in height but whose branches spread themselves out for several yards. We were about to cut down one of these for fire wood but our guide solicited us to spare them, and made us understand by signs that they had been long serviceable to his nation and we ought to content ourselves with a few of the smaller branches.

The "pedestrian" expedition reached the banks of the Coppermine River after a considerable walk, and immediately turned about and returned to Fort Enterprise. Hood and Back were at the camp when Franklin returned. They had been forced to leave their canoe and proceed on foot, and had reached Point Lake. This concluded the expedition's travelling for the year 1820.

The men continued to work diligently on the house. Besides the men employed there, two men were appointed to fish and others were occasionally sent for meat. This latter employment, although extremely laborious, was relished by the Canadians as they never failed to help themselves to the fattest and most delicate parts of the deer. Toward the end of the month the deer began to quit the barren grounds and came into the vicinity of the house, and the necessity of sending for the meat considerably retarded the building of the house. In the meantime we lived in canvas tents which proved very cold, although we maintained a fire in front of them.

On October 6th, the house being completed, we struck our tent and removed into it. It was a log building, fifty feet long and twenty-four wide, divided into a hall, three bedrooms, and a kitchen. The walls and roof were plastered with clay, the floors laid with planks rudely squared with the hatchet, and the windows closed with parchment of deerskin. The clay froze as it was daubed on and afterwards cracked in such a manner as to admit the wind from every quarter, yet compared with the tents our new habitation appeared comfortable. Having filled our capacious clay-built chimney with faggots, we spent a cheerful evening before the invigorating blaze. Our working party, who had shown such skill as house carpenters, proved themselves with the same tools—the hatchet and crooked knife — to be excellent cabinet-makers, and daily they added tables, chairs, bedsteads to the comforts of our establishment. The crooked knife, generally made of an old file, bent and tempered, serves an Indian or Canadian voyageur for plane, chisel and auger. Snowshoes and canoe timbers are fashioned with it, the wood of the sledges reduced to the proper thinness, and their wooden bowls and spoons hollowed out.

On the 7th there was a great herd of reindeer in our neighbourhood. On the morning of the 10th I estimated the numbers I saw during a short walk at upward of two thousand. The Copper Indians kill the reindeer with guns in summer or, taking advantage of a favourable disposition of ground, enclose the herd upon a neck of land and drive them into a lake where they fall an easy prey. In the rutting season and in the spring they catch them in snares which are simple nooses formed in a rope made of twisted sinew placed in the aperature of a hedge constructed of the branches of trees.

A party who had been sent to Akaitcho returned, bringing 370 pounds of dried meat and 220 pounds of suet, together with the unpleasant information that a still larger quantity of the latter article had been found and carried off, as he supposed, by some Dog-Ribs who had passed that way. Toward the middle of the month the reindeer began to quit us for more southerly pastures. Their longer residence in our neighbourhood would have been of little service for our ammunition was almost completely exhausted. We had, however, already secured in the store-house the carcasses of a hundred deer, together with a thousand pounds of suet and dried meat. The necessity of employing the men to build a house for themselves before the weather became too severe obliged us to cache some of the meat instead of bringing it to the Fort.

On the 18th Mr. Back and Mr. Wentzel set out for Fort Providence accompanied by two Canadians and two Indians. Mr. Back had volunteered to go and make the necessary arrangements for transporting the store we expected from Cumberland House, and to endeavour to obtain additional supplies from the trading post on Slave Lake. Ammunition was essential to our existence and a considerable supply of tobacco was also requisite, not only for the comfort of the Canadians but also as a means of preserving the friendship of the Indians.

Toward the end of the month the men completed their house and took up their abode in it. It was thirty-four feet long and eighteen feet wide, divided into two apartments. It was placed at right angles to the officers' dwelling and facing the storehouse, so that the three buildings formed three sides of a quadrangle.

On the 26th Akaitcho and his party arrived. This was a serious inconvenience to us for our being compelled to issue them daily rations of provisions from the store. The want of ammunition prevented us from sending them to the woods to hunt although they are accustomed to subsist themselves for a considerable part of the year by fishing, or snaring the deer, without recourse to firearms. On the present occasion they felt little inclined to do so, and gave scope to their natural love of ease as long as the storehouse seemed to be well stocked.

By the middle of November we had become anxious to hear of the arrival of Mr. Back and his party at Fort Providence. The Indians conjectured that the whole party had fallen through the ice or had been cut off by the Dog-Ribs. The matter was put to rest by the appearance of Solomon Bélanger on the 23rd. He reported they had had a tedious and fatiguing journey to Fort Providence, and for some days were destitute of provisions. He arrived alone, having walked constantly for the past thirty-six hours, leaving his Indian companions encamped at the last woods, they being unwilling to accompany him across the barren ground during the storm that had prevailed for several days. His locks were matted with snow and he was encrusted with ice from head to foot so that we hardly recognized him. We welcomed him with the usual shake of the hand but were unable to give him a glass of rum which every voyageur receives on his arrival at a trading post.

As soon as his packet was thawed we opened it eagerly to obtain our English letters. The latest was dated on the preceding April. We were not so fortunate with regard to our stores. Some of the most essential had been left at the Grand Rapid on the Saskatchewan, owing to the misconduct of an officer to whom they were entrusted to convey them to Cumberland House. Being overtaken by some of the North West Company's canoes, he had insisted on their taking half. They were unable to do so and the Hudson's Bay officer upon this deposited our ammunition and tobacco on the beach and departed, without any regard to the serious consequences that might result to us from the want of them. Two Eskimo interpreters [from Churchill] had arrived at Slave Lake on their way to join the party.

Having received a hundred balls from Fort Providence, we distributed them amongst the Indians, informing Akaitcho that the residence of so large a party as his at the house, amounting to forty souls, was producing a serious reduction in our stock of provisions. He acknowledged the justice of the statement and promised to remove as soon as his party had prepared snowshoes and sledges for themselves. Keskarrah, the guide, remained behind with his wife and daughter. His wife had been long affected with an ulcer on the face which had nearly destroyed her nose. I may remark that the daughter, whom we designated Green Stockings, is considered by her tribe to be a great beauty. Mr. Hood drew an accurate portrait of her, although the mother was adverse to her sitting for it. She said she was afraid her daughter's likeness would induce the Great Chief in England to send for the original. The young lady was undeterred by any such fear. She had already been an object of contest between her countrymen, and although under sixteen years of age had belonged successively to two husbands and would probably have been the wife of many more if her mother had not required her services as a nurse.

The weather during this month was the coldest we had experienced. The thermometer sunk on one occasion to 57° below zero. The trees froze to their very centres and became as hard as stones and more difficult to cut. Some of our axes were broken daily and by the end of the month we had only one left that was fit for felling trees. A thermometer, hung in our bedroom at a distance of sixteen feet from the fire but exposed to its direct radiation, stood even in the daytime occasionally at 15° below zero, and was observed more than once, previous to kindling the fire in the morning, to be as low as 40° below zero.

It may be intereting to the reader to know how we passed our time. A considerable portion of it was used in writing up our journals. Some newspapers and magazines we had received from England with our letters were read again and again and commented on. We occasionally paid the woodmen a visit or took a walk for a mile or two on the river. In the evenings we joined the men in the hall and took a part in their games, which generally continued to a late hour. In short, we never found the time to hang heavy

157

upon our hands. The Sabbath was always a day of rest. Divine service was regularly performed and the Canadians attended, and behaved with great decorum, although they were all Roman Catholics and but little acquainted with the language in which the prayers were read.

Our diet consisted almost entirely of reindeer meat, varied twice a week by fish and occasionally by a little flour, but we had no vegetables of any kind. With reindeer fat and strips of cotton shirt we formed candles, and Hepburn acquired considerable skill in the manufacture of soap from wood ashes, fat and salt.

On January 15th, 1821, seven men arrived from Fort Providence with two kegs of rum, a barrel of powder, sixty pounds of ball, two rolls of tobacco and some clothing. They had been twenty-one days on their march from Slave Lake and the labour they underwent was evinced by their sledge collars having worn out the shoulders of their coats. We were rejoiced at their arrival and proceeded forthwith to pierce the spirit cask and issue each of the household the portion of rum they had been promised on the first day of the year. The spirits, which were proof, were frozen; but after standing at the fire for some time they flowed at the consistency of honey. The fingers adhered to the dram glass and would doubtless speedily have frozen had they been kept in contact with it, yet each of the voyageurs swallowed his dram without experiencing the slightest inconvenience.

On January 27th Mr. Wentzel and St. Germain arrived with the two Eskimos. The English names bestowed on them at Fort Churchill are Augustus and Junius. The former speaks English. We now learned that Mr. Back had proceeded to Fort Chipewyan on the 24th of December in an attempt to procure stores.

On February 5th two Canadians came from Akaitcho for further supplies of ammunition. We were mortified to learn that Akaitcho had received unpleasant reports concerning us from Fort Providence and that his faith in our good intentions was shaken. He informed us that Mr. Weeks (the trader at Fort Providence) had refused to pay some notes for trifling quantities of goods and ammunition that we had given to the hunters who accompanied our men to Slave Lake.

On March 12th we sent four men to Fort Providence, and on the 17th Mr. Back arrived from Fort Chipewyan having performed, since he left us, a journey of more than a thousand miles on foot.

Back spent five weeks at Fort Chipewyan trying to obtain supplies. Although the North West Company co-operated as far as they could, the Hudson's Bay Company men refused any material assistance. Back had a very difficult and hungry time of it during the trip south, and not much better on the way north.

On the 4th of April our men arrived with the last supplies of goods from Fort Providence, the fruits of Mr. Back's arduous journey to Lake Athabasca. I also sent out our mail, including a letter for Governor Williams (of the Hudson's Bay Company) in which I requested that he would, if possible, send a schooner to Wager Bay (on Hudson Bay) with provisions and clothing, to meet the exigencies of our party should we succeed in reaching that part of the coast.

The commencement of April was fine and for several days a considerable thaw took place which produced a consequent movement of the reindeer to the northward and induced the Indians to believe that the spring was commencing. Many of them therefore quitted the woods and set their snares on the barren ground near Fort Enterprise. Two or three days of cold weather, however, dampened their hopes and they began to say that another moon must elapse before the wished-for season. In the meantime, their premature departure caused them to suffer from want of food, and we were in some degree involved in their distress. We received no supplies from the hunters, our net produced very few fish, and the pounded meat which we had intended to keep for summer use was nearly expended. The Indian families about the house, consisting principally of women and children, suffered most. As most of them were sick or infirm they did not like to quit the house, where they received medicines from Dr. Richardson. Now they cleared away the snow on the site of the autumn encampments to look for bones, deer feet, bits of hide, and other offal. When we beheld them gnawing the pieces of hide and pounding the bones for the purpose of extracting some nourishment from them by boiling, we regretted our inability to relieve them. Meanwhile, to divert the attention of the men from their wants, we encouraged the practice of sliding down the steep bank of the river on sledges. The officers joined in the sport and the numerous overturns we experienced seemed to form no small share of the amusement of the party. But on one occasion when I had been thrown from my seat and almost buried in the snow, a fat Indian woman drove her sledge over me and sprained my knee severely.

Fortunately, the deer soon returned to the area and the rest of the spring was spent largely in involved and long-winded conferences with the Copper Indians about their participation in the summer's plans. By the end of May preparations had been made to travel to the Coppermine River and descend it to the coast.

To the Coppermine

Dr. Richardson had volunteered to conduct the first party to the Coppermine River while the rest of the officers remained with me. On the 2nd of June the stores were packed up in proper-sized bales for the journey. I had intended to send the canoes by the first party, but they were not yet repaired, the weather not being warm enough to get the men to work on them without the hazard of breaking the bark. This day one of the new trading guns which we had recently received from Fort Chipewyan burst in the hands of a young Indian. Fortunately, it did not do him any material injury. This is the sixth accident of the kind which has occurred to us since our departure from Slave Lake. Surely the deficiency in the quality of the guns, which hazards the lives of so many poor Indians, requires the serious consideration of the principals of the trading companies.

On the 4th the party under Dr. Richardson started. It consisted of fifteen voyageurs, three conducting dog sledges; Bald Head and Basil, two Indian hunters with their wives; a sick Indian and his wife; together with Angélique and Roulante [the two Métis women], so that the party consisted of twenty-three exclusive of the children. The burdens of the men were eighty pounds each, exclusive of their personal baggage, which amounted to nearly as much more. Most of them dragged their loads on sledges, but a few preferred carrying them on their backs. The Indians also struck their tents, and the women, the boys and old men who had to drag the sledges took their departure too. However, it was three o'clock before Akaitcho and the hunters left us. I desired Mr. Wentzel to inform Akaitcho that I wished a deposit of provisions to be made at the Fort previous to next September, as a resort should we return this way. He and the guides promised to see this done.

While the Indians were packing, one of the women absconded. She belonged to the Dog-Rib tribe and had been taken by force. On the 5th this woman presented herself to us on a hill, but was afraid to approach until the interpreter went and told her that we who remained would not prevent her from going where she pleased. Upon this she came to solicit a fire steel and kettle. She was at first low-spirited, from the non-arrival of a country woman who had promised to elope with her. The Indian hunter having given her some directions as to the proper mode of joining her tribe, she became more composed and agreed to adopt his advice of proceeding to Fort Providence instead of wandering about the country all summer in search of her people, at the imminent hazard of being starved.

June 14th. The sleds for the canoes having been finished during the night, the party attached to them commenced their journey this morning. Each canoe was dragged by four men assisted by two dogs. After their departure, Hepburn, three Canadians, the two Eskimos and we officers quitted Fort Enterprise, most sincerely rejoicing that the long-wished-for day had arrived when we were to proceed towards the final object of the expedition. Due to our heavy loads we proceeded only five miles the first day. At Marten Lake we joined the canoe party and camped with them. We had the mortification of learning that the meat our hunter had put *en cache* here had been destroyed by wolverines, and we had to furnish supper from our scanty stock of dried meat. The few dwarf bushes we could collect afforded insufficient fire to keep us warm and we retired under our blankets, finding the night extremely cold. We had our tents but we had left our tent poles behind and could not now replace them. In crossing one lake with my bundle on my shoulders I fell through the ice but was extricated without receiving any injury. Mr. Back, who left us to go in search of stragglers, met with a similar accident in the evening. In proceeding to get upon the ice of the lakes, we found this could not be effected without wading up to the waist in water for some distance from its borders. We had not command of our feet in these situations and the men fell often; poor Junius broke through the ice with his heavy burden on his back, but fortunately was not hurt.

On the 20th of June we arrived at the western side of an arm of Point Lake, through which the Coppermine River runs. The men were much jaded by their fatiguing journey and several were lame from swellings of the lower extremities. The ice on the lake was still six or seven feet thick and there ·was no appearance of decay except near the edges. As it was evident that by remaining here until it should be removed we might lose every prospect of success in our undertaking, I determined on dragging our stores along the surface until we should come to a part of the river where we could embark. Directions were given to every man to prepare a train [sled] for the conveyance of his portion of the stores.

We found Akaitcho and his hunters camped here. We were extremely distressed to learn that they had expended all the ammunition they had received at Fort Enterprise without having contributed any supply of provision. Dr. Richardson had, however, kept with him two hunters and prepared two hundred pounds of dried meat which was now our sole dependence for the journey. The number of our hunters was now reduced to five, as two declined going any farther. Akaitcho, his brother, the guide, and three other men remained to accompany us. We were much surprised to perceive an extraordinary difference in climate in so short an advance to the northward as fifty miles. The snow here was lying in large patches on the hills. Vegetation seemed to be three weeks or a month later than at Fort Enterprise.

On June 25th the storm which had blown for two days abated, and we prepared to start. The canoes were mounted on sledges and nine men were appointed to conduct them, having the assistance of two dogs to each canoe. The stores and provisions were distributed equally amongst the rest of our men except a few small articles which the Indians carried. Our course led down the main channel of the lake, but we proceeded at a slow pace. We put up at eight p.m. and the party was much fatigued. The distance made was only six miles. The following day we accomplished only four miles. The suffering of the people in this early stage of our journey was truly discouraging to them and very distressing to us. I therefore determined to leave behind the third canoe and by this we gained three men to lighten the load of those who were most lame. In the evening of the 29th, having come twelve miles, we found a channel open by which Point Lake is connected with Rock Nest Lake.

The next morning the men, having gummed the canoes, embarked to descend the river. It was about two hundred yards wide and, the course being uninterrupted, we cherished a sanguine hope of now getting on more speedily—until we perceived that the waters of Rock Nest Lake were still bound by ice and that recourse must again be had to the sledges. The ice was much decayed. It cracked under us at every step, and the party was obliged to separate widely to prevent accidents. Once, on reaching an open channel, we were obliged to ferry our goods across it on pieces of ice. The fresh meat being expended, we had to make another inroad on our pounded meat. Our distance today was six miles.

It was not until four o'clock July 1st that some of our men came in with the agreeable information that they had seen the river flowing from the base of the Rock Nest Lake. We embarked at nine a.m. on July 2nd and descended a succession of strong rapids for three miles. We were carried along with extraordinary rapidity, shooting over large stones upon which a single stroke would have been destructive to the canoes; and we were also in danger of breaking them from the want of the long poles which normally lie along the bottom and equalize the weight of the cargoes. They plunged very much, and on one occasion the first canoe was almost filled with waves. But there was no retreating after we had once launched into the stream, and our safety depended on the skill and dexterity of the bowmen and steersmen. The banks of the river here are rocky and the scenery beautiful, with small wooded dales to the edge of the stream. But it is flanked on both sides at a distance of three or four miles by a range of round-backed barren hills upwards of six hundred feet high.

In one place the passage was blocked up by drift ice,

still covered in snow. A channel was made for some way with hatchets and poles but on reaching the most compact part we were under the necessity of transporting the canoes and cargoes across it—an operation of much hazard as the snow concealed numerous holes which the water had made in the ice. That evening the men were employed to a late hour in repairing their canoes. The hunters arrived in the course of the night after a long absence. It appeared that a dog which escaped from us two days ago came into their camp howling piteously. Seeing him without his harness they came to the hasty conclusion that our whole party had perished in the rapid and, throwing away part of their baggage and leaving the meat behind them, they set off with the utmost haste to join Chief Longlegs [another of the Copper Indian chiefs]. Fortunately, a messenger of ours met them on their flight. Akaitcho scolded them heartily for their thoughtlessness in leaving the meat which we so much wanted. They proposed to remedy the evil by going to a favourite spot for hunting about forty miles below our present encampment. Akaitcho accompanied them, but previous to setting off renewed his charge that we should be on guard against the great grizzly bears of the Barren Lands.

Our plan was now that no rapids should be run until the bowman had examined it and decided upon its being safe. When the least danger was to be apprehended, the ammunition, guns and instruments were to be put out and carried along the banks. At four in the morning of July 4th we descended a succession of very agitated rapids and notwithstanding our precautions the leading canoe struck with great force against a stone and the bark was split. Fortunately, the injury was easily repaired. We camped that day having gone twenty-four and a half miles and having met one of Akaitcho's hunters. That afternoon they brought us the agreeable intelligence of their having killed eight musk-ox cows, of which four were full-grown. All the party were immediately dispatched to bring in this

165

seasonable supply. A young cow, irritated by the firing, ran down to the river and passed close to me at a short distance from the tents. I fired and wounded it, when the animal instantly turned and ran at me, but I avoided its fury by jumping aside and getting on an elevated piece of ground.

As we now had more meat than the party could consume, we delayed our voyage for the purpose of drying it. The hunters were supplied with more ammunition and sent forward. On the 6th we passed out of the rapids and into a main stream of about three hundred yards wide interrupted by sandy banks covered with willows. At ten we rejoined our hunters who had killed a deer and halted for breakfast. One of them, while walking along the shore, fired upon two grizzly bears and wounded one, which instantly turned and pursued him. His companions in the canoe put ashore to his assistance but did not succeed in killing the bears. We encamped at the foot of a lofty range of mountains appearing to be from a thousand to fifteen hundred feet high. These are the first hills we have seen in the country that deserve the name of mountain range; they are probably a continuation of the Stony Mountains crossed by Hearne.

The next day we arrived at the encampment of Hook, the other great chief of the Copper nation. He had with him only three hunters, his brother Longlegs, and our guide Keskarrah, who had joined him three days before, communicating to him our want of provisions. As an introductory mark of our regard I decorated him with a medal. Hook then stated that he was aware of our being destitute of provision and of the great need we had of an ample stock, and gave his regret that the unusual scarcity of animals, together with having only just received a supply of ammunition, had prevented him from collecting the quantity of meat he had wished to give for our use. However, he offered to give us what he had, stating that their families could live on fish until they could procure more meat. His women brought out three and a half bags of pemmican, besides some dried meat and tongues. We would gladly have rewarded the kindness of him and his companions substantially but we were limited by the scantiness of our stores to a small donation of fifteen charges of ammunition to each of the chiefs.

I was rejoiced to be able to persuade Hook to remain in this vicinity, where the animals abound at all times, on the borders of Great Bear Lake. They promised to remain on the east side of Bear Lake until November, making deposits of provisions as a resource for our party in the event of our being compelled to return by this route. In the afternoon, passing the foot of a high range of hills, we arrived at the place where the portage leads to the Bear Lake, according to the Indians. The Indians say they travel from hence with their families in three days, so the distance cannot, I think, exceed forty miles. As we proceeded we picked up a deer the hunters had shot, and killed another from the canoe, and also received an addition to our stock of seven young geese which the hunters had run down with their sticks.

Proceeding farther we discerned proofs of there having been Indians near this spot and shortly met three old Copper Indians with their families who had supported themselves with the bow and arrows since last autumn, not having visited Fort Providence for more than a year. So successful had they been that they were able to supply us with upwards of seventy pounds of dried meat, and six moose skins fit for making shoes.

Below this point the river descends for three-quarters of a mile in a deep but crooked channel cut through the foot of a hill six hundred feet high. It is confined between perpendicular cliffs and the body of the river, pent in this narrow chasm, dashed furiously around the projecting rocky columns. After discharging part of their cargoes, the canoes ran through this defile without sustaining any injury. Soon after we perceived our hunters running up the river to prevent us disturbing a herd of musk-oxen they had observed grazing on the opposite bank. We put the hunters across and they succeeded in killing six, upon which we encamped to make dry meat. To the eastward and the northward of us at a distance of twelve miles lay the Copper Mountains which Mr. Hearne had visited.

On the 11th we rejoined our hunters at the foot of the Copper Mountains where they had killed three musk-oxen. We availed ourselves of the opportunity to search for specimens of ore, and a party of twenty-one persons set off on that excursion. We travelled for nine hours over a considerable space of ground but found only a few small pieces of native copper. Our guides reported that they had found copper in large pieces in every part of this range, for two days' walk to the north-west, and that the Eskimos came hither to search for it. The annual visits which the Copper Indians were accustomed to make to these mountains had now been discontinued since they had been able to obtain a supply of iron instruments from the trading post. The impracticability of navigating the river upward from the sea, and the want of wood for forming an establishment, would prove insuperable objections to rendering the collection of copper at this part worthy of mercantile speculation.

July 12th. We had now entered the confines of the Eskimo country and our guides recommended us to be cautious in lighting fires lest we should discover ourselves. Throughout the day's voyage the current was very strong. The river is in many places confined between perpendicular walls of rock, and large masses of ice twelve or fourteen feet thick were still adhering to many parts of the bank.

In the evening two musk-oxen, being seen on the beach, were pursued and killed by our men. While we were waiting to embark the meat, the Indians reported they had been attacked by a bear which sprang upon them while they were talking. His attack was so sudden that they had no time to level their guns properly, and they all missed except Akaitcho who, less confused than the rest, took deliberate aim and shot the animal dead. They do not eat the flesh of bear but, knowing that we had no such prejudice, they brought us some of the choice pieces which, upon trial, we found to be excellent meat.

Now being within twelve miles of the rapids where the Eskimos are found, we pitched our tents. A strict watch was appointed, consisting of an officer, four Canadians and an Indian. We immediately commenced arrangements for sending forward persons to discover whether there were any Eskimos in our vicinity. It was determined to send Augustus and Junius [the two Eskimos from Hudson Bay] who were very desirous to undertake the service. These adventurous men proposed to go armed only with pistols concealed in their dress, and furnished with beads, looking glasses and other articles, that they might conciliate their countrymen by presents. We felt great reluctance in exposing our two little interpreters, who had rendered themselves dear to the whole party; but this course of proceeding appeared to offer the only chance of gaining an interview.

Augustus and Junius not having returned next morning, we were much alarmed respecting them and determined on proceeding to find out the cause of their detention. It was eleven o'clock before we could prevail on the Indians to remain behind, which we wished them to do, fearing that the Eskimos might suspect our intentions if they were seen in our suite. We promised to send for them when we had paved the way for their reception. In the evening we had the gratification of meeting Junius who was hastening back to inform us that they had found four Eskimo tents at the fall which we recognized to be the one described by Mr. Hearne [Bloody Falls]. The Eskimos were asleep at the time but rose soon afterwards, and

Augustus presented himself and had some conversation across the river. He told them that white people had arrived who would make them very useful presents.

The information seemed to alarm them very much but one of them came nearer to him [in his kayak] and received the rest of the message. He would not, however, land on his side of the river, but returned to the tents without taking a present. His language differed in some respect from Augustus's but they understood each other tolerably well. We now encamped, having come fourteen miles. Junius set off again to rejoin his companion accompanied by Hepburn who was directed to remain two miles above the falls, to arrest our canoes on their passage lest we should too suddenly surprise the Eskimos.

At ten p.m. we were mortified by the appearance of the Indians with Mr. Wentzel who had in vain endeavoured to restrain them from following us. The only reason assigned by Akaitcho for his conduct was that he wished to reassure himself of my promise to establish peace between his nation and the Eskimos.

After supper, Dr. Richardson ascended a lofty hill and obtained the first view of the sea. It appeared to be covered with ice. He saw the sunset a few minutes before midnight from this elevated situation.

The next morning we experienced much difficulty in prevailing upon the Indians to remain behind. We left a Canadian with them and proceeded on our journey but not without apprehension that they would follow and derange our whole plan. We soon ran into many dangerous rapids, one of which we called Escape Rapid, from both the canoes having narrowly escaped foundering in its waves. We had entered it before we were aware, and the steepness of the cliff prevented us from landing. Two waves made a complete breach over the canoes and a third would in all probability have filled and overset them, which would have proved fatal to everyone.

At noon we perceived Hepburn lying on the bank of

170

the river and landed immediately. We regretted to learn that some of our men had appeared on the tops of the hills just at the time Augustus was conversing with one of the Eskimos who was almost persuaded to land. The unfortunate appearance of so many people revived his fears and he crossed to the eastern bank and fled with the whole of his party.

We learned from Augustus that the party, consisting of four men and as many women, had manifested a friendly disposition. From seeing all their property still strewed about, and ten of their dogs left, we entertained the hope that these poor people would return after their first alarm had subsided, and I determined on remaining until the next day. We sent Augustus and Junius across the river to look for the runaways, but their search was fruitless. They put a few pieces of iron and trinkets in the Eskimo kayaks which were lying on the beach. Under the coverings of their tents were observed some stone pots and hatchets, a few fish spears made of copper, two small bits of iron, and some dried salmon which was covered with maggots and half putrid. A great many skins of small birds were hung up to a stage, and even two mice were preserved in the same way. Several human skulls, which bore the marks of violence, and many bones were strewed about the ground near the encampment, and as this spot exactly answers the description given by Mr. Hearne of a place where the Chipewyans who accompanied him perpetrated the dreadful massacre on the Eskimos, we had no doubt of this being the place. We caught forty excellent fish of the salmon species [arctic char] in a single net below the rapids.

On the morning of the 16th three men were sent up the river to search for dry wood to make floats for the nets. We were preparing to go down to the sea in one of the canoes when Adam arrived in the utmost consternation informing us that a party of Eskimos were pursuing the men we had sent to collect wood. The orders for embarking were countermanded and we went with a party to their rescue. We soon met our people returning at a slow pace and learned they had come unawares upon an Eskimo party consisting of six men, with women and children, who were travelling towards the rapid with a considerable number of pack dogs carrying their baggage. The women hid themselves on the first alarm but the men advanced and, stopping at some distance from our men, began to dance in a circle tossing up their hands in the air and accompanying their motions with much shouting, to signify, I conceive, their desire of peace. Our men saluted by pulling off their hats and making bows, but neither party was willing to approach the other and at length the Eskimos retired to the hill from whence they had descended.

We proceeded in the hope of gaining an interview with them but, lest our appearance in a body should alarm them, advanced in a long line at the head of which was Augustus. We were led to their baggage, which they had deserted, by the howling of the dogs; and on the summit of the hill we found, lying behind a stone, an old man who was too infirm to effect his escape with the rest. He was much terrified when Augustus advanced and probably expected immediate death; but that the fatal blow might not be unrevenged he seized his spear and made a thrust with it at his supposed enemy.

Augustus repressed his feeble effort and soon calmed his fears by presenting him with some pieces of iron. His dialect differed from that used by Augustus but they understood each other fairly well. It appeared that his party consisted of eight men and families returning from a hunting excursion with dried meat [from the interior]. After being told who we were, he said he had heard of white people from parties of his nation residing on the sea coast to the eastward. He gave us much information about the coast but he knew it only to the eastward to the next river which he called Tree River. The old man said his name was Terreganoeuck, or White Fox, and that his tribe called themselves the Deer Horn Eskimos.

After this conversation White Fox proposed going down to his baggage and we perceived he was too infirm to walk without the assistance of sticks. Augustus therefore offered him his arm. We informed him of our desire to procure as much meat as we possibly could and he told us he had a large quantity concealed in the neighbourhood which he would cause to be carried to us when his people returned. I told him we were accompanied by Copper Indians who were desirous to make peace, to which he replied he would rejoice to see an end put to the hostility between the nations. We left Terreganoeuck in the hope that his party would rejoin him and sent Augustus and Junius back in the evening to remain with him. The tribe to which he belongs repair to the sea only in spring, and kill seals. As the seasons advance, they hunt deer and musk-oxen at some distance from the coast.

The next day we waited all morning in the expectation of the return of Augustus and Junius and when they did not come I sent Mr. Hood. He returned at midnight to say that none of the Eskimos had ventured to come near White Fox, except his aged wife who had concealed herself near by at our first interview. She told him the rest had gone to a river westward where there was another party of Eskimos. In the afternoon a party of nine Eskimos appeared on the east bank of the river below our encampment, carrying canoes and baggage on their backs; but they turned and fled as soon as they perceived our tents. The appearance of so many different bands of Eskimos terrified the Indians to such a degree that they determined on leaving us the next day, lest they be surrounded and their retreat cut off. I endeavoured by the offer of any remuneration they chose to prevail on them to remain, but in vain. I had much difficulty even in obtaining their promise to wait at the Copper Mountains for Mr. Wentzel and four men whom I intended to discharge at the sea.

The fears our interpreters, St. Germain and Adam, entertained were greatly increased and both came this evening to request their discharge, saying their services would no longer be needed as the Indians were going. As these were the only two in the party on whose skill in hunting we could rely, I was unable to listen to their desire of quitting us; and lest they should leave by stealth, their motions were strictly watched. We knew that the dread of the Eskimos would prevent these men from leaving as soon as the Indians were at a distance, and we trusted to their becoming reconciled to the journey.

The Indians left next morning promising to wait three days for Mr. Wentzel at the Copper Mountains. We afterward learned their fears did not permit them to do so, and that Mr. Wentzel did not rejoin them until they were a day's march to the southward of the mountains.

We embarked at dawn and proceeded toward the sea nine miles distant from Bloody Falls. After passing a few rapids, the river became wider and we camped at ten on the western bank at its junction with the sea. Our Canadian voyageurs complained much of the cold but they were amused by their first view of the sea and particularly with the sight of seals that were swimming about near the entrance of the river. But these sensations gave place to despondency before the evening had elapsed. They were terrified at the idea of a voyage through an icy sea in bark canoes. They speculated on the length of the journey, the roughness of the sea, the uncertainty of provisions, the exposure to cold where we could expect no fuel, and the prospect of having to re-traverse the barren grounds to get to some establishment.

On the evening of July 18th, our dispatches being finished, we parted from Mr. Wentzel with Parent, Gagnier, Dumas, and Forcier — Canadians whom I had discharged for the purpose of reducing our expenditure of provisions as much as possible. The remainder of the party, including officers, amounted to twenty persons. I told Mr. Wentzel that if we were far distant from this river when the season put a stop to our advance, we should in all probability be unable to return to it and would have to travel across the barren grounds towards some established post; in which case I said we would certainly go first to Fort Enterprise. Therefore, before he quitted Fort Enterprise, he was to be assured of the intentions of the Indians to lay up the provisions we might require.

The travelling distance from Fort Enterprise to the mouth of the Coppermine River is about 334 miles. The canoes and baggage were dragged over snow and ice for 117 miles of this distance.

The Hyperborean Sea

July 20th, 1821. We had intended to embark early this morning upon an element more congenial with our habits than the fresh water navigations we had hitherto encountered. We were detained, however, by a strong gale which continued the whole day and was the more provoking as we procured but few fish. Our only luxury now was a little salt which had long been our substitute for bread and vegetables.

It was not until the next afternoon, in a dense fog, that we commenced our voyage on the Hyperborean Sea. Shortly afterwards we landed on an island where the Eskimos had a cache. We took four sealskins to repair our shoes and left in exchange a copper kettle and some awls and beads. We travelled all day inside a crowded range of islands, to the east, and saw the "blink" of ice visible to the northward. On the 22nd we continued along a coast consisting of a gravelly or sandy beach skirted by green plains; but as we proceeded the shore became exceedingly rocky and sterile and at last projected to the northward in a high, deep promontory. Ice had drifted down upon this cape but we ventured into it, pushing the canoes through the small channels amongst it. After pursuing this dangerous and anxious navigation for some time, we encamped on a smooth and rocky point. The following day the Tree

River of the Eskimos was reached. The fishing nets were set, but obtained almost nothing. This part of the coast is the most sterile and inhospitable that can be imagined. Fortunately, our interpreters killed a reindeer upon an island. On the 24th, the ice having retreated some distance from shore, we effected with difficulty a traverse across Gray's Bay. That night we had thundershowers. The nets only furnished us with three salmon trout, which we attributed to the entrance of some seals into the mouth of the river. In the morning we paddled against a cold breeze until the spreading of a thick fog caused us to land.

So we continued along this dreary shore, seeking a channel between different masses of ice which had accumulated at the various points. In these operations the canoes were in imminent danger of being crushed, particularly when the ice was being tossed on the waves by gales. On the 26th a great deal of ice had drifted into the inlet where we had encamped, and though we attempted to force a passage, the first canoe got enclosed and remained for some time in a very perilous situation. We landed without having sustained any serious injury. Here we remained detained by the ice for some time in this place which we named Detention Harbour. On the 28th, the ice continuing in the same state, several men were sent to hunt and one of them fired no less than four times at deer but unfortunately without success. It was a satisfaction, however, to ascertain that the country was not destitute of animals. We had the mortification to discover that two of the bags of pemmican which were our principal reliance had become mouldy by being wet. Our beef, too, had been so badly cured as to be scarcely eatable. It was not the quality of our provisions that gave us most uneasiness, however, but [their] diminution and the utter incapacity to obtain any addition. Seals were the only animals that met our view at Detention Harbour and these we could never approach.

On the 29th we were at last freed and on July 30th we entered Arctic Sound where we were again involved in a

176

stream of ice, but after considerable delay extricated ourselves and proceeded towards the bottom of the inlet in
search of the mouth of a river. About ten that morning we
breakfasted on a small deer which St. Germain had killed.
Our stock of provisions being now reduced to eight days'
consumption, it became a matter of the first importance to
obtain a supply and, as we had learned from White Fox
that the Eskimos frequent the rivers at this season, I determined on seeking communication with them here with the
view of obtaining relief of our present wants, or even
shelter for the winter if the season should prevent us from
returning either to Hook's party or Fort Enterprise. Augustus, Junius, and Hepburn were therefore furnished with
the necessary presents and desired to go along the bank of
the river as far as they could in search of natives.

At two in the morning of August 1st our hunters
returned with two small deer and a grizzly bear. Augustus
and Junius arrived at the same time, having traced the river
twelve miles without discovering any vestige of inhabitants. We then embarked and ran along the eastern shore
of Arctic Sound [they were now descending into Bathurst
Inlet] opening another wide extremity of water. We spent
the remainder of the afternoon endeavouring to ascertain,
from the tops of hills, whether this was another bay or
merely a passage enclosed by a chain of islands. We determined on proceeding southward. During the delay four
more deer were killed, all young and lean.

Being detained by the continuance of a gale which had
overthrown our tents, on the 2nd of August some men
were sent out to hunt while the officers visited the tops of
the highest hills to ascertain the best channels. Much doubt
at this time prevailed as to whether the land on the right
was main shore or merely a chain of islands. In this state
of doubt we landed often, endeavouring from the summits
of the hills to ascertain the true nature of the coast, but in
vain. So we continued paddling through channels all night
against a fresh breeze which increased to a violent gale and

compelled us to land. The inlet, when viewed from a high hill adjoining our camp, exhibited so many arms that the course we ought to pursue was more uncertain than ever. It was absolutely necessary, however, to see the end of it before we could determine that it was not a strait. After paddling twelve additional miles on the morning of the 5th of August we had the mortification to discover that this was an inlet, terminated by a river. We were somewhat consoled for the loss of time in exploring this great inlet by the success of Junius in killing a musk-ox, the first we had seen on the coast, and afterwards by the acquisition of the flesh of a bear. This latter proved to be a female in excellent condition; and our Canadian voyageurs, whose appetite for fat meat is insatiable, were delighted.

Until August 15th the party continued coasting north on the east side of Bathurst Inlet, entered Melville Sound, and explored it thirty miles to the eastward before crossing over to the north shore and beginning to work westward again. During this time they sustained themselves largely on Barren-Land grizzly bears, of which they shot a surprising number.

We had now reached the northern point of the entrance into the Sound which I named in honour of Lord Melville, First Lord of the Admiralty. Shortly after the tents were pitched Mr. Back reported that both canoes had sustained material injury during this day's voyage. I found on examination that fifteen ribs of the first canoe were broken, some in two places; and that the second canoe was so loose in the frame that its ribs could not be bound in the usual secure manner, and consequently there was danger of its bark separating from the gunwales if exposed to a heavy sea.

Distressing as these circumstances were, they gave me less pain than the discovery that our people, who had hitherto displayed a courage beyond our expectation in following us through dangers and difficulties, now felt serious apprehension for their safety. They were not restrained from expressing them even by the presence of their officers. We even suspected that their recent lack of success in hunting excursions had proceeded from an intentional relaxation in their efforts to kill deer, in order that the want of provisions might compel us to put a period to our voyage.

I must now say that many concurrent circumstances had caused me to meditate on the approach of this painful necessity. The season was breaking up and severe weather would soon ensue when we could not sustain ourselves in a country destitute of fuel. Our stock of provisions was now reduced to a quantity of pemmican sufficient for three days' consumption. Though reindeer were seen, they could not be easily approached on the level shores and it was to be apprehended they would soon migrate to the south. The time spent exploring Arctic and Melville Sounds and Bathurst Inlet had precluded the hope of us reaching Repulse Bay, which at the outset of the voyage we had fondly cherished.[5] In the evening I announced my determination of returning after four days' more exploration, unless we should previously meet Eskimos and be enabled to make arrangements for passing the winter with them. This communication was joyfully received by the men.

The following day we found traces of Eskimos including the skull of a man placed between two rocks. We now had the pleasure of finding the coast trending north-east [they were now on the north coast of the Adelaide Peninsula] with the sea in the offing clear of islands. This afforded a matter of wonder to our Canadians who had not previously had an uninterrupted view of the ocean.

Our course was continued until eight p.m. when a

---

[5]Franklin must have been one of the world's most optimistic explorers. Repulse Bay, on Hudson Bay, lay over seven hundred miles east of the mouth of the Coppermine River *as the crow flies*.

threatening thunder squall induced us to camp, but the water was so shallow we found some difficulty approaching shore. Our tents were scarcely pitched before we were assailed by a heavy squall and a violent gale from west-nor'west which three times overset the tents in the course of the night. The wind blew with equal violence the following day and the sea rolled furiously upon the beach. The Canadians now had the opportunity of witnessing the effect of a storm upon the sea, and the sight increased their desire of quitting it.

The hunters were sent out and saw many deer but the flatness of the country defeated their attempts to approach them. Our allowance was limited to a handful of pemmican and a small portion of portable soup for each man per day. On the 18th, the stormy weather and sea continuing, there was no prospect of our being able to embark. The hunters found the burrows of a number of white foxes and Hepburn killed one of these animals, which proved excellent eating, esteemed by us as equal to young geese. This place, which we call Point Turnagain, is only six degrees and a half east of the mouth of the Coppermine River [about 170 miles], but we had sailed, in tracing the deeply indented coast, 555 geographic miles.

We were not able to escape from Point Turnagain till August the 22nd during which time the gales blew without diminution. The thermometer fell to 33°. Two men who were sent out with Junius to search for a deer that Augustus had killed did not make their appearance, and on the 20th we were presented with the most chilling prospect, the small pools of water being frozen over. A search for the missing men was finally successful. The stragglers were much fatigued and had suffered severely from the cold, one of them having his thighs frozen and, what under our present circumstances was most grievous, they had thrown away the meat they had shot.

My original intention, when the season compelled us

to relinquish the survey, had been to return by way of the Coppermine River and, in pursuance of my arrangement with Hook, to travel to Slave Lake by Great Bear Lake. But our scanty stock of provisions and the length of the voyage rendered it necessary to make for a nearer place. We had found the country between Cape Barrow and the Coppermine River would not supply our wants. Besides, at this advanced season we expected a recurrence of gales. I therefore determined to make for Arctic Sound, where we had found animals more numerous than at any other place, and enter the river which we call Hood's River, to advance up that stream as far as it was navigable, and then construct small canoes out of the larger ones, which could be carried with us in crossing the barren grounds to Fort Enterprise.

Our men, cheered by the prospect of returning, embarked with the utmost alacrity and paddled with unusual vigour a distance of twenty miles before noon. The wind then freshened too much to permit us to continue and the whole party went hunting but returned without success, drenched with heavy rain.

A severe frost gave us a comfortless night, and at two p.m. we set sail on a traverse of fifteen miles across Melville Sound before a strong wind and heavy seas. The privation of food under which our voyageurs were then labouring absorbed every other terror; otherwise the most powerful persuasion could not have induced them to attempt such a traverse. The waves were so high that the masthead of our canoe was often hid from the other though it was sailing within hail. The traverse having been made, we neared a high rocky lee shore on which a heavy surf was beating. The canoes drifted fast to leeward and, on rounding a point, the recoil of the sea from the rocks was so great that they were with difficulty kept from foundering. We looked in vain for a sheltered bay to land in and at length, being unable to weather another point, were obliged to put ashore on the open beach. The landing was fortunately effected without further injury than the splitting of the head of the second canoe.

The next day we risked sailing across the eastern entrance of Bathurst Inlet. Some deer being seen on an island, the hunters went in pursuit and killed three females which enabled us to save our last remaining meal of pemmican. Contrary to what we had experienced earlier in the month, the deer were now plentiful. The hunters killed two on the 25th and we were relieved from all apprehension of an immediate want of food. On the 25th we reached Hood's River and ascended as high as the first rapid where we encamped. Here terminated our voyage on the arctic sea, during which we had gone over 650 geographical miles. Our voyageurs could not restrain their expressions of joy at having turned their backs on the sea. The consideration that the most painful and most hazardous part of the journey was yet to come did not depress their spirits at all. It is due to their character to mention that they displayed much courage in encountering the dangers of the sea, magnified as it was for them by the novelty.

The Journey Home

Embarking at eight a.m. we proceeded up the river, which is full of sandy shoals. We encamped at a cascade of eighteen or twenty feet high and set the nets. Bear and deer tracks had been numerous on the banks of the river when we were here before, but not a single recent one was to be seen at this time. The next morning the nets furnished us with ten whitefish and trout. We pursued our voyage up the river but the shoals and rapids were so frequent that we [officers] walked along the bank the whole day. The crews laboured hard in carrying the canoes thus lightened over the shoals or dragging them up the rapids, yet our journey in a direct line was only about seven miles.

We camped at the lower end of a narrow chasm

through which the river flows upward of about a mile. The walls are upward of two hundred feet high, quite perpendicular, and in some places only a few yards apart. The river forms two magnificent and picturesque falls, the upper about sixty feet high and the lower one at least a hundred and perhaps considerably more. Messrs. Back and Hood took beautiful sketches of this majestic scene.

The river above this fall seemed so rapid and shallow that it was useless to proceed farther with the large canoes. We accordingly commenced breaking them up and making two smaller ones. By the 31st both the new canoes being finished, we prepared for our departure on the 1st of September. The leather which had been preserved for making shoes was now equally divided amongst the men, two pair of flannel socks were given to each person, and such articles of warm clothing as remained were issued to those who most required them. The men were also furnished with one of the officers' tents. This being done I communicated my intention of proceeding directly to Point Lake, opposite our spring encampment, a distance of 149 miles in a straight line. They received the communication cheerfully, considering the journey to be short, and we left in high spirits. Our luggage consisted of ammunition, nets, hatchets, ice chisels, astronomical instruments, clothing, blankets, three kettles and the two canoes, which were each carried by one man. The officers carried such a portion of their own things as their strength would permit. The weight carried by each man was about ninety pounds and with these we advanced at the rate of a mile an hour. In the evening the hunters killed a lean cow out of a drove of musk-oxen but the men were too much burdened to carry more than a small portion of its flesh.

On the 1st of September a fall of snow took place, and the canoes became a cause of delay by the difficulty of carring them in a high wind, and they sustained much damage from the falls of those who had charge of them. At the end of eleven miles we encamped and sent for a musk-ox and deer which St. Germain and Augustus had killed. The day was extremely cold with the thermometer varying between 34° and 36°. In the afternoon a heavy fall of snow took place. We found no wood at the encampment but made a fire of moss to cook supper and crept under our blankets for warmth.

Noticing that the river continued to the west and fearing that by pursuing it we might lose much time, I determined on quitting its banks the next day and accordingly we followed it only to a place where a musk-ox had been killed on the 3rd, after which we emerged from the valley of the river and entered a level but very barren country. Having walked twelve and a half miles we encamped at seven and distributed our last piece of pemmican and a little arrowroot for supper, which afforded but a scanty meal. Heavy rain commenced at midnight and continued without intermission until five in the morning when it changed to snow and the wind went north-west in a violent gale. As we had nothing to eat and were destitute of the means of making a fire, we remained in our beds all day; but the covering of our blankets was insufficient to prevent us from feeling the severity of the frost.

There was no abatement of the storm next day. Our tents were completely frozen and the snow had drifted around them to a depth of three feet, and even in the inside there was a covering of several inches on our blankets. Our suffering from cold with the temperature at 20° will easily be imagined; it was, however, less than what we felt from hunger.

The morning of the 7th cleared a little but we feared that winter had set in with all its rigour and we therefore prepared for our journey although we were in a very unfit condition for starting, being weak from fasting, and our garments stiffened by the frost. Just as we were about to commence I was seized with a fainting fit, in consequence of exhaustion and sudden exposure to the wind; but after eating a morsel of portable soup I recovered so far as to be able to move on.

The ground was now a foot deep with snow and the margins of the lakes encrusted with ice. The swamps were entirely frozen but, the ice not being strong enough to bear us, we frequently plunged knee deep in water. Those who carried the canoes were repeatedly blown down by the violence of the wind. The largest canoe was so much broken as to be rendered utterly unserviceable. This was a serious disaster, the remaining canoe having, through mistake, been made too small. It was doubtful whether it would be sufficient to carry us across a river.

As the accident could not be remedied, we turned it to best account by making a fire of the bark and ribs of the broken vessel and cooking the remainder of our portable soup and arrowroot. This was a scanty meal after three days' fasting. In the afternoon we got into hilly country where the ground was strewn with large stones. These were covered with lichens called *tripe de roche*.[6] A considerable quantity was gathered and, with half a partridge each, shot in the course of the day, furnished us with a slender supper.

The next morning we came to a river flowing with a rapid current to the westward. We had much difficulty in crossing this, the canoe being useless since it required gumming, an operation which, owing to the want of wood for fire, we were unable to perform. Several of the men slipped into the stream but were immediately rescued by the others.

On the 9th we came to the borders of a lake amidst a clump of stunted willows. The lake stretched to the westward as far as we could see, and its waters discharged by a stream a hundred yards wide. Being entirely ignorant where we might be led by following the lake, and dreading

---

[6]Rock tripe — a glutinous lichen which, when boiled, is the final resort of starving men in the Arctic.

the idea of going a mile out of our way, we determined on crossing the river. The canoe was gummed for the purpose, willows furnishing us with fire. But we had to await the return of Junius who had gone off the night before. He arrived in the afternoon and informed us that he had seen a large herd of musk-oxen and had wounded one but it had escaped. He brought about four pounds of meat, the remains of a deer that had been devoured by wolves. The poor fellow was much fatigued, having walked all night, but as the weather was favourable for crossing the river we could not allow him to rest.

Managed by St. Germain, Adam and Peltier, the canoe was able to ferry one passenger at a time if he lay flat on its bottom, by no means a pleasant position owing to its leakiness. The transport of the whole party was effected by five o'clock. Two young hares were shot by St. Germain which, with the small piece of meat brought by Junius, furnished the supper for the party. We subsequently learned from the Copper Indians that the lake was Cathawhachaga. Had we kept on the western side, instead of crossing the river, several days' harassing march and a disastrous accident would have been avoided.

It was now September 10th, the thermometer was at 18°, and in the course of our march this morning the ground became higher and more hilly and covered to a greater depth with snow. This rendered walking not only laborious but hazardous in the highest degree. It often happened that the men fell into the interstices between the rocks, with their loads on their backs, being deceived by the smooth appearance of the drifted snow. If any had broken a limb his fate would have been melancholy indeed; we could neither have remained with him nor carried him on.

We halted at ten to gather *tripe de roche* but it was so frozen that we were quite benumbed with cold before a sufficiency could be collected even for a scanty meal. About noon the weather cleared and to our great joy we saw a herd of musk-oxen grazing in the valley below us. The party instantly halted and the best hunters were sent forward. No less than two hours were consumed before they got within gunshot. In the meantime, we beheld their proceedings with extreme anxiety. At length they opened fire and we had the satisfaction of seeing one of the largest cows fall; another was wounded but escaped.

To skin and cut up the animal was the work of a few minutes. The contents of its stomach were devoured upon the spot, and the raw intestines, which were next attacked, were pronounced by the most delicate amongst us to be excellent. This was the sixth day since we had had a good meal. After supper two of the hunters went in pursuit of the herd but could not get near them.

We were kept in camp all the next day by a strong wind and were much incommoded by the drift of snow. We restricted ourselves to one meal today as we were at rest, and there was only meat remaining sufficient for one day. The gale had not diminished on the 12th but as we were fearful of its continuance for some time we determined on going forward. The snow was two feet deep and the ground much broken which rendered the marching extremely painful. We accomplished eleven miles today. Our supper consumed the last of our meat.

On the 13th, in thick heavy weather, we had the extreme mortification to find ourselves on the borders of a large lake which we subsequently learned from the Indians was named Contwoyto, or Rum Lake. Neither of its extremities could be seen so we coasted the western portion in search of a crossing place. The lake being bounded by steep and lofty hills, our march was very fatiguing.

Crédit was missing when we camped and did not return during the night. We supped off a single partridge and some *tripe de roche*. This unpalatable weed was now quite nauseous to the whole party and produced bowel complaints. Mr. Hood was the greatest sufferer from this cause. We were extremely distressed at discovering that our improvident companions had thrown away three of the fishing nets and burned the floats. Being thus deprived of our principal resource, that of fishing, and the men getting weaker every day, it became necessary to lighten their burdens of everything except ammunition, clothing and the instruments required to find our way. I therefore deposited at this encampment many of our instruments.

On the morning of the 14th, the officers being assembled around a small fire, Perrault presented each of us with a small piece of meat which he had saved from his allowance. It was received with great thankfulness, and such an act of self-denial and kindness, being totally unexpected in a Canadian voyageur, filled our eyes with tears.

Shortly afterwards we met Crédit, who had killed two deer. We instantly halted and shared the deer that was nearest us for breakfast.

While the other deer was being sent for, we went to the bank of a river which blocked our path. The canoe was placed in the water at the head of a rapid and St. Germain, Solomon Bélanger and I embarked in order to cross. In mid-channel the canoe became difficult to manage and the current drove us to the edge of the rapid when Bélanger unfortunately applied his paddle to avert the danger of being forced down it, and lost his balance. The canoe was overset in consequence. We kept hold of it until we touched a rock where the water did not reach above our waists and here we kept our footing. Bélanger then held the canoe steady while St. Germain placed me in it and afterwards embarked himself, in a very dexterous manner. It was impossible to embark Bélanger, however, as the canoe would have hurried down the rapid the moment he raised his foot from the rock on which he stood. We were therefore compelled to leave him in his perilous situation. We had not gone more than twenty yards before the canoe, striking on a sunken rock, went down. The place being shallow we were able to empty it and a third attempt brought us to the shore.

In the meantime Bélanger was suffering extremely, immersed to his middle in the centre of a rapid, the temperature of which was very little above the freezing point. He called piteously for relief and St. Germain on his return endeavoured to embark him in vain. An attempt was next made to carry a line out to him. This also failed. At last when his strength was exhausted the canoe reached him with a small cord belonging to one of the nets and he was dragged senseless through the rapid.

By this accident I had the misfortune to lose my portfolio containing my journal from Fort Enterprise together with all the astronomical and meteorological observations made during the descent of the Coppermine River.

Soon after leaving this river we discovered a herd of deer and after a long chase a male was killed by Perrault. After this we passed around the north end of a branch of the lake and ascended the Willingham Mountains near the border of the lake. The party was in good spirits this evening at the recollection of having successfully crossed the rapid and being in possession of provisions for the next day. Besides, we had taken the precaution of bringing away the skin of the deer to eat when the meat should fail.

On the 18th the country was level and gravelly but the snow was very deep. We went for a short time along a deeply beaten road made by the reindeer. We supped off *tripe de roche* which had been gathered during our halts in the course of the march. The next morning everyone was faint from hunger and marched with difficulty, having to oppose a fresh breeze and wade through snow two feet deep. However, we gained ten miles by four o'clock, and then camped. The canoe was unfortunately broken by the fall of a person who had it in charge. No *tripe de roche* was seen today.

We had now got around Rum Lake but on the 20th we were in hilly country and the marching was much more laborious. Mr. Hood was particularly weak. I was also unable to keep pace with the men, who put forth their utmost speed encouraged by their hope of seeing Point Lake. When they failed to see the lake that night they threatened to throw away their bundles and quit us, which rash act they would probably have done had they known what track to pursue. The following day the party was very feeble, and the men much dispirited. We made slow progress, having to march over hilly rugged country. Just before noon the sun beamed through the haze for the first time in six days and we obtained an observation which showed we were six miles to the southward of that part of Point Lake to which our course was directed. We altered course immediately and fired guns to apprise our hunters, who were out of view, and ignorant of our having done so. Two partridges were killed and these, with some *tripe de roche*, furnished our supper. At this point Dr. Richardson was obliged to leave his specimens of plants and minerals, collected on the sea coast, being unable to carry them any farther.

On the 22nd we came on the borders of a large lake and were grieved at finding it expand very much and incline to the east and south. We considered it must be a branch of Point Lake and we knew that only by by-passing round its south end could we reach the Coppermine River. Our course was continued in that direction. That evening the party became dispersed and when we found the men they were halted amongst some willows where they had picked up some pieces of skin and a few bones of deer that had been devoured by the wolves last spring. They had rendered the bones friable by burning, and eaten them, as well as the skins and some old shoes. Peltier and Vaillant were with them, having left the canoe, which they said was so completely broken as to be rendered incapable of repair. The anguish this intelligence gave me may be conceived, but it is beyond my power to describe it.

The men now seemed to have lost all hope of being preserved. On the following morning the rain had so wasted the snow that the tracks of Mr. Back and his com-

190

panions, who had gone on with the hunters, were traced with difficulty. The men became furious at the apprehension of being deserted by the hunters, and some of the strongest, throwing down their bundles, prepared to set out after them. The entreaties and threats of the officers prevented their executing this mad scheme. We overtook Mr. Back in the afternoon and after halting an hour, during which we refreshed ourselves with eating our old shoes, we set on in the hope of reaching the Coppermine. The bounty of Providence was manifested the next morning in our killing five small deer. This unexpected supply reanimated the drooping spirits of our men and filled every heart with gratitude.

We set out again on the 26th and after walking about three miles along the lake came to the river, which we at once recognized as the Coppermine. The rapids were carefully examined in search of a ford but, finding none, the expedient occurred of attempting to cross on a raft made of willows. This scheme was abandoned on the advice of the experienced voyageurs who declared they would prove inadequate to the conveyance of the party and that much time would be lost in the attempt. It therefore became necessary to search for trees of sufficient size to form a raft. To do this we considered it best to trace the shores of Point Lake in search of them and resumed our march. I now decided to send Mr. Back forward to hunt with the interpreters. I also had in view the object of enabling him to cross the lake with two men and convey the earliest account of our situation to the Indians. I instructed him to halt at the first trees he should come to and prepare a raft, and if his hunters had killed animals, so that the party could be supported while we were making our raft, he was to cross immediately and send the Indians to us with supplies as quickly as possible.

Mr. Back and his companions set out at six and we at seven. I desired the two Eskimos not to leave us, they having often strayed in search of the remains of animals.

Our people, through despondency, had become careless and disobedient and had ceased to dread punishment or hope for reward. At length we came to an arm of the lake running to the north-east and apparently connected to that lake which we had coasted between the 22nd and 24th of the month. The idea of again rounding such an extensive piece of water and of travelling over such barren country was dreadful, and we feared that other arms equally large might obstruct our path. While we halted to consider the subject, the carcass of a deer was discovered in the cleft of a rock into which it had fallen in the spring. It was putrid but was little less acceptable to us on that account. A fire being kindled, a large portion of it was devoured on the spot. Afterwards we concluded to return to the river and make another attempt to cross the stream on a raft of willows. But Crédit and Junius were missing at this point, and it was also necessary to send notice of our intention to Mr. Back and his party. Augustus, being promised a reward, undertook the task and we agreed to wait for him at the rapid. It was supposed he could not fail to meet the two stragglers on his way to or from Mr. Back. We supped on the remains of the putrid deer, and the men, having gone to the spot where it was found, scraped together the contents of its intestines which were scattered on the rock and added them to their meal.

That night Crédit rejoined us but we got no intelligence of Junius. We sat out before daybreak and at two in the afternoon encamped between the rapids where the river was at its narrowest. Some *tripe de roche* was collected which we boiled for supper with the moiety of the remainder of our deer meat. The men commenced cutting the willows for construction of the raft. I promised a reward of three hundred livres to the first person who should convey a line across the river by which the raft could be managed.

On the 29th, with a temperature of 38°, the men began to bind the willows into faggots for the construction of a raft which was finished by seven o'clock. The willows were green and it proved to have very little buoyancy and was unable to support more than one man at a time. Several attempts were made by Bélanger and Benoit to convey the raft across the stream, but they failed for want of oars. All the men suffered extremely from the coldness of the water in which they were necessarily immersed up to their waists in an endeavour to aid. At this point Dr. Richardson proposed to swim across the stream with a line and haul the raft over. He launched into the stream with the line around his middle, but when he had got a short distance from the bank his arms were numbed with cold and he lost the power of moving them. Still he persevered turning on his back, and had nearly gained the opposite bank when his legs became powerless and, to our infinite alarm, we beheld him sink. We instantly hauled upon the line and he came to the surface and was gradually drawn ashore in an almost lifeless state. He recovered strength gradually before a good fire of willows. I cannot describe what everyone felt at beholding the skeleton which the doctor's naked, debilitated frame exhibited. When he stripped, the Canadians simultaneously exclaimed, *"Ah que nous sommes maigres."* That evening Augustus came in. He had walked a day and a half but had seen neither Junius nor Mr. Back. Of the former he had seen no traces, but had followed Back's party for a considerable distance until the hardness of the ground made him lose the track. It was the opinion of Augustus that when Junius found he could not rejoin the party he would try to gain the woods at the west end of Point Lake, and follow the river until he fell in with the Eskimos who frequent its mouth.

Next morning the men searched out dry willows and formed a more buoyant raft than the former. The wind still being adverse and strong, they delayed attempting to cross until a more favourable time. They collected some *tripe de roche* and made a cheerful supper. In the afternoon of October 1st we were rejoiced to see Mr. Back and his party.

They had traced the lake about fifteen miles farther than we did and, dreading, as we had done, the idea of coasting its barren shores, returned to make an attempt at crossing here. St. Germain now proposed to make a canoe of the fragments of painted canvas in which we wrapped our bedding.

Crédit, who had been hunting, brought in the antlers and backbone of a deer that had been killed in the summer. The wolves and birds of prey had picked them clean but there still remained a quantity of the spinal marrow. This, although putrid, was esteemed a valuable prize and, the spine being divided into portions, was distributed equally. The marrow was so acrid as to excoriate the lips, but we rendered the bones friable by burning, and ate them also. The following morning there was a foot and half of snow and the weather was stormy. Men who had been sent to look for gum returned without having found any, but St. Germain said he could still make the canoe with the willows covered with canvas, and went off with Adam to a clump of willows for that purpose. The snowstorm continued all night and during the forenoon of the 3rd I set out to St. Germain to hasten his operation; but though he was only three-quarters of a mile distant, I spent three hours in a vain attempt to reach him, my strength being unequal to the labour of wading through the deep snow. My associates were all in the same debilitated state, and poor Hood was reduced to a shadow from the severe bowel complaint. Back was so feeble as to require the support of a stick in walking, and Dr. Richardson had lameness superadded to weakness. We officers were unable from weakness to gather *tripe de roche* ourselves, but Hepburn was indefatigable in his exertions to serve us and daily collected all the *tripe de roche* that was used in the officers' mess.

On October 4th the canoe was finished and St. Germain embarked and, amidst our prayers for success, succeeded in reaching the opposite shore. The canoe was then drawn back on a rope and in this manner one by one the party was conveyed over. I immediately dispatched Mr. Back with St. Germain, Solomon Bélanger, and Beauparlant to search for Indians, directing him to go to Fort Enterprise. We now had every reason to be grateful and our joy would have been complete were it not mingled with sincere regret at the separation of our poor Eskimo, the faithful Junius.

The want of *tripe de roche* made us go supperless to bed. Showers of snow fell during the night. We were all on foot by daybreak but from the depth of the snow, our advance was slow. Mr. Hood was now very feeble and Dr. Richardson, who attached himself to him, walked with him at a gentle pace in the rear. I kept with the foremost men to cause them to halt occasionally until the stragglers came up. The distance walked today was six miles. Crédit was very weak in the morning and his load was reduced to little more than his personal luggage. About noon next day Samandre came up to inform us that Crédit and Vaillant could advance no farther. The doctor returned and found Vaillant about a mile and a half in the rear. Having encouraged him to advance to a fire, he made every attempt, but fell down amongst the deep snow at every step. Leaving him in this situation the doctor went back about half a mile further to the spot where Crédit was said to have halted, but the track being nearly obliterated it became unsafe for him to go father. Returning he passed Vaillant who, having moved a few yards in his absence, had fallen down and was unable to rise. He could scarcely answer his questions. When J. B. Bélanger heard this melancholy account he went immediately to aid Vaillant and bring up his burden. When Bélanger came back with Vaillant's load he informed us that he found him lying on his back, benumbed with cold and incapable of being roused. The stoutest men of the party were earnestly entreated to bring him to the fire. They declared themselves unequal to the task. They urged me to allow them to throw down their loads and proceed to Fort Enterprise with the utmost speed. Compliance with their desire would have caused the loss of the whole party, for the men were totally ignorant of the course, and none of the officers could have directed the march, being insufficiently strong to keep up at the pace they would then walk.

Something had to be done, however, to relieve them as much as possible from their burdens, and we officers consulted on the subject. Mr. Hood and Dr. Richardson proposed to remain behind, with a single attendant, at the first place where sufficient wood and *tripe de roche* could be found for ten days' consumption. I should proceed as expeditiously as possible with the men to the house and send them immediate relief.

I was distressed beyond description at the thought of leaving them in such a dangerous situation and for a long time combated their proposal. The ammunition was also to be left with them. It was hoped that this deposit would be an inducement for the Indians to venture across the barren grounds to their aid. When we communicated this resolution to the men, they promised with great appearance of earnestness to return to those officers upon the first supply of food.

The next day we reached an extensive thicket of small willows and at this place Dr. Richardson and Mr. Hood determined to remain, with John Hepburn. The tent was pitched and the offer was made for any of the men who felt too weak to proceed to remain with the officers.

We set out without waiting to take any of the *tripe de roche* and, descending into more level country, found the snow very deep, and the labour of wading so fatigued us that we were compelled to encamp after a march of four and a half miles. Bélanger and Michel were left far behind and when they arrived at the camp appeared quite exhausted. They begged to be allowed to go back to the tent. Not being able to find any *tripe de roche*, we ate a few morsels of burnt leather for supper. We were unable to raise the tent, and found its weight too great to carry, so we cut it up and took a part of the canvas for a cover.

A strong gale came on after midnight which increased the severity of the weather. In the morning Bélanger and Michel renewed their request to go back to the tent. This was agreed on and, shortly after, Perrault and Fontano were seized with a fit of dizziness and other symptoms of extreme debility. Some Labrador tea was quickly prepared for them and, after drinking it and eating a few morsels of burnt leather, they recovered and expressed their desire to go forward. The other men, alarmed at what they had just witnessed, became doubtful of their own strength. When we had gone about two hundred yards Perrault became dizzy and desired us to halt, which we did until he recovered and proposed to march on. Ten minutes more had hardly elapsed before he again desired us to stop and, bursting into tears, declared he was totally exhausted and unable to accompany us farther. We proposed that he should return and rejoin Bélanger and Michel. Having taken a friendly leave of each of us and enjoined us to make all the haste we could, he turned back. During these detentions Augustus, becoming impatient of the delay, had walked on and we lost sight of him.

Before we had gone another two miles Fontano was completely exhausted, being seized with faintness and dizziness and falling often, and at length exclaiming that he could go no farther. We endeavoured to encourage him but the poor man was overwhelmed with grief and seemed desirous to remain at that spot. We proposed that he go back and join the others, or follow their tracks to the officers' tent. I cannot describe my anguish on the occasion of separating from another companion under circumstances so distressing. There was, however, no alternative. After some hestitation he set out and we watched him with inexpressible anxiety for some time. Antonio Fontano was an Italian who had served many years in De Meuron's regiment.

The party was now reduced to five persons, Adam, Peltier, Benoit, Samandre and myself. We made an attempt to gather some *tripe de roche* but could not, owing to the severity of the weather. Our supper consisted of tea and a few morsels of leather. Augustus did not make his appearance but we felt no alarm, supposing that he would go to the tent if he missed our track. Next morning we gathered some *tripe de roche* and enjoyed the only meal we had for four days. We enjoyed great benefit from it. After walking five miles we came to the borders of Marten Lake and were rejoiced to find it frozen. We encamped at the first rapid in Winter River amidst willows and alders and were gratified by the sight of a large herd of reindeer on the side of a hill. However, our hunter, Adam, was too feeble to pursue them. The following morning we reached our house.

When we reached Fort Enterprise, to our infinite disappointment and grief we found it a perfectly desolate habitation. There was no deposit of provisions, no trace of the Indians, no letter from Mr. Wentzel to point out where the Indians might be found. It would be impossible to describe our sensations after entering this miserable abode and discovering how we had been neglected. We all shed tears, not so much for our own fate as for that of our friends in the rear. I found a note, however, from Mr. Back stating that he had reached the house two days earlier and was going in search of the Indians at a part where St. Germain deemed it probable they might be found. If unsuccessful he purposed walking to Fort Providence and sending help from there. But he doubted whether either he or his party could perform the journey in their present debilitated state. It was clear to me that the only relief for our companions behind must be procured from the Indians. I therefore resolved to go in search of them; but my companions were absolutely incapable of proceeding, and I thought by halting two or three days they might gather a little strength.

We now looked around and were gratified to find several deerskins which had been thrown away during our former residence. The bones were gathered from the heaps of ashes, and these with the skins and the addition of *tripe de roche* we considered would support us tolerably well for a time. As to the house, the parchment being torn from the windows, the apartment we selected was exposed to all the rigour of the season. We endeavoured to exclude the wind as much as possible by placing loose boards against the apertures. The temperature was now between $-15°$ and $-20°$. We procured fuel by pulling up the flooring of the other rooms. While sitting around the fire singeing the deer fur for supper, we were rejoiced by the unexpected arrival of Augustus. He had seen two deer but had not had the strength to follow them. However, the next day he set two fishing lines below the rapid.

On October 13th the wind blew violently and the snow drifted and the party was confined to the house. The afternoon of the 14th Bélanger arrived with a note from Mr. Back stating he had seen no trace of Indians and desiring further instructions. Bélanger's situation required our first care, as he came in almost speechless, and covered with ice, having fallen into a rapid. He did not recover sufficiently to answer our questions until we had rubbed him for some time, changed his dress and given him warm soup. I now determined on taking the route to Fort Providence as soon as possible and wrote to Mr. Back desiring him to join me at Reindeer Lake.

Bélanger did not recover sufficiently to leave us before the 18th.

In making arrangements for our departure Adam revealed that he was affected with such swellings in some parts of his body as to preclude the slightest attempt at marching. It now became necessary to abandon the intention of proceeding with the whole party towards Fort Providence, and Peltier and Samandre having volunteered to remain with Adam, I determined on setting out with Benoit and Augustus. I instructed Peltier and Samandre to forward help, immediately on its arrival, to our companions in the rear. I thought it necessary to admonish Peltier, Samandre and Adam to eat two meals every day in order to keep up their strength, which they promised me they would do.

The first day we camped on Round Rock Lake where Augustus tried for fish but without success. Our fare was skin and tea. The night was bitterly cold and the wind pierced through our famished frames. The next morning I had the misfortune to break my snowshoes and this prevented me from keeping pace with Benoit and Augustus, and in the attempt I became quite exhausted. I therefore resolved on returning to the house and letting them proceed alone in search of the Indians. On arrival at the house I found Samandre very dispirited and too weak to render any assistance to Peltier, upon whom the whole labour of getting wood and collecting the means of subsistence had devolved. I undertook the office of cooking whenever food could be procured, but as I was too weak to pound the bones, Peltier agreed to do that in addition to his more fatiguing task of getting wood. Neither Adam nor Samandre would quit their beds and scarcely ceased from shedding tears all day. Our situation was indeed distressing, but in comparison with that of our friends in the rear, we considered it happy. The *tripe de roche* had hitherto afforded us our chief support; now we naturally felt great uneasiness at the prospect of being deprived of it by its being so frozen as to render it impossible to gather it.

Our strength declined each day and every exertion began to be irksome. By the 28th of October Peltier had difficulty lifting the hatchet; still he persevered. Samandre and I assisted him in bringing in the wood, but our united strength could only collect sufficient to replenish the fire four times each day. The inside of our mouths becoming sore from eating bone soup, we stopped the use of it and boiled our skin, which made a mode of dressing more palatable than frying it. On the 29th we saw a herd of deer sporting on the river about half a mile from the house but none of us felt strong enough to go after them.

While we were seated round the fire this evening discoursing, the conversation was suddenly interrupted by Peltier's exclaiming with joy, "Ah, le monde!" imagining that he had heard the Indians in the other room. Immediately afterwards, to our bitter disappointment, Dr. Richardson and Hepburn entered. My mind was instantly filled with apprehension which was immediately confirmed by the doctor's melancholy communication that Mr. Hood and Michel were dead. Perrault and Fontano had neither reached the tent nor been heard of by them. This intelligence produced a despondency in the minds of my party. We were shocked at beholding the emaciated countenances of the doctor and Hepburn, as they strongly evidenced their extremely debilitated state. We were all little more than skin and bone. The doctor particularly remarked on the sepulchral tone of our voices. Hepburn having shot a partridge, the doctor tore out the feathers and having held it to the fire a few minutes, divided it into seven portions. Each piece was ravenously devoured as it was the first morsel of flesh any of us had tasted for thirty-one days.

Next day the doctor and Hepburn went out in search of deer but, though they saw several herds and fired some shots, they were not fortunate enough to kill any, being too weak to hold their guns steady. My occupation was to seek for old skins under the snow but I had not the strength to drag in more than two of those which were within twenty yards of the house until the doctor assisted me. We then made up our stock to twenty-six skins although several were putrid and scarcely eatable. That night after our supper of singed skin and bone soup, Dr. Richardson told me the story of the death of Hood and Michel.

Dr. Richardson's Narrative

On the morning of September 29th I went out in quest of *tripe de roche*, leaving Hepburn to cut willows for a fire. I had no success and on my return found that Michel had come with a note from Mr. Franklin stating that he and Bélanger were about to return to us and that about a mile beyond our present camp was a clump of pine trees which he recommended. Michel informed us that he had quitted the party yesterday but had missed his way and passed the night in the snow a mile or two northward of us. Bélanger, he said, being impatient, had left the fire two hours earlier and as he had not arrived, he supposed he had gone astray. Michel now produced a hare and a partridge which he had killed in the morning. We looked upon Michel as the instrument chosen to preserve all our lives. He complained of cold and Mr. Hood offered to share his buffalo robe with him while I gave him one of two shirts which I wore.

Next morning Hepburn, Michel and myself carried the ammunition and the other articles to the pines. Michel was our guide. Hepburn and I then returned to the tent and arrived in the evening much exhausted with our journey. Michel preferred sleeping where he was, and requested us to leave him the hatchet, which we did. Mr. Hood remained in bed all day. Seeing nothing of Bélanger we gave him up for lost.

On the 11th Hepburn and I loaded ourselves with the bedding and, accompanied by Hood, set out for the pines. Mr. Hood was much affected with dimness of sight and other symptoms of extreme debility. On arrival we were alarmed to find that Michel was absent. We feared he had lost his way in coming to us in the morning. Hepburn went back for the tent, returning with it at dusk completely worn out with the fatigue of the day. Michel too arrived at the same time and reported he had been in chase of some deer which passed near his sleeping place in the morning. He said he had found a wolf which had been killed by the stroke of a deer's horn, and had brought a part of it. We implicitly believed his story then, but afterwards became convinced from circumstances, the details of which may be spared, that it must have been a portion of the body of Bélanger or Perrault. A question of moment here presents itself — namely, whether he actually murdered these two men, or either of them, or whether he found the bodies in the snow. Capt. Franklin suggests the former. When Perrault turned back, Capt. Franklin watched him until he reached a small group of willows which was immediately adjoining to the fire. Capt. Franklin conjectured that Michel, having already killed Bélanger, completed his crime by Perrault's death, in order to screen himself from detection. His asking for the hatchet seemed to indicate that he took it for the purpose of cutting up something that he knew to be frozen. These opinions, however, are the result of subsequent consideration. The following morning the tent was pitched and Michel went out early, refusing my offer to accompany him, and remained out the whole day. He would not sleep in the tent at night but chose to lie at the fireside. On the 13th there was a heavy gale and we passed the day by the fire. Next day, the gale abating, Michel set out as he said to hunt, but returned unexpectedly in a very short time. This conduct surprised us, and his contradictory answer to our questions excited some suspicions.

On the 16th Michel refused either to hunt or cut wood, spoke in a very surly manner and threatened to leave us. Under these circumstances, Hood and I deemed it best to promise that if he would hunt diligently for four days we would give Hepburn a letter for Mr. Franklin, a compass, inform him what course to pursue, and let them proceed together to the fort. The following day Michel went out, proposing to remain all night and to hunt next day on his way back. He returned in the afternoon of the 18th, having found Vaillant's blanket, together with a bag containing two pistols. We had some *tripe de roche* in the evening but Mr. Hood was unable to eat more than one or two spoonfuls.

On the 19th Michel refused to hunt or even to assist in carrying wood to the fire. Mr. Hood endeavoured to point out to him the duty of exertion but the discourse, far from producing any beneficial effort, seemed to excite his anger and amongst other expressions he made use of the following: "It is no use hunting; there are no animals; you had better kill and eat me." At length he went out, but returned soon with a report that he had seen three deer but was unable to follow them, having wet his foot in a small stream.

Sunday, October 20th. After reading morning service, I went to gather *tripe de roche*, leaving Mr. Hood arguing with Michel before the tent at the fireside. Hepburn was employed cutting down a tree a short distance from the tent. A little while after I went out I heard the report of a gun, and about ten minutes later Hepburn called to me in a voice of great alarm to come directly. When I arrived, I found poor Hood lying lifeless, a ball having apparently entered his forehead. I at first was horror-struck with the idea that he had hurried himself into the presence of his Almighty Judge by an act of his own hand, but the conduct of Michel gave rise to other thoughts and excited suspicions. I discovered that a shot had entered the back part of his head and passed out at the forehead, and that the muzzle of the gun had been applied so close as to set fire to the night-cap behind. The gun could not have been placed in position to inflict such a wound except by a second person. Upon inquiring of Michel how it happened, he replied that Mr. Hood had sent him into the tent for the short gun, and that during his absence the long gun had gone off and he did not know whether by accident or not. He kept the short gun in his hand at the time he was speaking to me.

Hepburn afterwards informed me that, previous to the report of the gun, Hood and Michel were speaking to each other in an elevated and angry tone; he said that on hearing the report he looked up and saw Michel rising from before the tent door and going into the tent. He thought the gun had been discharged for cleaning it and did not go to the fire until Michel called that Mr. Hood was dead, a considerable time later. I thought Michel guilty of the deed, though he repeatedly protested that he was incapable of committing such an act. We removed the body into a clump of willows behind the tree, and returning to the fire read the funeral service in addition to the evening prayers.

Michel tried to persuade me to go to the woods on the Coppermine River and hunt for deer instead of going to the Fort. In the afternoon a flock of partridges coming near the tent, he killed several which he shared with us.

On the morning of the 23rd, we set out carrying with us the remainder of a singed skin. Hepburn and Michel each had a gun, and I carried a small pistol which Hepburn had loaded for me. In the course of the march Michel alarmed us much by his gestures and conduct. I overheard him muttering threats against Hepburn, whom he openly accused of having told stories against him. He also assumed such a tone of superiority in addressing me as evidenced that he considered us to be completely in his power.

I came to the conclusion that he would attempt to destroy us at the first opportunity and that he had hitherto abstained from doing so only because of his ignorance of the way to the Fort, but that he would never suffer us to go thither in company with him. Hepburn and I were not in condition to resist even an open attack. Our united strength was far inferior to his and, besides his gun, he was armed with two pistols, an Indian bayonet and a knife. In the afternoon, coming to a rock on which there was some *tripe de roche*, he halted and said he would gather it while we went on, and that he would soon overtake us.

Hepburn and I were now left together and he confirmed me in the opinion that there was no safety for us except in Michel's death, and he offered to be the instrument of it. I determined, however, to take the responsibility upon myself and immediately upon Michel's coming up to us I put an end to his life by shooting him through the head with a pistol.

Up to the period of Michel's returning to the tent his conduct had been good, and respectful to the officers, and in a conversation between Capt. Franklin, Mr. Hood and myself at Obstruction Rapid, it had been proposed to give him a reward upon our arrival at a post. His principles, however, unsupported by a belief in the Divine Truth of Christianity, were unable to withstand the pressure of severe distress.

On the following two days, we had mild weather and found a species of lichen that was good to eat when moistened and toasted over the fire. On the 26th we saw a large herd of reindeer and Hepburn went in pursuit of them; but his hand being unsteady through weakness he missed. Next day we set out early, and about noon fell upon little Marten Lake, having walked about two miles. In the afternoon we crossed a recent track of a wolverine which appeared to have been dragging something. Hepburn traced it, and upon the borders of the lake found a spine of a deer that it had dropped. It was clean-picked and at least one season old but we extracted the spinal marrow. We camped within sight of Dog-Rib Rock.

At dusk on the 29th we came in sight of the Fort and Hepburn killed a partridge after firing several shots. It was impossible to describe our sensations when, on attaining the eminence that overlooks it, we beheld the smoke issuing from one of the chimneys. Upon entering the now desolate building, we had the satisfaction of embracing Capt. Franklin, but no words can convey an idea of the filth and wretchedness that met our eyes on looking around. Our own misery had stolen upon us by degrees, and we were accustomed to the contemplation of each other's emaciated figures, but the ghastly countenances, dilated eyeballs and sepulchral voices of Mr. Franklin and those with him were more than we could at first bear.

So ends Dr. Richardson's account of what happened. Most historians have accepted his version as it stands. Dr. Richardson was, after all, a white man, a medical man, and an officer in the Royal Navy; while Michel was an Iroquois

Indian. Nevertheless, there is good reason to doubt Rich-
ardson's account. While it appears likely that Michel killed
Hood, in a fit of rage, having been goaded beyond endur-
ance by the petulant railings of the unhappy midshipman,
there is no evidence that he killed Bélanger, Perrault or
Fontano either for food or to conceal a murder. These three
were very near death when Franklin deserted them and
they must soon have died of exhaustion, starvation or expo-
sure. Michel seems to have found one or more of the bodies
and, reasoning that it was better to engage in cannibalism
than to lie down and die, he ate of the meat and supplied
it to Hood, Richardson and Hepburn. One thing is abun-
dantly clear: despite Richardson's pious horror at the can-
nibalism imputed to Michel, neither he nor Hepburn could
possibly have survived to return to the Fort unless they had
followed suit. It can be assumed that Michel's corpse did
not go to waste after he was "executed." Hepburn and
Richardson were in comparatively good condition when
they reached the Fort—in much better condition than those
who were already there—and yet they had killed nothing
but a single partridge and had not even been able to find
much tripe de roche.

Franklin's narrative continues:

The morning of the 31st was very cold with the wind from
the north. Hepburn went out in quest of deer, and the doctor
to kill some partridges. Both were unsuccessful. The
doctor and Hepburn began this day to cut the wood,
and also brought it to the house. Being too weak to aid
in these laborious tasks, I was employed in searching for
bones, and cooking, and attending to our more weakly
companions.

On November 1st Hepburn went hunting but, as usual,
was unsuccessful. As his strength was declining, we advised
him to desist from the pursuit of deer and to endeavour to
kill a few partridges. The doctor gathered a little *tripe de*

roche, but Peltier could not eat any of it and Samandre only a few spoonfuls. In the afternoon Peltier was so much exhausted that he sat up with difficulty; and at length he slid from his stool upon his bed, and in this composed state he remained for two hours without our apprehending any danger. We were then alarmed by hearing a rattling in his throat and, on the doctor examining him, he was found to be speechless. He died in the course of the night.

Samandre had sat up the greater part of the day, even assisting in pounding some bones; but he now became very low and began to complain of cold and stiffness of the joints. He did not appear to get better and I deeply lament to add he also died before daylight. We removed the bodies of the deceased into the opposite part of the house.

Adam now became very low and despondent and I was distressed by the thought that the labour of collecting wood must now devolve upon Dr. Richardson and Hepburn and that my debility would disable me from affording them any material assistance. They were occupied the whole of the next day carrying down the logs of which the storehouse was built. Our stock of bone was exhausted by a small quantity of soup we made up on the 3rd. The toil of separating hair from skins, which was now our chief support, had become so wearisome as to prevent us from eating as much as we should otherwise have done.

On November 7th Adam passed a restless night with gloomy apprehensions of approaching death. He was so low that I remained in bed by his side to cheer him as much as possible. The doctor and Hepburn went to cut wood. They had hardly begun their labour when they were amazed at hearing the report of a musket. They immediately spied three Indians close to the house. These Indians had left Akaitcho's encampment on the 5th of November, having been sent by Mr. Back with all possible expedition. They brought but a small supply of provisions so they could travel quickly. It consisted of dried deer's meat, some fat, and a few tongues. Dr. Richardson, Hepburn and I eagerly devoured the food which they imprudently presented to us in too great abundance, and in consequence we suffered dreadfully from indigestion and had no rest the whole night. The note I received by the Indians from Mr. Back communicated a tale of distress with regard to himself and his party, as painful as that which we had suffered.

Mr. Back's Narrative

October 4th, 1821. Mr. Franklin having directed me to proceed with St. Germain, Bélanger, and Beauparlant, to Fort Enterprise, I took leave and set out on my journey through swampy country against a keen north-west wind accompanied by frequent snow showers. We scarcely got more than four miles when we halted for the night and made a meal of *tripe de roche* and some old leather. On the 6th we set out at an early hour being close to the woods. We were making considerable progress when Bélanger unfortunately broke through the ice and sunk up to the hips. He was in danger of freezing, but some brushwood on the border of the lake enabled us to make a fire to dry him. We halted at five and made a scanty meal of an old pair of leather trousers.

The following morning we crossed several lakes and at noon reached Marten Lake. A simultaneous expression of "Mon Dieu, Nous sommes sauvés" broke out from the whole. We hoped to reach Dog-Rib Rock that night but an unforeseen and almost fatal accident prevented the prosecution of the plan; Bélanger (who seemed a victim of misfortune) again broke through the ice in a deep part near the head of a rapid, but was saved by our fastening our worsted belts together and pulling him out. By urging him forward as quick as his icy garments would admit of, to prevent freezing, we reached a few pines and kindled a fire, but it was late before he even felt warm, though he was so near the flame as to burn his hair twice. Because of storms it was not possible to travel on the 7th and 8th and it was not until the 9th that we reached Fort Enterprise where we perceived neither any marks of Indians nor even of animals. The men then began absolutely to despair. When we crossed the ruinous threshold of that long-sought-for spot, what was our surprise at beholding everything in a most desolate and neglected state. For the moment, hunger prevailed and each began to gnaw the scraps of putrid and frozen meat lying about, without waiting to prepare them. Later a fire was made and the neck and bones of a deer lying in the house were boiled and devoured.

I now listened to St. Germain's proposal, which was to follow the deer into the woods (so long as they did not lead us out of our route to the Indians), and if possible to collect sufficient food to carry us to Fort Providence. We set about making mittens and snowshoes while Bélanger searched under the snow and collected a mass of old bones, which when burned and used with a little salt, we found palatable enough, and made a tolerable meal.

On the 11th we began our journey, but at the point where the river leaves the lower lake, St. Germain fell in, which obliged us to camp directly to prevent his being frozen. The next day was excessively cold and our meal at night consisted of scraps of old deerskins and swamp tea. The following morning I sent St. Germain to hunt, but the weather became exceedingly thick with snowstorms and prevented us from moving. We had nothing to eat this day.

I decided to send a note to the commander, whom I supposed to be by this time at Fort Enterprise, to inform him of our situation; not that I imagined he could better it, but that by all returning to the Fort we might perhaps have better success in hunting. I therefore dispatched Bélanger, much against his inclination, and told him to return as quickly as possible to a place about four miles further on where we intended to fish until his arrival. The other men were so weak this day that I could get neither of them to move; and it was only necessity that compelled them to cut wood for fuel, performing which operation Beauparlant's face became so dreadfully swelled that he could scarely see.

On the 15th we did not get more than three-quarters of a mile from our last encampment before being obliged to put up, but in this distance were fortunate enough to kill a partridge. I was now so much reduced that my shoulders were as if they would fall from my body, and my legs seemed unable to support me.

We waited until two the next afternoon for Bélanger and not seeing anything of him set out to camp at the narrows, the place which was said to be good for fishing. We had not proceeded far before Beauparlant began to complain of increasing weakness. This was the usual thing with us so no particular notice was taken of it. He inquired where we were going to put up; St. Germain pointed to a small clump of pines near us, the only place that afforded fuel. "Well," replied the poor man, "take your axe, Mr. Back, and I will follow at my leisure. I shall join you by the time the encampment is made." This is a usual practice of the country and so St. Germain and myself went on towards the spot. Near there we saw a number of crows perched on the top of some high pines. St. Germain immediately said there must be some dead animals thereabout and proceeded to search, whereupon he found the heads of several deer buried in the snow and ice, without eyes or tongues.

An expression of "Oh Merciful God. We are saved!" broke from us both. It was then twilight and a fog was darkening the surface of the lake when St. Germain commenced making the encampment — the task was too laborious for me to render him any assistance. Had we not thus providentially found provisions I feel convinced that the next twenty-four hours would have terminated my existence. Darkness stole on us and I became extremely anxious about Beauparlant. I told St. Germain to go and look for him as I had not the strength. He replied that he could scarcely find his way back from a pine branch he had put on the ice, and if he went now he would certainly be lost. In this situation I could only hope that as Beauparlant had my blanket and everything requisite to light a fire he might have encamped at a little distance from us.

In the morning, being much agitated, I desired St. Germain to search for Beauparlant. It was late when he arrived back with a small bundle which Beauparlant was accustomed to carry and, with tears in his eyes, told me he had found our poor companion dead. He had been stretched on a sand bank three-quarters of a mile away, frozen to death, his limbs all extended and swelled enormously, and as hard as the ice that was near him.

October 18th. While we were this day scraping together the remains of some deer meat from the heads, we observed Bélanger coming around a point, scarcely moving. I went to meet him and made inquiries about my friends. Five, with the captain, he said, were at the house, the rest were left near the river unable to proceed, but he was too weak to relate the whole.

Bélanger and St. Germain insisted upon remaining at this spot until they had recovered sufficient strength to have some hope of reaching either Fort Providence or the Indians. Back, on the other hand, tried every means to persuade them to move on immediately; an act which would have been suicidal.

Having collected with great care, and by self-denial, two small packets of dried meat or sinews, sufficient (for men who knew what it was to fast) to last for eight days at the rate of one indifferent meal a day, we prepared to set out on the 30th. I calculated we should be about fourteen days reaching Fort Providence. We set out against a keen northeast wind. Seeing a number of wolves and crows in the middle of the lake, and supposing such an assembly was not met idly, we made for them, and came in for a share of a deer which they had killed a short time before. On the 3rd of November we set out before daylight, though in fact

212

we were better adapted to remain where we were, from the excessive pain which we suffered in our joints, and proceeded until one o'clock without halting when Bélanger, who was ahead, stopped and cried out, "Footsteps of Indians!" St. Germain inspected the tracks and said three persons had passed the day before. On this information we camped and, being too weak to walk myself, I sent St. Germain to follow the tracks with instructions to the Chief of the Indians to provide immediate assistance for our friends at Fort Enterprise as well as for ourselves. I was so exhausted that had we not seen the tracks this day, I had determined on remaining at the next encampment.

Shortly afterwards an Indian boy made his appearance. St. Germain had arrived before sunset at the tents of Akaitcho whom he found at the spot where he had wintered last year.

Rescue

On November 8th the Indians who had come to Fort Enterprise requested us to move to a camp on the banks of the river as they were unwilling to remain in the house in which the bodies of our companions were lying exposed to view. We agreed to move but the day proved too stormy and so Dr. Richardson and Hepburn dragged the bodies to a short distance and covered them with snow, and the objections of the Indians were removed. They cleaned our room of an accumulation of dirt and fragments of pounded bones. The improved state of our apartment, and the large and cheerful fires they kept up, produced in us a sensation of comfort to which we had long been strangers. In the evening they brought in dried wood which was lying on the riverside and which we had been unable to drag up the bank. They set about everything with an activity that amazed us. These kind creatures next turned their attention to our personal appearances and prevailed upon us to shave and wash ourselves.

The next day Crooked Foot caught four large trout on Winter Lake which were very much prized, especially by the doctor and myself. Though the night was stormy and our apartment admitted the wind, we felt no inconvenience; the Indians were so very careful in covering us up and in keeping a good fire.

It was of consequence to get amongst the reindeer before our present supply of food should fail, so we made preparations for quitting Fort Enterprise, and on the 16th left the house. The Indians treated us with the utmost tenderness, gave us their snowshoes, and walked without, themselves, keeping by our sides so that they might lift us when we fell. The Indians prepared our encampment, cooked for us and fed us as if we had been children; evincing humanity that would have done honour to the most civilized people.

From this period to the 26th of November we gradually continued to improve under the kindness and attention of the Indians. On that day we arrived in safety at the abode of our Chief and companion, Akaitcho. Here we learned that Mr. Back, with St. Germain and Bélanger, had gone to Fort Providence. We found Augustus, the Eskimo, here in perfect health.

On December 11th we arrived at the Fort. Here we determined to await the arrival of Akaitcho and his party in order to present their rewards to them. They arrived on the 14th with their whole band. We discovered at the commencement of Akaitcho's speech to us that he had been informed that our expected supplies had not arrived.

"The world goes badly," he said. "All are poor. You are poor, the traders appear to be poor, I and my party are poor likewise. Since the goods have not come, we cannot have them. I do not regret having supplied you with provisions, for a Copper Indian cannot permit white men to suffer from want of food on his lands. And at all events," he added in a tone of good humour, "this is the first time that the white people have been indebted to a Copper Indian."

There are two points in the Franklin journals which are not adequately dealt with by him. One is the failure of Akaitcho to obey the instructions to make a large meat cache at Fort Enterprise, which the Franklin party could fall back on. It has been said by many historians that this failure amounted almost to treachery, and certainly displayed a callous disregard of a promise on the part of the Indians. The facts are that when Akaitcho and his people got to Fort Resolution, in a near-starving state, they were unable to obtain ammunition either from the Hudson's Bay Company post or the North West Company trader. Without ammunition it was touch and go whether they themselves could hope to survive the coming winter, and it was impossible for them to return to Fort Enterprise and lay in supplies for Franklin. That the Copper Indians did all in their power to help Franklin's men is forcefully stated in the journals.

Another unanswered question is what became of the two Canadian women and their children who accompanied the expedition north from Fort Enterprise. If Roulante and Angélique went with the party along the coast, they did not return with it. They are not present amongst the survivors. Perhaps they turned back from the mouth of the Coppermine with Mr. Wentzel and his party of five Canadians; Franklin does not say.

He paid his debts of gratitude to young Hood, and eulogized him eloquently. Unfortunately, he did not see fit to do as much for others of his party who died in his service, and who died largely because Franklin was unable to comprehend, and deal with, the world in which he found himself, and was too stiff-necked and intransigent to accept the advice of those who did understand the country. We must make amends for his omission.

Of the seventeen voyageurs hired by Franklin, eight died of starvation and/or exhaustion. They died at the very end of their tethers, having accomplished prodigies in the way of endurance and service in a cause which, to them, could have had but little meaning. And they died primarily because their lives were foolishly hazarded.

These men were Joseph Peltier, Matthew Crédit, Ignance Perrault, François Samandre, Gabriel Beauparlant, Antonio Fontano, Registe Vaillant and Michel Teroahauté. To this list we must also add the name of Junius, the unfortunate Eskimo from Hudson Bay who vanished into silence somewhere on the plains to the east of Point Lake.

Franklin speaks glowingly of seaman Hepburn, who deserves no less. But he fails to give his proper due to another man, without whose efforts the entire expedition would probably have perished. This was Pierre St. Germain. If ever a man deserved recognition for steadfastness, indomitable courage and intelligent humanity it was St. Germain.

Franklin returned to the Mackenzie country in 1825, remaining until 1827, in order to map sections of the arctic coast east and west from the mouth of the Mackenzie River. On his return to England he was rewarded with a knighthood and the governorship of Tasmania. This ought to have made a respectable end to his career as an explorer, but such was not to be. In 1845, at the age of fifty-nine, he took command of what was intended to be the final expedition for the Northwest Passage. In the spring of that year he sailed from England with two ships and a goodly company of British seamen . . . and he and they sailed to their deaths. But that is another story—one that I have touched on in Ordeal by Ice.

I   An idealized view of Prince of Wales Fort on Hudson Bay, from which Samuel Hearne set out on his incredible travels across the Barren Lands.

II The ferociously difficult "rock barrens" at Nueltin Lake lie on the route Hearne followed during his third attempt to reach the Coppermine River.

III This is a pingo, a huge upheaval of the tundra caused by frost action. This one is near the mouth of the Coppermine. As Hearne noted, Barren-Land grizzly bears made use of pingos as denning sites.

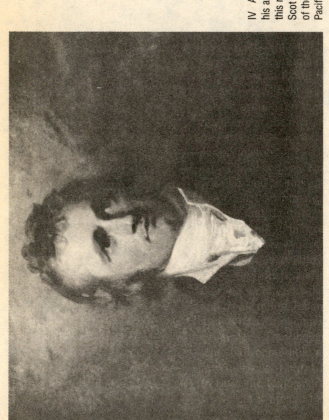

IV Alexander Mackenzie looked like this in his affluent later years but, even in this rather stuffy portrait, one sees the hard Scot tenacity that took him to the mouth of the Mackenzie River and later to the Pacific coast.

V This is the great river of disappointment—for Mackenzie—since it did not lead him to the Pacific. Nevertheless, this mighty river which bears his name may well have been his greatest discovery.

VI   The canoe journey down the Mackenzie to Great Slave Lake was a pleasant jaunt for the Franklin expedition. It provided no foretaste of what lay in store for the explorers when they entered the Barren Lands.

VII Something of the atmosphere of a winter carnival seems to hang over this engraving, but at this early stage of John Franklin's attempt to reach the shores of the Arctic Ocean overland, he and his people still had reason to feel a trifle jaunty.

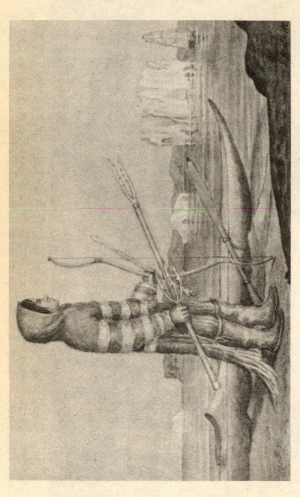

VIII Tattannæuk-Esquimaux Interpreter, named, by the English in Hudson's Bay Augustus, the faithful follower of Captains S. John Franklin, & S. Geo. Back, & D. Richardson, in their Arctic land Expeditions in N. America.

IX When Franklin finally reached the arctic coast he found a savage ocean that, time and again, very nearly brought the expedition to a fatal end. This was not the kind of naval expedition that Lt. John Franklin, Royal Navy, was accustomed to.

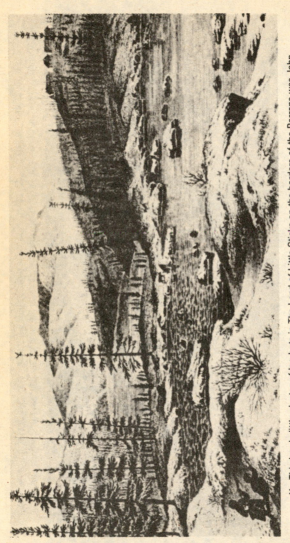

X This lonely little cluster of log huts in The Land of Little Sticks on the borders of the Barrens was John Franklin's headquarters and, very nearly, his tomb. It might better have been named Fort Starvation rather than Fort Enterprise.

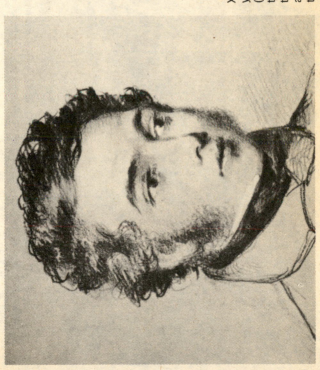

XI This drawing of George Back was made in 1833, the year he set out on his second major arctic expedition (he had accompanied Franklin on his journeys across the Barren Lands), yet he still looks to be little more than a boy. Looks are deceptive. He was a tough and competent explorer who has received far less than his just due in history.

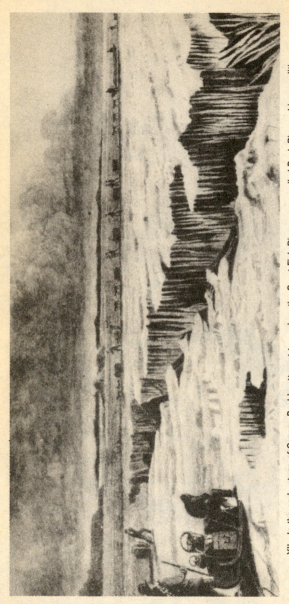

XII In the early stage of George Back's attempt to explore the Great Fish River — now called Back River — his expedition almost foundered trying to cross the rotting ice of the great tundra lakes, like Aylmer Lake where Back made this sketch.

XIII Back, the explorer, was almost matched by Back, the artist. This sketch catches the excitement and trepidation of the explorers when they met their first Eskimos near the mouth of the Great Fish River.

XIV It is almost impossible to comprehend the nature of the tundra plains from a point on its surface. But from the air much of it is seen to be a morass of lakes, ponds and rivers — a watery chaos that seems to be impassable to travellers on the ground.

XV These Dog-Rib Indians landing their boats on the shores of Great Slave Lake were photographed in 1900, only a few years after young Frank Russell accompanied a band of them far into the winter tundra on their annual musk-ox hunt.

XVI The Indians of the Land of Little Sticks travelled light and hard, as Frank Russell discovered. But he learned to live with them, almost as one of them. It was that . . . or perish.

XVII The improbable-looking musk-ox, a hold-over from the time of the ice age, was once abundant everywhere in the tundra region. But it was as easily hunted as a cow in a pasture, and now it is found only in the Thelon Reserve and on a few of the arctic islands.

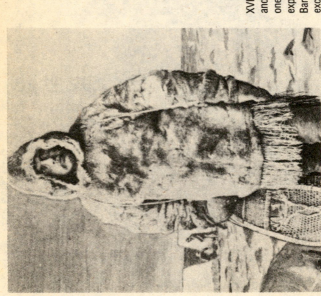

XVIII Despite his pompous appearance in this retouched and posed photograph, Joseph Burr Tyrrell was one of the arctic region's greatest truly Canadian explorers. His two epic journeys through the Barren Lands are exploits unmatched by any man except Samuel Hearne.

XIX One of J. B Tyrrell's major discoveries was the existence of a tribe of inland Eskimos — later named the Caribou Eskimos — who knew nothing of the sea and nothing about white men. These stone-age people may have lacked the benefits of our culture but they obviously weren't bothered by that fact.

XX Between them the two Tyrrell brothers, J. B. and J. W., explored and ran most of the rapids on the three major rivers in the Barren Lands: the Thelon, Kazan and Dubawnt. The rapid they are running in this photograph was a minor one compared to some they dared.

XXI Moving in herds that sometimes numbered a quarter of a million, the caribou were the true lifeblood of the tundra. Reduced to the danger level by ferocious over-hunting, they are now beginning to recover but, like the buffalo, the truly great herds of the past are probably gone forever.

XXII Whatever else they may have done, the Royal North West Mounted Police have earned, and well deserve, a place in history for their patrol work in the Arctic in the days before aircraft and motorized toboggans. Commissioned to celebrate the centenary of the Force, artist David Blackwood chose this aspect of their work above all others.

XXIII One of the most dramatic of the R.N.W.M.P. patrols took place in 1916, to investigate the disappearance of two priests near the Coppermine. Led by Inspector Denny LaNauze, the patrol is here seen making camp close to Bloody Falls, where Samuel Hearne watched an Eskimo massacre in the year 1771.

XXIV Inspector LaNauze found that the two priests had been killed by the Coppermine Eskimos so he continued on into what was virtually unknown territory for several weeks until he located and arrested the killers, Sinnisiak and Uluksak, with whom he is pictured here at Bernard Harbour.

XXV With only the little schooner North Star to support him, Vilhjalmur Stefansson carried out an almost inconceivable exploration of the high arctic islands, discovering several previously unknown ones in the process.

XXVI Stefansson was a fanatic proponent of the principle of living off the land. To the incredulity and chagrin of many arctic explorers, he thoroughly proved his point. Here he is seen on the sea-ice with a seal he has just killed.

XXVII John Hornby was one of several wanderers from abroad who fell in love with the tundra plains during the years before the First World War. Here he is seen with a pack dog and a young Eskimo friend near the Coppermine.

XXVIII In 1912, on the shores of Coronation Gulf, Hornby was living the life that he loved best—a nomad amongst nomads. He was one of the first white men to meet these Eskimos who still hunted with bows and arrows, living the life their people had known since prehistoric times.

XXIX In this log shanty, set in a strange oasis of spruce trees on the banks of the Thelon River in the very heart of the Barren Lands, John Hornby and two companions died of starvation. The macabre account of their fate was preserved in the diary of one of them, an English schoolboy named Edgar Christian.

XXX It was not until the 1920's brought a great demand for white fox skins that commerce discovered the arctic interior. Here one of the first traders, Thierry Mallet, is seen helping load a canoe as his small party prepares to leave the edge of timber and enter the tundra plains.

XXXI One of Thierry Mallet's earliest posts was at Windy River in south-central Keewatin. Here he made contact with the Caribou Eskimos, first discovered by J. B. Tyrrell. This picture, taken at Windy River in 1949, shows some of the last survivors of the Caribou Eskimos having a small drum dance on a summer evening. Mallet sensed that these people were doomed when the traders came among them.

XXXII When the blizzards roar across the rolling plains, the tundra seems impossibly hostile. Yet it was once, and for millennia remained, home to the inland Eskimos and to the Idthen Eldeli Indians. Now all of these are gone. No men live in all the vast sweep of the Barren Lands.

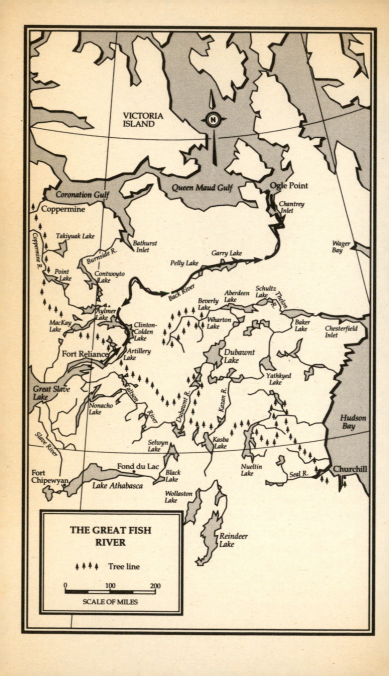

VICTORIA
ISLAND

N

Coronation Gulf

Queen Maud Gulf

Ogle Point

Coppermine

Chantrey
Inlet

Takiyuak Lake

Coppermine R.

Bathurst
Inlet

Garry Lake

Wager
Bay

Burnside R.

Pelly Lake

Point
Lake

Contwoyto
Lake

Back River

MacKay
Lake

Aylmer
Lake

Beverly
Lake

Aberdeen
Lake

Schultz
Lake

Thelon R.

Clinton-
Colden
Lake

Wharton
Lake

Baker
Lake

Chesterfield
Inlet

Fort Reliance

Artillery
Lake

Dubawnt
Lake

Great Slave
Lake

Thelson
River

Dubawnt R.

Kazan R.

Yathkyed
Lake

Hudson
Bay

Slave River

Nonacho
Lake

Kasba
Lake

Selwyn
Lake

Fort
Chipewyan

Fond du Lac

Black
Lake

Nueltin
Lake

Seal R.

Churchill

Lake Athabasca

Wollaston
Lake

Reindeer
Lake

THE GREAT FISH
RIVER

🌲🌲🌲🌲 Tree line

0   100   200

SCALE OF MILES

IV

The Great Fish River

GEORGE BACK TRAVERSES THE BARREN GROUNDS FROM WEST TO EAST, 1833-35

Franklin's discoveries along the arctic coast did nothing to dissipate the chimera of a usable Northwest Passage, and many men were still anxious to pursue it. Among these was Captain John Ross who, in 1818, had rediscovered the mouth of Lancaster Sound, down which his junior, Parry, was sent by the Royal Navy in two fruitless bids to achieve the glory of making the Passage. Ross felt, with justification, that the Navy had treated him shabbily and that he had been shoved into the background by Parry. So in 1829 he led a private expedition in search of the Passage. He did not find it, but he did discover the Magnetic Pole, and he carried his little crew through one of the most amazing arctic adventures on record by spending four winters in the ice.[1]

---

[1]Ross's story is told in *Ordeal by Ice,* the first volume in the *Top of the World* trilogy.

During his long incarceration, Ross had no way of communicating his predicament to the outside world, with the result that it was assumed he had lost his ship and that he and his men were trapped. The British government at first refused to send a search expedition, but eventually public pressure forced them to relent; and in 1833 Captain George Back, on leave from the Navy, was picked to conduct an overland searching expedition to the arctic coast.

Back, who had been with Franklin on both of his arctic land expeditions, was the most capable of the Englishmen involved in those two ventures. He remembered what the Chipewyan Indians had told Franklin many years earlier about the Thlew-ee-choh-desseth (Great Fish River), a mighty river flowing north across the tundra plains to the arctic sea from the vicinity of Great Slave Lake. Back now planned to find this river, explore it to its mouth, and so reach the arctic coast within striking distance of the area where Ross was supposed to have vanished.

Although assisted by the government, the expedition was largely financed by public subscription. It was taken under the wing of the Hudson's Bay Company which provided men, canoes and supplies, and made the arrangements to get the party to its starting point on Great Slave Lake.

The group from England consisted of George Back, a young and eccentric doctor named Richard King, and three "men," two of them shipwrights, the brothers Thomas and William Matthews. When Back reached Canada he acquired four volunteers from a British artillery regiment including Ptes. Malley and Carron. The main body of the expedition consisted of local men, including Scotch-Canadians, French-Canadians, Iroquois, Chipewyans and Copper Indians. These men, only incidentally mentioned in Back's book, included James McKay, George Sinclair, John Ross, William Rowland, Thomas Anderson, Malcolm Smith, Donald McDonald, Morrison Morrison, James Spence, Peter Taylor, Charles Boulanger, Pierre Kanaquasse, Thomas Hassel, Antoine de Charloit, La Charité, Olivier Seguin, Pierre Ateasta, François Hoole, two unnamed Iroquois, and the now venerable Copper Indian Chief, Akaitcho, together with a large part of his band. A number of these people were Hudson's Bay Company men, and the Company also provided the services of Factor A. R. McLeod, who was Back's invaluable right hand and to whom a very considerable portion of the credit for the expedition belongs.

Back's outward journey was a classic tour, for he sailed to Montreal and was then carried over the voyageur routes west and north to Great Slave Lake, travelling by canoe and bateau. On reaching Fort Resolution, the "tripper" part of the journey came to an end and work began.

Having first entrusted McLeod with the task of building a winter headquarters (named Fort Reliance) at the extreme north-eastern end of Great Slave Lake, Back set out with half of his party to search for the headwaters of the Great Fish River. Guided by the Indian Maufelly, he set out up the Hoar Frost River and, after a fearsome struggle with rapids and portages, his canoemen at last brought him to the north end of Artillery Lake. From there the going was fairly easy through Clinton-Colden into Aylmer Lake, beyond the north-west bay of which Back saw the headwaters of the river he was seeking.

This reconnaissance accomplished, Back returned to the newly built Fort Reliance, having become the first European to visit the great chain of lakes curving north and west into the tundra from the east end of Great Slave Lake.

Winter at Fort Reliance was somewhat less trying than the ghastly winter with Franklin at Fort Enterprise. But the cold was just as fierce, and the local Indians were without food and were dying of starvation and disease so that they could not contribute much to the stores Back was trying to amass for his northern thrust. However, the party suffered no casualties — except for the tragedy of Augustus.

It will be remembered that Augustus was the survivor

of the two Hudson Bay Eskimos who were with Franklin on his first expedition. During the winter of 1833-34, Augustus set out from Churchill to join the new expedition. He got to Fort Resolution all right, but somewhere between there and Fort Reliance he encountered a fearful winter gale and, unable to find shelter, froze to death.

By the spring of 1834, things were being made ready for what was to be the deepest penetration of the Barren Grounds since Hearne's time. Back sent his two English shipwrights to the shore of Artillery Lake to build a boat that would carry him downstream to the sea and which would also be fit for coastwise navigation when he got there. Then, in the midst of the spring activity, word arrived that the missing Captain Ross had successfully extricated his crew and had arrived safely home in England. Some of the steam went out of Back's expedition, but he decided to carry on, if only to add what he could to man's knowledge of the unknown plains to the north and west and, we suspect, in the hopes of achieving geographic immortality by some new discovery along the arctic coast.

In early June, McLeod and a party of Copper Indians set out into the Barrens as an advance party to kill and lay up supplies of deer. On the 7th, Back followed with the balance of the party (strengthened by a contingent of Copper Indians), dragging the great boat which had been built for the voyage. Constructed of solid timber in good English fashion, this boat was about as unsuitable a craft for northern rivers as could be imagined. She weighed about two tons, was thirty feet long, and required the combined efforts of every available man to keep her moving even on iron runners over the still-frozen lakes. Presumably the voyageurs who were expected to man her kept their opinions of her to themselves, but we can imagine their gloomy thoughts at the prospects ahead. It was not until July 1st that the party was able to manhandle her as far as the headwaters of the Big Fish River, where she was finally launched on Musk-Ox Lake.

In the excerpts that follow, I have foreshortened Back's voyage considerably, since one rapid is much like another, and the account is essentially the story of a journey down a myriad of rapids, with all too little time for observing the countryside or its inhabitants.

THE ARCTIC LAND EXPEDITION TO THE MOUTH OF THE GREAT FISH RIVER

Having crossed the ice on Musk-Ox Lake, at four p.m. we reached Musk-Ox Rapids, the point from which I had returned the previous year. Several Indians who were camped here paddled to us in their small canoes and assailed our ears with the familiar but annoying cry of "Etthen-Oolah, Etthen-Tahouty," — no deer, the deer are gone away. It appeared that the scarcity of animals had driven Akaitcho a short distance to the north where he was forced to live on the flesh of the musk-ox, the flavour of which is not a delicacy even to a Copper Indian, who certainly is not fastidious in his taste.

July 2nd. The Indians were directed to go with our interpreter and deposit their respective loads of pemmican at the north end of the portage, there to be released from their servitude — an order which was received with wonderful satisfaction, as they were yet puzzled to comprehend why we should take such pains to plunge into the dangers which they considered assuredly awaited us. The thirst of enterprise and the zeal of discovery were notions far beyond the conception of these rude children of nature, whose only desires are for food and raiment. The length of the portage being four miles the people were occupied all day.

On the 3rd the bundles of pemmican, which had been a continual subject of anxiety to me from the commencement of the winter, were counted and examined and I was happy to learn that eleven had been brought without injury or spoilation. We had altogether twenty-seven bags of pemmican weighing eighty pounds each; two boxes of macaroni, some flour, a case of cocoa, and a two-gallon keg of rum. It does not become me to enlarge upon the difficulty of transporting a weight, all things included, of nearly five thousand pounds over ice and rocks from Fort Reliance. The Indians were not more astonished at their own voluntary subjection to our service than at the sight of a boat manned by Europeans and stored with provisions of the southern country, now floating on the clear waters of the Barren Lands.

It was now unnecessary for Mr. McLeod and his party to proceed farther; and it was satisfactory to me at parting with him that I could make over a tolerable stock of dried meat for his party, which would consist of ten persons and fourteen dogs, entirely dependent on the success of the hunters who were to guide them back [to Fort Reliance].

The boat was conveyed to the open water and launched. The river flowing from this lake cuts through a chain of craggy rocks and mountains, thickly strewn with boulders and debris but with sufficient pasturage in the valleys and the declivities to attract musk-oxen and deer.

An increasing current brought us to a strong rapid and fall with an island in the centre, and just above it a moss-covered rock where we perceived Akaitcho's son and another Indian waving and shouting to warn us of the danger.

Akaitcho had chosen this bleak tract for his hunting grounds and had pitched his lodge on the very peak of the highest hill a few miles off, which being too distant for me to visit, I sent him some tobacco and presents with a request that he detain his men at his lodge, as we were too busy to talk to them. Scarcely, however, had I returned from taking my bearings when I saw the old man and several others close alongside. The interpreter declared he could not prevail upon him to remain at home. He said, "I have known the Chief [Back] a long time and I am afraid I shall never see him again — I will go to him.''

The boat was now pushed off with four good hands aboard, quite empty [of cargo], to run the fall. Unfortunately, the steersmen kept her rather too much to the left and she was drawn on a shelving rock which brought her up with a crash threatening immediate destruction and calling forth a shriek from the prostrate crew. The immense force of water drove her farther on so that she hung only by the stern. A steersman jumped on a rock and in an instant her stem was swept around by the large fall. I held my breath expecting to see her dashed to shivers against a protruding rock but the steering oar caught the rock and twirled her broadside to the rapid which then carried her down without further injury.

I was, upon the whole, not sorry for the adventure as it not only gave the men a memorable proof of the strength of these waters, but afforded me an occasion for cautioning them against running any rapid for the future without first studying the lead of the channel.

Seeing that I was now about to depart, Akaitcho looked very melancholy and cautioned me against the dangers of a river which, he plainly told me, none of the present race of Indians had the least knowledge of. Especially did he warn me against Eskimo treachery, which he said was always perpetrated under the disguise of friendship. ''I am afraid I shall never see you again,'' he continued, ''but should you escape from the Great Water [the sea], take care you are not caught by the winter and thrown into a situation like that in which you were on your return from the Coppermine, for you are alone, and the Indians cannot help you.''

Having recommended him to collect plenty of provisions for me by the autumn, and in two moons and a half to look for the smoke of my fires, and shaking him by the hand I stepped into the boat.

It is really remarkable that for nearly a month past

there had not been two consecutive days of fine weather; but now, as we hoped, the charm was broken; [however] the clouds began to gather with the declining sun, and by midnight assumed a decidedly stormy aspect. It looked as if that watery saint, Old Swithin, had taken it into his head to leave his abode in England just to travel north a little, and was then on his passage hereabouts.

However this may be, the rain poured and the wind blew in hollow gusts, and last of all there was a downright heavy gale sufficient to have laid low the tallest, stoutest pines in the forest, but the only trophy of its prowess was the upsetting of our tent, even though secured with a rampart of heavy stones. The storm raged through the whole of July 5th and July 6th. On the 7th it gradually moderated and at last the sun peeped faintly through.

On the morning of the 8th I had the boat launched and laden with her full cargo which, together with ten persons, she stowed well enough for a smooth river. The weight was calculated at 3,360 pounds exclusive of awnings, masts, yards, sails, spare oars, and the crew. The crew as finally reduced consisted of—

James McKay—Highlander
George Sinclair—Half-breed
Charles McKenzie—Highlander
Peter Taylor—Half-Breed
James Spence—Orkney
John Ross—Highlander
William Malley—Lancashire
Hugh Carron—Irish

In addition there was the surgeon, Mr. Richard King, and myself.

We pushed off at ten o'clock and found that the recent rains had caused a rise of a full eight inches in the river which varied in width from two hundred yards to a quarter of a mile as long as it kept between the rocky ridges of the mountains. A wide and deep channel terminated in a rapid which we ran with full cargo and which brought us to a small lake perfectly free of ice. The river now became contracted and formed an easy rapid, upon the north bank of which I made our first cache of pemmican for the return voyage. At six p.m. we reached another lake and McKay and Sinclair were dispatched to find out the most likely place for getting through, since this lake was still filled with ice. A north-west breeze sprang up and opened a channel along the western shore barred by only a few pieces through which a passage was cut. On the 9th we found the ice we met in shallow water was porous and rotten so that it yielded to the united effect of axes and the weight of our men; and after an hour and a half the boat was got through onto an easy rapid. The shelving shore encouraged the hope that the river would turn out favour- ably, but that illusion was soon dispelled by a very long rapid where the boat was only saved by all hands jumping into the breakers and keeping her stern upstream until she was clear from a rock that had brought her up. We were carried on with considerable velocity past pasturages of musk-oxen and deer. The latter scampered away as we approached, but the former stood stupidly gazing at us; luckily for them we were not in want of their carcasses.

Late that day we came to an appalling rapid, full of rocks and large boulders; the sides hemmed in by a wall of ice and the current flying with the velocity and force of a torrent. The boat was lightened of her cargo and I stood on a high rock, with an anxious heart, to see her run it. I had every confidence in the judgement and dexterity of my principal men McKay and Sinclair, but could not help know that one crash would be fatal to the expedition. Away they went with the speed of an arrow and in a moment foam and rocks hid them from view. I heard what sounded like a wild shriek, and saw Mr. King a hundred yards away make a sign with his gun and run forward. I followed with an agitation which may be conceived; but to my inexpres- sible joy found the shriek was the triumphant whoop of the crew, who had landed safely in a small bay below. I could not but reward them with a glass of grog apiece and they immediately applied themselves to the fatiguing work of the portage with as much unconcern as if they had just crossed a mill pond.

On opening a bag of pemmican tonight the upper part was found mouldy, and on removing it a stone was found, and then layers of mixed sand, stones and green meat — the work of some rascally Indian who, having pilfered the contents, had adopted this ingenious device to conceal his peculation. As it was now uncertain whether we might not be carrying a heap of stones instead of provisions, every bag underwent a severe probing, and much to our satisfaction the remainder proved sound and good tasting.

July 11th commenced with heavy rain and a gale from the north-west and we were consequently prevented from moving, as the boat could not be taken down the rapids on account of spray hiding the rocks, as well as the impossibility of keeping her under control. A combination of foul and boisterous weather, a chaos of wind, storm and rain, against which it was vain to struggle, continued until July 13th. By then my patience was exhausted and we started, finding ourselves in what might be called a continuous rapid. Two or three hundred deer and, apart from them, herds of musk-oxen were grazing or sleeping on the western banks which looked green and swampy. For the first time in nine days the sun shone and our hunters, unable to resist the tempting neighbourhood of so many animals, were allowed to go in pursuit. In less than an hour they returned with four bucks. The change of food was palatable but as we had abundance of provisions and the boat was already too heavily laden, I discouraged all such pursuits for the present.

We now ran a line of deep rapids with full cargo, and a white wolf, some geese and partridge were observed here. The river now spread itself into several branches which not a little puzzled me, but we pulled into the right channel and shortly opened a view to the south-east so extensive that the extreme distance was definable only by a faint blue line.

I was a little alarmed at such a siphon-like turn; yet I endeavoured to persuade myself that the river would not ultimately deviate far from its original course.

Back thought the river might take him to the arctic coast in the vicinity of Bathurst Inlet, lying due north of him. He had no idea of the tremendous distance he had still to travel to reach the river mouth.

A range of low mountains stretched in a north-west and south-east direction seeming to oppose an insurmountable barrier to the onward course of the river in the direction of my hopes, yet I was unwilling to abandon all hope. All my plans and calculations rested on the assumption of the northerly course of the river, but this determined bend to the south-east and the formidable mountain barrier ahead seemed to indicate a different course and determination not, as had been anticipated, in the polar sea, but in Chesterfield Inlet on Hudson Bay.

However, be the issue what it might, Hudson Bay or the polar sea, I had no alternative but to continue on.

A fresh and fair wind now relieved the men from the labour of the oars and we ran under the foresail down a long, narrow lake [Beechey], whose termination could not be seen. At eight p.m. we were stopped by a ridge of ice reaching from shore to shore and we hauled into a deep bay and secured for the night. The country had assumed a mountainous and imposing appearance, rugged and desolate. Many parts bore a close resemblance to the lava fields around Vesuvius. However, the intermediate spaces were filled with green patches of meadow which literally swarmed with deer, not fewer than twelve or fifteen hundred having been seen within the last twelve hours.

That night a gale blew up and the ice became so closely packed, with so heavy a surf running, that any attempt to approach it would have stove the boat. There was nothing left but to remain patiently until the violence of the wind should demolish the ice and make a passage for us. This was gradually effected and we got away early the next morning, July 15th. Our direction continued south-east though the mountains had dwindled to hills which soon gave way to sand banks. The lake, which I have named after my friend Captain Beechey, visibly decreased in breadth and at length discharged itself in an awful series of cascades nearly two miles in length, making a descent of about sixty feet. The steersmen were dispatched to examine it and they reported that it was possible; the boat might be got down, but they did not see how she could ever be got up again. This was a consideration of no great moment, while we were still within walking distance of the house at Fort Reliance. Accordingly, having portaged our supplies and made a cache, the trial was made with the boat. She was lifted over some obstacles and cautiously lowered with a rope down the different descents, until she was safely brought to the eddy below.

The next day a loud roar of rushing waters, heard for the distance of miles, prepared us for a long line of rapids which now appeared, breaking their furious way through mounds and ranges of precipitous sand hills of the most fantastic outline. Some resembled parts of old ruins or turrets. The river's course became more tortuous and as we drew away from the influence of the cold winds coming from Bathurst Inlet, an agreeable change took place in the weather. The level character of the land to the eastward made three detached and lofty hills serve as marks for any wanderers whom chance should bring to this far country. Indeed they had already been made use of as was indicated by numbers of piled stones resembling those I remembered to have seen along the banks of the Coppermine River, evidently the work of the Eskimos, on whose frontiers we had arrived.

These traces of the tenants of the arctic zone did not

a little surprise me since on former occasions we had not found them at any distance from the coast. Was it possible, I asked myself, that we were nearer the sea than I had imagined?

The river now contracted to about fifty yards and this narrow space had projecting rocks within it. We ran through and were lifted considerably higher than the side water as we shot down with fearful velocity. Familiar as I was with such scenes, I could not but feel thankful that we escaped safe, and I determined in the future to lower the boat down other similar chutes. We now swept past a magnificent river as broad as the Thames at Westminster, and I gave it the name of Baillie's River. We then entered an alluvial plain so flat as scarcely to rise beyond the horizon, and to raise our hopes of being near the sea. Once, indeed, some of the party imagined they saw tents but as we advanced these proved to be nothing but a luxuriant border of willows, the retreat of hundreds of geese which, having lately cast their large quill feathers, were unable to fly. In the water they had recourse to diving—but on land they either had a fair run for it, or plunged into any cover that happened to be near.

Early the next morning we pushed into a roaring and gloomy defile. The boat was twirled about in whirlpools against the power of the oars and, but for the amazing strength of McKay who steered it, must inevitably have been crushed against the protruding rocks. There was a deep and settled gloom in the abyss—the effect of which was heightened by the hollow roar of the rapids and by the screaming of three large hawks frightened from their aerie and hovering high above us. Once past the defile the boat drove with the current at a velocity of not less than six miles an hour amongst whirlpools and eddies. As we advanced, still most provokingly to the eastward, a large river nearly as broad as that we were descending came in through a low country to the right. I named it McKinley. We now began to see a great number of stone piles on commanding eminences, apparently placed there for the purpose of frightening the deer into a particular course where ambushes could be laid. At certain distances along the lines of marks were semi-circular screens built of stones facing toward the open country, under the banks of which hunters would be effectually hid.[2]

On the morning of July 19th the current lost itself in a large lake full of deep bays, with a clear and uninterrupted horizon, but glimmering with firm ice. Having taken a more northerly course we passed two open reaches of about fifteen or twenty miles in extent and landed on an island to make a third cache of pemmican against our return. From here I got a view of another opening almost entirely covered with unbroken ice, and found a piece of old kayak blanched with age. The opening was distinguished by the name of Lake Pelly. An observation now determined that, indefatigable as our exertions had been, we had gained but little or nothing and had abundance of hard work in prospect before we should be permitted to taste salt water. The men inclined to believe a tale told by an Indian that before arriving at the sea they would find an immense lake, with such deep bays that no Indian had ever been around them. Indeed here was a large lake with bays answering to that description. The strong current from a rapid which we encountered now gave us some hope that the tediousness of winding and groping our way in the lake was at an end, but to our chagrin we soon found ourselves in a wide indefinable space, studded with islands of sand hills, and with the difficulty of finding the river increasing as we advanced amidst this labyrinth. The unwelcome glare of ice was also seen. From time to time we found a current; still we were baffled and had often to turn on our track. Towards evening our hopes were again blighted by the

---

[2]These were stone ''deer fences'' used by the interior Eskimos to channel herds of migrating deer to selected river crossings from which they could be attacked by spearmen in kayaks.

startling fact of extensive and unbroken fields of ice stretching to the extremest point of vision. There being no chance of further progress I camped on a spot that, judging from the circles of stones [tent rings], had doubtless been used by the Eskimos for the same purpose.

We were on an island and when I climbed a ridge it was with indescribable sorrow that I beheld a firm field of old ice which had not yet been disturbed from its winter station. Nevertheless, the next morning at three a.m. we made an attempt. The shore lane got narrower as we proceeded until there was barely room for the boat to pass with poles. The ice, far from being decayed, was thick, green, and compact, and gave ominous token of what was in reserve for us farther north. We now ascended the highest nearby hill only to see one wide and dazzling field of ice extending far away in every direction.

However, by means of my telescope I discovered a strip of what I took to be water away to the north-east, and patches were also visible in the ice between the water and the opposite land. We therefore continued to creep slowly to the southward, sometimes wedged in the ice, at others cutting through it with axes. Towards evening we were stopped completely and after portaging the supplies for some distance over extremely rotten ice, the boat was lifted over the remaining obstructions after which our progress was more satisfactory. The crew, half benumbed as they were from being so long in the water, could not reach land until past ten p.m. In sixteen hours we had come only fourteen miles. During the whole of the next day we followed the same proceedings until some hours later brought us to a sheet of water terminating in a rapid. This, though seldom a pleasing object to those who have to go down them, was now joyfully hailed by us as the end of a lake which had occasioned so much trouble and delay. I bestowed upon it the name of Lake Garry.

Congratulating one another on our release we went on with renewed spirits. The following day we got away early and in about an hour reached a strong rapid, the descent of which looked exceedingly like going down a hill. The steersmen were desirous of lightening the boat but the water was too shoal for landing and as no place could be found above or below, we decided to risk the descent with the whole cargo. So off we pushed and in a few minutes plunged into the midst of curling waves and large rocks. By the coolness of the crew and the dexterity of bow and sternman we avoided each danger as it arose. At length, however, one towering wave threw us on a rock and something crashed. Luckily we did not hang, for nothing could have resisted the force of the torrent, and the slightest check at such a moment would have meant inevitable destruction to the whole party. After being whirled to and fro for some time we escaped without damage other than a broken keel-plate. I was not a little rejoiced when we were again in smooth water. Much to our satisfaction the river now kept to the northward and gave us the hope of making a little latitude. Soon after, however, we entered MacDougall Lake and caught the faint sound of falls which took us off due south in the direction of Chesterfield Inlet — the proximity of which, I will not deny, began to give me serious uneasiness.

Bending short round to the left the whole force of the water glided smoothly between two stupendous rocks, from five to eight hundred feet high, rising like islands on either side. Our first care was to secure the boat in a curve on the left near where the river disappeared, sending up showers of spray. We found this was not one fall, as the hollow roar had led us to believe, but a succession of falls and cascades and whatever else is horrible. It expanded to about the breadth of four hundred yards, having near the centre an insulated rock about three hundred feet high with the same barren and naked appearance as those on each side. The rapid, yawning and cavernous, swallowed huge masses of ice and then again tossed the splintered fragments high into the air. A more terrific sight could not well be conceived and the impression which it produced was apparent on the countenances of the men. The portage was over scattered debris of rock and afforded a rugged and difficult way about a mile distant. The boat was emptied of her cargo, but was too heavy to be carried more than a few yards; whatever the consequences, there was thus no alternative than to try the falls.

Every precaution that we could devise was adopted. Double lines to the bow and stern were held on shore by the most careful of the men, and McKay and Sinclair took their stations at each end of the boat with poles to keep her from dashing against the rocks. Repeatedly the strength of the current hurled the boat within an inch or so of destruction, and as often did these able and intrepid men ward off the danger. Still she did not escape without some severe shocks, in one of which the remaining keel-plate was entirely stripped away. But cool, collected, prompt to understand and obey the mutual signs which each made to the other by hand — for their voices were inaudible — the two gallant fellows finally succeeded in guiding her down to safety at the last fall. Here she was taken out of water and with the assistance of Mr. King and myself was carried below it. I gave the men each a good glass of grog with praises which they had well earned.

On the 23rd, when the people were carrying the pemmican and boxes across, a task which the loose and slippery stones made by no means easy, and aware that it would take them until noon, I gladly availed myself of the opportunity to make some observations. The prospect before us, viewed with the telescope from a commanding eminence, in no manner cleared up the doubt of what would be the ultimate course of this river.

When I turned around I noticed to my amazement that there was no spray rising from the rapid and that its deafening roar had subsided into a grinding noise. A phenomenon so utterly at variance with what had existed an hour before made me hasten down. This was the disruption of the main body of the ice on Lake MacDougall being carried over the falls. With this new obstacle there was no contending, for in such a torrent the boat would have been crushed to atoms. By five p.m. the river had so far cleared itself as to allow of our loading our boat, not without risk from the floating pieces which yet remained beating about in the eddy.

When we started on July 25th the river was near a mile broad. The banks on either side were low and the river was soon broken by a mile of heavy and dangerous rapids. Although the boat was lightened and every care taken to avoid accidents, she and those in her were twice in the most imminent danger of perishing. We called this Escape Rapid and made another cache of pemmican at the foot of it. We had not gone more than two miles further when a thick fog and pelting rain obscured the view and obliged us to land for shelter. When it cleared we renewed the attempt. The current, always swift, now rushed still faster and soon became a line of heavy rapids which more than once made me tremble for our poor boat. Not being able to land we were compelled to pull hard at the oars to keep her under command and thus flew past rocks and other dangers with a velocity which seemed to forebode some desperate termination. About eight p.m. we arrived near a detached mountainous rock, in which quarter the descent now manifest, as well as the hollow roar, plainly indicated something which at that late hour it was prudent to avoid. The very élite of my men were beginning to evince a cautiousness which was quite new to them and the order for camping was executed with significant alacrity.

Within a few hundred yards nine white wolves were prowling around a herd of musk-oxen, one of which we shot. Being a bull it was too strongly scented to be eaten. In the morning we ran the rapid which we named Wolf Rapid. Some of the animals whose name it bore seemed to be keeping a hopeful and brisk lookout for what might happen. Several other rapids (for there was no end to them) worked their way between high rocks which, for the first time since the river had turned so much to the eastward, lay on the eastern side. I thought this augured well for a northerly bend at no great distance. The late suspicious trending to the eastward had again created doubts in my mind and set me speculating whether the river might not yet terminate in Wager Bay [Wager Inlet in Hudson Bay].

After a course of six miles to the south-east, the river again veered northerly rushing with fearful impetuosity amongst rocks and large stones which raised such whirl-pools in the rapids as would have put the strength of a canoe in jeopardy. The boat's breadth of beam and steady trim kept her up in such trials, but though we escaped the rapid we had a narrow chance of being dashed on the beach by the eddy. To the westward the rocks had, comparatively speaking, become mountainous. They were desolate, rugged and barren. We camped that night under the lee of a high rock beside which the musk-oxen and deer had tramped deep tracks. It was opposite to a solitary bank of sand that formed the entrance to a small river, a favourite resort of geese, which having frequented it during the moulting season had left thousands of the finest quills strewn on the sand. Carts might have been laden with them.

The swollen river now rolled on in sullen and deathlike silence, long undisturbed by anything louder than an occasional bubbling caused by the unevenness of the bottom. But the shores got nearer and nearer, and for a space it was quite uncertain in what quarter we should go. This was the beginning of a rapid that looked as even and smooth as oil and in that supposition, having taken the precaution to lighten the boat forward, we pushed off and in the next minute were in it. I shall never forget the moment of the first descent down what cannot be more fitly described than as a steep hill. There was not, it is true, a single break in the smoothness of the surface, but with such wild swift-ness were we borne along that it required our extremest efforts to keep the boat clear of the gigantic waves below;

and we succeeded only to be tossed about in the Charybdis of its almost irresistible whirlpools.

Six miles farther on was another rapid which was more civil than the last. We had now entered fairly mountainous country and the river had taken a decided turn to the northward. I contemplated having to run many more rapids and falls and my astonishment will be understood when, from the foot of this rapid, we emerged into the expanse of a spacious lake bounded only by the horizon and stretching north-north-west. I climbed the summit of a tolerably high hill and could not descry any land: there was, however, much ice and the space between the western shore and us was quickly filling up with drifting masses. It was therefore important to push on as fast as possible. A short breaking sea and the ice together considerably impeded our progress, but on reaching an island we opened upon a bay into which I pulled, for the purpose of finding the river if it were there, or of creeping under a weather shore if it were not.

After a couple of miles we had the satisfaction of finding the current was running with us. Leaving the lake which, as a token of my sincere regard, I called after Captain Sir John Franklin, we followed this stream which as usual broke into a rapid. A fine open reach ahead at first held out the prospect of repaying us for this lost time but two miles later the river again became pent in by almost-meeting rocks of considerable altitude. The disappearance of the surface line of water, and the jets of mist thrown up against the grey rocks, gave unequivocal tokens of a fall. We had noticed the usual upright marks of rocks set up upon the summits by the Eskimos. We now perceived that, beside the marks, there were many active and bustling figures, either pressing in a close group or running about from place to place in manifest confusion.

These were the Eskimos of whom we had so long and ardently wished to get a sight. Some called out to us and others made signs, warning us as we thought to avoid the fall and cross over to their side of the water. But when our intention of doing so was apparent, the men ran towards us brandishing their spears, uttering loud yells and motioning to us not to land.

For all this I was not unprepared, knowing the alarm which they must feel at beholding strangers coming from a quarter where the scourge of merciless warfare only had visited their tribes. As the boat grounded they formed into a semi-circle twenty-five paces distance and with the same yelling of some unintelligible word, and the alternate elevation and depression of both extending arms, continued in the highest state of excitement until, landing alone, and without visible weapon, I walked deliberately up to them. Imitating their own action of throwing up my hands I called out *Tima*—"Peace."

In an instant their spears were flung on the ground; and putting their hands on their breasts they also called out *Tima*. I endeavoured to make them understand that we were not Indians, but Kabloonds—Europeans—come to benefit, not to injure them. I then adopted the John Bull fashion of shaking each of them heartily by the hand. Then patting my breast, according to their own manner, I conveyed to them that the white man and the Eskimo were very good friends.

All this seemed to give great satisfaction and was not diminished by a present to each of two new shining buttons. These, some fish-hooks and other trifles of a like kind, were the only articles which I had brought for this purpose, being strongly opposed to the customary donation of knives, hatchets, and other sharp instruments which might be turned to use against the party presenting them.

Concluding that I had now in some degree gained their confidence, though not so entirely but that each held the knife or stiletto-shaped horn grasped in his hand by way of precaution, I directed McKay and Sinclair to examine the fall with the view to running it, and so avoid making a portage, fearing lest the sight of our baggage might tempt the natives to steal and so provoke a rupture.

They understood at once what we were about, so I went with them to their tents, which were three in number, one single and two joined together. On our arrival I was struck with the sight of a sort of circumvallation of piled stones, similar to those which we had passed, and arranged, as I conjectured, to serve for shields against the missiles of their enemies. Besides the bow and arrow, and spear, these people make a most effective use of the sling. Many dogs of inferior size basked in the sunshine, and thousands of fish lay all around split and exposed to dry on the rocks, their roes appearing to be particularly prized. These, which were whitefish and small trout, had been caught in pools below the falls constructed for the purpose.

By this time the steersmen reported the impracticability of getting down the fall owing to a rock near the centre, and were instructed to have the baggage carried over the portage in such a way that one person would always be with the depot, while Mr. King would superintend the whole. While the crew was thus occupied, I took upon myself the part of amusing the Eskimos by sketching their likeness and writing down their names. This gratified them exceedingly, but their merriment knew no bounds when I attempted, what was no easy task, to pronounce what I had written.

As far as I could make out they had never seen Europeans before. They had a cast of countenance superior to that of such of their nation as I had hitherto seen, indicating less of low cunning than is generally stamped on their features. The men were of the average stature, well knit and athletic, and had nurtured a luxurious growth of beards and flowing mustachios.

They had only five kayaks, and the few implements they possessed were merely such as were indispensable for the procuring of food: knives, spears and arrows. The blades of the latter were of rough iron and had probably been obtained by barter from their eastern neighbours. One of the most intelligent took my pencil and at my request drew the coastline which, he said, we would reach on the following day.

Information was now brought that the crew were quite unequal to the task of conveying the boat over the portage. So, like a prudent general, I changed my tactics and, taking advantage of the good humour of our new acquaintances, requested them to give us a helping hand. The request was cheerfully complied with and with their assistance we succeeded in carrying the boat below the falls; so that, in reality, I was indebted to them for getting to the sea at all. They seemed, moreover, to have some notion of the rights of property; for one of them, having picked up a small piece of pemmican, repeatedly asked my permission before he would eat it.

By four a.m. on July 29th we were afloat, and in the afternoon while threading our way between some sand banks, we caught sight of a majestic headland in the extreme distance to the north which had a coast-like appearance. The sand banks were also cut by several channels, shallow, and not navigable. The country on both sides was swampy. This may be considered as the mouth of the Thleweechoh, which after a violent and tortuous course of 530 geographical miles, running through an iron-ribbed country without a single tree on the whole line of its banks, expanding into fine large lakes with clear horizons, pours it waters into the polar sea in latitude 67° 11' N. and longitude 94° 30' W.

Back and his men had reached the Arctic Ocean but they did not realize that they had come to it at the bottom of a great bay—Chantrey Inlet. Having calculated that he was not much more than three hundred miles east of Point Turnagain—the most easterly point reached by Franklin, Hood and himself in 1821 — Back was sanguine about being able to sail west and close the gap. But he had had his share of luck. Pack ice in Chantrey Inlet made progress north and west almost impossible. The party eventually managed to reach Cape Ogle, the north-west point of the Inlet, and from there they caught a dim and distant glimpse of what was later to be called King William Island where, not much more than a decade later, the frightful Franklin tragedy was to take place.

Back evidently wished to keep on trying to reach Point Turnagain but his men had better sense. They were mostly experienced canoemen and they knew only too well how hellish the task of taking the boat back upstream would be. To complicate matters, King became insubordinate and insisted that they ought to sail due north, a course which would have been tantamount to suicide considering the lateness of the season, the lack of supplies, and the unsea-worthiness of the boat. With their leaders wrangling and at odds, it appears that the men precipitated the only sane decision possible; in any event, Back turned for home on August 14. It was none too soon.

It is typical of the explorers of this era that Back slips as lightly over the return trip as if it had been a pleasure jaunt upon the Thames. But those who have travelled on Barren-Land rivers will know that Back's men could only have forced that unwieldy monster of a boat over the innu-merable falls and rapids upstream to Musk-Ox Lake by superhuman effort. Although the return journey has little place in Back's book, it must stand as one of the greatest feats of rivermanship in all the annals of the Arctic.

When the exhausted voyageurs regained Musk-Ox Lake, it was already September 17 and winter was at hand. Fortunately, they were met by the indefatigable McLeod, with a goodly store of supplies and plenty of Indian helpers. The entire party hastily retreated to Fort Reliance where winter caught them in earnest and held them prisoner until the spring of 1835.

Despite its paucity of incident, Back's story is the account of a truly remarkable river voyage through the great plains, and it makes a fitting end to the days of the old-fashioned European explorers in the Barren Grounds. It was an achievement that stood alone for a long time. Until as late as 1948 Back's map of the Great Fish River — now called Back River, in his honour — remained the only map in existence.

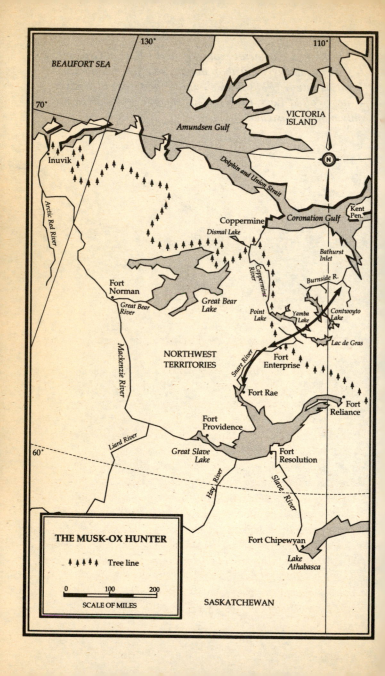

THE MUSK-OX HUNTER

♦♦♦♦♦ Tree line

0   100   200
SCALE OF MILES

V

The Musk-Ox Hunter

FRANK RUSSELL GOES HUNTING WITH THE DOG-RIB INDIANS, 1892

Back's expedition marks the end of an era. During the next half-century the Barren Grounds were rarely, if ever, visited by white men. The incentive that had drawn Franklin and Back into the interior had been the desire to reach and explore the arctic coast. They had had no interest in the Great Plains themselves, seeing in them only a fearsome obstacle to be surmounted before the coast could be reached.

But there were easier ways to explore the coast. In 1837 Thomas Simpson of the Hudson's Bay Company travelled down the Mackenzie and surveyed the coast west to Point Barrow in Alaska. The following year he used the route blazed by one of the parties on Franklin's second expedition, and reached the coast from Great Bear Lake. In two seasons he travelled by boat all the way east to Chantrey Inlet. What little remained to be mapped of the continental arctic shores was explored by another Hudson's Bay Company man, John Rae, in 1846 and 1847—

but neither of these journeys, great voyages that they were, concerned the interior of the Barren Grounds.

Ironically, it was Franklin himself who drew the next Europeans into the interior. After his disappearance, a massive search was mounted — mostly sea-borne, but including two land expeditions. These were undertaken in the hopes of finding some clue to the mystery of their disappearance after all likelihood of finding any of the Franklin people alive had passed. The first was a canoe trip down the Back River in 1855 by Hudson's Bay Factor James Anderson, and was a repetition of Back's journey. The second was a more ambitious venture by Lieut. Schwatka of the U. S. Army who, between 1878 and 1880, led an expedition overland north-west from Chesterfield Inlet to King William Island in search of Franklin relics — making the first crossing of the formidable hill barrens in a region that is, even now, virtually unknown. But, again, neither journey was directed at exploring the Barren Grounds. It was not until the final decade of the century that Europeans began to think of the mighty tundra wilderness as anything other than an obstacle to be crossed en route to somewhere else.

In 1889 the first of a new breed of tundra travellers appears on the scene, men of independent means who, impelled by no real necessity, chose to risk death and to endure hardship simply for the sake of travelling in the wildest regions of the world. They were born wanderers who often masked their compulsion under the guise of sportsmen or sportsmen-naturalists. One of them, an Englishman named Warburton Pike, made a remarkable winter journey in the company of Indians to the north and east from Great Slave to Beechey Lake, nominally to hunt musk-oxen. He wrote a first-rate book about his trip[1] — one in

---

[1]Warburton Pike, *The Barren Ground of Northern Canada*, Macmillan, 1892.

which, for the first time since Hearne, the people, the animals, the very nature and quality of the tundra world are dealt with in detail for their own sake. But it is a book that does not lend itself to our purpose and so, instead, I have chosen part of the story of another of these new men in the Arctic.

Frank Russell had barely graduated from an American university when, in 1892 (probably also inspired by Pike's experiences), the urge seized him to visit the mysterious arctic plains. He came north travelling the hard way, on snowshoes, to Great Slave Lake where he wintered in an abandoned cabin. Nominally he was there to "collect" musk-oxen for the University of Iowa; in truth he was one of the wanderers upon whom the Barrens were to exert a strange and steady fascination throughout the next half-century. He was typical of the company that includes Warburton Pike, Buffalo Jones, Henry Toke Munn, Caspar Whitney, Alfred Harrison, George Douglas and a score of others who, from 1889 to the beginning of the First World War, haunted the western doorways into the Barren Grounds that had been opened by Franklin and Back, appearing and disappearing with the same apparent lack of purpose that seems to characterize the drift of the caribou herds themselves. Their kind is gone now, but throughout the western Arctic they will long be remembered as a mysterious and almost inexplicable phenomenon.

Russell's account, succinct as it is, gives us a glimpse of what life was like amongst the aboriginal people of the western Barren Grounds. Through Back's eyes we have seen the land in summer. Here we see it at a season when the hunt for musk-ox robes, eagerly sought by the traders, lured the Dog-Rib Indians far out into the roaring wastelands of the winter tundra.

EXPLORATIONS IN THE FAR NORTH

I reached Fort Rae on Great Slave Lake on the 6th day of February, 1894. I suffered from the *mal de racquette*[2] the last day which, fortunately, had not before troubled me on the 650-mile journey north.

The prospects for a successful musk-ox hunt, which was the chief undertaking of the expedition, were not promising, so that my spirits were at the lowest ebb during the month of February, which I spent in a cold and lonely half-breed's cabin at Rae.

During this month Mr. Hodgson, the Hudson's Bay Company manager, and I maintained a trapping track, or rather a line of poisoned baits, thirty miles in length. The Dog-Rib Indians were so afraid of strychnine that they would not even touch an animal killed by it. They knew that it was very bad medicine indeed — for did not one of their number, Kwatse, die in the springtime from using the water of the Great Slave Lake a few miles from where a bait had been left in the winter snow? The people of the Lower Mackenzie are not so timid; they use strychnine without fear. Nearly every clerk [the white employees of the various trading posts] sets a few baits each winter, which usually succeed in killing the favourite dog of the trading post, a red or cross fox, or very rarely a silver fox.

I occupied the few hours of daylight at that season in cutting firewood and in writing up my journals. I could not work at night as I had neither lamp or candle. I had great difficulty in keeping the cabin warm enough to prevent the ink from freezing even when I sat beside the fireplace which was kept well filled. I several times found

---

[2] An agonizing pain in the ankles and legs due to the strain of walking on snowshoes.

that the ice had formed upon my hair in a few seconds so that the comb would not pass through it readily. The fireplace was only large enough to contain a few billets of wood in an upright position. The northern fireplace is never broad or deep. It is designed to throw out as much heat as possible from the small billets of quick-burning pine and sprucewood. It was provided with two hooks, one for the tea kettle and the other for the kettle in which meat or fish was boiled. I preferred to cook my own venison, of which I had secured an abundance, and occasionally indulged in a bit of whitefish roasted by suspending it from the rafters above.

Without the daily visits of Mr. Hodgson I should have found the monotony of Fort life hard to endure, but his long residence in the Far North had furnished him with a store of experience that enabled him to make the most of the pleasures of solitude. Stalwart of frame — standing six foot three inches in height — he was respected by the natives as a man not to be trifled with. The prestige of "The Honourable, The Hudson's Bay" has been in no small degree acquired through the personal valour of its representatives.

Each evening the watchman's whistle at the Hudson's Bay Company storehouse called some members of the families of the two engaged servants to receive the rations for the following day. These were called the "pret," and "giving out pret" was the principal event of the day. At some of the posts the servants are summoned for rations by a bell or by a gong, but whatever the signal it is promptly obeyed. A labourer's ration is four fresh fish a day, or four pounds of half-dry, or three pounds of dried, caribou meat; one and one-half pounds of tea, and two pounds of negrohead tobacco each month, forty pounds of white pressed sugar and one hundred pounds of flour each year.

Toward the end of February the Indians gathered in bands along the edge of the Barren Grounds, where they killed caribou in preparation for the musk-ox hunt. A considerable portion of the Yellowknives and Dog-Ribs depend entirely on the sale of musk-ox robes to obtain credit at the Company's stores, from which they must buy tea, tobacco, ammunition, etc. Since they had given up the [usual] fall hunt the previous year, owing to the severity of the season, it became all the more necessary that they should succeed in the spring.

They were unwilling to run the risk of admitting a white man to the great hunting ground which is peculiarly their own. Although they looked on any white man not connected with the Company as lawful prey who was to pay exorbitant prices for their services because "he is rich and we are poor," their superstition was stronger than their cupidity. Naohmby sent a message to the effect that I might come to his camp if I wished. True, he had promised to take me to the musk-oxen, but now he and his followers were starving and it was doubtful if they could kill any caribou for the hunt. This was not encouraging, and as I knew that Naohmby followed the longest route to the Barren Ground, reaching it at a point north-west of the Great Bear Lake, I gave up the plan of accompanying him and determined to pounce upon the first band of Dog-Ribs which made its appearance at Rae.

On the 4th of March I told a party of four, who had come to the Fort for ammunition for the hunt, that I was going with them whether they wanted me to do so or not. With the aid of the Fort interpreter, we discussed the matter until midnight. Johnny Cohoyla, a petty chief, was the leader of the party. He had been engaged by the Company in his younger days as a boatman, when he had acquired a limited vocabulary of Red River French. He finally consented to "look after me," which meant to look at me doing my own work, and to cook for me — if I purchased meat for him and his family, which became surprisingly large in a short time. I also agreed to pay two skins or one dollar a day, and supply tea for our party during the trip.[3]

We started late on March 5th for the Indian camps at the edge of the timber. I was not in a cheerful mood as I hitched in my dogs for the long journey which, the Dog-Ribs emphatically declared, would kill me, as they, accustomed to such a life, "found it hard." I would have to walk or run on snowshoes the entire distance, and not lie in a portable bed or cariole[4] as do most white travellers in the interior of the Far North, while some native driver attends to the team. I would not hear an English word for two months, and the antagonism of the unwilling Indians must prove a source of constant annoyance.

My outfit consisted of a .45-.90 Winchester and ammunition, fifteen pounds of dried caribou meat, eighteen pounds of frozen bread, several pounds of tea, and a few ounces of salt. My bedding consisted of a single four-point blanket sewed to a light caribou-skin robe.

Johnny tried to exhaust me on the 150-mile trip to the camps. He would have walked that distance in two days, but his dogs were not equal to the task, and though they were beaten until their heads were bruised and bleeding they could not reach our destination in less than three days. My ankles troubled me with the torturing *mal de racquette*, which made me very glad to see the dirty, smoke-begrimed lodges with their swarm of dogs and half-naked children. The whole camp was soon wrangling over my last pinch of salt. I was now dependent upon my rifle or the Indians for meat, which with tea made up the bill of fare for the next two months.

---

[3] A "skin" represented a made beaver and was valued at approximately one dollar in trade goods by the Hudson's Bay Company. The Hudson's Bay Company even issued its own metal currency in the form of tokens marked "One Made Beaver."

[4] A toboggan with high canvas sides.

The Dog-Ribs were not ready for the great musk-ox hunt. They must first make new snowshoes, sled lines, and moccasins; caribou must be killed and pounded meat and grease prepared.

We moved our camps twice during the next three weeks, and thus interrupted the drearily monotonous rub-dub of the noisy drums, to the beating of which the men sat and gambled from early morning until midnight. They were not willing to venture as yet upon the bleak desert of snow, known to them as "no-wood country." At last it was finally decided that we should start after the Easter festivities were concluded.

On Easter Sunday we gathered for prayers at an early hour in the chief's lodge. The men, their hair and faces freshly greased, were the first to arrive and took their places in a semi-circle round the fire opposite the entrance. The women seated themselves in a group near the door flap. "Jimmy-the-Chief" occupied the post of honour at one side, on his right side sat his wife, beyond whom were the other women and the children. On his left was Johnny Cohoyla, the choir leader, and I the guest of the band; next came the older men in order of rank. We all sat cross-legged upon blankets spread on the floor of spruce boughs. The women brought the family tinware, a plate and cup for each person, wrapped with the hymn books in a piece of coffee sacking which afterwards served as a tablecloth. Over the fire hung a ten-gallon kettle of boiling meat, while beside it stood other copper kettles containing several gallons of tea.

We usually had a few fresh caribou tongues each Sunday, but on this occasion there was one for each person, and a ball of freshly made pemmican. Grace was repeated in concert, then the chief threw a tongue and a small ball of pemmican into the fire and the feast began. As the meat was cut from the bones, they were cracked for the marrow.

Two hours later we had a second meal of boiled meat, and as I had given them a little flour before leaving the post, a kettleful of the much-prized *rubaboo* was also prepared. This was made by cutting up a quantity of back-fat into small cubes and boiling, stirring in flour to thicken it.

On the evening of March 28th my dogs were not to be found at feeding time. "The wolves will eat your dogs tonight," said Johnny. "Yes, the wolves are very numerous," said the others. Without the dogs I could do nothing. Missing this opportunity to secure musk-oxen, I must remain another year in the country or go back to Iowa without these, the most difficult to obtain of American mammals. After a long search the next morning I found two of the dogs feeding upon the remains of a caribou six miles from camp, and by three o'clock, just as I was concluding arrangements to buy two miserable little local dogs, my other two made their appearance. I felt that a year of my life had been restored.

An hour later we started on the grand hunt, in which only the best men engaged; the women and children, of course, remained at the camp in the woods. There were eleven Indians in the party, with two lodges — Johnny in charge of mine, with three other Indians.

We occupied the great part of the second day in traversing a long narrow lake called Ten-en-di-a Tooh [probably Snare Lake]. In the afternoon from the summit of a lofty granite hill I beheld the Barren Grounds for the first time. Behind us lay the rugged hills, their slopes clothed with stunted pines upon which a bright sun was shining; before us were hills still more precipitous and barren, everywhere strewn with angular blocks of granite—a cold and dreary waste from which a snowstorm was quickly approaching. Half-acre patches of spruces, from one to three feet high, still appeared for a few miles, but our lodge poles were cut that day. These were trimmed down so slender that they would afford little fuel for the return trip; each sled carried four poles, fourteen feet in length. The country was so rough that we only travelled thirty-five miles.

Before starting on the morning of the fourth day the regular Sunday service was performed, as it was on the following Sundays which we spent in the Barren Grounds. Notwithstanding the need of haste we knelt for an hour with only a blanket between our knees and the naked rock on which our lodge was always pitched. The service was marked by a seriousness which I thought resulted more from a superstitious desire to propitiate the wrath of a savage storm god than from a feeling of reverence toward a beneficent Creator.

We camped that night in a little clump of pines on the Coppermine River. The Dog-Ribs called this stream Tson Te. This was the last outlier of the timbered country and we must henceforth carry fuel on our sleds. We left the Coppermine with our sleds loaded as heavily as the dogs could haul with wood which we had cut and split into billets of convenient size. What a luxury a good oil stove would have been! As we were about to start, Jimmy, who was leader of the band and by far the most intelligent man amongst them, after a long look eastward turned to me and said: "This is the woodless country where the blizzards blow and it is always cold." Then drawing his old grey blanket closer about him, and shouldering his double-barreled smooth-bore encased in a greasy guncoat, he set off at a rapid pace, the seven dog-trains falling into line upon the track of his snowshoes. We followed the course of a small stream for about forty miles until we reached a lake at least thirty miles in length called Yam-ba Tooh [Yamba Lake].

As we advanced on the seventh day the hills became more rolling, with gravel and pebbles. Wherever the wind had swept the surface clear of snow, the reindeer moss and tufts of low grass appeared. Toward evening we passed a few old musk-ox tracks.

On the ninth day we traversed the largest lake seen north of the Great Slave Lake, which I think must be the Rum Lake of Franklin [Contwoyto Lake]. Away toward the northern end of the lake four or five peaks were visible; two of them were lofty cones standing pure white in their snow mantles.

We crossed two gravel ridges trending south-east, and again encountered the hills of naked granite, strewn with great angular boulders, which necessitated constant watchfulness to prevent our sleds from being broken. These vehicles were the common birch flat sleds [toboggans] of the North, fifteen inches in width and seven feet in length. Their bottoms soon became grooved from end to end by the sharp points of rocks lying just below the surface of the snow. Still Jimmy's old grey blanket led the way, straight over the hills, never swerving from a north-east course. Sometimes we would ascend for an hour, and then go pell-mell down a steep incline for two or three hundred feet, holding back our sleds with all our strength yet landing in the drifts at the bottom with the last dog dragging under, and the rest of the team tangled in the harness.

The caribou were now quite abundant and we had little difficulty in killing enough for men and teams. My dogs were keen hunters and were always ready to dash after the herds of caribou which swept over the snowy slopes like the shadows of swift-flying clouds. The only way I could restrain them was to overturn the sled. In the evening, when they were released from the harness, they would pursue any caribou which might appear near camp, which caused me considerable anxiety, as the dismal howl of the never-distant wolves gave warning of their certain fate if they left the camp.

On the tenth day [April 8] Johnny, with three other Indians and myself, separated from the rest and turned a little more to the northward. We were now in what the Dog-Ribs designated the Musk-Ox Mountains [they were in the angle between Burnside and Mara Rivers]. After running about ten miles, Esyuh, who was in advance, suddenly turned and began to make frantic gestures. Over the hills, a mile away, appeared a black object closely followed by another and another. No need for him to urge us to hasten forward or to tell us what those huge rolling balls were. A few seconds later the dogs were all released and scattering out over the country — some in pursuit of the three musk-oxen, some on the backtrack, and others trotting complacently along at their masters' heels. They were not well-trained hunters; at sight of the musk-oxen even the threatening whip did not prevent them from breaking into howls and many of them were too spiritless to be of any assistance in stopping the game. We followed as fast as we could run. It was then I discovered the advantage of having light clothing, light gun, and little ammunition. The dogs soon overtook the clumsy musk-oxen, which turned to defend themselves as from a pack of wolves. They were not held long at a time, but their flight was so hindered that they were overtaken by my companions, who had outdistanced me after a run of three miles.

Our lodge was set up that night beside the fallen carcasses and our teams for once had all they could eat. There were several hundred pounds of meat with fat two inches in thickness on the backs, meat of excellent quality without the faintest trace of musk. The meat from one of the animals was tender and as well flavoured as any venison I ever ate. The other two were tough, but the Dog-Ribs preferred tough meat to walking a dozen yards to get the meat of the younger animal. The complexion of our diet was now changed; before we had enjoyed caribou ribs boiled, garnished with a handful of coase grey hairs; now we had boiled ribs of musk-ox with hairs of a brownish-black.

I awakened next morning with a sense of weight upon my blanket and my ears were greeted by a rushing roar caused by a north-east gale which had covered everything inside our lodge to a depth of a foot or more with fine, flour-like snow. It was impossible to face such a blizzard without freezing in a few minutes. All landmarks were obscured so that we could not continue upon our course in any case. As we had only wood enough for the time that we expected to be engaged in actual travel, we could have no fire on days like this, when we were compelled to "lay to." We remained in our blankets until midday, when a kettle of meat was (half) boiled and we turned in again.

In the evening a fire about the size of a cigar box was kept up long enough to boil a kettle of tea, one cup for each man. No meat was cooked, for our appetites were soon satisfied with the large sticks of white frozen marrow from the long-bones of the musk-ox.

We usually drank snow water, as soon as snow could be melted after the campfire was started. Each individual carried a tin plate on which a block of snow was placed and inclined toward the fire. As the lower side became saturated we drank the water as from a soggy snowball, and so avoided the cinders and hairs which quickly covered everything about the diminutive fire. Before leaving the woods we had melted snow by fixing large blocks on the end of poles before the log campfire. A steady stream soon trickled from the lower end which was trimmed to a point by a few strokes of a knife.

Throughout the trip we washed our hands and faces daily by melting water in tin plates and squirting it, à la Chinese Laundryman, upon our hands. The whole party possessed two pieces of soap and one towel. A Dog-Rib towel is never washed; its owner's face is often greased and the colour of the towel is affected accordingly.

Throughout the following day the storm continued with increased severity, and we were forced to lie in the snow another twenty-four hours.

My dogs never came inside the lodge at night but coiled themselves up in the lee of the lodge where the snow soon drifted over them, giving warmth and shelter. The twelve Indian curs came inside as soon as the last man rolled up in his blanket at night. At first they spent a few minutes fighting over the bones about the fireplace, then they rummaged through everything that was not firmly lashed down. As a dog walked over a prostrate form the muffled "marche!" would quiet them for an instant, when their snarling and snapping would break out anew, until some of us would pick up a billet of wood and "pacify" them. After we had once fallen into the sleep of exhaustion we were seldom awakened by their fighting over us. In the morning I usually found two or three coiled up in the snow upon my blanket; the heat of their bodies melted the snow, which froze as soon as they left it and made my scanty bedding hard and stiff.

After sixty hours of such "resting" we were quite ready to move on, as the thirteenth day dawned bright and clear. Early in the day we caught sight of a band of forty musk-oxen already in flight a couple of miles distant. We chased them six miles, but only one of our party — Wisho — reached them and killed four. We were very much fatigued from our long run, and covered with perspiration which froze on our outer garments as we walked back with the dogs to bring up the sleds. It was after nightfall before we set up the lodge; and cold, tired and hungry, we sat shivering around a column of smoke over which hung a kettle containing both meat and drink — for our supply of tea was exhausted and we had to quench our thirst with the greasy bouillon in which the meat was boiled.

The temperature was falling rapidly, giving us some concern about Johnny Cohoyla, who had not returned. The next morning I was awakened by the monotonous wailing of his brother, Esyuh, who was chanting the virtues of the lost reprobate, and entreating the fates in general and the north wind in particular, to spare him.

"A man is lost!" he cried.

The Dog-Ribs repeated the phrase with significant glances at me as if my accompanying them had offended the Great Spirit, so that he had wreaked his vengeance upon the man who had allowed me to enter the Dog-Rib hunting ground. A terrific gale prevented us from searching for the lost man; we could only spend the day in our blankets while the snow drifted in and over everything. That was one of the most miserable days I ever spent. I had tried twice to run with the Indians, and failed to reach the musk-oxen, and there seemed to be no immediate prospect of my getting any. The musk-oxen were not numerous, they said, and our wood might fail before we secured any more. Johnny must have perished, as no human being could live through a night of such storm without protection, and it was thirty-six hours before we could leave the camp to search for him. We spent that time shivering in our blankets, even the Indians saying, "It is cold, very cold."

The next morning proved to be calm and we set off in search of Johnny. I had as great difficulty to keep my cheeks from freezing as at any time during the winter, though there was scarcely any wind blowing.

After running about ten miles, I was recalled by the signalling of another searcher. Johnny had been found by his brother, safely and snugly rolled up in a couple of musk-ox skins which he had secured, where he had been warmer than if in the lodge, and had had plenty of frozen marrow to eat so that he had been quite comfortable.

On the sixteenth day we continued the journey northward. With the field glasses I discovered a band of fourteen musk-oxen on the summit of a high hill, so far away that it was impossible to distinguish them from the surrounding boulders with the unaided eye. In a couple of hours we were within half a mile of them and released the dogs, which soon disappeared over an intervening ridge.

My companions had concluded, from the way that I had run, or failed to run on the two previous occasions, that I could not run very far, and that their best plan to keep me from bringing a magazine-loading gun into competition with their muzzle-loaders was to give the musk-oxen time to get far enough away so that they could exhaust me in the race. I had prepared for this by taking off some of my clothing, and only carrying the ammunition actually required, so that when they did begin to run at a swift pace, my snowshoes clanked close behind them.

We soon came upon eleven musk-oxen standing at bay in two little clusters, hardly lowering their heads at the dogs, whose ardour had been cooled by the statue-like immobility of the noble animals. Their robes were in prime condition; the long hair and heavy, erect mane gave them an imposing appearance. To kill them was simple butchery, yet I had no choice but to fire as rapidly as possible and get my share of them, as they were all doomed anyway.

On leaving Fort Rae, Johnny had agreed to assist me in skinning the game killed; he now found that his own affairs would require all his attention. Esyuh helped me to skin two, while I finished the third by moonlight, freezing my fingers in the operation.

It was impossible to skin the heads in darkness. [Since these musk-oxen were required as museum specimens, the skull too was needed.] I therefore wrapped the skins around them so they would not freeze during the night. Another blizzard was raging in the morning, which prevented moving but enabled me to attend to the heads which had not frozen very much; but the skins around them were stiff and solid, so that it was impossible to fold them up for easy transportation.

I spent the day sawing the skulls in halves, so that they might be loaded on the sled, sitting beside a little smoke arising from the bones of the musk-oxen, which contained enough grease to burn though not very readily. Our fires were started with birch bark, a small roll being carried by each man for that purpose. The wood was cut in sticks a foot in length and finely split, then built up in a "log cabin" or a cone. Each man took his turn blowing to keep it alight, as the wood was not dry and the quantity so small that it required constant attention.

We were destined to spend the next day in the blankets, with the clouds of powdery snow settling down upon us through the smoke hole of our lodge. We had had but two meals a day since leaving the Coppermine, and when lying stormbound we ate but one. When travelling, although we were voraciously hungry before nightfall, it was thirst which troubled us the most, as we were running most of the time.

Early on the nineteenth day we sighted musk-oxen while yet a long distance from them. While ascending a steep hill I was delayed by my sled sinking in the soft snow until the great awkward balls into which the skins had frozen, projecting at the sides, made the load drag heavily. When I reached the top the others were a quarter of a mile in advance, and instead of waiting for me to come up they had released their dogs and were likely to kill every musk-ox before I could reach them.

Johnny, remembering the havoc which my Winchester was liable to make in his fur return, thought best to "suspend the rules" of the hunting code and let me buy off them if I wanted any musk-oxen.

Without releasing my dogs, which were wildly tugging at their collars, I started forward with little hopes of killing any musk-oxen, but in excellent humour for slaughtering a few Dog-Ribs. Fortune, however, smiled upon me. Four bulls of the largest size broke away together, without a dog in pursuit, and came within range. This was not so much like butchering them; they were running much faster than I could on snowshoes and had a chance for their lives. I killed two as they passed me about a hundred yards distant and wounded the others so that they were bagged after a run of half a mile.

I had now killed seven musk-oxen and already had as many on my sled as the Hudson's Bay people had told me it was possible to haul. When Johnny returned from chasing the scattered herd, I stated my plain and unbiased opinion of him in all the Red River French and Dog-Rib that I could command. His deprecatory "yaz-zi" changed to a sheepish "ne-zi" — good — when I informed him that

I had secured all the robes I wanted. He refused to carry a skeleton for me at any price — not even a head or half a split skull would he carry — so I gave him two robes for carrying back to the lodge.

The next day was spent in camp. The others were engaged in skinning the animals killed, and in boiling bones for grease to eat on the return trip. I thus had an opportunity to prepare the two skulls for transportation.

On the twenty-first day of the hunt we started homeward — the turning point of the expedition. We were all heavily loaded with the loose, bulky skins. The sleds were frequently overturned, and if our dogs had not been in unusually good condition they would never have been brought out at all. My load extended over both ends of the sled, and was nearly as high as my shoulders. With the four lodge-poles on the top, it was no easy matter to keep everything lashed firmly in place.

On the twenty-third day a blinding snowstorm prevented moving before midday, when we pushed on through the soft snow without meat for ourselves or the dogs. On the return trip we only secured five caribou, which was less than half rations for five men and sixteen dogs.

We were now burning our lodge-poles for fuel; on the night of the twenty-fifth day the lodge was set up for the last time, with two poles only. With our sled lines made fast to the circle of sleds, which were always enclosed, these gave sufficient support.

We started at six a.m. the next morning determined to reach the Coppermine, some fifty miles distant, before camping. In the afternoon we came upon a lodge-pole standing beside a sled track which we had followed all day, upon which a line was written in syllabic characters, informing us that Jimmy's party was intending to reach the wood that evening also.

At half past ten, after sixteen and a half hours of continuous travelling, we reached a little grove of trees, which seemed more welcome than any harbour to the storm-tossed sailor. We were all too fatigued to cut much brush [to sleep on], and fell asleep in a little hole scooped in the snow, before a few logs which made such an uncomfortably hot fire that we did not enjoy it as we had anticipated. But we would no longer have to sleep upon snow or flat rocks; we would not have to sleep with our moccasins and frozen blanket footings [duffel socks] next to our bodies to dry them, and at noonday we could have tea to quench our thirst.

After five hours' rest we were awakened by Jimmy arriving, and reminding us that there was nothing to eat and that we must push rapidly on. Our load weighed over five hundred pounds and the dogs were getting pitifully weak. I pushed on the sled and carried a load on my back to assist them.

We only rested five hours at the first camp inside the wood and then hurried on, as the teams were failing rapidly from want of food. On the twenty-eighth day the first sign of thaw appeared and the snow softened just enough to cause it to stick to our snowshoes which made them heavy and, worse still, lumps of ice would accumulate every few minutes which soon blistered the bottom of our feet over the entire surface.

During the last two days before reaching the camp the heavy snowshoes caused the *mal de racquette* to reappear, which made it simply torture to move; yet we were now in the woods where soft snow required heavier work in the management of the sleds.

At two in the afternoon of the twenty-ninth day we reached the vicinity of the camping place from which we had started and fired several rounds to announce our arrival. A few minutes later we dashed into a deserted camp! The lodges were gone; snow had drifted over their sites. Their skeleton poles offered a dreary welcome to us as, tired, hungry and disappointed, we turned away in no pleasant humour to follow the track along which a line of slanting poles indicated the direction of departure.

We were now upon an old, hard track from which the sled frequently overturned into the soft snow on either side, and my dogs were about to give up altogether. More powder was burned as we approached the camps, three hours later. As I passed one of the first lodges, my sled swayed off the track and caught against a tree, much to the amusement of a couple of young women who, after watching my attempt to right it, remarked, "The white man is weak, indeed." One of them then grasped the sled line to show me how to straighten up a load, and tugged and hauled and tugged again without producing the slightest effect. I am afraid that I laughed very ungallantly as the discomfited maiden fled to the shelter of the lodge.

Mrs. Jimmy came to me with a very cordial greeting, exclaiming, "Merci! merci — tco!" — "Thanks, big thanks, for the good musk-ox hunt!" She evidently ascribed our success in a measure to my presence. We had been absent twenty-eight days from the camps, twenty-two of which were spent beyond the Coppermine River.

There was very little meat in the lodges and the caribou were moving out into the Barren Grounds, so that the Indians must lead a more than usually precarious existence for the next two months until they could follow the caribou by water. For three days they were quite content to lie about the camp, feasting upon the store of dried meat and grease which remained. They would not sell me any of this, though I needed a supply very much for a projected journey down the Mackenzie River.

I had left a small bag of articles in Johnny's lodge during the hunt, which they had opened and discovered contained a few ounces of compressed tea that I had reserved for the trip back to Rae. They did not appropriate the tea, but the day after our return they began to clamour for it to make tea for a Sunday feast. First Johnny, and then the whole band, came to me with smiles, whines, and finally threats. Johnny boiled a large kettle of water and placed it before me with an insolent demand for "lee tea."

I could contain myself no longer. I felt dependent on them to guide me to the post. It was utterly impossible for me to reach it, through two hundred miles of trackless forest with my load of musk-oxen, without their assistance. But three days of nagging, culminating in that defiant act, over-came my power of self-restraint and I turned loose my wrath upon Mr. Cohoyla with a vehemence which seemed to have a salutary effect.

On the 30th of April I started for Fort Rae accom-panied by three Indians with two empty sleds, on which they refused to haul any of my load although I offered to pay them; they were still sulky about the tea.

From the experience gained during that 800-mile trip, I am satisfied that Fort Resolution is a much better post from which to hunt musk-oxen than Rae. The Dog-Ribs now trade at both stations, and Beniah, one of the most enterprising of that tribe, for the last five years has killed musk-oxen within two days' travel of the woods at the east end of Great Slave Lake.

My advice to sportsmen is to keep out of the musk-ox country if life and health are valued. To be sure, there is a satisfaction in overcoming the obstacles which must be encountered before the musk-oxen are reached, but at the end, when you are within rifle shot of the long-sought game, you find after all that it is a cruel butchery; you do not feel the triumphant exhilaration which results from successfully pursuing the noble moose or elk. In fact, you can duplicate the sensation felt on such an occasion, at far less expense and less hardship, by hiring a pack of hungry curs for an afternoon, and turning them into your neigh-bour's sheep pasture. When they have rounded up the flock, you can take your stand at a safe distance and shoot down the sheep; the musk-ox is not a "sporty" animal.

Russell was luckier than he knew. The demand for musk-ox robes became so great that in a matter of a few decades these strange beasts, who seem to have survived out of some prehistoric age, had been hunted to the verge of extinction.

Although European man had, as yet, no more than nibbled at the edges of the vast arctic prairies, the disruption he had brought to the neighbouring forest regions was already having its effect upon the hidden land to the north. The lives of Indians and Eskimos were already changing, mostly for the worse. Disease, malnutrition, social disintegration, and servitude to the steel trap and to the trader for the goods they had once made themselves, and the food they had once hunted for themselves, were already beginning to take a heavy toll of their numbers, of their strength, and of their pride of being. The animals, too, were beginning to experience terrible attrition. The musk-oxen were rapidly being destroyed. The wood buffalo, which had filled the open glades to the south-west of the Barrens, were almost gone. The unique Barren-Land grizzly bear was becoming scarce, for not even these giants could stand against the rifles which trade had put in the hands of the Indians. And the greatest of all the tundra animals was also beginning an inevitable decline (although no man realized it for many years to come): the Barren-Land caribou, which in 1890 may still have numbered as many as four million animals, were being slaughtered by whites and Indians on a colossal scale (its precedent was the slaughter of the plains buffalo).

In 1890 Hearne's Barren Grounds would no longer have been recognizable to him in terms of their fauna or their human occupants. Soon the rate of change was to increase drastically. The time was coming when the white man, who had thrown his shadow so far before him, would begin to thrust and hack his way into the Barren Grounds in deadly earnest.

But before this happened, there was to be one more great journey of exploration.

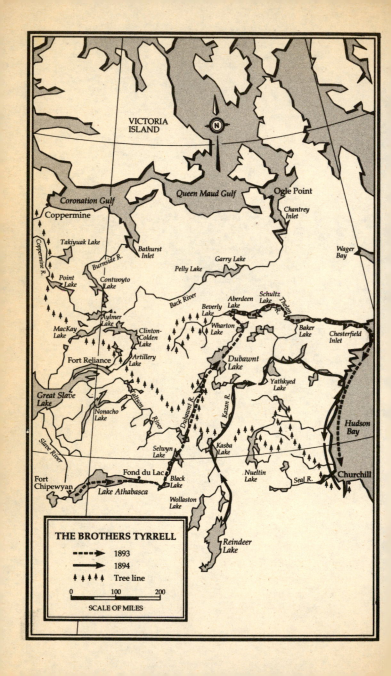

VICTORIA
ISLAND

Coronation Gulf
Coppermine

Queen Maud Gulf

Ogle Point

Chantrey
Inlet

Wager
Bay

Takiyuak Lake

Coppermine R.

Bathurst
Inlet

Burnside R.

Pelly Lake

Garry Lake

Point
Lake

Contwoyto
Lake

Back River

Aberdeen
Lake

Schultz
Lake

Thelon R.

Beverly
Lake

MacKay
Lake

Aylmer
Lake

Clinton-
Colden
Lake

Wharton
Lake

Baker
Lake

Chesterfield
Inlet

Fort Reliance

Artillery
Lake

Dubawnt
Lake

Great Slave
Lake

Nonacho
Lake

Hanbury River

Dubawnt R.

Kazan R.

Yathkyed
Lake

Hudson
Bay

Slave River

Selwyn
Lake

Kasba
Lake

Nueltin
Lake

Seal R.

Churchill

Fort
Chipewyan

Fond du Lac

Black
Lake

Lake Athabasca

Wollaston
Lake

Reindeer
Lake

THE BROTHERS TYRRELL

- - - → 1893

⟶ 1894

🌲🌲🌲🌲🌲 Tree line

0   100   200

SCALE OF MILES

VI

The Brothers Tyrrell

EXPLORING THE INTERIOR OF KEEWATIN BY CANOE, 1893

By the late 1800's the burgeoning new nation of Canada (which had been born in 1867 as a somewhat scrawny infant consisting of Ontario, Quebec, New Brunswick and Nova Scotia) had grown to include most of what now lies within her boundaries. But much of what lay within those boundaries in 1890 still remained terra incognita. *The whole of the Northwest, as it was called, was occupied by only a handful of fur traders, a few white trappers, and Indians and Eskimos; and there were vast areas which had not even been visited by white men. The largest of these unknown regions lay inside the Barren Grounds.*

A nation needs to know what it consists of, and so, about 1890, the fledgling Geological Survey of Canada was given the task of finding out. It had little money and few men for the job, but one of its few men was worth a platoon. He was Joseph Burr Tyrrell, born near Toronto in 1858, and trained as a geologist.

In 1892 Tyrrell was sent to explore and map the huge

*region north of the Churchill River between Reindeer Lake
on the east, and the Athabasca River on the west. This was
the mother country of the Chipewyan Indians who, in
Hearne's time, had ranged far to the north onto the tundra
plains. By 1890 these once mighty people had been so
reduced that they had almost abandoned the Barren
Grounds. Where once they had numbered perhaps four or
five thousand, they now numbered fewer than three or four
hundred. But what was left of them still occupied the ances-
tral grounds.*

*Joseph Tyrrell came among them in the spring of 1892
and spent that summer exploring their country. While he
was mapping Black Lake, to the east of Lake Athabasca,
his Chipewyan guides casually pointed out a stream on the
northern shore and remarked that it was the beginning of
a canoe route which their ancestors had once followed far
out into the Barrens. Tyrrell pricked up his ears. For many
years he had felt the fascination of the land of Hearne, and
this seemed like an omen.*

*Back in Ottawa that fall he proposed to his superiors
that they let him attempt a traverse of the Barrens from
south to north, starting from Black Lake. Since the area
he wished to explore represented a blank patch on the map
of better than half a million square miles, he had little
difficulty obtaining permission to try his luck.*

*Tyrrell was about to open the third door into the tundra
world — the southern one. To do it he made two journeys
which, in sum, represent as magnificent a feat of travel
and exploration as any in the history of North America.*

*Tyrrell had all the right instincts and attributes for the
task ahead. Instead of mounting a huge and cumbrous
expedition, he chose to make the journey in three light
cedar canoes carrying a party consisting of himself, his
younger brother James (who had spent a winter among the
Eskimos of Hudson Strait), and six picked canoemen. Three
of these were Iroquois: the brothers Pierre, Louis and
Michel French from the Caughnawaga Reserve near Mon-*

treal. Louis, the middle brother, had won distinction while serving with Lord Wolseley in the Egyptian campaign as a voyageur on the Nile. Pierre, the eldest, was a renowned white-water man who once ran the ice-filled Lachine Rapids on Christmas Day as a demonstration of his virtuosity. The three remaining canoemen were John Flett, James Corrigal and François Maurice, all of them Métis, and all with long experience as voyageurs with the Hudson's Bay Company.

James Tyrrell was a land surveyor who abandoned his business and joined the expedition for the joy of the adventure. It is fortunate that he did so, since Joseph was not given to writing popular accounts of his explorations. It is to James that we owe the story of the first part of a twofold venture which was to result in the exploration of over a thousand miles of river routes through an area never before visited by any white man except Samuel Hearne.

The ventures of the Tyrrells into the Barrens have special significance for Canada. They were the first northern exploring voyages of real note to have been conceived and carried out solely by Canadians.

ACROSS THE SUB-ARCTICS OF CANADA

Fort Chipewyan is an old and important trading post of the Hudson's Bay Company. Before many of our American and Canadian cities came into existence, Chipewyan was a noted fur-trade centre. From here Alexander Mackenzie started, in 1789, on his famous journeys. The Fort now consists of a long row of eighteen or twenty detached buildings connected by a high, strong wooden fence or wall.

Here we engaged the best Indian guide available to accompany us through Lake Athabasca and as far beyond as he knew the country. The guide's name was Moberly — a Christian name, though before we were through with him he proved himself to be anything but a Christian. He was acquainted with our proposed route for about one hundred miles to the northward from Black Lake.

Before noon all our supplies were ready to be loaded. The total weight of our outfit consisted of about four thousand pounds. It included bacon, axes, flour, sugar, dutch oven, mustard, geological hammers, pain killer, canned beef, mathematical instruments, and a box of ammunition.

A sailboat rode at anchor before the Fort and for a time we thought we might make use of it to carry all our stuff as far as the east end of the lake. Moberly particularly urged the necessity of taking the big boat, for his home was at the east end of the lake and he had a lot of stuff which he wished to carry there; but as we were not on a freighting tour for his benefit we decided to take only the canoes. At this he became sulky and thought he would not go. At last we told him to go where he chose, as we were in no way dependent on him.

On the morning of the 21st of June our outfit set out for the east end of the lake. Old Moberly was also on hand with his family and a big bark canoe. We made but slow progress in the face of an east wind and pitched camp at nine-thirty p.m. in a little sandy bay, worthy to be remembered because of the swarms of mosquitoes which greeted us on arrival. We had been reminded of the existence of these creatures at Chipewyan but here it was a question of the survival of the fittest. Mosquito nets, already fixed to the hats, had to be drawn down and tightly closed and mosquito oil or grease smeared over our hands.

Our second day on the lake was even less successful than the first, for though we made an early start in the morning we were soon obliged to put to shore by reason of the roughness of the water and a strong head wind. That evening we met a party of Indians in their bark canoes, sailing with hoisted blankets before the wind. As they bore down upon us they presented a picturesque and animated scene. François was on hand to interpret and, as we met, a halt was made. The first and most natural question asked by the Indians was, "Where are you going?" "To hell," was François's prompt but startling reply.

In order that we might have the opportunity of securing information about the country (not that to which François had alluded) we decided to go ashore and make tea. From one old hunter named Sharlo we obtained interesting sketch maps of canoe routes spreading northward from Lake Athabasca; of course tea and tobacco had been served out before such information was sought, for no man of experience would think of approaching an Indian for the purpose of a favour without first conferring one.

After many days of bad weather we reached Fond du Lac on the 29th of June. Fond du Lac is a Fort only in name. It consists of two or three small log shanties and a little log mission church situated on a bare, exposed and sandy shore. One or two Indians were living at the place, and letters were left with one of them in the hope that they might be taken safely to Chipewyan and thence forwarded by the Hudson's Bay Company's autumn packet to Edmonton. This was undoubtedly the last chance, though only a chance, of sending any news to our friends until we should return to civilization.

From Fond du Lac eastward Lake Athabasca is narrow, having the appearance of a broad river, being about five miles in width but extending a distance of fifty miles. On the south shore could be seen a large group of Indian lodges and at this camp was the home of our guide. It was here his family was to be left. Moberly himself now appeared to be very indifferent as to whether or not he should go any farther with us. Finally, after the offer of liberal inducements, he promised to secure a companion canoeman and follow our track in the morning. We parted and proceeded along the south shore until evening when, finding an inviting camping ground in the open jackpine woods, we went ashore for supper.

At lunch the next day we were joined by Moberly and

his companion, an old Indian named Bovia. We were surprised to see them for we had had a suspicion that the guide had no intention of keeping his promise. During the afternoon his canoe lagged far behind, not so much because of his inability to keep up with us as because of his serene indifference and laziness. The paddles used by him and his comrades were like spoons as compared with our broad paddles, and the position of old Bovia, as he pulled with one elbow resting on the gunwale of his canoe, was most amusing. We decided that the guides were going to be a drag rather than a help so it was resolved that before proceeding further a definite understanding must be reached.

On the 1st of July we arrived at the end of the lake, having proceeded 210 miles from Chipewyan. Here there were several Indian families living in substantial log houses. One of these, we learned, was the property of our brave Moberly, and in front of it he and old Bovia deliberately went ashore and drew up their canoe. The action struck us as suspicious, but presently they made an open demand for a division of our bacon, flour, tea and tobacco. Some pieces of tobacco and a small quantity of tea had already been given, but any further distribution was declined. At this Moberly feigned to become very angry and said he would go with us no farther. There was no use in trying to force him to continue with us and nothing could be gained by punishing him for his deception. He was given one last opportunity but, still refusing, we parted company with him without wasting strong language which he would not have understood.

With our three canoes we thereupon commenced the ascent of what had been named the Stone River, the outlet of Black Lake.

Sunday was spent in camp at the foot of a wild and beautiful cataract. The weather was warm and the black flies and mosquitoes swarmed so thickly that we could nowhere escape from their ceaseless hum and dreaded bite. In this neighbourhood they did not appear to have the customary respect for the smudge. Dense smoke was made about camp, but the flies only appeared to revel in it. The men fished in one of the rapids and took two salmon trout measuring three feet one inch and three feet two inches respectively.

On Monday began one of our most laborious days. Our camp was at the foot of a fall and in consequence was at the lower end of a rough and rocky portage, three miles in length. The canoes were all heavily loaded, containing some four thousand pounds of cargo which had to be transported. James Corrigal was laid up for the time with an ugly gash in the knee so we only had five packers. They went at their work with a rush, notwithstanding a rocky hill of two hundred feet which had to be climbed, and a deep muskeg which obliged them to wade. Before nightfall, however, their spirits were away down as a result of this slavish work. Feet were fearfully blistered and all complained of pains in one place or another. Each man had carried six loads to the upper end of the portage, representing a walk of thirty-three miles, eighteen of which were travelled with 100-pound loads upon their backs over rocky hills and through swamps knee deep with mire. The work was resumed next morning in hot weather, and the flies were out in swarms. Two more trips were needed to get everything across. We then loaded the canoes and pushed out into the lake, heading for the opposite shore where we discovered the mouth of the river we were to ascend. While yet far out on the lake we could see its foamy water and as we drew near could plainly hear the unmistakable roar of a cataract.

Because of the condition of the men, camp was ordered to be pitched so as to give them some chance to recruit. My brother and I walked across the portage and found it to be three and a half miles in length. Its upper end terminated on the shore of Black Lake where we had hoped to find Indians who would help us across, but in this we were disappointed and, instead of Indians, found old forsaken tepee poles and blackened fireplaces. Just here I am reminded of an Indian tradition which says that it was on these very portages that the Great Spirit first made the black flies. Our experiences would tend to bear out that belief.

On the 7th of July we skirted the shores of Black Lake (first mapped by my brother in 1892) for about a distance of sixteen miles until we reached a hunting trail which, we had been informed by the Indians, led away to the northward. Beyond this point nothing was known of the road or of the country through which it would lead us. We had expected to be guided by that old humbug Moberly, but he having deserted us we were now on our own resources.

On Saturday without guide or map we commenced our journey into the great untravelled wilderness. The work of portaging was soon begun. During the remainder of the day, and indeed until ten o'clock at night, we continued our labour. It was amusing to note the craftiness of the Iroquois, who invariably tried to secure light articles such as biscuits, tents or dunnage bags. With immense loads of comparatively little weight they would stagger off, reminding one of old Atlas carrying the world on his shoulders.

On the 11th Wolverine Lake was discovered. It is only three by six miles but its coastline of forty or fifty miles was large enough. After exploring the uttermost recesses of several deep bays without discovering any trace of the river, it was nightfall when we pitched camp, and obtained shelter from a cold and drizzling rain.

One evening camp was pitched on an island a little distance from shore upon which a lonely grave was discovered. This island camp recalled an incident connected with John, our baker. For some time past his bread had not been giving satisfaction. Some of the party were afraid to eat it on account of the possibility of canoeing accidents which, if occurring, would almost certainly result fatally, for with John's bread in one's stomach there would be no hope of remaining afloat. At first John had confined his baking to the making of grease bannocks, which after being formed in a pan, were removed and cooked on a stick before the fire. So long as he baked in his accustomed way he was fairly successful, but as soon as he undertook the use of baking powder and a reflector or camp oven, he grievously failed. Being anxious to uphold the dignity of his profession he sat up all night endeavouring to improve on his methods but with no success. The next time he prepared to go to work my brother observed him. John opened the flour sack and the top of it was rolled down until it formed a ring over the flour, in which a hollow was then made with the hands. Into this hollow a quart or more of water was poured and into the water the prescribed quantity of baking powder was stirred and allowed to effervesce before being stirred into the flour. The secret of John's failure was thus disclosed. After this we enjoyed better bread.

A week had now passed since leaving the end of the long portage out of Black Lake and during that time we had made only about eighty miles. This was a slow rate of travel that had to be improved upon.

During the evening of the 17th we met some Indians on Selwyn Lake who paddled across to where we were and from some of their sketch maps useful information was obtained. But their attention was chiefly diverted to filling our men with alarming stories of the fearful dangers and disasters which we would encounter should we pursue the route we were following. They said we would meet with impassable canyons and that the country through which it led was inhabited by savage tribes of Eskimos who would undoubtedly eat us. These stories produced a deep impression on the minds of some of our men and might have given rise to serious trouble and even disorganized the whole party. Jim went to my brother with a sad face and unbosomed his trouble. He said if he were a single man he would not feel so badly, but having a family dependent on him he could not run into such destruction as he now learned awaited us. We told our men that the Indians were a set of miserable liars who were only trying to prevent us from going to their hunting grounds; that I had lived with the Eskimos for nearly two years and had found them to be far better people than these Indians who were trying to deceive them. At length we persuaded them to disbelieve their stories.

From Lake Athabasca our course had been constantly upstream, but we had now reached the height of land and from this point to the sea our way was ever with the current. Having launched our little fleet in the lake on the north side of the watershed the new stage of the journey was begun by crossing a large lake which we named Daly Lake. Near the centre of it we were delayed for a day and a half by a gale. So wild was the lake that water spouts were whirled up from its billows and carried along in great vertical columns for considerable distances. Remarkable features of the vicinity were certain eskers composed of clear sand and gravel, sixty or seventy feet in height, trending north-easterly, and quite narrow at the top. They were so level and uniform that they might have been taken for the remains of an embankment of ancient railways.[1]

During the morning of the 22nd the beginning of the Dubawnt River was discovered. It was indeed a great, broad and rapid river, broken up into many shallow channels whose water seemed to have been spilled over the edge of the lake. This was the river we had set out to explore, and with nothing more than conjectures as to where it would lead us, we pushed our canoes into the stream and sped away to the northward.

Many rapids were run but our veteran steersman,

---

[1] Eskers are the "inverted" beds of extinct rivers which once flowed through, or over, the glaciers that covered this portion of the North. When the ice melted, the sand and gravel was deposited on the land below and these sinuous embankments are one of the most startling features of the Barren Grounds.

Pierre, with his skilled judgement and unflinching nerve, was usually able to map out a course and steer it successfully. On one occasion Pierre led the way through the centre of a wild, rocky rapid. We saw that he was making for a chute between two great boulders, where the channel was barely wide enough to allow us to pass. I determined to follow, but our third canoe sought a channel nearer the shore. By keeping straight in the centre of the current, Pierre was shot through the notch in safety, but my steersman, less skilful, allowed our canoe to be caught by an eddy. Like a flash it was hurled end for end but, happily for us, struck the chute stern first instead of sideways and was carried through safely. The third canoe fared worst of the three, for it was dashed upon a great flat rock and broken. Its occupants, by jumping out, managed to hold it until assistance could be given them.

We were now fairly beyond the limit of woods which, for some time past, had been gradually becoming thinner, more scattered and of more stunted growth.

By the evening of July 28th, when we had reached the north end of Barrow Lake, we were becoming very short of food. If game should not be found within a week or ten days, we would have to return, or proceed with the prospect of starvation before us. We had only begun to think seriously on this question when a moving object was seen on a little island in the lake. With field glasses it was made out to be a caribou and no time was lost in manning a canoe and pulling for the island. As we approached, the caribou galloped to the farther side, plunged into the water, and struck out for shore. The rate at which the frightened animal tore straight through the water was really marvellous, and for a time it looked as though we would not be able to overtake it with our light canoe and four paddlers. Every muscle was strained, of deer and man, so that the hunt resolved into a veritable race for life. Unfortunately for the poor animal the course was too long, and before it could reach the shore we had overhauled and shot it.

The following day, passing through Carey Lake, one of our party called attention to movement on the distant shore. It turned out to be not one but a band of caribou. Our canoes were headed to leeward of the band and, drawing near, we found there was not one band but a great many bands, literally covering the country over wide areas. The valleys and hillside for miles appeared to be moving masses of caribou. To estimate their numbers would be impossible. They could only be reckoned in acres or square miles.

After a short consultation, a landing was made near a grove of tamarack. Rifles were examined and a supply of cartridges were provided. I was given fifteen minutes to run around a mile or so behind some rising ground. Meanwhile, the rest of the party scattered in different places and at the given time my brother opened fire. At this first shot the whole band was thrown into confusion and rushed to and fro. Simultaneously with my brother's shot I opened fire from the rear and our men from the sides, two of them being obliged to take refuge on a great boulder to avoid being trampled to death. This band was speedily scattered but not before a woeful slaughter had been made, yielding an abundant supply of fine fresh meat. It was fortunate there was wood at hand with which to make a fire and dry the meat. Having slain as many animals as we required, the men were set to work to prepare dried meat for the rest of the trip.

Several days were spent in drying the eighteen or twenty carcasses which were selected, and while this was going on I roamed the hills and photographed the bands of deer which were everywhere about us. We could walk to and fro through the herds, causing no more alarm than one would by walking through a herd of cattle in a field. The following excerpt from my brother's diary will give a fairly clear idea of the number of deer seen:

"July 30th. Yesterday was the first clear warm day we have had for a long time but today is clear and warm also, with a gentle breeze from the west. We spent the day skinning and cutting the fattest of the bucks we had killed yesterday. Our camp was a hundred yards from the lake. All day the caribou had been around us in vast numbers, many thousands being collected together in single herds. One herd collected on the hill behind the camp and another remained for hours in the bog on the point in front of us. The small fawns were running about everywhere, often within a yard or two of us, uttering their sharp grunts as they stood and looked up at us or as they turned and ran back to the does. About noon a large herd collected on the sides and summits of the hill behind us. We walked quietly amongst them and as we approached within a few yards of the dense herd, it opened to let us in and then formed a circle around us, so that we were able to stand for a couple of hours and watch the deer as they stood in the light breeze or slowly rubbed past each other to keep off the black flies.''[2]

On August 2nd the journey was resumed and during the day a remarkable grove was found on the north shore of the lake. As a whole, the country was now a treeless, rocky wilderness, but here by a little brook grew a clump of white spruce trees, perhaps thirty in all, of which the largest measured eight feet in circumference two feet above the ground. Such a trunk would be considered unusually large in a forest a thousand miles to the south. Here it stood with its fellows far out in the Barren Grounds.

All day and part of the next was spent in finding the exit from the lake. It commenced with a wild rapid and was followed within a distance of twenty miles by seven others, all of which together had a fall of about twenty feet. This took us to a new lake which we named Markham.

---

[2]This appears to have been the largest herd of caribou ever seen by white men. Dr. Tyrrell later estimated that between one hundred and two hundred thousand animals were seen during the time the party halted at Carey Lake. The total of all the caribou still surviving in the entire Canadian Arctic is now hardly larger than the numbers that went to make up this one gigantic herd!

We now noticed a decided change in climate. For the first time since early in the season, snowbanks were seen on the hillside and the weather became decidedly colder. Towards the north of this lake we passed great piles of rafted ice on the shore. Such conditions during the month of August were highly suggestive of the character of the climate which must exist here in the winter.

Towards the north end of Markham Lake we found some old moss-grown tepee poles and fragments of birch bark indicating that, in days gone by, the spot had been visited by Chipewyan Indians, though it was not now known to them except in legends. Probably it was near this grove that Samuel Hearne, our only white predecessor in this part of the Barren Grounds, had crossed the Dubawnt River in company with Indians 120 years before.

On August 5th the canoes successfully ran six rapids for a descent of over a hundred feet. As we were approaching a seventh we found ourselves enveloped in a dense and chilling mist which so obstructed the view that we were unable to proceed. We went ashore at the head of the rapids and discovered, much to our delight, a small patch of stunted black spruce trees. During the day's run we had been soaked by the spray of the rapids and therefore were glad to enjoy the warm and cheerful blaze of a fire.

The following afternoon as my brother was tramping in the interior, he reached the summit of an adjacent hill where a most dreary and chilling scene opened to his vision. To the east and northward, not many miles away, and extending as far as the eye could see, there appeared a vast white plain shrouded in drifting clouds of mist. It was evidently a great lake, still covered in the month of August with a field of ice, and was probably the Dubawnt or Tobaunt Lake known in a legendary way to the Athabascan Indians and sighted by Hearne when on his journey to the Coppermine River. Its rediscovery was now a matter of deepest interest to us. Was it to form an insurmountable obstacle in our path? Judging from appearances, most of the men were of the opinion that it would.

On the 7th of August we broke camp early and, bidding good-bye to the last vestige of growing timber, we continued downriver toward the frozen lake over four more rapids to the broad mouth of the river.

The body of the lake was covered with ice and overhung with mist so that we were unable to paddle out into it, but turned northward in a channel of open water. We struck across to a long point. Here the pack ice was tight in against the shore defying further advance by canoe. Towards the edge of the pack, however, the ice was much broken and honeycombed but it was far too heavy to be tackled by canoes or even stout boats. It was decided therefore to turn into what we supposed was a bay, and get a view of the pack from the shore. We then discovered that the point was a long island and that the supposed bay was a channel through which we might pass unobstructed by the ice.

By this time the wind was blowing strongly and a heavy rain settled in and drove us to camp. During the night the wind increased to a gale, accompanied by torrents of rain which flooded the tents and saturated our clothing. Not a vestige of fuel was to be found in the country. For three days the storm continued. On the fourth it turned to snow and the temperature went down to freezing — rather inhospitable weather for the 10th of August. Next morning we continued on our way through the channel we had entered until eight a.m. when we again found ourselves hemmed in by heavy ice, some of which was ten feet in thickness. To advance was impossible so a landing was selected. Not far from the landing was a high hill so we provided ourselves with field glasses and climbed its summit. As we tramped across country we found the ground frozen and all the little ponds covered by new ice. Such a condition was not the most enlivening, and it was a point of discussion with us whether the season here was spring or autumn. Upon reaching the hill we noticed that to the south and east as far as we could see the ice field extended, but to the north there lay open water, and near the base of the hill was a neck of land across which we might portage into the open water.

This we did but, before nightfall, were again blocked by the pack. Meeting with so much ice at this season made the prospects of further advance northward anything but encouraging, but we resolved if possible to push on and see the end of the great river we had thus far descended.

Although the morning of the 12th broke cold and dreary, and new ice covered the ponds, we discovered that the ice pack had moved offshore leaving a channel of open water. Into this we made our way and once more we paddled lustily. During the day we encountered much ice, solid fields of which extended out from the land, but we were able to get along. Several white wolves were seen on shore and, at some places where landings were made, numerous little ermines were observed.

Until the evening of August 15th we paddled on through varied seas of ice and open water, following the barren western shoreline, in search of the outlet of Dubawnt Lake. We were awakened on the 16th by a howling gale. The tent occupied by my brother and myself was only prevented from being blown away by scrambling out in the darkness and securing it with new ropes and piles of stone. This storm continued with unabated fury for two days, and during this time our only spark of comfort was in the brewing and imbibing of hot chocolate prepared over the spirit lamp. When, on the second day, the rain ceased and the wind fell sufficiently, we heard to the north the roar of heavy rapids. Stimulated by the sound, we struck camp and started out for what we hoped to be the Dubawnt River flowing out of the lake; and after a long pull we were gratified to find our hopes realized.

On the 18th we launched in the clear strong stream of

the Dubawnt and soon found ourselves at the head of the rapids we had heard. At the second rapids, signs of Eskimos were discovered. They consisted of rings of camp stones, an old bow, and numerous broken or partly formed willow ribs of a kayak or canoe.

About six miles from Dubawnt Lake we arrived at the head of a wild rapid where the broad river rushes down to a narrow, rocky gorge not more than fifty yards wide and two and a half miles in length. The river forms one continuous, boiling, tumbling stream of foaming water. When we had run this rapid, camp was pitched and near it were found bones of musk-oxen. Later, on the opposite side of the rapid, two of these strange animals were seen.

Toward evening we sighted, some distance ahead of us, the solitary lodge of an Eskimo. In front of the doorway stood a man gazing toward us and, behind and around, excited women and children were gathered. They were all quickly chased inside the tent and the doorway laced up securely. But the man remained outside, watching us intently. Our canoes were no doubt taken to be those of the *Itkilit* (the Indians) from the south — their hereditary enemies — so they expected nothing good from our coming.

Our own men, recalling the stories of the "savage Eskimos who would undoubtedly eat them," were scarcely less fearful than the solitary native who, as we drew near, was observed through our glasses to be nervous and trembling. As soon as we had approached within calling distance, I stood up and shouted "Chimo! Chimo! Chimo!" (Hello, Hello). Before my words were finished the doorway of the tent was torn open and with great rejoicing and excited gestures all the inmates scrambled out to meet us at the shore as we landed.

The male Eskimo was a tall, well-built, stalwart man with a shrewd, intelligent face. With him were his two wives and six children. The tent was a large, clean-looking one made of deerskin parchment supported by stout spruce poles.

We were cordially invited inside and seats of deerskin were offered by the hostess, and venison placed before us, while we in return handed around presents of beads, tobacco, matches and such things. About us were to be seen evidence of communication with traders, such as a large tin kettle, two old guns, and a pair of moleskin trousers.

Upon inquiry I was told they had received these things in trade from other Eskimos. The family were accustomed to meet with Eskimos from Hudson Bay, who trade at Fort Churchill, and for this reason the Dubawnt must in all probability flow into the Bay. About camp there appeared to be an abundance of venison for the present support of the family, but the hunt for musk-oxen was what had brought this venturesome hunter far up the river in advance of his tribe.

After a pleasant but brief visit, during which time we received some valuable information about the route, we parted. As we did so, Louis, my Iroquois steersman, with an expression of pleasant disappointment, exclaimed, "They are not savage, but real decent people."

These people had told us that from there to the sea [Hudson Bay] was about twenty days' journey and though we thought we could likely make it in half that time, we were impressed and spurred on by the knowledge of the fact that we were now far into the interior of the country and, at the least, eight hundred miles by our road from the nearest Hudson's Bay Company post, Fort Churchill. As we glided downriver, several white wolves were seen upon the shore gnawing at the carcass of a deer. By this time — the 22nd of August — the skins as well as the carcasses of the deer were at their best, and we saved the centres of several hides and dried them for use as sleeping mats, while all of the fine fat meat secured was applied to the replenishing of our severely taxed larder.

After canoeing around almost the entire circumference of Wharton Lake we found the outlet, much obscured by a labyrinth of islands. Nearby was an Eskimo cache consisting of a komitik (sled), snow shovels, musk-ox horns, etc., and here we pitched our camp. As no moss or fuel could be found in the vicinity, some of the men considered they had "struck a bonanaza" in finding the komitik and carried it to camp intending to use it to boil the kettle. A slat or two had already been knocked off when, happily, I arrived in time to prevent its destruction and preserve our good name with the natives.

From here we continued downstream into Marjorie Lake and, passing out of the north-western extremity, we gained the river. It began with a rough rapid, in running which my canoe struck a rock and was badly injured and nearly filled with water. After a delay of some hours we were again in the stream, being borne away to the *westward*, the direction opposite to that which we were now anxious to follow. The river here was a noble stream, deep and swift, with a well-defined channel and high banks of rock or sand. During the whole of the 25th our course continued to the westerly and north-westerly and because of this we began to feel very anxious. We had now passed the latitude of Baker Lake whither, according to information obtained from the Eskimos, we were expecting the river to take us. Instead of drawing nearer to it we were heading away towards the Arctic Ocean.

Just at dusk, to our surprise and pleasure we suddenly came upon an abundance of driftwood — not little sticks of willows, but the trunks of trees six or eight inches in diameter. No growing trees were to be seen in the district, nor had we seen any during the previous three or four hundred miles. At first the occurrence of this wood seemed unaccountable but the theory was suggested that we must be close to the confluence of some other river flowing through some wooded country. This theory was borne out by the discovery, within a short distance, of a river as large as the Dubawnt, flowing in from the westward and with it mingling its dark-coloured waters. [This was the Thelon River.]

According to information obtained from an Eskimo at a later date, some distance up this river [to the west] there were great numbers of his people engaged in the building of kayaks. We would have been pleased to visit them, but deeming it unwise at this late season to go out of our way, we pulled on with the stream which was now double its former strength and flowing again to the northward. That night, camp was pitched on an island and we had a great blazing, roaring fire of driftwood. We hoped that for some time to come the supply of fuel might continue, for of late we had been entirely without fire. The following morning the river still flowed toward the Arctic, but at latitude 64° 41′ N. it suddenly swerved around to the east and then to the south-east and bore us down to the western extremity of a magnificent body of water which has since been named Aberdeen Lake. It was a lovely calm evening when the track of our canoes first rippled the waters of this lake, and as we landed on a bluff point on the north shore and from it gazed to the eastward over the solitary but beautiful scene, a feeling of awe crept over us. We were undoubtedly the first white men who had ever viewed it, and in the knowledge of this fact there was inspiration.

During the next few days we had good weather — something unusual in the Barren Grounds, and this enabled us to explore the large lake without delay. We found it to be about fifty miles long, and at one point of landing the remains of an old Eskimo camp with parts of a human skeleton were found.

Towards the east end other remarkable traces of Eskimos were seen in the shape of stone pillars, well and uniformly built, but for what purpose I confess I cannot tell.[3]

Borne down by the river, we had launched on the bosom of Aberdeen Lake without effort, but not so easy a

---

[3]These pillars formed a stone "fence" which acted to deflect the migrating caribou towards selected crossing points on rivers and lakes where they could be ambushed by the inland Eskimos.

matter was it to find our way out. But by the morning of the 29th, enshrouded in a dense fog, we re-entered the river and later in the day entered the west end of Schultz Lake. The next day the old story of looking for the ''hole'' out of the lake was repeated. But by climbing a hill an outlet was discovered four or five miles distant on the opposite side. About seven miles down stream a very rocky rapid was discovered and the contents of the canoes being all safely landed below the rapids, they themselves were run by the Iroquois. Had it not been for our good steersman, Pierre, many and many a rapid through which our little craft were guided in safety would have cost us much laborious portaging. If a rapid could be run at all in safety, Pierre had the skill and nerve to do it.

About twelve miles below Schultz Lake, tents were pitched and within them our soaked and shivering party sought comfort. Little was to be found, however, for the wind continued to increase in violence, driving rain through our shelters, saturating blankets and making us generally miserable. It was impossible to make a fire, supposing moss or other fuel could have been found. A little dried venison comprised our menu. As those who have used it well know, this description of meat is not the most palatable. It is good, strong, portable food, but may better be compared to sole leather than any article of diet.

Late in the forenoon of the 1st of September, an Eskimo and his kayak was sighted ahead and, much to our amusement, he was soon seen much *farther* ahead. The poor fellow, seeing our fleet of canoes, evidently thought his safest move was to get out of the way, and this he did, leaving us farther behind at every stroke.

He did not slacken pace until he reached an Eskimo encampment of several tents. Here he landed and informed the others of our approach, and all eyes keenly watched us. As we drew near, they observed by our canoes and appearance that we were not Indians and they responded to our greeting with cheers and wild gesticulations and, as we landed, we were received with hand shakings and great rejoicings. None showed the least sign of hostility. Indeed the ladies exhibited an embarrassing amount of cordiality, so much so that it was thought wise to make our visit as brief as possible. Having "greeted" all the brethren, I proceeded to obtain what information I could from them regarding our route to the sea, and was much pleased to learn that we were close to the mouth of the river.

There was now no doubt as to the route. We were to reach Hudson Bay through Chesterfield Inlet, which was not too far distant, and at this certain knowledge we felt much encouraged. Several skins were obtained from the natives and also some skin clothing. One very old man asked to be given a passage down the river a few miles to another native village.

As we proceeded we found the current both strong and swift, and quite rough in places, but the Eskimos in their kayaks shot ahead from time to time and showed us the best channels. Sometimes they fell behind for the sake of having the opportunity of showing how quickly they could re-pass us. By the time we had descended eight or ten miles farther, our native escorts commenced hallooing and acting in a most hilarious manner. We wondered what possessed them, but the cause was soon disclosed as we switched around a bend in the river and found ourselves close upon a large Eskimo village. On going ashore, the first thing which attracted by attention was a small tent constructed of beautiful musk-ox robes. I felt inclined to doubt my own eyes, for it seemed such a strange waste of luxury. I entered this princely dwelling and finding the owners — three young brothers — I began negotiations for its purchase. The value asked was moderate; the robes were secured and made into a snug bale. The owner of another batch of musk-ox skins appeared and I offered to buy the four best ones. After a little discussion the crafty hunter came to the conclusion that he wanted a small kettle and some gun caps (for he had an old gun) and so offered me one of the robes for these articles. After some "serious" consideration, I concluded to let him have the kettle and some caps for the skin. It was then my turn to make an offer. I produced a telescope, a jack-knife and an old shirt, and offered them for the three remaining robes. The temptation proved too great; the skins were handed over and accepted with great delight.

Although it was now time to camp, and many pressing invitations were extended, it was thought wisest for the moral well-being of our party not to do so. Before we left the village one old Eskimo surprised us by making a remark in English. I said to him, "Oh, you understand English?" whereupon he made the amusing reply, "No, he no understand English." I tried then to find out where he had learned to speak our language but the only reply I could get from him was that he had always been able to speak it. It may be that he had accompanied Sir George Back, Dr. John Richardson or John Rae on one of their Franklin search expeditions.

As we had been informed by the natives, we soon found ourselves at the mouth of the Great River and as we passed out into the broad, shallow delta [of Baker Lake] and gazed over the deep blue, limitless waters beyond, the gratifying fact forced itself upon us that we had accomplished what we had started out to do — viz, to explore a route through the heart of the Barren Grounds where no other white man, if indeed Indian or Eskimo, had ever passed. We were still, of course, a long way from being out of the Barren-Grounds country, but once on the waters of Baker Lake the remainder of the road was to some extent known to us.[4]

Since leaving the shores of Black Lake we had travelled a distance of just 810 miles through unknown country. We had occupied more time in doing so than we had expected. We still had 750 miles to go to Churchill before

[4]Baker Lake had been explored by Capt. Christopher in 1762.

the close of navigation. In order to stimulate the men to greater exertion, it was thought best to explain our position to them, for up to this time they had little idea as to where they were, whether in the vicinity of the North Pole or within a few days of civilization. The effect produced by this information was to make them resolve to make longer days and put forth greater exertion.

The wind being fair, our canoes were loaded and with many good-byes to the natives we started out to the eastward. But the wind soon grew too strong and caused such a high sea to run that we were forced to seek shelter after only fourteen miles. The high wind continued all night and during the following day, accompanied by snow and sleet. The fresh-water ponds were now frozen over. Such a condition of climate, together with our small and rapidly diminishing stock of provisions, made us chafe at the delay. On the morning of the 5th we were able to launch again and during the day made a good run of about forty miles.

During the afternoon of the 6th the northerly of the channels leading out of Baker Lake was reached. When we had advanced a distance of about two miles, a stiff current — almost approaching a rapid — was met but instead of moving with us as would naturally be expected, it was flowing to the westward. At first sight it caused doubts as to whether we were on the right road. The canoemen were all persuaded that we were ascending some big river, and would have turned back at once; but concluding that we had already reached tide water, though sooner than expected, we pulled on and before long we witnessed a seemingly strange phenomenon of a river changing its direction of flow. One night was spent in this rocky cut, and the following day, being fair and bright, saw us on the waters of Chesterfield Inlet. On the 10th of September, extremely rough water forced us into a sheltered cove. While the cooks were preparing the midday meal, my brother and I set out for the summit of an island a mile away. While taking sights from its crest there appeared from behind it what seemed a phantom ship. For a moment I gazed in amazement, but then realizing that the appearance was a real one, I called my brother's attention to it. The object was clearly made out to be a two-masted sailboat heading to the westward. By whom could it be manned? We could not imagine, but there it was with two square sails set to the wind and tearing up the inlet. By the aid of field glasses we could make out many moving figures, but as to whether they were whalers, Hudson's Bay Company's traders from Churchill, or who else, we could not conceive. If, however, they were to be more to us than a vision it was necessary to bestir ourselves, for they were rapidly passing. From my pocket I drew an immense red handkerchief and waved it most energetically, while my brother discharged several shots from his revolver. We soon saw from the boat's movements that we were observed, but instead of coming in towards us they only bore away more to the southward. Still I vigorously waved the red handkerchief, and finally, much to our delight, the sails flapped loosely in the wind, then in a moment were refilled by the strong breeze and the boat swept in toward us.

When they had approached sufficiently near we could see that there were Eskimos on board, and a moment later their anchor was cast out, and several of them, making a sort of raft out of three kayaks they had in tow, paddled in to the rocky shore where we stood. In vain did we look for the face of a white man. They informed us they were moving up into the interior from the coast to spend the winter, and so it was not surprising that nothing we could offer would induce them to consider the question of taking us down to Churchill or of selling their boat to us. We offered what to them would have been fabulous wealth, but to no purpose. There they were with all their belongings on their way to the westward, and westward they were determined to go.

Though we were not able to purchase or charter the

boat from the natives, we obtained much valuable information and a sketch-map of the coast of the Bay from the
mouth of the Inlet down to Fort Churchill.

Next morning we were up early. The wind had fallen
somewhat and the canoes were soon launched. We managed to travel until after eleven o'clock, when, because of
the light wind and rough water, we were again obliged to
make for the shore, and in order to do so had to pull through
a heavy surf breaking over the low sandy beach. During
the afternoon at this point observations for longitude were
obtained and close by upon a prominent hill a large cairn
of rocks was erected to mark the spot for the benefit of
future explorers.

The two following days were marked by rough
weather and little progress, but finally we reached the
mouth of the great Inlet through which for several days we
had been paddling.

For having completed another stage of the journey we
were exceedingly glad, but coupled with this fact there was
another, viz, that before us was a 500-mile voyage to be
made in open canoes down an exposed sea coast. Here we
would be surrounded by entirely new conditions and confronted with new difficulties.

Starting southward down the coast of Hudson Bay on the
13th of September, with the weather beautifully calm, we
made a capital run past a rocky coast, skirted by a succession of shoals and reefs, and at night camped upon the
shore about twelve miles north of Marble Island, whose
snow-white hills of quartzite could be distinctly seen on
the horizon.

Marble Island—so called because of the resemblance
its rounded glaciated rocky hills bear to white marble—
is well known as a wintering station for New England
whalers.

We had been informed by the Eskimos that there were
no whalers now at the island. Near camp, on the shore,

we found part of the skeleton of an immense whale, but unfortunately not the part that is of commercial value. This doubtless had been carried away by the Eskimos or by some whaling crew.

During the following day the weather continued fair and feeling that nature was favouring us we made good use of our time.

Though we saw little game, we still had some dried meat left, and at this rate of travel two weeks would take us to Churchill. By carefully rationing ourselves we had meat enough to last for five or six days, and the balance of the time could, if necessary, be spent without provisions.

On the night of the 15th, however, being camped upon a little sand island in the mouth of Corbet's Inlet, our hopes were blighted by the approach of a gale, and all the next day we lay imprisoned upon the sand-bar without any fresh water to drink. Toward evening the wind was accompanied by a chilling rain, which continued all night and the greater part of the next morning. On the following afternoon the wind suddenly fell, and though a heavy sea continued to roll in from the east, the waves ceased to break.

Fearing to lose one hour when it was possible to travel, we launched our canoes upon the heaving bosom of the deep and started across the mouth of the inlet on an eight-mile traverse. As we passed out beyond the shelter of the island, we found the seas running fearfully high but so long as they did not break upon us we had little to fear, and this was not likely to occur unless the wind rose. But when we were in the middle of the inlet this is just what happened. The wind rose from the opposite quarter and increased in force until our situation was perilous. Every effort was made to guide the canoes so as to brook least danger, but in spite of all we could do the seas dashed in upon us and it looked as if we would never reach shore. My brother and I laid down our paddles and with tin kettles vigorously began bailing out the water. Many times the tumbling waves seemed as if they would surely roll over us, but our light cedar canoes, though sometimes half-filled with water, were borne up on the crest of the waves. At length we neared a rocky shore towards which for several hours we had been struggling fiercely but to our dismay found it skirted by a long line of rocks and shoals upon which the wild sea was breaking. What were we to do? One rock could be seen standing up in advance of the others, and behind this we managed with a supreme effort to guide the canoes. Then, in shallow water, with the force of the seas broken, we all sprang out and with great exertion succeeded in landing the boats in safety.

The storm continued for two days longer and as our provisions were now about exhausted, attention was chiefly devoted to hunting, but all that could be found was a small duck and two gulls. On the morning of Sept 20th, camp was called at four o'clock and without breakfast, our journey resumed. Later in the day each man had a small piece of dried meat, insufficient to satisfy his appetite; but hungry though we were the motto plainly written on every man's face was, "Speed the paddle." Thus we pressed on for two days until we were again storm-bound by a heavy gale with snow which lasted four days.

During this time we suffered considerably from the violence of the storm as well as want of food. When it had abated a little, which was not until the morning of the 25th, two of the men, Pierre and Louis, were sent out with shotguns to hunt while with rifles my brother and I set out for an all-day tramp into the interior. Shortly after we left camp a hare jumped out from amongst the rocks and was perforated by a slug from my Marlin. By three o'clock, after a long and laborious march, we had secured nothing in addition except a solitary ptarmigan. We made a fire, roasted and ate the ptarmigan, and then started back to camp. In some places the fresh snow was deep and soft, adding greatly to the fatigue of our march. We had not proceeded far before we met with encouragement in the discovery of deer tracks. They were a day or so old, for they were frozen, but they led away nearly in the direction of camp so we eagerly followed them and from every hilltop keenly scanned the country.

Darkness came on while we were several miles from camp and we found ourselves groping through a field of water-worn boulders. We had to feel our way with hands and feet between and over the rocks. We reached camp thoroughly used up, but were not obliged to go to bed hungry for Pierre and Louis had been more successful than us and had secured several ptarmigan and rabbits.

The next day, again storm-bound by a gale, the whole party hunted for food. We were not altogether unsuccessful, assembling in the evening with five marmots [small ground squirrels]. The following morning, though a strong breeze was blowing, we determined to make a start, for to remain where we were meant that we must soon starve to death. We were already much reduced and weakened from the effects of cold and hunger, and the conditions of the weather had been most disheartening. Churchill was still nearly three hundred miles distant. We had not one bite of food. The country was covered with snow and the weather piercingly cold. No fuel was to be had and, worst of all, the weather was such the greater part of the time that we were unable to travel.

About eight miles along the coast a band of deer was seen upon the shore. Our course was quickly altered and a landing effected, though with great difficulty as the tide was falling and the water rapidly receding [the waters of the west side of Hudson Bay are extremely shallow and the tidal flats extend for many miles out to sea at low tide]. The men were left to keep the canoes afloat while my brother and I went in pursuit of the deer which were at this time much more difficult to hunt than earlier in the season. At first the deer trotted about in confusion but, soon locating their enemies, fled straight away across the plains. For several hours we followed, vainly seeking to get nearer them. Being unsuccessful we retraced our weary steps to the shore where we arrived faint and exhausted. We found the men had been unable to keep the canoes afloat because of the ebbing tide. They were now high and dry and the water of the bay was barely visible in the distance — such was the extremely low and flat character of the coast.

As it was impossible to launch until the return of the tide, Pierre and Louis were given our rifles and set off to try their fortunes. Anxious hours of waiting followed. By evening Pierre and Louis were seen returning in the distance, but as none of them appeared to be bringing any game, I confess my heart grew sick. As they came nearer, however, Louis held up the claw of a polar bear saying, "I got him!" We learned with joy, sure enough, he had killed a polar bear.

The encounter had taken place six miles inland and Louis was alone at the time, his brother having gone off on another track. The meeting was a mutual surprise, for the bear, lying on the snow near the ice, being very white himself, was unobserved until the hunter's approaching footsteps aroused him. There was then not fifty yards between them and no time for consideration. The bear made straight for Louis who met his charge with a slug and brought him to his knees. He was up in an instant and following the Indian, who had taken to the ice, thinking that in the conflict he would have an advantage there. But in this he found he was mistaken. The bear was quickly overtaking him so he turned and with a second shot again knocked the animal down. As Louis made for the shore the bear regained his feet and with blood streaming from his wounds made one more desperate charge. He was now within a few feet of Louis. The hunter turned quickly and with one well-aimed shot laid his savage pursuer dead at his feet.

This was a most fortunate shot for our whole party as well as for the Indian. We all gladly followed him to the scene of the combat. On a hill nearby some dry moss was discovered and, even before the skinning had been completed, some of the flesh was toasted and greedily devoured. The effect produced upon the spirits of our party was marked. Though the flesh of the polar bear is famed for its rankness we would not have exchanged it for its weight in silver.

The carcass was extremely poor, the only food in the stomach being the droppings of reindeer. At the first meeting, therefore, Louis must have been considered a very desirable prize by the bear. Fortunately for us, the Indian proved to be the fittest survivor. No part of the carcass was wasted but every scrap, amounting to between three and four hundred pounds, was placed in bags and carried to the canoes which we reached with much difficulty long after dark.

We now hoped to proceed rapidly towards Churchill but, alas for our hopes, the gale which had arisen increased in fury until it became a terrific storm, accompanied by sleet and snow, and this continued for five long days. One night the tent occupied by my brother and I was ripped apart by the force of the gale and with difficulty kept from being carried away. So piercingly cold was the wind that without shelter we must soon have perished. We were already numb with cold, but in the midst of snow and darkness I managed to find in my bag a sail needle and having lowered the tent to the ground while my brother held it, I stitched up the rip.

Besides the discomfort occasioned by the storm, I suffered a serious poisoning. Our cook, thinking to give my brother and myself a treat, provided a dish of fried bear liver. Perhaps because of its rank flavour my brother took sparingly and so partially escaped, but I ate of it freely and at once became fearfully ill. For a day I lay in the tent retching and straining, though throwing off nothing but froth, till I thought I should have died. Towards evening, finding out I would have to take something or give up the ghost, I took a little brandy and soon began to recover. I have since learned that polar bear liver is considered to be poisonous, both by the Eskimos and by the North Sea whalers.

After the five days' storm, which lasted until October 4th, the whole country was buried in snow and the possibility of finding even moss for fuel was excluded. Winter had overtaken us. Ice was forming along the shore of the bay and it was evident that within a very few days travel by canoe must end.

After a long portage out to meet the tide, we launched the canoes in light snow; but in spite of our most vigorous exertions we were only able to make ten miles, and that through a chilling spray which froze upon and encased canoes and men in an armour of ice. We had great difficulty in getting ashore at night, having again to portage over the low-tide boulder flats. The following day the waters of the bay were out of sight and it was not until about noon that we were able to float the canoes. We were then obstructed by the new ice and a head wind so we were not able to make more than a mile or two before being forced to struggle back to shore. We had now been more than three weeks on the coast and were still at least 250 miles from our haven.

Some different mode of travel had to be adopted or we would never get in. The shore ice was forming rapidly and might now block up at any moment. We only had enough bear meat for another day or two and game had all left the country. My brother and I talked the matter over during the night and the plan suggested itself of abandoning everything but rifles and blankets and starting down the shore on foot. But then, how could the numerous large rivers, which were still open, be crossed? The only other feasible plan was to abandon dunnage, instruments, geological collections, etc. — everything except notebooks and essentials — and with these start out in only two light canoes, and with this increased force, travel for our lives.

This plan was decided on and in the morning the men cached our stuff. Then with heavy hearts we turned toward the shore. After launching the two canoes it was with great danger we were able to force our way through the broken shore ice to the open water beyond. Having once gotten clear we were able to make good progress even at great risk of being smashed upon some of the many rocks. We paddled far into the night; but at a late hour, being sheathed in ice, we landed, and without supper lay down to sleep upon the snow.

Eight more dreary days passed, six of which were spent battling the elements, and two lying storm-bound in our tents. During this interval our party suffered much from cold and lack of food, and to make matters worse, dysentery attacked us and it appeared as if one of our men would die.

The ice had been all the while forming, rendering it more difficult to launch or get ashore. Our frail canoes were badly battered and often were broken through by the ice. Still, with hollow cheeks and in feeble strength, we struggled on, until on October 14th the ice became so heavy, and extended so far out to sea, that in order to clear it we had to go quite out of sight of land.

That evening we began to look for some opportunity of going ashore but nothing could be seen before us but a vast field of ice, with occasional protruding boulders. We pushed on, hoping to find some point or channel but the appearance of things did not change. We stood up in the canoes or climbed upon boulders, hoping to get a glimpse of the land. Soon night began to fall and our canoes were leaking badly and the weather was bitterly cold. Failing to reach shore we resolved to wait for high tide, hoping we might do it better then. The tide came and went and we were no more able to penetrate the ice or gain the shore than before. It had become intensely dark and we were in danger of being smashed on ice or rocks. We were utterly helpless and could do nothing but remain where we were or go where the tide chose to carry us.

The hours of that night were the longest I have ever

experienced and the odds seemed to be against our surviving until morning. My brother was badly frozen, having
been obliged to sit or lie in icy water all night. Poor little
Michel had both his feet frozen and the rest of us were
badly used up. We could not hold out much longer; we
must gain the shore or perish. At high tide the ice loosened
somewhat and by great exertion we manged to haul out
our little craft. We had been in them just thirty hours
battling with ice, chilling winter blasts, our clothing
saturated and frozen, our bodies faint and numb with
starvation.

My brother was in a perishing condition. I wrapped
him up as warmly as I could and administered half a bottle
of Jamaica ginger, the last of our stock. We then set about
hauling the canoes over the ice to shore which we soon
reached and we were fortunate in finding some driftwood.
The three Western half-breeds were still fairly strong, but
the remaining five of us were very weak. We knew now
that we could be no great distance from Churchill, for we
had again reached wooded country. This was a consoling
fact. As for launching our canoes again, that was entirely
out of the question. If we were to reach Churchill at all, it
must be by land.

A plan was proposed for a party to go to the Fort and
bring back a relief party, and two of the Western men, Jim
and John, volunteered. On the morning of the 16th these
two men set out on their journey while those of us remaining proceeded to move our tents back from the shore to
the nearest woods where we might make ourselves more
comfortable. Clothing and blankets were now dried and,
with some ptarmigan which we shot in the grove, we were
soon comparatively comfortable, with the exception perhaps of poor Michel who suffered much from frozen feet.

On the morning of the 17th, I undertook to go hunting
for ptarmigan, which were plentiful in the woods. But since
we only had a dozen or two cartridges the opportunity for
living on feathered game was limited to a short period.

Before I had walked a hundred yards I was forced to realize how weak I had become and after making a circuit of half a mile and shooting only two or three birds, I was scarcely able to crawl back to the tent. François took the shotgun then and went out, returning in the evening with a fine bag of game.

About one o'clock we were suddenly startled by the exclamation "Hello, Jim!" The eagerness with which we scrambled over dishes to the tent door can be imagined and on looking out, sure enough, there was Jim returning. Was he alone? No, thank the Lord! Behind him a moment later emerged from the woods a number of men followed by teams of dogs and sleds. They had travelled the thirty miles of snowy plains which separated us from Churchill.

Most men who had done what the Tyrrells had would have been content, and justifiably so, to rest on their laurels, forget the hardships they had suffered, and regain their strength in the comparative luxury of Fort Churchill until summer brought a ship to take them home. Not so with the Tyrrells and their Iroquois and Métis companions. They decided to go straight off home. There was only one way to get there, and that was to walk.

It was a longish walk — almost a thousand miles on snowshoes to the south and west. Leaving Churchill on November 6, the party reached Selkirk at the south end of Lake Winnipeg on January 1, 1894. All in all they had travelled close to 3,500 miles by canoe and on foot since leaving the end of steel the previous spring.

The achievements of the party were spectacular. Not only did they make a tremendous journey, without loss, but they brought back with them the first really accurate and detailed description of the interior of the Barren Grounds. Joseph's geological and glacialogical survey of the route remained the standard by which studies of the arctic plains were measured well into the 1940's. These accomplishments ought to have satisfied him, but they only whetted his appetite. No sooner had he returned to Ontario than he began preparing for a second journey in order to find out what lay between the Dubawnt River system and Hudson Bay.

In early June of 1894 he set out to discover an entirely new route northward through the Barrens, beginning from Reindeer Lake in what is now northern Manitoba. To reach his starting point he had first to paddle north from Selkirk to the Saskatchewan, into the Churchill River, up Reindeer River, and across Reindeer Lake to the remote trading post of Fort DuBrochet, a distance of over eight hundred miles. His party consisted of three Métis (of whom John Flett was one) and David Crane, a Cree Indian. He was accompanied by R. Munro Ferguson, an aide-de-camp to the Governor General, who was anxious to see what Canada was really like. He seems to have seen enough to strike him dumb, for this time Joseph Tyrrell had no Boswell. The story of this epic journey was never written, except in the form of official reports.

At Reindeer Lake Tyrrell hired two Chipewyans to guide him by the ancient water routes to the north. The Indians took him to the headwaters of the Kazan River, at Ennadai Lake, and then, their duty done, returned south. Tyrrell and his men continued on downstream meeting, to their great surprise, large numbers of Eskimos of a previously unknown culture—the Caribou Eskimos—who had never before been visited by white men and whose very existence was unsuspected. Continuing north through the great Yathkyed Lake of Hearne, Tyrrell decided that there was insufficient time to allow him to follow the Kazan to its mouth, and so with the aid of the Caribou Eskimos, he portaged east into the Ferguson River. Running down this then-unknown river he reached Hudson Bay on September 16, at the same point where he had camped in deep snow on September 25 of the previous year.

Once again Tyrrell had to endure the torment of canoe travel on the shores of what is, to all intents and purposes, an open ocean — and in winter weather. But this time the party got through with their canoes, reaching Churchill on October 1. To Tyrrell's disgust the inland rivers and lakes were not sufficiently well frozen to allow him to walk south again and he had to sit impatiently at Churchill for six weeks before he could stretch his long legs and set off to snowshoe the thousand miles to the railway.

Although James Tyrrell missed the Kazan trip, he was not through with the Barren Grounds. In 1900 he accepted a commission from the government to explore a route from Great Slave Lake to Baker Lake, and this he did, making the first discovery and survey of the main headwaters of the Thelon River. This lateral traverse of the Barrens was at least the equal of the Kazan voyage. It genesis was spectacularly imaginative, since James's primary task was to see if it was feasible to build a railroad from Baker Lake to Great Slave Lake — a railroad which, presumably, was to serve the caribou, the Indians and the Eskimos.

Between them the Tyrrell brothers contributed more to our knowledge of the arctic plains than any other men, before or after their time. It was fitting that this should be so, for, unlike most explorers of the Canadian North, the Tyrrells were citizens of that young country of which the Barren Grounds formed such an immense portion.

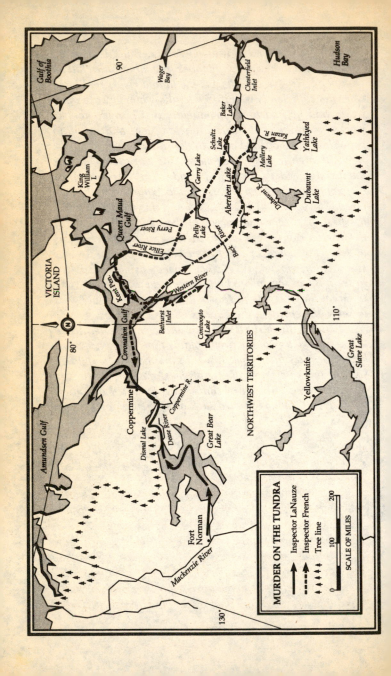

MURDER ON THE TUNDRA

→ Inspector LaNauze
⇢ Inspector French
⟶⟶ Tree line

SCALE OF MILES
0   100   200

Hudson Bay

Gulf of Boothia

Wager Bay

Chesterfield Inlet

Baker Lake

Schultz Lake

Kazan R.

Yathkyed Lake

Mallery Lake

Garry Lake

Aberdeen Lake

Dubawnt R.

Dubawnt Lake

King William I.

Queen Maud Gulf

Perry River

Pelly Lake

Back River

Ellice River

Kent Pen.

Western River

Coronation Gulf

Bathurst Inlet

Contwoyto Lake

Victoria Island

N

90°

80°

110°

130°

NORTHWEST TERRITORIES

Amundsen Gulf

Coppermine

Coppermine R.

Dismal Lake

Dease River

Great Bear Lake

Yellowknife

Great Slave Lake

Fort Norman

Mackenzie River

VII

Murder on the Tundra

THE ROYAL NORTH WEST MOUNTED POLICE PATROL TO COPPERMINE AND BATHURST INLET, 1916-18

The explorations of the Tyrrell brothers did more than open new ways into the tundra world — they caught the imaginations of many diverse men whose natures impelled them to seek out the lonely places, the wild and silent places. James Tyrrell's book was widely read and, though it was hardly a tourist brochure, it attracted a considerable influx of strangers into the tundra.

In 1899 a clipped and briskly military English gentleman named David Hanbury arrived on the scene, pockets well lined with cash, and with a driving urge to see as much of the tundra as he could. He saw a lot. In two years of travelling, mainly with Eskimo companions, he crossed the Barren Grounds via the Thelon route both ways and then, for variety, pioneered a route north-west from Baker Lake to Lake Pelly on Back River, then north to Queen

Maud Gulf, then west along the arctic coast to the Coppermine, and so to Great Bear Lake. This done he disappeared as suddenly as he had appeared.

Hanbury was one of the true wanderers, but other and more prosaic men were also heading north—some of them under orders. In 1904 the Royal North West Mounted Police made a patrol to Baker Lake, taking a first cautious sniff at the edges of what was to become an immense new addition to their bailiwick. Again, in 1908, Inspector Pelletier patrolled some distance up the Thelon; but since there were no people in the inland plains except the Eskimos, and therefore no crime, the police saw little need for further patrols. Things were to change with a vengeance during the next few years.

It was at this time that the Barrens saw one of their most illustrious visitors in the person of the famed Canadian naturalist and author, Ernest Thompson Seton. He entered the Barrens briefly in the western region, and his ecstatic book The Arctic Prairies gave the Barren Grounds a romantic cast they had not known before.

Beginning in 1910 a perfect spate of invaders struck the north-western corner of the arctic plains. A young man named Vilhjalmur Stefansson wintered close to the Coppermine, at the beginning of what was to be a meteoric career as an arctic explorer. In 1911 the western bays of Great Bear Lake, which now formed a main port of entry into the Barrens, became positively crowded. A British big-game hunter improbably named Cosmo Melvill arrived there, accompanied by a lean, blue-eyed English mystic, John Hornby, a man who was to epitomize the breed of Barren-Ground wanderers. A handful of white trappers and a free trader also showed up. Two gently educated Canadian brothers named Douglas appeared. Cabins sprang up until they almost formed a settlement of self-exiled devotees of the tundra plains. The early arrivals were shortly joined by two Belgian oblate missionaries, Fathers Rouvière and LeRoux, men with the true martyr *complex, who had decided it was their duty to die, if need be, in order to save the souls of the Copper Eskimos.*

These were all strange men, most of them fanatical individualists, and the tensions that built up among them were fierce and pervasive. It was perhaps inevitable that tragedy would be the outcome; yet when it struck it took a form no one could have anticipated.

In September of 1913 Fathers Rouvière and LeRoux set out from an advanced cabin they had built far out on the Barrens to the east of Great Bear Lake, intent on travelling to the mouth of the Coppermine to meet the Eskimos on their own ground. They vanished into silence. When almost two years had passed with nothing heard from them, their superiors asked the police to investigate, and in July of 1915 Inspector Denny LaNauze was dispatched to solve the mystery. He began his patrol from Fort Norman on the Mackenzie River.

REPORT OF INSPECTOR LaNAUZE ROYAL NORTH WEST MOUNTED POLICE

I left Fort Norman on July 23rd with a York boat for Great Bear Lake in search of the missing priests, Reverend Fathers Rouvière and LeRoux. Our route was up the Bear River and then across Great Bear Lake to the north-eastern extremity where I proposed to establish winter quarters. I had already sent the bulk of our supplies on ahead by scow, and nine Indians, who were to track the scow as far as Great Bear Lake.

My party consists of Constable Withers, Constable Wight, Special Constable Eskimo Ilavinik, with his wife Mamayuk and his daughter Nagosak, Special Constable D'Arcy Arden and myself.

Our York boat was fairly heavily loaded as we had all our personal baggage and some freight, and two canoes aboard. Our dogs followed along the shore. We rowed the half-mile down the Mackenzie to the mouth of the Bear River where we landed, got our track lines ready, and started up the river. The going at first was fine but we soon got into shoal water and the trackers and crew had to take to the water. We camped at six-thirty p.m. having made only seven miles. The next day we could make only ten miles and all hands were waist deep in the cold waters, and farther up we ran into mud slides which gave the trackers a mud bath for variety.

On the 26th we were obliged to unload the York boat and take all our stuff up to the head of the rapids by canoe, a distance of about ten miles. Arden and an Indian, Ilavinik and myself took two loads through that evening. It was cold and pouring rain and we were in the ice water till ten p.m. Two days later we pulled the York boat through the rapids after a hard struggle.

The next day we met an old white trapper named Stone coming downstream. He told us the ice only left Great Bear Lake on July 17th and he had been held up *sixty-three days* with an east wind. The river got worse as we proceeded, and on August 1st, we took four hours to get one mile. The channel was twisting all over the river, the edges were too shallow for the boat, and we were obliged to cross and re-cross, poling along the edges of the swift channel. We reached the entrance of the river at one a.m. of August 4th.

Our own York boat could not hold all our freight with all dogs, sleighs and ourselves, so I was confronted with the proposition of trying to make two trips across Great Bear Lake with our boat. Fortunately, two white trappers named Sloan and Harrison had preceded us to the lake with a small home-made schooner, the *Wild Duck*. I offered them the freight and they accepted and I arranged with them to take it to Dease River at three cents per pound.

On August 12th we got a light south-west wind and started on our long voyage across Great Bear Lake. We sailed fifteen miles before anchoring because of a head wind. On the 16th it was so rough and squally that, even in harbour, some of us were sick in the boat. We decided it was too rough to tackle it, but on the 18th we made twenty miles to another harbour in Russell Bay.

On the 19th we were away at three a.m. and made about fifty-five miles before the wind changed. The next day we found shelter behind a point and found Sloan and Harrison with a broken rudder; they had crossed in a gale ahead of us and had had a hard time. On the 21st Arden took us to the only harbour on the coast. It is not a good one, and the *Jupiter*, of G. M. Douglas, lies here, where she was beached in a storm by Mr. Hornby. Here we were held for eight solid days with a north-east wind. The gale blew so that we could not get out to our boats which rode at their homemade anchors. The white-topped breakers roaring into our little bay had a 200-mile sweep from McTavish Bay. Had it not been for a small rock bar outside the bay, the boats would have surely swamped and beached.

On September 5th we made the Narezzo Islands. It was very cold at night now but we were only twenty-five miles from the mouth of the Dease River. On the 8th we tracked along the shore and arrived at a cache opposite the priests' house that Arden had made the previous fall. We had now arrived at our destination and I decided to establish [our base] at the priests' house here chiefly on account of it being a good fishing place.

I was now at liberty to take stock and get ready to start overland across the Barrens to a cabin where the missing priests had started from on their projected journey to the sea coast. The voyage across Great Bear Lake was about 350 miles and very interesting if at times exciting. It is a vast inland sea and has every appearance of enormous depth. The scarcity of good harbours along the coast we sailed is the chief drawback to navigation in open boats. Dangerous storms rise quickly and the lake is so deep and the bays so open and long that the rollers have a great sweep and are of a great size. The lake is full of fish and our nets never failed us. We caught enough for our dogs and ourselves all the way. The average trout is about eight pounds but we caught them up to eighteen and have since caught two twenty-eight pounds each. Great Bear Lake will bear much exploration; it has never been surveyed to any extent.

I left my base on Dease Bay September 19th on patrol to Lake Rouvière where the missing priests had established a mission to the Coppermine Eskimos. Winter had already set in and we were obliged to travel overland with pack dogs. Our destination lay seventy miles north-east in the Barren Lands. We arrived at the edge of the Barren Lands at two p.m. the following day and upon climbing a ridge, a fine view lay before us: to the south-west the hollow of the Dease valley and the river winding through dark green spruce; to the north a high bare range of mountains a long way off; Dease Bay and its islands a long way to the west; and, to the north-east, the Barren Lands stretched off in gently rolling hills not unlike the Saskatchewan prairies. On the slopes of a rocky hill facing us we could see a herd of eighteen caribou quietly grazing. We pushed on and, tying up our dogs, struck off to hunt and killed three of the herd. We made camp by a clump of spruce and the following day cached our meat and killed eight more deer. We were in the Eskimo hunting grounds and deer were viewed everywhere in small herds, but of the Eskimos we did not see any.

We continued our journey. The Dease River was entirely frozen over and all inland lakes were solid enough to cross. On the 24th we camped on an island of small spruce overlooking the north-east branch of the Dease. It was somewhere here that Vilhjalmur Stefansson camped in 1910-11, and his house was found by Constable Wight on a later patrol in this area.

The 25th was bitterly cold and we were just breaking

camp when I observed two moose come out of the valley. Ilavinik had never seen a moose before and was anxious for the chase so he and the Indian Harry set out and returned in three hours packing a moose rib. They had killed both, which proved to be two old bulls. The weather held us in camp the rest of the day but next morning we proceeded over rolling hills to Big Stick Island on one of the most beautiful days I have ever seen.

On reaching the top of the high hill we saw the valley of the Big Stick Island, known to the Eskimos as the sled-making place. A veritable oasis of tall dark spruce about two miles long nestled at the foot of a high rocky hill and, to the north, blue lakes lay tucked away amongst the frowning hills. To the east bald grassy plains stretched as far as the eye could see and small herds of caribou were everywhere.

On the afternoon of the 27th we ascended a mountain of about fifteen hundred feet and another valley lay before us with Lake Rouvière stretching away in the distance. We descended the valley, passing a fairly recent Eskimo cache and some Eskimo tracks. We were now in regular "kopje-like" country with stones placed on top of one another, which is one of their deer-hunting devices. Evidently they drive the deer amongst these kopjes and ambush them there. On the 29th we crossed Lake Rouvière on the ice. This lake has been named by G. M. Douglas in honour of the missing priest Father Rouvière, who established a mission here in 1911. The priest's cabin is built in a small clump of dry spruce at the north-east end of the lake. At eleven a.m. we arrived at this tiny cabin we had come so far to find, and found everything in ruins and not a sign or clue to show the whereabouts of the missing priests. The season was already far advanced and so I decided to turn back from here. We made the thirty miles to Big Stick Island in one day's hard march. Ilavinik hunted meat for the coming winter and killed ten more deer. On October 2nd we must have seen over four hundred caribou travel-

313

ling in large bands to the north-east. We were living on straight meat and tea and thrived on the diet. We reached our base in a heavy snowstorm on October 4th having travelled over 180 miles.

During the winter of 1915-16 Inspector LaNauze and his party remained at Dease Bay preparing for a sledging expedition across the Barren Grounds to the Coppermine River. They were unable to leave their base before late March owing to the impossibility of procuring supplies for themselves and for their dogs.

On March 29th, 1916, accompanied by Constable Wight, Special Constable Ilavinik, Mr. D'Arcy Arden, and two toboggans with four dogs to each toboggan, I left our base on Great Bear Lake.

We carried an eighteen-foot cruiser canoe on top of one load which I thought we might need later on the Coppermine River. My plan was to proceed to Coronation Gulf via the Dismal Lakes and the Coppermine River, to get in touch with Eskimos who inhabit the Gulf and so do all in our power to clear up the mystery of the "missing priests." We carried fish nets and a good supply of ammunition and intended to live off the country as much as possible, building caches for our return along the route.

On the 30th of March we left the Bear Lake woods and struck east across the Barren Lands. The snow was hard-packed and afforded splendid travelling but the country was singularly desolate of game and not a deer track anywhere. The next day near Big Stick Island wolf tracks were observed; and a cache set out in advance for us by Constable Withers on March 19th was intact, but we just arrived in time as there was a beaten trail made by wolverines all around it and they had already gnawed partly through the roof.

On April 1st the Indians who had accompanied us from Great Bear Lake returned so that we now had to make double trips with our toboggans on account of our heavy loads and carrying the canoe. So far we had killed no deer and I thought it advisable to hunt for a day or two here. I struck out north-west and came into a woefully bare and stony country without a sign of anything living. But Ilavinik got back to camp at nine-thirty p.m. having killed five deer and having seen over two hundred. This was splendid; the deer had evidently started their northern migration and we hoped to travel north in their company.

From April 2nd to 4th we were held in camp by a heavy snowstorm. The 5th broke dull and cloudy and we started out for the Dismal Lakes expecting to strike them in two days' travel. Owing to a regular gale from the north-east we got into a bad blizzard and could not see a yard ahead. Heading down a hill we struck a large lake which we crossed and got into a deep ravine full of spruce. It was a fortunate find in the blizzard; the ravine was well sheltered, and we were soon in our comfortable tent with the storm raging around us.

On the 7th, travelling on the ice, we came to a distinct narrows with Eskimo signs of stones placed on end. I was sure we were now on the Dismal Lakes. We were held up by a storm till eleven a.m. on the 8th when it cleared slightly and travelling south-east for about eight miles we viewed the ridge of the Kendall River valley. It is a splendid camping ground and there is sufficient timber for building purposes. We were again out of fresh meat and as we had such a good camp I thought it advisable to hunt here and make dried meat before pushing on to the Coppermine. Accordingly, we spent the next day hunting and deer were found in hundreds on the Barrens south of the Kendall River and were very easily approached. We killed thirteen, which was all we needed; they were chiefly cows going north to drop their young and were in good condition.

On the 10th Mr. Arden and Constable Wight went back to Lake Rouvière to bring across the remainder of our stuff and the canoe. They returned on the 12th having had a hard trip through soft snow and rain on the Bear Lake end of the divide. Meantime, Special Constable Ilavinik and I had been smoke-drying the meat, Indian fashion, and feeding our dogs up.

Not being able to wait for the weather to improve, we started on the 16th for the Coppermine River. The hills we had been travelling over end abruptly in a precipitous peak facing south and from this the deep valley of the Coppermine was plainly seen. To the north-west lay the Coppermine Mountains, which are a series of high rocky hills. The woods extended over a mile from the river and, passing through these, I noticed the depression of a small creek which I headed for. We followed the creek down a good grade and struck the Coppermine at four-thirty p.m. It was a great pleasure to see a good-sized river again, flowing as it does through the heart of the Barren Lands between its high, spruce-covered banks. Noticing a blaze on a tree, I went to look at it and found an empty cache with the following writing on it:

> "Canadian Arctic Expedition. Mail party. Fort Norman. R. M. Anderson, Arnout Castel. February 24, 1915. Returned down river March 19, 1915."

This party had evidently failed to reach Fort Norman, as we had heard no news of their arrival there last fall. I now realized that we might contact the Canadian Arctic Expedition[1] somewhere in Coronation Gulf. We cached our load here and made open camp as there was plenty of big dry spruce and brush, and the following day returned to the Kendall River to bring down the rest of our gear.

It was now April 18th and willows were seen budding and the first hawk was observed; spring was arriving in the valley of the Coppermine. We were still being forced to make two trips between each pair of camping places in order to move all our supplies, food and dried meat. On Easter Sunday camp was located in a small bluff of spruce

---

[1]Commanded by Vilhjalmur Stefansson.

on the barrens overlooking the canyon of the river, and to
the north we could see a high range of rocky hills which
Ilavinik said looked like the coast range. A dull morning
turned into a beautiful afternoon, which was indeed a pleasant change from the blizzards and bad weather we had been
having. Unfortunately, Mr. Arden developed a very bad
attack of snow blindness, and was totally blind. On the
24th Constable Wight and Ilavinik set out to locate a suitable place to build a cache downstream. I shod the toboggans with iron runners we had carried all the way from
Bear Lake for spring use. Mr. Arden's eyes were still very
bad but were improving under frequent application of bor-
acic acid solutions.

The next few days were spent building a strong cache
in which we could leave the majority of our stuff and about
one month's provisions. I expected to return here and hunt
the surrounding country thoroughly when the snow left the
ground in case we could get no news of the missing priests
on the coast. On the 29th we started for the coast with
about two hundred pounds to each toboggan; it was a relief
to proceed ahead without any further double tripping.

The Coppermine ran between high clay banks with
many bends, and we were able to travel fairly directly
across the Barrens and thus avoid the rough ice. The snow
was hard-packed and our toboggans, with the runners now
on, slipped along easily. Breaking camp early on the 30th
we headed north-west to avoid some high hills, and upon
reaching an elevation got a distant view of the arctic coast.
The blue haze over the ocean was unmistakable. We soon
got into a very broken-up country, full of deep ravines, but
Mr. Arden located a good route to the west around these
and, travelling along the base of the ridges, we struck the
mouth of the Coppermine at five p.m.

We had now been a month coming from Great Bear
Lake to the arctic coast. We were singularly fortunate in
the matter of game, killing deer as we needed them, and
we were practically dependent on the country for our dog

feed and our own meat. Although several old camp signs were observed along the route, we saw nothing that we could attribute to the missing priests.

The first thing we noticed upon our arrival on the sea ice was fresh sled tracks leading across to an island opposite the mouth of the river, and a group of deserted snow houses on the island. Going across we came upon a freshly broken camp of, evidently, white men; and a small cache of canned pemmican with fresh sled tracks leading east. I judged we must be close behind a travelling party of the Canadian Arctic Expedition and decided to follow their tracks the following morning.

May 1st broke fine and we proceeded east following the sled tracks. After about ten miles' travel we came upon and killed four bull caribou and renewed our stock of dog food. These deer were poor, their skins like paper, and the marrow like blood in their bones. At eight p.m. we struck a lot of fresh sled tracks and, rounding a precipitous cliff, saw an Eskimo village on the ice about a quarter of a mile away. We were promptly recognized as strangers, and a group of people came running out, stopped and began jumping up and down holding their hands over their heads. As soon as we answered this sign they advanced and our dogs, seeing the tents, started to run, and we soon charged headlong into a group of laughing and excited Eskimos who pulled on the sleds, dragging them into camp. We were invited to camp, and as I did not like to refuse such spontaneous hospitality I accepted and there was great rejoicing.

We learned that there were two white men and a western Eskimo family in a camp across the bay and that there was a big ship about four days' travel to the westward. It was indeed a relief to have a competent interpreter [Ilavinik] with me on our first visit to a strange people. There were about fifteen Eskimos at this camp and they were living in roomy deerskin tents, with snow sleeping-benches and snow passageways.

On this occasion we did not pitch our own tent, and the women started to cook deer meat for us in a large stone pot suspended over a seal oil lamp. The operation was taking so long and we were getting so hungry that I got the primus stove going and eventually, after midnight, we had supper, surrounded by the admiring populace. They were entirely clothed in deerskins. Some had rifles and the majority had a few tin kettles. We learned that this place was the Kugaluk where Captain Bernard, the pioneer trader of Coronation Gulf, wintered in 1910-11 with his schooner *Teddy Bear*.

The following day leaving Ilavinik in camp with the Eskimos I set out to look for the white men. Crossing a bay about eight miles wide we saw a white man ahead and were soon heartily greeted by Mr. Chipman, topographer of the Canadian Arctic Expedition. I was surprised and pleased to hear that Corporal Bruce, R.N.W.M.P. of the Herschel Island detachment, was with him and that his sled was not far ahead. Their headquarters and their ship, the *Alaska*, were situated at Bernard Harbour in the Dolphin and Union Straits. Corporal Bruce informed me that he had been instructed to endeavour to contact my patrol. No news had yet been gained of the missing priests.

On May 3rd we experienced an arctic blizzard. We had thought the blizzard on the Coppermine had been bad, but one could not stand up in this one. Mr. Arden left us at this point to go east with Mr. Chipman, and Corporal Bruce joined my party, acting as guide. It was my intention to proceed west and visit the native camps. The next day we returned to the Eskimo camp and spent a day in interviewing the people and preparing for our trip across Coronation Gulf. On this occasion we pitched our own tent and found it much more satisfactory than camping with the Eskimos, in spite of their hospitality. I could not gain any information re the missing priests at this camp. About five in the afternoon we struck a large Eskimo village near Point Lockyer where we were greeted by about forty people and accorded another hearty welcome. These people were still sealing, and shortly after our arrival several men came into the camp with two bearded seals. They said Stefansson was the first white man they had ever seen. One man named "Koomuck" told me he had been with Stefansson when he brought the Indians and Eskimos together, but that was all I could get out of him. I felt convinced that this man knew something about the priests but I did not like to excite his suspicions. He said he had heard of Arden but knew of no other white men on Bear Lake.

At eight o'clock we came upon another large Eskimo village on the ice beneath Cape Lambert in the Dolphin and Union Straits. Ilavinik and I started out to get acquainted with the people here. We met a man named Nachim and his wife Kanneak who knew of Ilavinik from Stefansson's man Natkusiak. Nachim and his wife had nursed Natkusiak on the Dismal Lakes when he had burned his face badly with powder. They seemed to be very straightforward people and had fine open countenances. I told them we had found a cache south of Lake Rouvière last fall but no Eskimos. Nachim and his brother promptly said: "That was our cache. We were hunting north-west of there at the time." I saw at once, as did Ilavinik, that some information was to be gained here, and Ilavinik suggested that we should go to Nachim's house, and we were escorted to a small snow hut in the middle of the village.

And there in this faraway spot in the Arctic, the mystery of the missing priests was at length revealed to us.

I sat back and let Ilavinik do the talking. I heard him question Nachim and I could see him trembling. I saw that something was happening, but I never moved, and in about five minutes he turned to me and said: "I got him. The priests were killed by Husky,[2] all right; these men very,

---

[2] Most white men in the Arctic at this period referred to Eskimos as Huskies.

very sorry." And indeed they appeared to be; they both had covered their faces with their hands, and there was a dead silence in the igloo.

I told Ilavinik to go ahead while I went out for Corporal Bruce and when we got back Ilavinik said: "Now you write down these two names Uluksak and Sinnisiak, you got that? Now I find out some more." Meanwhile, several other Eskimos had entered the igloo, and while Ilavinik was taking, an elderly man named Koeha was joining in the conversation in the usual Eskimo manner. Ilavinik ordered only one man to speak at once, and they said Koeha had better speak as he knew all.

Without any hesitation Koeha gave a clear and concise account of the whole affair.

The two white men that were killed came with us in the fall to the mouth of the Coppermine River. They came from the Imaerinik (Lake Rouvière) across the Barren Grounds with a sled and they reached the coast when the ice was not yet strong. The two white men were Kuleavik (Father Rouvière) and Ilogoak (Father LeRoux). Kuleavik had a short black beard about three inches long and he was not much shorter than Ilavinik and about one foot shorter than you are. Ilogoak was more bigger than the other man; he had a small moustache and a small beard.

Both men wore long black coats buttoned down in front to the feet; both men could talk good in our language; when we talked together we could understand them. Eight tents (of people) went to the coast with the priests, including Kormik, Hupo, Uluksak, Sinnisiak and some others. A white man named Hornybeena (Hornby) returned to Bear Lake but Ilogoak and Kuleavik came this way with our people. I was afraid of these people (the two priests).

The white men stayed with us for five nights. They lived in a tent with Kormik. Kormik took the priest's rifle and hid it in a corner of the tent. Ilogoak found it and got very angry with Kormik. Kormik got very angry and I watched him. He wanted to kill the white men. I am speaking the truth and am not talking foolish. I did not want to see the white men killed, and I helped them to get away. I helped them to load up the sled. I held Kormik close to the door of the tent by force and after that I told Kormik's mother, "You hold your son; I go outside." I stood outside the door. I hurried up the priests to pack their sled and they were talking together quickly. Neochtellig helped me to get the white men started, and I started with them, pulling the sled in the harness. The white men had two dogs of their own and one they got from me and one from Noweina.

I went up the river with them as far as I could see the tops of the tents behind. Then I said to the two white men, "There are no trees here so you go as far as you can, and after that you can travel easy; I like you and I do not want anyone to hurt you." Ilogoak was running ahead of the sled and Kuleavik was driving the sled. He shook hands with me. The sun was very low when the white men left and there was not much daylight at that time.

In two nights after the white men left two men named Uluksak and Sinnisiak left to go up river. Some people knew that they started, as they said they were going to help some people coming from Bear Lake; they took dogs and no sled. These men caught up with the priests and stayed with them for one day. The next day Uluksak and Sinnisiak started ahead but the white men stayed in camp. The two white men had no tent; it was cold weather. The two Eskimos came back the same night and camped with the white men again. The next morning the white men started and Uluksak and Sinnisiak went with them

322

At this point in Koeha's narrative we interject the account given later by Sinnisiak.

I was stopping at the mouth of the Coppermine River one morning. A lot of people were going fishing. When the sun had not gone down I returned to camp and saw that the two priests had started back up the river; they had four dogs; I saw no other men.

I slept one night. Next morning I started (with Uluksak) and with one dog to help some people that were doming down (the Coppermine). All day I walked along and then I left the river and travelled on land. I was following the priests' trail. I met the priests near a lake. When I was close to them one man came to meet me.

The man Ilogoak, the big man, came to me and told me to come over to the camp. Ilogoak said, "If you help me pull the sled I will pay you in traps." We moved off the same day I arrived, in order to get near the woods; Uluksak was with me and we pulled the sled. We could not reach the trees (that night); it was hard work and we made camp.

The next day we started back but the priests kept going ahead; it started to storm and we lost the road. After that the dogs smelt something and Uluksak went to see what it was and I stayed behind. Uluksak found it was a cache of the priests and told me to come over. As soon as we came there the priests came back. Ilogoak was carrying a rifle. He was mad with us that we had turned back, and I could not understand all his talk.

I asked Ilogoak if he was going to kill me and he nodded his head. Ilogoak said, "Come over to the sled," and he pushed me with his hand. The priests wanted to start again and he pushed me again and wanted me to put on the harness, and then he laid his rifle out on top of the sled. I was scared and I started to pull.

We went a little way and Uluksak and I started to talk, and Ilogoak put his hand on my mouth. Ilogoak was very mad and was pushing me. I was thinking hard and crying and very scared and the frost was in my boots and I was cold. I wanted to go back [to Coppermine] but I was afraid. Ilogoak would not let us. Every time the sled stuck, Ilogoak would pull out the rifle. I got hot inside my body and every time Ilogoak pulled out the rifle I was very much afraid.

I said to Uluksak, "I think they will kill us." I can't go back now, I was thinking, I will not see my people anymore; I will try and kill him. I was pulling ahead of the dogs. We came to a small hill. I took off the harness quick and ran to one side and Ilogoak ran after me and pushed me back to the sled. I took off my belt and told Ilogoak I was going to relieve myself, and I did not want to go to the sled. After that I ran behind the sled; I did not want to relieve myself. Then Ilogoak turned around and saw me; he looked away from me and I stabbed him in the back with a knife. I then told Uluksak, "You take the rifle." Ilogoak ran ahead of the sled and Uluksak went after him. The other white man wanted to come back to the sled; I had the knife in my hand and he went away again.

Uluksak and Ilogoak were wrestling for the rifle, and after that Uluksak finished up Ilogoak. I did not see Uluksak finish him. The other man ran away when he saw Ilogoak die. I asked Uluksak, "Is he dead?" and he said, "yes, already." I then said to Uluksak, "Give me the rifle." He gave it to me. The first time I shot I did not hit him [the running priest] but the second time I got him. The priest sat down when the bullet hit him. I went after him with the knife. When I was close to him he got up again; both of us were together. I had the knife in my hand and I went after him when he got up again.

Uluksak told me, "Go ahead and put the knife in him." I said to Uluksak, "Go ahead you. I fixed the other man already." The Father fell down on his back. Uluksak struck first with the knife and did not strike him; the second time he got him. The priest lay down and was breathing a little, when I struck him across the face with an axe I was carrying; I cut his legs with the axe; I killed him dead.

After they were dead I said to Uluksak, "Before when white men were killed they used to cut off some and eat some." Uluksak cut up Ilogoak's belly; I turned around, Uluksak gave me a little piece of the liver, I ate it; Uluksak ate too.

We covered up both bodies with snow when we started to go back. We took only a rifle and cartridges. We took three bags of cartridges. We started back in the night time. We camped that night; next morning we got back to camp as soon as it was light. I went to Kormik's tent. Kormik was sleeping and I woke him up. I told him I killed those two fellows already; I can't remember what Kormik said. Kormik, Kocha, Angebrunna, Kallun, and Kingordlik went to get the priests' stuff. They started in the morning and came back the same night. Kormik sold the two church shirts to Natallik. I can't tell anymore. If I knew any more I would tell you.

We now return to Koeha's account.

Uluksak and Sinnisiak came back in the night. After this five people went after the priests' stuff. I was very sorry that the two white men had been killed and I wanted to go and see them. When we got to the place, I saw one man dead lying by the sled. It was Ilogoak. I took two dogs and a small pot and one pair of white man's boots and a small cod line and I put these inside

325

the pot. The other stuff the other people took. Sinnisiak went back to Victoria Land. Uluksak lives to the
eastward.

The man Uluksak had told the tale of the murder to all
present [at the mouth of the Coppermine] and said he had
been urged to assist in the crime by Sinnisiak. Father
LeRoux had been stabbed in the back by Sinnisiak and
finished off by Uluksak, and Father Rouvière had made a
dash for the sled where his rifle was. Sinnisiak evidently
was too quick for him and he started to run away, when he
was shot by Sinnisiak. Koeha with three others had then
visited the scene of the murder. Upon being asked why
they did not tell of this before, they said they were afraid;
they wanted to tell it to Arden but no one they met could
understand their language. They had carried it in their
heads a long time. They were afraid to tell it to the man at
the Igloopuk [the headquarters of the Canadian Arctic
Expedition] as there were so many there, and Hornby had
told some of them if they killed white men, the white men
would kill them.

Learning that the Eskimos Kormik and Hupo were in
the next village we started for there on May 9th. There
were two large Eskimo villages here comprising about a
hundred people and the natives were all living in deerskin
tents and killing seals preparatory to making caches of
blubber to leave on the coast before proceeding inland to
their summer caribou hunt.

A dance was held in a huge tent on the 9th, the per-
former beating a very large skin drum about ten feet in
circumference, accompanying the beating by jumping up
and down and flourishing the drum. Women and men alike
performed and joined in the singing.

I now had the evidence; the next step was to arrest the
murderers. Sinnisiak was supposed to be somewhere near
Victoria Land on the ice, and Uluksak east of the
Coppermine.

Following this singularly flat and dreary coast, we arrived at Bernard Harbour, the southern headquarters of the Canadian Arctic Expedition, on May 10th. The *Alaska* was wintering in the ice here and the members of the party lived in a small house made of sod. The Arctic Expedition had plenty of fine seal meat for dog feed, but as our Mackenzie River dogs would have to be starved before they would touch this diet, we fed them deer meat as they still had strenuous work ahead of them. On the 11th, Corporal Bruce laid information before me against Uluksak and Sinnisiak, and I issued warrants for their arrest.

On the 12th, accompanied by our guide, Mayuk, we struck northward across to the Liston and Sutton Islands. Our guide was looking for a deserted snow village where he had seen the murderer during the winter, and we would follow the tracks from there. On the 13th an old village was located with fairly fresh sled tracks leading north from it; following these we passed a somewhat recently deserted village about ten miles farther north where skin tents had been used, and at midnight we came to a freshly deserted village with a fresh trail still leading north.

I thought perhaps our man had received word and fled, but we had not gone very far the next day when the low stony coast of Victoria Land showed up quite plainly and, proceeding north, we soon located a village of skin tents situated on the ice just off the shore.

As we approached, men and women separated into groups, the peace sign was not shown, neither did the people run out to meet us; but as we got quite close they all came running out and we were welcomed as usual. There were about forty people. Sinnisiak was not seen but our guide led us to a tent where Sinnisiak was found sitting down engaged in the manufacture of a bow, and he was formally arrested by Corporal Bruce. The man was absolutely paralyzed with fear. I explained to him and the people that he had to come with us and though he did not want to come, the usual Eskimo audience advised him to go, and did not hinder us in the least. Special Constable Ilavinik told me afterwards that the first words he said were, "What do you men want?" When he was told, "The white men here want you to go with them," he replied, "If the white men kill me, I will make medicine and the ship will go down in the ice and all will be drowned." I told him he could take his wife and his effects along and after this we had no more trouble and got the prisoner quietly away from the camp. After we got out on the ice a few miles, I told him he had to leave his effects with another family who shared his sled, as they were travelling too slow for us. At this camp I secured a valuable piece of evidence in the actual .44 rifle belonging to Father Rouvière.

When we arrived back at Bernard Harbour Dr. Jenness[3] was there. Taking turns on guard we endeavoured to get the prisoner to lie down and sleep, but he would not, and we learned from Dr. Jenness that Sinnisiak was afraid of being stabbed while he slept. Eventually he slept from sheer weariness.

On the 17th I took his preliminary hearing. He stated that he had been the chief instigator of the crime, that they had murdered the priests in self-defence because the priests had threatened them with their rifles and beaten them, and he thought he had better kill the priests before they killed them. I committed Sinnisiak for trial on two charges of murder. I was now obliged to leave Corporal Bruce in charge of him while Constable Wight and myself had no time to lose to get east again on the chance of finding the second murderer, Uluksak.

I had information from an old Eskimo that Uluksak intended to hunt that summer in the Dismal Lake district and that I would probably find him at the mouth of the Coppermine when the Eskimos gathered before going inland.

---

[3] Dr. Diamond Jenness, the anthropologist of the Canadian Arctic Expedition.

Mr. Jenness kindly lent me his own Eskimo boy "Patsy" and his sled and team of dogs so I could return to Bernard Harbour and not have to take my own men back again at this already late season. On the 17th we struck out for the mouth of the Coppermine, arriving there on the 21st to find that no Eskimos had arrived as yet. However, from the top of an island Patsy located through the field glasses six sleds far out on the ice travelling towards us very slowly. Six hours later they had disappeared behind another island. Long before we reached this island we located the skin tents of the Eskimos and while we were yet far away the peace sign of holding up hands was in evidence. As we got closer the people ran down to greet us, all except the man Uluksak who hung back. He was immediately recognized by Patsy and as Constable Wight and myself approached him he ran forward holding up his hands and saying, "Goana, Goana (thank you). I'm glad."

I asked him if he knew why we had come, and he said, yes, he knew well; were we going to kill him? "The other two white men hit me over the head, will you do this?"

Our problem now was to get our prisoners back to civilization. Leaving Constable Wight at the mouth of the Coppermine to make a visit to the scene of the murder, my party proceeded back to Bernard Harbour from where we planned to go out by Herschel Island on the S.S. *Alaska*. I judged it best from all points of view to take the prisoners out via the Herschel Island route. [This would mean a ship passage around Alaska and down the coast to Vancouver or Victoria.] There was always the danger of losing them on the long trip overland to Great Bear Lake, probably accompanied by a number of Eskimos who frequent that country. Moreover, they still had a dread of the Indians and asked me if I was going to take them into Indian country. If we had not connected with the Canadian Arctic Expedition, I would have tried to take them out via Great Bear Lake. In conclusion, I might mention that we were dealing with a still practically primitive people, a people

329

who six years ago were discovered living in what might be termed a Stone Age, hidden away in the vast sub-Arctic spaces of the northland of Canada.

While LaNauze was carrying out his patrol, the police were busy elsewhere in the Barrens. In 1910 an American named H. V. Radford, who claimed to be a collector for the Smithsonian Institute, and who was accompanied by a young Canadian named T. G. Street, had entered the Barrens from the east end of Great Slave and descended the Thelon to Schultz Lake, where the two men wintered with some of the inland Eskimos. After a brief visit to Baker Lake the following spring, the white men set out with Eskimo guides overland for Bathurst Inlet. A year later, in June of 1913, reports began to trickle back that both men had been killed. The story, from Eskimo sources, asserted that Radford had deliberately struck an Eskimo with a whip and threatened to kill him, and that the Eskimos had struck back in fear of their lives.

It was necessary to investigate. But how? There was then no way of reaching Bathurst Inlet except along some variant of the route Hanbury had followed. The R.N.W.M.P. were game to try; but it was not until 1915 that an advance post was set up at Baker Lake as a starting point for the patrol. For some reason things went so badly that in the following year the officer in charge was relieved and the command passed to Inspector F. H. French, who arrived at Baker Lake in September of 1916. He was unable to begin his patrol until the spring of the following year but, once under way, he proved himself to be an arctic traveller of the first quality. He was also a modest man. He concludes his official report with these words:

"I have not attempted to make this report flowery, or to go into descriptive details, but have simply dealt with cold-blooded facts."

French does himself an injustice. His is a succinct and

vigorous account of one of the most memorable and difficult patrols ever undertaken by the Force in all its years of arctic service.

REPORT OF THE BATHURST INLET PATROL ROYAL NORTH WEST MOUNTED POLICE

In the summer of 1916 Inspector Beyts was relieved by Inspector F. H. French; the latter arrived at Baker Lake on the 20th of September. The autumn and winter were spent making preparations. Writing in January, 1917, Inspector French observed: "I hope to make a successful trip, commencing in March next; my only difficulty is the inevitable dog feed question which seems to rise at every point a man moves in this country, so devoid of timber and vegetation. If I can only procure the game along the line of march, I feel sure I shall be able to bring the patrol to a successful termination. We shall be unable to carry enough rations for the return trip, and will have to take our chances, along with the dogs, and depend on the country. As far a being able to establish a friendly footing amongst the Killinemuit [Bathurst Inlet Eskimos], I have not the slightest doubts, if we can only get across the Barrens dividing us, without a hitch."

Inspector French's Report

On March 21st, 1917, I left Baker Lake detchment with Sgt. Major Caulkin, Police Natives "Joe" and "Bye-and-Bye," and hired native "Quashak" and native woman "Solomon," taking three teams of dogs [25 dogs], sleds, and two canoes. One month's rations for six were all we were able to take with us along with our camp equipment and coal oil and at that we were heavily loaded. After the month's rations were finished, we were to subsist as best we could. We cut overland from Baker Lake to Schultz Lake following a series of small lakes. Up to the 26th it had been clear and cold, but on this date a storm commenced and continued until April 2nd with such intensity that we were not able to break camp until that date. We then proceeded to Aberdeen Lake [on the Thelon River]. During this part of the patrol it was continually storming and we were frequently held up. We reached the east end of Aberdeen on April 5th and there found an encampment of Harvaktormiut and one Padlermiut family.[4] We built our igloo alongside and camped with them.

The next day I sent Sgt. Major Caulkin and natives deer hunting and they returned in late afternoon after they had shot twelve. From the time of our arrival at Schultz we had been able to kill sufficient deer to feed ourselves and dogs although the deer were never plentiful. On the 7th I made an arrangement with a native to come with us two days with his dog team and help carry dog feed and also act as guide across the height of land, as from this point I decided to proceed overland and to make for Lake Garry on Back River. The native was only agreeable to come on condition that his son could accompany us as well.

Leaving Aberdeen Lake we went in a north-westerly direction following a zig-zag course along ravines as there was no snow on the ridges. The weather was fine and clear and travelling was good. The deer appeared to be getting more plentiful as we proceeded farther north. On the 10th our native guide and son returned to their camp and we were alone in a strange country with which none of my natives were acquainted. The weather also changed and became very foggy and stormy and we were unable to continue. We holed up until the 12th but had to camp again

---

[4] The Harvaktormiut were the Eskimos of the Baker Lake region while the Padlermiut came from the region east of Yathkyed Lake.

on that date due to a blizzard coming on, which continued unabated until April 15th when we were finally able to continue our journey to the north-west. Again on this date travelling was very bad and it was surprising to see how little snow there was on the land. Ahead of us appeared to be a long stretch of absolutely barren rocky country which we found, upon coming nearer, impossible to cross so that we were forced to make a wide detour to the north-east. Eventually we arrived at Lake Garry on April 16th and found that it did not compare in any way with the map we carried.

Our object at the moment was to locate the Hanningormiut encampment and we spent two days looking for it without success. We travelled west to Lake Pelly and as it still continued foggy we were unable to locate the outlet from this lake into Back River, and so made camp. It remained foggy until April 24th when we made a break and found the outlet, down which we continued until we arrived at the encampment of the Hanningormiut where we built our igloo.

The Hanningormiut are but a small band consisting of about twenty-nine persons and as far as I could understand they never leave the Back River vicinity and have never seen the sea. They said they had never seen white men but once before and from what they told me it was D. T. Hanbury's party they saw [in 1902]. They still hunt with bows and arrows.

Up to this time I had intended to follow Back River up to Beechey Lake and strike north from there, but we were losing so much time what with fog and storms and having no knowledge of the country that I felt anxious as to whether we should get back, since the snow was now beginning to melt off the land. However, on meeting the natives here, I was told that to proceed on such a course was impossible since between Beechey Lake and Bathurst Inlet there was a stretch of country consisting of high, barren, rocky hills on which there was usually very little snow and practically considered impossible by the natives for sleds. One of the natives suggested the route travelled over by the natives coming south from the arctic coast, following a river which extended inland east of Bathurst Inlet, and stated that he himself used this river and had been along that route as far as the arctic coast.

I tried to obtain this man's services as a guide across country. At first he demurred, saying it was a country of starvation and hardship, but I offered him a rifle and ammunition to accompany us, and it was not before considerable more conversation had ensued that he consented to do so.

We left this camp on April 26th proceeding north and the next day struck a large lake and then continued northwest until May 1st when we were held up by a very bad blizzard. On May 3rd we reached the river that the native had mentioned and continued down it coming to the arctic coast on the night of May 7th. As far as I was able to judge, we hit the coast about fifteen miles west of the Ellice River. On May 9th we touched Melbourne Island and there killed some deer and a little later picked up some recently made native sled tracks. These we followed and they took us down into a deep, narrow bay which we continued to follow until it brought us into Elu Inlet, from which we made our way into Melville Sound.

On the 10th we were again held up by a blizzard but on the 11th proceeded to the west until the blizzard came again forcing us to camp. This storm continued to the night of May 12th during which time we had to remain in our igloo. The 13th broke fine and clear; our first experience of a really warm day since starting out. The following day we saw several sled tracks leading south-westerly [into Bathurst Inlet] and on following these we eventually came to a large Eskimo encampment on an island, consisting of thirty-six natives. Only the women were in the camp, as the men were a mile away at the seal-hunting holes. When the women sighted us they ran into their tents and igloos, but seeing us raise our hands above our heads, they came out and our natives approached them and commenced talking.

The men all ran from the seal holes and gathered around an elderly native and then advanced toward us at the double and in extended order, each carrying seal spear or snow knife; but seeing that our attitude was friendly, everything was all right and our natives understood them pretty well when talking.

While we were standing talking with these natives, the majority of whom had never seen a white man before, another band arrived with five sleds from the west side of Bathurst Inlet and there were twenty-seven in this party. All the natives greeted us in a friendly manner and when we camped alongside them were eager to help in building our igloos and fixing our camps. When they heard we were out of coal oil they sent us bladders of seal oil for the small native lamps we had, and they always appeared anxious to furnish any information we required. We spent a whole month travelling with and amongst these people, including bands of Killinemuit and Killishiktlmuit from the west side of Bathurst Inlet, and Wadlearingmuit who ranged between Bathurst and the Coppermine River. We were constantly meeting fresh bands of natives and carrying out our investigation of the murders of Messrs. Radford and Street. Their stories were all the same and corroborated the information received from different sources. In the first encampment I took statements from three men and one woman who were present, the first being a native named Aningnerk, who was a head man and had under his control a band of thirty-five people.

About five winters ago, two white men came from the south and they had three Eskimos with them and they came to an island on the salt water called Kwogjuk. One was named Ishumatok, the other Kiuk. The one white man called Ishumatok was bad, but the other

335

white man named Kiuk was good. The three Eskimos who came with the white men went away again to the south and the white men could not speak to us and we did not understand them, but they made us understand a little by making signs.

They wanted two men to go with them to the west. Two men, Harla and Kaneak, were going with them but Kaneak's wife was sick. She had fallen on the ice and was hurt and Kaneak did not want to leave her there. The white man called Ishumatok got very mad at Kaneak and hit him with a whip. The other white man tried to stop him. The white man was shouting all the time. He dragged Kaneak to the water's edge. The other white man went with him and they were going to kill Kaneak in the water. Everybody was frightened that the two white men were going to kill Kaneak. Two men, Okitok and Hulalark, ran out and stabbed Ishumatok. He fell on the ice. The other white man ran off shouting towards the sled and Okitok ran after him and caught him, and Amegealnik stabbed him with a snow knife. He was running towards the sleigh; he tried to get a rifle. The two white men were covered over and left on the ice. I do not know what became of their property; some the Eskimos took and some I think was left on the island. Their rifles were broken up and made into tools after the cartridges were used up.

I do not think this would have happened if the white men had not beaten Kaneak with the dog whip, or if we had understood the white men. Kaneak and Hulalark are away on the Salt Ice Land [probably Victoria Land]. Amegealnik I think is away to the west near the big river [probably the Coppermine].

We do not want trouble with the white men; we want them to come here and trade with us.

I engaged a native to take us to Kwogjuk Island and show

us where the murder took place. This was done but nothing whatever was to be found. It was evident that if the bodies were placed where this man pointed out, they must have been carried into the waters of the inlet by the first stormy period and carried out to sea. It is also evident that Mr. Radford used very little discretion or judgement in handling these natives when trying to obtain their services. He appears at all times to have used rough methods along his route of travel from Chesterfield Inlet, as I have heard stories of previous occurrences of a similar nature. One of these reports referred to Mr. Radford as threatening to shoot a native named ''Bosun'' at Baker Lake because he would not accompany him from that place to Bathurst Inlet; and also chasing a native at Schultz Lake because the native had cheated him out of a fish in a trade deal. Undoubtedly the previous incidents occurring along the route had been told to the Killinemuit by some of the natives accompanying Radford and Street to Bathurst Inlet. Had Radford, instead of resorting to chastisement, used discretion when Kaneak said he did not want to go with him, and tried to get another native, I believe he would have succeeded in so doing and that Messrs. Radford and Street would be alive today.

The weather now began to be warmer and finer. On May 16th we struck south down Bathurst Inlet on our return journey and on the 17th came up with a large band of Killinemuit travelling in our direction. They were a little too friendly and insisted on travelling with us all day and camped alongside us at night. We were held up by a rain and sleet storm which cleared in the afternoon so we stayed in camp and traded with these natives and I was fortunate in being able to procure from them some fish for dog feed, as we were now entirely out and did not know how soon we would come across deer again.

Some of the Killinemuit had not seen a white man before and had very few white men's goods in their possession, but I noticed that two had two old muzzle-loading rifles which they had obtained from native traders coming from the west. Most of their arrowheads were made from bone or native copper which they obtained in Bathurst Inlet.

One thing I noticed in particular about the arctic coast Eskimos is the absence of infants, particularly of the female sex, and from different sources I found out that it is correct that they do away with the majority of female born babies. I lectured them severely on this matter, endeavouring to show them how eventually their tribe would become extinct.

We made our last igloo on the 19th. It collapsed during the heat of the day and fell in on us while we were all asleep; so we pitched our tent for the first time and continued its use, although they were wretched conditions under which we camped owing to the wet condition of the land. We travelled as long as we could and camped when conditions were favourable, going on two meals of half-raw deer meat during the day, and found it not very agreeable to keep on the go for fourteen to sixteen hours between meals. From the 18th the travelling got very bad; the sea ice became bare and jagged and cut the dogs' feet so that the majority were lame. I had an outfit of sealskin boots made and put on all the dogs, but the ice was so sharp that they would wear out a pair in one night.

We arrived at the foot of Bathurst Inlet on the 21st and here found the ice covered with water fifteen inches deep from the Western River. We proceeded up the Western River for about twenty-five miles travelling along the snow on the sides, and having to cross frequently at the bends; these were over knee deep in fast-running water which was entering our sled loads. We now made camp and examined the land to the south and found it to be practically devoid of snow and absolutely impossible to travel with dogs and sleds.

Inspector French had hoped that there would still be time to make a dash south from Bathurst Inlet and reach the

upper Thelon before the melting snows made sledding
impossible. Once on the Thelon he could have returned
downstream to Baker Lake by canoe. But this was clearly
impossible and he now had to make other plans.

We now returned to the south end of Bathurst Inlet intending to wait there for open water and endeavour to get out
[along the coast] by canoe. In that event I would have been
obliged to abandon the dog sleds and part of the outfit. But
on the 24th we met a band of natives who had followed
our trail down the Inlet. They came from the west, and
from them we learned that there were three ships along the
arctic coast to the west which they said were only about
nine days' travel away.

As we were entirely out of supplies and living on a
straight meat diet, which was not agreeing with Sgt. Major
Caulkin or myself, and also finding our ammunition to be
insufficient to return with, I decided to make west to these
ships and try to obtain supplies and ammunition to last me
through the summer, then to return again to the foot of
Bathurst Inlet and wait till freeze-up next fall and return
overland to Baker Lake.

The dogs were beginning to show signs of lameness
again and we changed to day travel, as going at night was
harder on their feet than during the day when the sun
thawed most of the points of ice. We met many bands of
natives of different tribes and camped at different places
along the coast. I did not like the look of some of them and
were told they were born thieves, although as soon as they
were told who we were they were very meek and did not
attempt to purloin anything from our outfit.

At these encampments I gave them a lecture on the
murdering of white men, and regarding pilfering from
them, and also dwelling on the laws of civilization generally. They appeared to be greatly impressed. They had
heard of Inspector LaNauze's patrol and the taking out of
the murderers of the Roman Catholic missionaries, and

this seemed to have created a great impression amongst them.

The weather was now getting very warm but on June 2nd it commenced to snow heavily and continued to do so throughout the next day. We had to refrain from walking ahead of the dogs after Sgt. Major Caulkin and two natives fell down cracks in the ice and were wet through. We reached Tree River on the night of June 4th, meeting a small encampment of Eskimos on an island there. They told us there was a white man living along the river and so we proceeded up about five miles and met a Swede by the name of Albin Keihlman, who was trapping. This man told us there was a trading vessel three days west from his camp. We traded for some Barren-Land grizzly bear meat from the natives here, and were made very sick from eating it, although the meat tasted pretty good.

After much hard travelling, on the night of June 8th we arrived at the schooner which was frozen in near an island east of the mouth of the Coppermine. She turned out to be the United States gasoline schooner *Teddy Bear*, with Captain J. Bernard in command. He greeted us kindly and gave us what provisions he could. We obtained five gallons of oil for our primus lamp and it seemed good to get some civilized cooking again. We were unable to obtain any ammunition for our rifles and so could not carry out my intention of summering at the foot of Bathurst Inlet, but Captain Bernard informed me that the Hudson's Bay Company had a trading post at Bernard Harbour and that I might be able to obtain supplies there.

As it was now out of the question for the patrol to return to the foot of Bathurst Inlet without ammunition, I decided to continue onwards. If possible I hoped to get out by way of Herschel Island. After two days at the *Teddy Bear* we continued on our journey and reached Bernard Harbour on June 13th. Mr. Phillip, the manager, informed me that it would be impossible to proceed farther west by sled as the break-up was liable to occur at any time. He suggested that the Hudson's Bay Company boat would arrive as soon as the ice cleared and that our best way out was to go with her to Herschel Island. This I decided to do and so I disbanded my dogs and outfit and we pitched camp near the post.

Needless to say, this has been a hard trip. I must say that it has been the hardest trip I ever made, and we suffered much from cold and exposure. These we felt all the more when our supplies ran out toward the end of our journey, and our deerskin clothing got the worse for wear, and the hair started falling out and the wind pierced through the seams and holes. Most of us were continually frozen about the face and the hands, and with regard to snow blindness we were suffering from this more or less during the whole journey. Both myself and Sgt. Major Caulkin were in very poor shape, as regards health; during the past six weeks we had been eating only quantities of deer, seal and bear meat, to which we were unused, and even this eaten mostly half raw. We had covered 1,835 miles over our route, but including expeditions for hunting and looking for native camps, our total was well over 2,400 miles.

Inspector French waited in vain for the arrival of the Hudson's Bay Company supply ship. That summer the ice conditions were so bad that no vessels were able to get east of the Mackenzie River. When it became obvious that none would arrive, Inspector French made up his mind to return to Baker Lake by the overland route.

During the latter part of August at Bernard Harbour, game such as deer, fish, and seals began to get scarce and as the supplies at the Hudson's Bay Company post were little more than sufficient to carry them through the coming winter, I determined to move camp to the Coppermine River and wait there till freeze-up. I purchased about two months' supplies from the Hudson's Bay Company for the party. I

341

was unable to get ammunition for our .303 rifles and so was forced to purchase two .30-.30 rifles from the Hudson's Bay Company. Mr. Phillip provided two whale boats to convey our outfits to the Coppermine, a distance of about 150 miles eastward.

On September 1, 1917, we left Bernard Harbour and arrived safely, with a new member of the party in the person of a white man named Albin Keihlman, whom I previously mentioned having met at Tree River last spring.

This man had been left behind by Captain Bernard of the schooner *Teddy Bear*, and owing to no vessel arriving, he was unable to get out to civilization. He did not possess sufficient supplies to see him through the oncoming winter so I considered it better to see him out of the country overland, as in all probability he would have become destitute if left on the coast.

During our stay at the Coppermine we hauled a quantity of driftwood to tide us over until we were ready to start south. We employed our time fishing and put a quantity on racks [to dry] and in caches along the river. Also, we had to make new harnesses for all our dogs and refit the sleds and overhaul the outfit generally. I intended to leave as soon as possible, either overland from the Coppermine and strike the south end of Bathurst Inlet or, if the coast froze first, to follow it as before.

While here, a band of seventeen Indians arrived overland from Fort Rae and Great Bear Lake district on a visit to a white settler who was located at the mouth of the Coppermine River. His name was Charlie Klinkenberg, and he was employed in trapping and trading in a small way. I gave one of these Indians a letter giving a few details of our patrol and instructed him to give it to the first white man he might meet, thinking in this way I might get word outside of our whereabouts.

In early October it began to get colder and the local natives, who were at Bloody Falls, moved down to the mouth of the river where during their stay I gave them lectures regarding civilized laws, etc., through our interpreter Joe. On October 16th we made a start from the Coppermine River proceeding east along the shore. But the rivers and lakes were hardly frozen enough to bear the sleds. In view of this and the fact that the country appeared rough, I considered it advisable to return to the arctic coast and continue along the sea ice. On October 20th we arrived back at the coast about eighteen miles east of the Coppermine. Here we remained until the 28th. Our dogs, thirty in number, were in fair condition to commence the overland patrol, and I considered they would take us through if we could procure game until we reached the Thelon River.

We broke camp again on the 28th and proceeded east along the arctic coast towards the mouth of Bathurst Inlet. Our journey was very strenuous as a man had to proceed ahead of the team with a spear and test the ice and many times we had a narrow escape of a sled going through. One day we saw a huge herd and several smaller bands of deer crossing the ice from Victoria Land and we procured eleven of them.

Barren-Land caribou were the chief game we encountered. Sometimes we might go all day and see none and we would begin to think they were getting scarce, but around camping time a band would show up and we would be able to procure the night's dog feed. Many times we saw bands too numerous to commence counting, but from time to time they got scarcer. Our total kill of deer during the journey was 168, and these were used for dog feed and our own consumption.

We reached Tree River on November 6th and at this point had to make a detour inland and back again to the coast owing to a gale having broken up the ice and driven it out to sea. On the 12th we reached Bathurst Inlet. Our dogs had not been very well fed of late and were beginning to look poor after the hard hauling, but on this date we saw five deer in the Inlet and shot them, which came in time to give our dogs a good feed.

The travelling down Bathurst Inlet was very heavy, the snow soft and deep, and we made slow progress. On November 15th we camped on the south side of Arctic Sound and met some Killinemuit, with whom we traded for dried deer meat, fat and skins. By November 18th our grub was low and not one-third of our journey was completed. On an island west of Gordon Bay we found a camp of three igloos, one native being Mayuk, who was employed by Inspector LaNauze on the Roman Catholic missionary case. At this point there were several relations of the native woman Solomon who had so far accompanied the patrol all the way from Baker Lake. Owing to the fact that she had been suffering from an abscess in the ear all summer and fall, the natives said it would be best to leave her here. She is to be brought back to Baker Lake by her uncle in the spring.

It had been our intention to proceed to the foot of Bathurst Inlet and south from there, but we heard now that there was a river in Gordon Bay so I determined to proceed along this as I thought the sooner we struck land the better off we would be for obtaining deer meat. We broke camp on the 21st and travelled south-east to the mouth of the river. Here we found a large quantity of deer carcasses strewn all along the banks of the river under the snow. These had been speared from kayaks by the natives before freeze-up and the skins only taken. It was a great waste of meat but it came handy to us. We made camp and turned our dogs loose, and we also picked out a few good carcasses and packed them on the sleds. Prior to our arrival there had been a great gathering of wolves, wolverines, ravens, etc., all feasting on the carcasses.

From the 23rd to the 27th of November we continued overland but found the going so rocky that we were compelled to return to the river again. At this point we were molested continually by bands of wolves. These same animals are the biggest wolves I have ever seen. They are dark brown and rangy and they got away with one of our dogs while we were passing through these mountainous regions.

Wolves seemed very numerous from time to time, and several times our camp was attacked by them and a general mêlée would ensue amongst the dogs. Once a pack of wolves came around our igloo and it was not before we had killed two of them that they went away.

A similar occurrence took place on Back River. These were much larger than we had previously seen and we shot one out of this band. At periods these wolves would follow us for days, evidently being hungry and looking forward to the time when we left camp when they could come up and clean anything left behind. On our outward journey they were our constant companions across the Barrens to Bathurst Inlet, where we appeared to leave them.

On December 1st we continued on over a very rocky and barren country on which there was little snow. The weather was fine and calm and continued so throughout the month, much to our sorrow, as we were not able to get near the deer and obtain food and dog meat which we so badly needed. Our clothes at this time were showing signs of needing repair as they had been wet with the fall travelling and were now continually frozen. Our foot gear [caribou or sealskin boots] was a real cause of worry as we had only a small quantity, and with the continual walking we were kept busy patching.

On December 5th we sent the natives deer hunting and they saw huge herds of them but owing to the calm, clear weather could not get near them and only after shooting lots of ammunition at long range did they succeed in knocking down five.

By the 12th we had reached Back River which we followed for three days, feeding our dogs the last small portions of dried meat. On the 15th we left Back River proceeding south for the Thelon, hoping to locate a cache made at the timbered place there in 1916 by Inspector Beyts. If we could reach and find this it would mean a lot to us. The dogs were now showing signs of weakness, and matters looked tough. We abandoned one sled and split the dogs among the other teams. During the past week all spare men were out in extended order ahead of the teams endeavouring to get close to the deer, which were plentiful, but all to no avail. It was hardly credible but we could not get near them, and they would be off, as it was so calm and clear, and one could not avoid the deadly scrunch of feet on the snow which always alarmed the deer and put them in flight. On the 18th the dogs stole a bag of deerskin clothing which they ate. The next day there were three men ahead of the sleds all day but only saw three deer, but the Sgt. Major succeeded in bringing one of these down.

December 20th and 21st we proceeded over rolling prairie land but saw no game and very few tracks. We fed the dogs one deerskin cut up in small pieces. On this date we came upon a river running south and presumed it ran into the Thelon. On the 22nd we continued along this river and came on the first signs of stunted spruce trees. Several dogs were exhausted and fell from time to time. At noon we saw fresh mush-ox tracks crossing the ice to the westward. I sent two natives on foot to look for same and proceeded ten miles farther along the river to where we could be near timber and get water, and there made camp. On this night we shot five of the exhausted dogs and skinned and fed them to the others.

At two-thirty the next afternoon our hunters arrived from the west and almost knocked us down with the news that they had shot twenty musk-oxen about ten miles from the igloo. I sent all natives and dogs up to the scene of the killing. Here they were to dress the musk-oxen, feed up and rest the dogs. On Christmas Day Quashak and Joe arrived with two sled-loads of musk-ox meat and we enjoyed a big feed. We remained in this locality until January 3rd, 1918. The dogs were getting all they could eat and were picking up again. On the 31st of December Sgt. Major Caulkin and native Joe went south-west to look for the cache put in by Inspector Beyts, which they found about sixteen miles away. It had broken down and what remained of the stores was under snow but they salvaged about seventy pounds of flour, four tins of Oxo, ten pounds of tobacco, four pounds of chewing tobacco and thirteen pounds of candles. The wolves had evidently been at the cache, for the Sgt. Major reported that one sack of flour was scattered, the lard pails were bitten through and cleaned up, even the molasses keg was shattered. However, we greatly appreciated what we did get as we were out of tobacco and had been smoking dried-out tea leaves for some time. To get a meal of bannock from the flour was a great boon to us.

On the 4th of January we reached Beverly Lake and camped on an island. Here were were held up two days by a heavy blizzard. We were fortunate in being able to find a little driftwood. On the 10th we reached Aberdeen Lake and on this date saw deer for the first time since leaving the height of land.

On January 12th there was a heavy ground drift from the north-west which developed into a bad storm. During this storm, which lasted for several days, our natives got lost and took us some seventy or eighty miles to the south. We should not have travelled in such weather had it not been for the fact that our dog-meat supply was again getting low and we wished to push on and to get as near as possible to Baker Lake with the dogs [before they all died]. On January 15th we were somewhere south of Schultz Lake and we broke up and burned a sled, leaving us now with two sleds. The next day our dogs were very down in condition and I was forced to kill three to feed the others. On the 17th one bitch had a litter of seven pups and these were all eaten up by the dogs. The next day we saw native signs and two [old] igloos, and came to the conclusion that we were in the vicinity of the Kazan River. By the 20th we were down to soup only and none of us were feeling any benefit from it, although it kept us alive, but we felt rather groggy about the knees after tramping all day and were now feeling the cold and our clothing was sadly in need of repairs.

Good fortune came our way on January 21st. We were heading on a north-east course to Baker Lake when we came over a hill and saw a band of fifteen deer below us. We shot ten after some smart manoeuvring. This put a new aspect on matters and the natives were much brighter, as they had been very downhearted and ready to quit us. In fact, native Joe told me that two of the Eskimos wanted to take some of the meat and run off and leave us, as they were still under the impression that we were going in the wrong direction.

However, the deer cheered us up, the dogs were well fed and we had a big banquet of back steak and blood soup. On the 24th we remained in our igloo as it was very stormy and cold. Native Bye-and-Bye went ten miles north-east and found a river running north with sled tracks on it. On the 25th we followed this river, and on the 26th of January, at nine-thirty a.m., came to its mouth and found ourselves at the south-west end of Baker Lake. The day was fine and clear and we could see the island where the Hudson's Bay Company post was, and we were all greatly overjoyed to see some land we knew after an absence of over ten months.

The Eskimos who killed the two oblate priests were duly tried and convicted of murder. Their sentence was life imprisonment, to be served at Fort Resolution on Great Slave Lake. However, in 1919 it was decided that they should be released, and they were freed and returned to their own country. It had become obvious by this time that they had acted under provocation and that the killing of the priests had been—in their eyes—an act of self-defence.

No attempt was made to arrest the killers of Radford and Street. Showing a surprising understanding of the situation, the Commissioners of the Royal North West Mounted Police concluded that Radford had brought his own murder upon himself, and that nothing was to be gained by prosecuting the Eskimos who had killed these two white men.

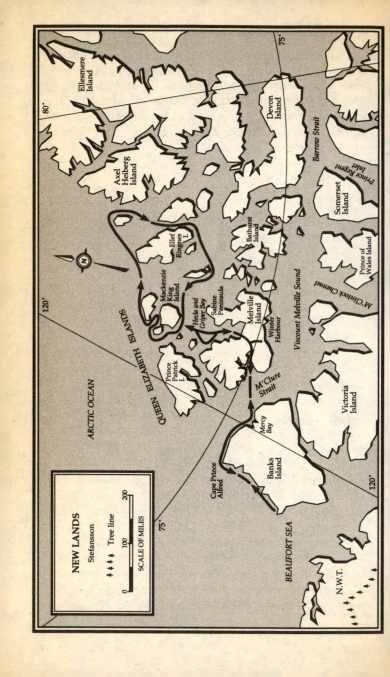

NEW LANDS

Stefansson

▲▲▲▲ Tree line

SCALE OF MILES

0   100   200

ARCTIC OCEAN

Ellesmere Island

Axel Heiberg Island

QUEEN ELIZABETH ISLANDS

Ellef Ringnes I.

Mackenzie King Island

Prince Patrick I.

Hecla and Griper Bay

Sabine Peninsula

Bathurst Island

Devon Island

Melville Island

Winter Harbour

Viscount Melville Sound

M'Clintock Channel

Barrow Strait

Prince Regent Inlet

Somerset Island

Prince of Wales Island

M'Clure Strait

Mercy Bay

Cape Prince Alfred

Banks Island

Victoria Island

BEAUFORT SEA

N.W.T.

N

VIII

New Lands

VILHJALMUR STEFANSSON DISCOVERS NEW ARCTIC ISLANDS, 1916

Born of Icelandic parents in southern Manitoba, Vilhjalmur Stefansson was, all through his adult life, a figure of controversy, since it was his nature to take nothing for granted and to believe nothing until he had tested it for himself. This attitude brought him into constant conflict with the opinions and conclusions of many other arctic explorers, and the fact that he was generally right did nothing to endear him to his fellows in the field. Now that he is dead, much of the vindictive pettiness that assailed him during his lifetime has faded, leaving the man to stand in his full stature as one of the towering figures in arctic exploration.

His work in the Canadian North began in 1908 when he entered the north-west corner of the Barren Grounds and spent the succeeding three years investigating the arctic coast east from Point Barrow in Alaska to the western portion of Victoria Island. During this time he made a

351

major ethnographic study of the then-almost-unknown Eskimos of this region, and he worked out principles for arctic travel (based on the concept of living off the land) which were to establish his pre-eminence as an explorer in the years ahead.

In 1913 he went north again at the head of the Canadian Arctic Expedition, sponsored by the Canadian government. The work done by this expedition under Stefansson's leadership resulted in the exploration of a vast area of the arctic island archipelago ranging north from Coronation Gulf to Meighen Island in latitude 80°, and in establishing the location and nature of all the lands in the western part of the archipelago. The expedition was in the field for almost five years and its detailed story is so complex that it is impossible to synopsize it here. Those who wish to read all the enthralling details must go to Stefansson's book The Friendly Arctic.

Strictly speaking, this expedition has no real place in a book about the mainland tundra; however, since the islands Stefansson discovered and explored are, in reality, extensions of the Barren Grounds — true arctic tundra — even though separated from the mainland by ice-filled straits and channels, I make no apologies for including an account of one of Stefansson's most spectacular journeys.

In 1913 Stefansson set out from the Alaskan coast to cross the ice of the Beaufort Sea direct to Banks Island. Ninety-six days and five hundred miles later he completed the crossing, having sustained himself and his companions on the sea ice almost entirely by hunting. He wintered near Cape Kellett on the west coast of Banks Island; but his plans for pushing farther north had been torpedoed by the failure of his second-in-command to send a supply ship to meet him at Banks Island — the assumption being that he and his party must necessarily have perished on the Beaufort Sea ice.

Nothing daunted, Stefansson pushed on with a skeleton outfit in the spring of 1914. He drove north to explore

*Prince Patrick Island and Brock Island and to glimpse
other new lands beyond. But now a shortage of essential
supplies, including ammunition, forced a return to Cape
Kellett and from there he had to travel all the way back to
Herschel Island in order to reassert command of the expedition and to obtain the materials he needed to continue
the northern work. At Herschel he purchased the* Polar
Bear *to carry supplies westward, and instructed a young
Australian, Hubert Wilkins, to sail the little vessel* Star *as
far as possible up the west coast of Banks Island to provide
an advanced base. One of his best men, Storkerson, was
told to travel even farther north with a party of Eskimos
and establish caches of caribou, bear and musk-ox meat.
In the spring of 1916 Stefansson planned to follow Storkerson with a small party of his own, and then strike out
into the unknown.*

THE FRIENDLY ARCTIC

On the 23rd of January, 1916, I started for Cape Alfred
from Sachs Harbour near Cape Kellett, with two sledges,
sixteen dogs, and the Eskimos Emiu and Alingnak, his
wife Guninana, and their daughter, Ikiuna, a girl of ten or
eleven. We travelled without adventure until near Bernard
Island. The last evening in January we passed the east end
of the island and camped about two miles beyond. The
previous fall Thomsen and Knight had placed on the east
end a depot of pemmican and kerosene. I now wanted to
pick these things up. The next day was beautifully clear
and at noon the sun came almost to the horizon. Emiu was
told to fetch the things from the cache some time during
the day.

Emiu had spent a large part of his life around Nome
and had there absorbed the Alaska idea of fast dog driving.
He took great delight in hitching a large number of frisky
dogs to a light sled and dashing across country at twelve
or fourteen miles an hour. It should not have taken him

more than an hour to go from our camp, pick up the two or three hundred pounds at the depot, and come home. No one in the camp knew exactly when he left but presumably it was about three o'clock, when daylight was nearly gone. When at five o'clock I went outdoors and found Emiu and his sled missing, I was not immediately disturbed. But at five-thirty I placed a lighted lantern as a precautionary measure on top of the snowhouse.

By eight o'clock we were genuinely alarmed. We pictured what had happened. Emiu could not have failed to reach the island for that was silhouetted against the fading daylight in the southward. He must have found the cache, packed his load, and started for home. Here he would fall victim to one of the weaknesses due to his upbringing with white men in Alaska, who generally overestimate the intelligence of dogs. Emiu had a naive belief that his dogs could find the way when he himself could not. Doubtless he had sat down on the sled, shouted to his dogs and they had dashed off at high speed in the general direction of home. They must have gone by the camp without stopping, not realizing where it was or possibly going on through mere excess of high spirits. Our snowhouse was on the bay ice with no landmarks near except the starlit trail.

We went to bed expecting to get up at five o'clock to pick up his trail and follow it, but as ill luck would have it a storm sprang up during the night. We could do nothing till past ten o'clock when Alingnak and I then went out to search. Alingnak found the trail less than a hundred yards to leeward of the camp. Apparently the dogs must have taken Emiu right through the camp without giving any warning. In spite of his best efforts, Alingnak could bring back no other information except that the trail led toward the land and could not be followed under present conditions of light. That afternoon and evening we worried much over what might have happened to Emiu. He had been lightly clad and had with him no snow knife except his short hunting knife. He was not yet skilful in snowhouse-building. The question was whether he might become so panic-stricken as not to do the sensible and obvious things. A snowhouse located on the sea-ice is the most inconspicuous of objects and difficult to find in a blizzard. But the black bulk of a ship is one of the easiest things found in dark weather. On his trip with Thomsen, Emiu had been at the *Star* and must have known that she lay about twenty miles to the northward. I took it for granted that Emiu, when he realized he could not find camp, had proceeded to the *Star*. Accordingly I struck out for the *Star* while Guninana and the girl maintained the camp and Alingnak again took up the sledge trail.

The day was beautiful until noon but I did not walk directly towards the *Star* but zigzagged about, spending a good deal of time on ice hummocks looking around with field glasses. In the early afternoon the weather suddenly changed into the beginning of a steady snowfall. I estimated that I was some twelve or fourteen miles from the *Star* and now started directly toward her, walking rapidly. But darkness came with strides more rapid than mine and I was still seven or eight miles away from where I supposed the ship to be when it became so dark that even the cut banks along the coast could not be discerned at more than ten or fifteen yards. The weather got even thicker and eventually one could scarcely speak of visibility at all, except that now as in any blizzard there was hope of seeing a body conspicuous as to its height, for no matter how heavily the snow may be blowing along the ground it is only in the most violent gales that it flies very thick at fifty or a hundred feet above the surface. My expectation now was to come in sight at any moment of the lantern which Wilkins was to keep burning at the masthead of the *Star* every night until I should arrive.

On the assumption that the ship was on the beach, my task was to follow the beach. In the darkness it was not easy. The only certain way was to zigzag at sharp angles, going first inland until you were sure you were on land

and then to seaward until you were sure you were on the ice. As usual under such circumstances, I frequently had to drop on my knees and dig with my knife until I found whether I was on ice or land. On account of this same thickness of weather I made the angles by which I turned landward and seaward so sharp that I probably had to walk four miles to advance one. But this is a game which always interests me, and although the advance was slow I did not find it tedious. I have always found that the pleasure of home-coming is keener the more difficult it is to find the way, and I looked forward with lively anticipation to my entrance into the warm camp.

At the rate of one mile of advance for four miles of walking, I must have been forging ahead at the rate of perhaps three-quarters of a mile per hour. This should have meant arrival before midnight. But midnight came and I had discovered nothing. I could not have missed the *Star*, so I kept on and on until about five o'clock in the morning. I knew that by any sort of calculation I must be far beyond my destination. The sensible thing to do was to stop where I was until the weather cleared and find the ship on the way back.

The best of all means for passing time is sleep. I felt neither sleepy nor tired but I lay down on top of a little knoll with my back to the wind and tried to sleep, covering my face with my arm in such a way as to keep off the drifting snow. A belief that has in the past handicapped polar explorers is that when you are lost in the Arctic you must not go to sleep. Not only is it thought that you will not waken, as you become colder, but it is actually supposed that the cold itself tends to make you sleepy. The first result of sleepiness is the slowing down of the pulse which seems to be the proximate cause of a general lowering of body temperature. People who are wakened from sleep from being too cold in bed become warm through mere wakefulness, providing the cold to which they are exposed is not too intense. This is exactly what happens in reality to a person who lies down as I did now. The approach of sleep brings on a chill that wakes you up, so that I have never under such conditions been able to sleep more than a quarter of an hour or so at a time, and more often I have not been able to go to sleep at all. With clothing a little warmer I could have taken longer naps. As soon as one brings common sense to bear on a situation of this sort, it becomes evident how dangerous is the ordinary procedure of trying to keep awake at all costs. It has been the cause of probably dozens of deaths that I have heard of. Men would get lost and, with the obsession that going to sleep would necessarily be fatal, would try to keep awake indefinitely by continuing to walk up and down. Through a semi-panic brought on by the fear of freezing, these men walk faster than they should, becoming gradually more fatigued and frequently perspiring violently enough to make their clothes wet, thus changing their clothes into good conductors of heat, no longer of much value as protection from the weather. But he who lies down without panic as soon as he feels tired or sleepy, and especially before his clothing gets wet with perspiration, is safer and better off the more naps he can take.

Before daylight, flickers of aurora through the clouds showed they were getting thinner. I started south again at six o'clock. With good visibility I made good progress, searching the mainland not only so much for the ship, which I now knew must be at an island, but for traces of people who would have been ashore abreast of her and for probable sledge trails leading from the land toward the camp. I zigzagged about half a mile out on the ice without having to make the angles nearly so sharp as the night before, so that now I was proceeding perhaps a mile and a half per hour. At half past eleven I picked up a track going south. To my surprise this trail did not run parallel to the land but curved and took me inland. After half a mile of going I came to a camp site where two or three men had spent the night. The trail led from this camp site straight out to seaward. When interpreted by Sherlock Holmes' methods, these and other signs showed that the men who had camped there had done so because they were lost in the evening and had the following morning been able to see the ship or some landmark which they knew. A few minutes' walk verified this conclusion, when the mast of the *Star* appeared through the storm three or four hundred yards ahead. This was at half past one, and I had left the camp at Bernard Island about eight the previous morning, twenty-nine and a half hours before.

My welcome at the *Star* was warm and cheerful. Food was brought at once, but I could not begin eating until plans had been arranged to continue the search for Emiu. He had not arrived and his absence looked serious. But early in the morning Wilkins and Martin started south and had gone only a few miles when they met Alingnak's party and Emiu with them.

The usefulness of the *Star* was now gone except in so far as it had contributed to our advancement towards Melville Island, and I arranged for its abandonment. The ship was safely hauled high upon the land. The remaining stores were unspoilable or of so little value that it did not pay to leave men for their protection. I was planning that a hunting party should spend the summer in Melville Island killing game, sun-drying the meat, putting the fat into bags or otherwise storing it, tanning the skins for future use as clothing, and doing everything to prepare for wintering on that island in 1916–17 by a party of between fifteen and twenty men and thirty to fifty dogs. The ultimate aim was to have a base as far north as the 76th parallel.

On April 5th we crossed from Mercy Bay to Cape Ross [on Melville Island] where we came upon Storkerson's trail and later found one of his camps. Here we killed a polar bear which had been prowling around for a day or two, eating entrails of killed bears and scraps he found lying about. The bear had touched neither a depot of pem-

mican and other provisions, which Storkerson had protected by a heap of rocks in a ravine, nor the musk-ox meat
which had been sunk into a sort of well made with pickaxes
in the top of an old ice hummock. Storkerson had left no
more than a note saying that he was proceeding with his
party to the head of Liddon Gulf. On the third day after
our arrival a sled arrived from the north with Herman
Kilian and Pikalu. Herman reported that Storkerson and
Thomsen, Noice, Anderson, Illun, two sleds and nineteen
dogs were now probably at the head of Hecla Bay on the
way to the New Land.

As we travelled northward from Liddon Gulf following Storkerson's trail, we had beautiful weather and the
opportunity to see whatever game there was on either side
of the Gulf. We saw on the average half a hundred cattle[1]
per day. From the top of Hooper Island on a clear morning
114 were counted. We killed none of these as Storkerson
had left for us caches of fresh meat. The huge black ovibos
can be seen whether on a snow field in winter or against
the green hillside in summer, as far away with the naked
eye as caribou can with the best six-powered glasses.

We crossed the isthmus from Liddon Gulf to Hecla
Bay in the vicinity of Point Nias. There was either a mis-
calculation on our part or a fault in the chart, for Sir
Edward Parry's monument of 1820 described by M'Clintock as still standing and conspicuous in 1852 should have
been visible but was not. At Cape Fisher we found M'Clintock's conspicuous monument — a barrel on top of a rock,
the rock itself on a hilltop against the skyline. The heavy
iron hoops were not much rusted although the top one had
loosened. We could not conceive what the use had been of
a heavy sheet-iron box resembling a modern camp stove
which had no holes in it beyond an opening at one end. It
is strange that with transportation such a problem heavy

---

[1]Stefansson prefers to use the word *ovibos* or "cattle" for
musk-oxen.

articles like sheet-iron boxes and a most massive barrel should have been hauled such a distance.

Beyond Cape Grassy we found that Storkerson had struck away from the land, but four miles from the Cape we found where the sledges had stopped briefly. Later we learned the reason had been one of the remarkable mirages that have deceived so many arctic explorers. Storkerson told me later that the fog had suddenly lifted, showing a land with bold cliffs apparently only fifteen or twenty miles away. After consulting his companions, both Eskimos and whites, he made up his mind that he could reach this new land that day. But for two or three hours as they advanced, the land kept receding and getting lower, until finally without becoming obscured by any fog or mist it sank beneath the horizon as if it had been some heavenly body setting.

In general my polar experience has been nearly free from the hardships that most impressed me in the books I read before going north. For nine polar winters I have never frozen a finger or a toe nor has any member of my immediate party. My only experience was on my first expedition when I got my feet wet in an overflowed river and froze one of my feet enough to raise a slight blister. But just north of Cape Grassy I suffered my first and thus far only serious accident of my career.

We were travelling at the rate of five miles an hour through some rather good going when my left foot broke through a perfectly ordinary snowdrift giving me a twinge in the ankle. We should have stopped right there and camped or I might have ridden upon the load, for when the going was so good the dogs could have made easy progress. But I foolishly kept walking for two or three miles, my foot getting continually worse. An hour after camping, the pain in the foot had become extreme and I could not flex the ankle joint at all. The next day I rode on top of the sled and found it about the most unpleasant experience I ever had. It was not only difficult and uncomfortable but there was a continual mental distress of being no longer useful but a handicap.

We were near Eight Bears Island when we met Thomsen and Illun with a light sledge who said they had left Storkerson, Charley [Anderson] and Noice the day before at Cape Murray with one sled and nine dogs. They had killed five caribou but it appeared to them that the caribou were fewer and the wolves far more numerous than the preceding spring.

I sent Emiu then, with his fast dogs and empty sled, to overtake Storkerson, asking him to wait where he was until we caught up. On May 3rd we arrived at Storkerson's camp at Cape Murray. Since leaving Cape Ross we had travelled so strenuously that the dogs had lost a good deal of flesh and were tired in spite of their abundance of food, so we stopped at Cape Murray three days to rest. Meanwhile I formulated plans for the year. The central idea was that Melville Island must be next year's base of operation. Captain Gonzales was to bring the *Bear* there if he possibly could. Storkerson was to take his family and some other Eskimos back to Melville Island where during the summer he would be in charge of the meat-gathering operations and other preparations for wintering. He was also to look around for coal mines so that if one were found we could use all our fat for light and food. I decided to take Castel, Emiu and Natkusiak with me for some distance farther before sending them back in ample time to get to Melville Island to help Storkerson.

With us we had for the use of our advance exploring party three Mannlicher-Schoenauer rifles and five hundred rounds. Two rifles were carbines which we carried ready for use in light canvas hunting cases on top of the sleds.

On May 7th Storkerson, Martin and Illun started south. The day after, Natkusiak, Emiu and I started north with two sleds, one bearing me as a passenger. We made over thirty miles that day overtaking Castel's party at their third camp. The weather was clearing and we could see from the camp where caribou were grazing. Natkusiak and Emiu went after them and got to them.

Spring is the worst of all seasons on the arctic islands. The total snowfall of the year would not amount to two or three inches of water when melted, but most of it falls in the form of snow between late April and late June. As we advanced along the coast of this [first] new land [Brock Island] we had to contend at all times with these unfavourable conditions. One of our teams consisted of big, long-legged dogs, another of smaller dogs that were used to soft snow, and the third of Eskimo dogs from Victoria Island that were unused to it. The big dogs waded through the snow without difficulty, the small Alaska dogs struggled along bravely and did their best, but the Eskimo dogs appeared bewildered and floundered helplessly through the snow that came to their bellies.

The day after we overtook Castel, we were travelling east when the weather cleared and we saw the Leffingwell Crags straight ahead and nothing but ice horizon and sky to the south. It was obvious that Cape Murray was therefore on an island twenty or thirty miles in diameter [Brock Island] separated from a larger island to the east by a strait. When we realized this we headed north-east and were soon following northward the coast of the larger island [Borden Island]. We gradually realized that we were in a big bay for we followed the land first west, then south-west and south until we got around the end of the peninsula when, on May 15th we found ourselves again on the west coast going north. During this time we got little idea of the topography inland except for low rolling hills. Continual fog and cloud with diffused light caused considerable suffering to the eyes and consequent delay at this time. Sitting in the sled because of my ankle, I needed no protection for I could close my eyes whenever I wished, and I was the only member of the party exempt from snow blindness. Occasionally we had to stop two or three days at a time when more than one member of the party was severely affected.

The strained ankle had been troubling me for more than three weeks and I began to feel more and more that I was a serious handicap to the party and finally decided to go no farther than Cape Isachsen on the north-west corner of Ellef Ringnes Island, and then turn back leaving the advance work to a party of two, Castel and Noice. We had provisions enough to outfit two men and nine dogs for about thirty days if the remaining three men and two dog teams depended entirely on game, and this accordingly was the arrangement. I gave Castel and Noice practically all the provisions. They were to follow the coast of our New Land [Borden Island] north-east and east but whenever it began to run south they were to leave it and strike directly for Cape Isachsen. They left us on the afternoon of the 21st. Natkusiak, Emiu and I struck north-west and camped on the shore floe.

Hunting conditions were bad both as to thick weather and unfavourable ice. I came to the conclusion that the food question was getting serious and I had better see if I could hobble around and do something. Walking carefully on snowshoes over level snow I did not seem to be hurting my foot at all. To the west I saw a seal about a mile off and as the ice seemed level I decided to try for it. On setting out for the seal I had an adventure that has several points of interest. Here is the copy of the adventure from my diary:

> On descending in the direction of the seal I found a three-foot tide crack that in my crippled condition I could not safely jump. I turned to follow one of the low ridges near the foot of the hummock. I am not sure what I was thinking, but probably of finding a crossing of the tide crack that would not expose my foot to a wrench, when I found myself falling.
>
> As there is a belief that one reviews his past in

falling, when the fall is likely to end disastrously, I set down here while fresh my experience. First I expected to fall only to my waist, as often has happened, and to support myself on the edge of the crack by my arms. When I found the crack was too wide and I kept on falling, I thought that this was just like a typical Antarctic crevasse. Then it occurred to me that it differed from the Antarctic in that there you could rely on landing on something to stop your fall, but here I might fall into the water. Then I decided, on the principle that is habitual with me now, not to speculate further but to wait and see if I dropped on ice or in the water.

When I struck, it proved to be glare ice. I seemed to have struck on my feet but they slipped and I fell on my left side. The crack was not wide enough for me to fall either backward or forward for my face was toward one wall, my back to the other, and the crack at the bottom only just wide enough so I could crawl along it. I began to wonder if I might be much hurt, and how long it would be before anyone came along my trail to look for me. I concluded six to ten hours. I arose a little stiffly and looked up to find that in falling I had made through the treacherous snow roof of the crevasse a nearly round hole three or four feet across which gave most of the light where I was. I now crawled about thirty yards in the direction in which I knew the hummock was lowest; and came to an opening where the sky showed nine feet above the floor. By cutting steps with my knife I got out here. On standing up and putting on my snowshoes — one badly broken by the fall — I found my foot seemed no worse. I therefore went for the seal and got him without incident at 135 yards. On the way home I unluckily slipped once and gave my ankle a wrench that seemed to hurt more than the fall.

The hunting continued bad not through any real scarcity

of seals, but because of thick weather. On such occasions I have envied the explorers who operated farther east. Sverdrup, for instance, three or four hundred miles east of us kept running into polar bears, but along the floe edge between latitude 76° and 80° we never saw even a single track in two years. We had to make our living from the elusive seal, which is on the whole the most difficult of all north polar animals to get.

Luck turned after a few days and when we had three or four hundred pounds of meat and blubber to take with us, the dogs were in such good condition and excellent spirits that we were able to make great speed toward Cape Isachsen, where we arrived the last day of May. The sand bar where we camped we thought was sure to be Cape Isachsen, yet we began to doubt it next day when in clear weather we found no trace of Castel's party. We supposed that he would have been here four or five days before. His instructions had been to erect a conspicuous monument, and the land was so flat that no such monument could possibly conceal itself. We did not have long to worry, however, for greatly to our surprise I saw through my glasses toward evening some black specks on the ice eight or ten miles south. We put up a flag on an ice-cake thirty or forty feet high to guide them to us but apparently Castel was as sure of our being behind him as we had been of his being ahead, so that he failed to look around with his glasses and did not see our flag. In spite of all we could do, Castel pitched camp three or four miles away, and I had to send Emiu with a message to bring him over to our camp.

Comparison of notes between Castel's party and mine brought out clearly once more the great advantages of living off the country. We had given him nearly all our provisions, but this had not turned out to be for his advantage, for hauling the food had made his progress slow and had tired out his dogs. Even with the men harnessing themselves to the sleds their progress had been only eight or ten miles a day. We were carrying loads less than half as heavy, and even with me on one of the sleds and the other men riding occasionally, we travelled at such a speed as to cover in one day what it took Castel three to make.

During the last week or two I must have been suffering from an attack of nerves brought on by my helplessness and inactivity. As I lay in the camp or rode bundled up in the sled I became unreasonably irritated by hearing Castel and Emiu talking continually about the delights of tinned sardines, which was Emiu's favourite food, or boiled potatoes, which was Castel's dream. After two days of this I lost patience and decided to send them where they could have them to their hearts' content. I had the self-control to wait till the first irritation had passed before speaking.

Once resolved to send Castel back instead of going back myself, my mind began working on various schemes and dreams connected with this altered program. I was already committed to wintering on Melville Island the next winter whether the *Bear* got there or not, but it now appeared to me that we could do much better than that. We could divide our party, the larger number wintering in Melville Island, and a few of us spending the winter at Cape Murray [on Brock Island]. I expected that making a living at Cape Murray would be a great deal more difficult than Melville Island, but had little doubt that we could do it. The plan was to have only a few dogs with us there during the winter.

It took two days to get everything ready for sending Castel back.[2] Both Castel and Emiu experienced something of a change of heart with regard to potatoes and sardines, and asked me not to send them back to the *Bear*, professing eagerness to spend the summer in Melville Island and willingness to accustom themselves to a meat diet. Without agreeing at the time, I wrote Storkerson that he should

---

[2] All of the Eskimos returned with Castel, leaving Stefansson with two white companions to carry on.

have a talk with them when they arrived and decide whether to keep them or not.

On the evening of June 4th, Harold Noice, Charley Anderson and I began to follow the edge of the land floe north-eastward from Cape Isachsen. One of the first things we noticed was the gradual increase of seals. On June 5th the ice was unusually level and there was bright sunshine, so thinking that if I wore snowshoes and stepped carefully I should be unlikely to twist my ankle, I decided to make the attempt to walk, going slowly with a long bamboo staff to steady myself. I struck out an hour ahead of the sleds and walked at the rate of a mile an hour until they caught up. They then stopped and waited until I got a mile ahead of them again. In this way I was able to walk six miles. Our progress was slower than it would have been had I ridden on the load but I was afraid that these men, being new, might be unduly depressed unless I showed signs of ability to help myself. Before making camp that night I shot an ugrug [seal] on level ice at thirty-five yards. From a pressure ridge at the camp I saw other seals and for practice went after two. I got a large male seal at sixty yards.

So my resulting optimism was founded not only on being able to walk for the first time in thirty-seven days, but on the foundation of two seals killed and hauled to camp where one was more than we could use. I have always found it good tactics in the early part of a trip, where an attempt is being made to convince new men that living off the country is safe, to kill a few animals to throw away. I get no pleasure from the killing of animals and disbelieve in waste of any kind, but the effort is not wasted, nor the meat either if it creates confidence.

Eight dogs were in our present team. Seven were originally chosen but in the last moment we added Jack, because he was fat and promising. But the day after we separated from Castel's party Jack began to show symptoms of severe illness. He did not become delirious as many sick dogs do in the north, nor did he refuse to eat, which is the commonest of all early symptoms, but behaved as if he might have severe inflammation of the bowels. Altogether our expedition lost perhaps a quarter of its dogs by one form or another of dog disease, but most of these died at home in winter quarters and it was seldom that any disease broke out in our advance teams. We were disturbed by the illness through its threat to the rest of the team. Although none of us had ever driven Jack before, he took his illness so bravely that before he died we were thinking more of hoping he would get over it than of the possible effect on our plans.

The Discovery of Meighen Island

The first hint that we might be approaching undiscovered land we got from the fact that when there was a current shown in our observations, it was running either southeast or north-west, and appeared therefore to be of tidal origin. The map as it stood, before our lands were placed upon it, showed a big open bight, which Sverdrup named Crown Prince Gustav Sea.

I have always thought that the discovery of land which human eyes have never seen is about the most dramatic of possible experiences. I don't pretend to be used to it or past the thrills that go with it. It is still my dearest dream to discover more lands or, if there are found to be none, finally to establish that fact for the half million or more square miles that still remain unexplored in the north polar regions.

The morning of June 12th Noice thought he could see land from the top of an exceptionally high pressure ridge and when I got up there and could see nothing that resembled it, Noice maintained that this was because the fog banks had somewhat shifted. Just before we went to bed, Charley reported seeing what he took for land on the temporary lifting of the fog, but this could not be verified. The next morning was moderately clear and no land was in sight, but after travelling about five miles to the east, from the top of a hummock I saw indubitable land to the north-east. As the ice was very rough, we had to camp after approaching six miles nearer. On June 14th we pitched camp on the sea-ice a hundred yards from the new land. It had accordingly been fifteen miles distant when we sighted it.

This land when first seen was barely visible against the clouded sky. The top of it was snow-covered with a smooth and oval skyline such as I have never seen on any land. It occurred to me that it might be covered with a glacier. As I was still unable to walk far and as the boys were enthusiastic about exploring, I asked Noice to go inland as far as he could while Charley followed the beach a little way, coming back before eight o'clock. A beacon was built by Noice on a hill three-quarters of a mile east from camp. It was about three and a half feet high. We shall put up a mark of boxwood there, so: "CANADIAN ARCTIC EXPEDITION—JUNE 15TH, 1916."

There is also a record wrapped in a malted-milk paper wrapper and enclosed in a New-Skin can, and that wrapped in a Kootenay cocoa tin — all three stand for things that have been useful to us on this trip but which now all survive only in their wrappers.

Since separating from Castel's party we had been cooking exclusively with kerosene in a primus stove. How economical such cooking may be is shown by the fact that between June 4th and June 16th we had used only one gallon. This had cooked two meals some days and three meals others. Perhaps half a dozen times we had found thaw water to cook with, but most of the time the fuel had had to melt snow. Of course such economy would not have been possible had we cooked more than one sort of food. We had a few items of groceries with us, but nearly every meal consisted of boiled seal meat with the broth for drink.

We started the exploration of this new land on June

17th, the sledges following the coast while I crossed overland. In spite of light fog I had no difficulty in keeping track of the team, but the men had greater difficulty in keeping track of me. After hobbling along ten miles overland at a slow rate I went down to the sea and waited about two hours for the sleds to come along. When they did not appear I started back along the coast and after six or seven miles found the camp. They had got the impression that I was behind them, had stopped and waited for me a while and eventually made camp.

Sea shells were scattered over the land and there were peculiar ice-built elevated beaches. It appears that this land has been rising in recent times, in common with most or all others in this part of the Arctic.

On his discovery of Prince Patrick Island, Sir Leopold M'Clintock was also the discoverer of the eggs of the Ross's Gull. But to this day such eggs are rare in collections. On June 18th on a reef between Second Land [Meighen Island] and a smaller island to the north, I saw with the glasses some gulls sitting while two others flew about my head, screaming and behaving like terns that have a nest. On the chance I walked half a mile out of my way to the reef and found a nest of two eggs. The nest was little more than a bowl of dry dust, lined with a few grass roots and small shells. Knowing these eggs to be so rare, I took the nest, what there was of it, and the two eggs.

Second Land (which I have sinced named Meighen Island) is the most nearly barren land I have seen in the Arctic. There is a little grass in places and there are some lichens and mosses, but a dozen caribou would find it difficult to spend a season there and they certainly could not live there permanently. Almost certainly no animals stay there more than a few days at a time. We found no lemmings and no owls but found owl pellets; balls of lemming bones and hair. But it is a paradise for the Hutchins Goose, whose eggs supported us for some time.

By June 22nd the sun had gone as far north as it

intended, and so had we. I had talked much with Peary about his Crocker Land to the north-west, and for twenty-four hours in clear weather Noice, Charley and I took turns in watching from a 200-foot elevation the skyline to the west and north. There were appearances on the horizon which might have been taken for land had one known it to exist but there was nothing that might not equally well have been fog clouds from open water.[3]

June 23rd. We were at the north tip of our land and started, about four p.m., to follow the coast south-east. Following the coast really means that we are now turning back and that the hope of further discoveries of land is renounced for another year.

The season was now advancing rapidly, uncomfortable to men and dogs, difficult for walking and for hauling sleds that stick in slush much worse than they do in any soft snow of winter. Most of the time we were fairly wading as we walked. On July 2nd we landed on the west coast of Amund Ringnes Island and proceeded to follow it south. Bearings taken showed that the strait between the two Ringnes Islands was much wider than the three miles indicated on the map, and in few if any places is less than fifteen miles wide.

Although it was midsummer, or rather because of it, Hassel Sound proved rather disagreeable:

"July 4th: Charley is much worse (with snow blindness), groaning and in great pain. He could not eat anything until afternoon but was a little better in the evening. A northerly gale slackened to a strong breeze in the afternoon but increased to a gale again in the evening. So as not to risk my ankle I sent Noice inland to hunt. Two miles away he saw a cow and calf caribou, fired at them and wounded

---

[3]Robert Peary had claimed the discovery of new lands out in the polar sea, which he named Crocker Land. Crocker Land does not exist.

the cow. He then chased them and they ran off. Too bad, for we are getting near the point where we must have meat.

"July 5: Started seven a.m., telling the others not to start for at least two hours to give me a chance to hunt. South of camp I saw a seal, was prevented from approaching nearer than three hundred yards by open shore lead, shot him at that range and had to go half a mile around to get to him. It turned out he was shot through the neck just back of the head and above the spine. He was merely stunned. I had pulled him ten feet or so from his hole and was about to leave him when he began to come to life. I expected the others to come along and pick him up. This seal was needed. I have never seen so protracted a spell of weather unfit for men or dogs as we have had since June 22nd and this is the first seal that has come out of his hole."

A day or two after this when I was walking overland and the men taking the sled along the ice in the Strait, they had the misfortune to have it upset in the deep water. Most of the bedding and clothing got soaking wet. It was a marvel that it had not happened before and still more of a marvel that it did not happen frequently after, for conditions under which one must travel over sea-ice in summer are such that it might seem impossible to keep anything dry. This is because in the spring the thaw water sinks until it finds or makes deep channels, and by midsummer the ice is cut up into a network of such channels a few inches or several feet deep and separating ice islands of all shapes and sizes. If the ice is three or four years old, these islands resemble mushrooms or champagne glasses — a narrow stem with a sort of wide table on top. Progress is a continual climbing up on such "islands" and plunging into the water beyond. Frequently the dogs have to swim and the sled must float, buoyed up by tin cans kept in the bottom of the load for that purpose. When the sled is actually in the water there is no danger of upsetting, and the task of the drivers is to keep the dogs and the sleds in the water most of the time, avoiding the ice islands and climbing out upon them only occasionally. The great danger is when the sled is crossing one of these islands, especially if they are rounded hummocks, as the sled is then likely to slide sideways into the water. This condition of ice is bad for sealing as well, since the least splash will send the seal into his hole. Thus we must make our living in July and August from caribou on the land or from the occasional seal that happens to lie near enough to land to be shot from shore.

Caribou signs were more abundant in Ellef Ringnes Island than they had been east of Hassel Sound. Traces of wolves were also numerous. We continued south along the coast of Ellef Ringnes for about fourteen miles on July 21st and were approaching land [an islet off Ellef Ringnes] after crossing a bay when we came upon the skeleton of a polar bear. I suppose polar bears must die now and then of illness or old age, but the sight of the skeleton brought the thought that the animal had been killed by men. An inspection gave no proof for I could find no bones that had been broken by a bullet. Before finding the bear's skeleton I had noticed a mound at the top of the point we were approaching. Presently we could see pieces of board sticking up. This was, then, a place that had been visited by white men.

I knew that Donald MacMillan's Crocker Land expedition had its base at Etah in North Greenland, but I hardly expected them to be working down in this vicinity. Yet the distance from his base at Etah is no greater than the distance from our base at Cape Kellett to the north end of Meighen Island, so that if both of us went equally far from home our fields of work would overlap by two hundred miles. Even before we found the record I was sure that the monument had been built by MacMillan. His expedition and ours had purchased pemmican from the same packers and here were scattered all about the peculiar red tins. MacMillan was a disciple of Peary's and the boards were chiefly from condensed milk boxes, and condensed milk was one of the four items of the standard Peary rations.

The only other white men who could have been in this region were Isachsen and Hassel [of the Sverdrup Expedition] in 1901.[4]

The beacon was probably a conspicuous one when MacMillan built it, placing in a corner a tin can containing his record. But since then summer had come on, the mud had softened and in part flowed away in the form of semi-liquid. We were much excited over the neatly written record dated April 23, 1916, some three months before our visit. It was east meeting west for the second time in arctic explorations, the other case being that of McClure and Kellett at Melville and Banks Island in 1853.

We were also meeting a method of exploration different from ours. MacMillan had three Eskimos with him and no white men, and was depending mainly on his Eskimos to do whatever hunting was necessary, while I had with me white men because I thought them better suited for the work. He had lost eight dogs and still had thirty-nine at his farthest point. We had lost one and now had seven. He had been hurrying so much that between hard driving and perhaps short rations three of his dogs had dropped in the harness and had been either killed or left behind to die, while ours had travelled in such easy stages and had been fed so well that they were continually fat and suffered from nothing except occasionally from sore feet.

Round the MacMillan monument were the tracks of a "small wolf" which we had noticed some time earlier. The explanation now seemed to be that this was not a wolf at all but one of MacMillan's dogs which had not died on being left behind on the trail but had revived after resting, had followed the trail to the monument, and had probably lived a long time on the remains of the bear carcass. Since then he had been able to make his living on lemmings and

[4]Stefansson, who was a supporter of Peary in the north polar feud, makes no mention of Dr. Cook, who passed through Hassel Sound on his way south after his attempt on the Pole in 1908.

birds eggs and was doubtless somewhere inland. We kept a sharp watch so far as the weather allowed, in the hope of being able to find him and take him home with us.

We rebuilt MacMillan's cairn with mud and tin cans, for we grudged to leave behind any of the boards except a sliver to which we fastened the same can that had contained MacMillan's record with our own record inside.

Stefansson and his party now turned westward to visit what showed on the maps as King Christian's Land. After some days of difficulty, evading open leads in the ice, he approached the west end of a smallish island lying to the north-east of him. We now pick up the narrative.

The great King Christian's Land of Sverdrup's map and the Admiralty chart does not exist.[5] In clear weather, from the tops of the highest hummocks, no land could be seen to the west, to the north-west, south-west or south, or indeed in any direction except north-east. Now, though the substantial middle of King Christian Island on the map had disappeared, I had no doubt that there was land in the direction where [Lieut. Shepard] Osborn had dotted in his discoveries of 1853. Heading south we travelled in that direction for twenty-five or thirty miles and I have never seen travelling conditions worse. In some cases the dogs had to swim continuously as much as half a mile at a time, towing the sledge behind them. I had to walk ahead picking a trail and especially careful now, for there were holes in the ice underneath into which the dogs would have swum as readily as where there was bottom. Part of the time the water was shallow enough so that the men could ride, but at other times they had to wade so as to allow the sled to float and thus prevent our gear from getting wet. The stray ice islands here and there were worse than the water.

When the sun was shining the dogs splashed and swam

---

[5]Only a small island, now called King Christian Island, exists in this region.

willingly enough, but on colder days it was my task to drag the leader against all his strength off each ice island and into the water. When the team was once in the water they behaved quietly and everything went well so long as their feet touched bottom, but when they began to swim the rear dog, which was the largest and the fastest, would catch up to the ones ahead and all would be bunching up around me.

We had now crossed the centre of Findlay Island [King Christian's Land] as mapped on Admiralty charts and found an average depth of over two hundred metres (maximum depth 315 metres) while all signs of nearby land are wanting. The going in this area could be called impossible — the water deep and the mushroom islands so high that a man who has been wading needs to put his hands and knees on them to scramble out. It is very hard to get a sled on one, for most have not room on top for the team to pull and there is not often room for the sled and dogs after you do get on top.

Now came an unusually cold spell and we had to break through a quarter of an inch of young ice on top of the water. The dogs could not advance at all, wading or swimming, until a way had been broken for them through this ice. August 1st it was warmer but there were heavy showers with periods of drizzling rain between, and this was one of the few days on the ice when we were soaking wet from top to toe. We had to zigzag so much that it was hard to keep careful reckoning and the continually cloudy weather made observation difficult. King Christian Island had long since sunk beneath the horizon when, the day after the rainstorm, August 2nd, we sighted an island to the south-west. After a few miles of advance two other islands a little to the left appeared. It took us the rest of that day, all of the third, and seven miles of travel on the fourth to get within half a mile of the largest island. We camped on the ice for we could not at once find a crossing [of the open shore lead] and were not, in fact, sure whether we cared to land. However, on foot I was able to make a landing after having followed the shore lead for half a mile. From a high hill, caribou could be seen on the middle and smallest islands, so I crossed over and shot seven out of nine fat bulls.

Obviously seven fat caribou was much more than we could carry. The reason for killing them was [that] on account of the deep water on top of the ice it was now almost impossible to get seals, and the ice itself had been moving and cracking during the last few days so I was afraid that the complete summer break-up might come any day, possibly marooning us on one of these small islands. I was so much worried by the instability of the ice that I should have gone ashore and made a summer camp on the largest of the three islands had I not seen from the top of it a still larger one to the north-west. We loaded seven or eight hundred pounds of boneless meat and fat on the sled and proceeded towards this new land. We knew it was a risky proceeding for, although the sled was strong enough to stand almost any kind of load in ordinary winter going, no sled could stand indefinitely the repeated shocks of diving off one ice island into the next, coming up each time with a shock like the blow of a thousand-pound hammer.

Our landing place should have been the nearest point but as we would have to live on caribou during the summer, I was reluctant to camp near a promontory. We accordingly tried to follow the coast of the north-east land and did so for three miles. It was an especially heavy shock that finally broke the hickory fender on the front end of the sled which decided us to go ashore and call sledge travel for that season ended. We found no place where we could land except by water. Having no tarpaulin intended to convert the sled into a boat, we were relying instead on sealskins. We inflated these each into an air bladder having a buoyancy of two or three hundred pounds. Four of them lashed to the sled converted it into a raft. It took the men several hours to inflate the sealskins and make the landing, and I got ashore meanwhile over some ice that was far too rough for the sledge and went in search of caribou. We had seen six with our glasses the day before, and I had them skinned and cut up by the time camp was well pitched. This was on August 9th.

This Third Land (which I have since named Lougheed Island) proved in most respects a delightful summer resort. There was not a single mosquito. The country was rolling hills, well covered with vegetation. The island's length is about forty-five miles, its main axis running a little west of north, its average diameter perhaps twelve miles. One wolf appeared soon after landing but he must have left the island. Absence of wolves and mosquitoes, together with an abundance of vegetation, made the caribou the fattest for the season that I have seen anywhere. There were perhaps three hundred of them on the island, which was many times more than we needed.

The only trouble was fuel. Of every resinous plant known to me as good fuel not one was found. Neither did we find willows. I made experiments with moss and with dried mushrooms. They would not burn, probably because we did not have a long enough time to dry them between the frequent rains. A few seals were on the ice but the chance of getting them was small. It would have been no fun for a seal hunter to find himself drifting off on the ice. A whole party with sledge and outfit might have enjoyed it more, but a man alone would have found it an unpleasant adventure.

So the only thing to burn was caribou fat, and boards, chiefly those we had picked up at MacMillan's Beacon. We stuck them up on edge to dry in the sun and wind and protected them from the rain. Most of them were about three-eighths of an inch thick and from eighteen inches to two feet long, and we made them into standard fuel portions consisting of a piece about three inches wide. One such piece whittled or split and burned with about a quarter of a pound of caribou suet sufficed to cook a meal. For the first part of our stay on Lougheed Island we used to cook two meals of this sort daily, but later when we had been able to dry some caribou meat to eat we used to have but one cooked meal.

The long weeks of wading through ice water before landing on Lougheed Island, and the summer spent there with inadequate fuel, came nearer to being hardship than any of my other experiences in the north. We had come ashore because we feared the break-up of the ice and the break-up, too, of our sled. During the middle of August Noice took care of the camp while Charley and I made a trip for several days with pack dogs exploring the island. From hills near the southern end we were able to get bearings of points on Bathurst Island. From other hills north of the middle we were able, on a clear day, to see King Christian Island, and from near the north end were even able to see cliffs which probably were on Ellef Ringnes Island. As with our other lands, we found considerable evidence of recent uplift in the form of a sprinkling of sea shells and some raised beaches. There were no traces of ovibos either past or present. Nor were there any traces of Eskimos. A few zoological specimens collected were chiefly such small things as could be preserved in the one-pound malted milk tins, but it seemed so interesting to try to get a caribou specimen from a district so far from where any had been taken before, that I decided to try it. One night I cleaned a young caribou while the boys were asleep, took all the measurements carefully, removed the skin according to the ideas of the taxidermist, and carried it home along with all the leg bones. I then went to sleep. Noice, under the influence of my lectures and the pressure of circumstance, had given up most of his views on meat and how to eat it, but he had persisted in preferring boiled fat caribou meat to the raw marrow which I had told him was much better. Noice now unrolled the skin and thought he would make himself useful by separating the bones from the hide. It then occurred to him that he would try to see if raw marrow was really good, and so he broke the bones for the marrow. I had taken so much pains with getting this specimen home in good condition that, when I woke, it was some time before I could see the amusing side of the incident and console myself that Noice had overcome the last of his food prejudices.

Toward the end of August it began to snow occasionally and on the 3rd of September we started the autumn sledge travels. The shore lead was not yet frozen, so we had to go overland. The only difficulty was to find ways across the few precipitous ravines. By September 8th we were at the north-west corner of Lougheed Island ready to cross to Borden Island but a reconnoitering excursion proved that the ice covering the thaw of the old ice was not yet strong enough. However, it froze exceptionally hard between the 8th and the 9th and the cold continued all day so that we considered it safe. Our sentiments on leaving Lougheed Island are shown by the diary on September 9th: "We left at 4:20 p.m. today. It is a hospitable if not a very pretentious place. We have not been hungry nor uncomfortable and are taking away with us food to last two or three weeks and skins for bedding and for clothing."

Soft snow and rough ice meant slow progress, so that it was not until September 14th that we sighted land. We reached Borden Island next day and found the ice on the shore lead weak. We tried to rush the load over quickly but the sled broke through just as we were getting it to land. Before us now were rather trying conditions. The black headlands that would have been conspicuous a week or two before were now white and indistinct against a leaden sky. Daylight was rapidly waning and it was one of our main concerns to reach Cape Murray while there was yet enough light that our party could be of some use in the fall hunt. We were counting on finding Natkusiak's party waiting for us there. The men took the sled along the land, as usual, while I travelled overland looking for caribou and learning what I could of the country. A typical diary entry follows:

"September 16: Started 8:30 a.m. following coast about south by west twelve miles. Then saw caribou six miles to south-south-west and went after them. When within half a mile of five I had first seen, I started three others out of a ravine where they had been hidden till they heard me. They were in long range but I did not fire so as not to scare the other five. I had fine cover but it was a clear frosty day and they heard me at five hundred yards and ran and did not stop for at least eight miles as I could see through my field glasses. The other three had run north. Went down to the coast and six or eight miles back along the shore to where I found a camp for the night, which is eighteen miles from yesterday's camp.

"September 17: The team followed the coast. I found a caribou trail averaging west in direction and caught up to them in thick fog at 2:30 p.m. Shot one only as I thought it probable we should find it too far to fetch the meat. A wolf came to within three hundred yards to get my wind. It was going to run off when I shot him — a fine male in medium flesh in nearly uniform yellowish-white, weight over a hundred pounds. I carried fifty pounds of caribou meat and travelled south for three and a half miles through thick fog. I walked to the beach and out on the ice but saw no trail. I concluded the team had not reached this point so walked east five miles when I came down to a bight where I found the trail. This was 9:30 p.m. Followed the trail west till 11 p.m. when it got too dark to see it.

"September 18: Found the camp after a steady walk with a 50-pound pack of about ten and a half hours. Got a little footsore from sharp slivers of rock frozen at all angles into the mud. These had in a day worn a hole in a nearly new boot sole that would have lasted a thousand miles on snow. No sign of Castel or of a depot he was supposed to make for us on this coast. We can, of course, get along as we are, but a gallon of kerosene and some new boots would be a good thing to have. I fear this failure to find Castel's depot presages Natkusiak's absence from Cape Murray, as something must have gone wrong.

"September 26: This is an uncomfortable time, while the snow is yet too soft for house building and the temperature nevertheless too low for comfort in a tent. We have searched the whole south coast of Borden Island without finding the depot. This is a setback. We can now have no winter base at Cape Murray. Castel was to cache for us boots, ammunition and other equipment, and due to failure to find these, we are not in a position to put up meat. The best we can now do is to go to Melville Island and help prepare things there for the spring work. Noice suggested we might all stay near Cape Murray for as long as the daylight lasted, putting up meat; and when the darkness came on, he would stay there alone to protect the meat while we went to Melville Island. I dared not accept this offer as we might possibly find conditions so bad in Melville Island that it would be difficult to send a sled back to him."

We started for Melville Island on September 26th. The journey south was an anxious one, our progress had been slow since leaving Lougheed Island and uncomfortable, for even now that the temperature had begun to drop well below zero, we were still forced to use the tent, having met with not a single snow drift hard enough for igloo-building. The hunt over Borden Island had given more knowledge of the country than game, and we were all depressed at not finding Castel's expected depot or Natkusiak's party at Cape Murray. These things had the effect of inclining us to think that all sorts of mishaps had occurred and that not only were prospects for next spring considerably darkened but the situation might be bad in Melville Island. We even talked of the possibility of finding nobody there, although it was difficult to assign any reason for thinking so remarkable a thing could happen.

We touched on the way at Emerald Island. I hunted overland while the sleds followed the east coast, but no game could be seen through the continual snowstorms. In following the beach the men strangely happened on a seal — strangely, because seals, though they live in the water and should not mind getting wet, do not usually expose themselves either to rain or snow. Charley tried shooting at eighty yards and missed, which is unusual for him. He said it was due to the excitement of realizing how much depended on the shot, for we were out of food and fuel and he knew that my chances of getting game in the interior of the island were small on account of the storm.

As the days got shorter and darker, the snow on the ice became deeper and softer and progress slower. We made as little as seven and a half miles in a long day of work, that was hard not only for the dogs but for the men, who pulled on the sled to help them. After taking seven days for the crossing, instead of three, we came inside of Melville Island near Cleverly Point the afternoon of October 2nd. We saw it only for a few moments through a temporary cessation of snowfall. When the snow cleared after sundown I could see a band of eight ovibos about eight miles south-west of our prospective camp. They were too far away to reach before dark but I did not worry about finding them tomorrow, for a farmer's cow is as likely to break through a stone fence and get lost as a band of ovibos is to travel beyond reach during a single night.

The diary records that for the last two or three days the dogs had eaten forty of their own sealskin boots, and had also eaten several pairs of our worn-out sealskin boots. We had been taking these home for new soles but now sacrificed the uppers rather than let the dogs get too thin. The next morning the men moved camp and came inland with a light sledge for fetching meat while I went ahead and killed a bull and an old cow. I saw a second band of fourteen but did not bother them. I cannot resist saying that the word ''sport'' has a curious meaning when applied to killing ovibos. I have heard of long journeys being made and even of ships being outfitted for the purpose of hunting ovibos. There may be much to say for the pleasures and even the adventures of the journey itself, but as for the "hunting" I would suggest that equally good "sport" could be secured with far less trouble and expense by paying some farmer for the permission of going into his pasture and killing his cows.

It was wonderful luck that on the evening of landing in Melville Island we had enough clear weather to see the ovibos herd and the next morning enough to kill them. Just afterwards the weather became so thick that, although the men with the team were only a mile away and in full sight coming toward me, they got lost. It was impenetrably thick the rest of the day and the day following, so that we talked a good deal about having secured the meat in the nick of time.

Plans and worries were badly mixed in our minds at this time. We made new guesses each day of what might be wrong but they were influenced by how we felt, and varied so much in tone that they were not worth writing down. A suggestion by Noice — I sincerely hoped might not be so — that Castel's party might have had sickness soon after leaving us and might still be in Isachsen Land. If that be so, we should learn of it at Melville Island so late that it would be difficult to reach them till the sun came back.

On the 5th of October we started travelling south-east, the team following the coast and I hunting overland. Because of the toughness of the ovibos meat, which we could well use for dog feed if we had something else, I shot three out of four caribou found about a mile from the beach, the team coming right up to the spot and taking on the meat without a special trip inland.

On October 7th "I left camp about 10 a.m., the others a half-hour later. I failed to see any game and came down to the coast some five or six miles south of Cape Grassy at half-dark. Found a sled trail badly snowed up by a wind that blew for an hour about noon. I started following it south (assuming it was our own sled trail) but soon noted that the footprints, although badly snowed over, showed by the turning out of the toes that the man was walking north. My suspicions aroused, I soon verified this by a dog track on a hard snow drift also going north. This was not our trail. I next took it to be that of two men travelling light to look for us in Borden Island. Followed the trail and found it turned west around Grassy, keeping near the land.

"Soon I saw a light, which proved that a camp other than ours was ahead, for we had been saving fat and had used no light as yet and the light would not show so clearly through our tent anyway. When I got nearer a man came running to meet me. It was Natkusiak, apparently quite as glad to see me as I was to see him, which is saying much."

We were overjoyed not only to get in touch with people but to find them this far north. Having once ascertained that they were not at Cape Murray, we had not been expecting to find them this side of Liddon Gulf; most likely, we thought, they would all be gathered in the vicinity of the *Bear* which would be at Winter Harbour south-east from Liddon Gulf.

The best news to reach me was the fire which was blazing in an open fireplace when I entered the comfortable ovibos-skin camp. They had discovered an excellent coal mine half a mile from the camp, good lignite in inexhaustible quantity, from our point of view, at least. "This is better than a gold mine," says the diary. "Had I a wishing cap, I could not have wished for things more valuable to the expedition than coal on north-western Melville Island convenient for our spring work."

We spent October 8th talking and rejoicing while the women got our clothing in order. It was especially our boots that needed fixing. The following day we left the camp and one week later met Storkerson, Castel, Lopez and Emiu with two sledges on the east side of Liddon Gulf. There were so many things to learn from Storkerson that we camped immediately and began to review the summer. He had done his work well and had been well assisted by every member of his party. They had killed and converted into dried meat ninety ovibos, twenty-seven seals and two or three polar bears. When autumn came, they had built a house out of ovibos hides with a floor space of twenty-eight by twelve feet and an additional sleeping alcove of about eight feet by eight. It had been our intention to spend the winter in snowhouses lined with skins, but now that we had coal to burn, the tallow could be used for candles and the seal oil for food for men and dogs.

So ended one of the last truly great arctic adventures. It did not, however, end Stefansson's work. During 1917 an almost equally impressive journey was made north through the archipelago, with a diversion far out over the sea-ice east of Meighen Island to establish once and for all the non-existence of Peary's Crocker Land. No more new lands were found, for the reason that there were none left to find. Stefansson had filled in the last remaining gaps in the map of the high arctic regions.

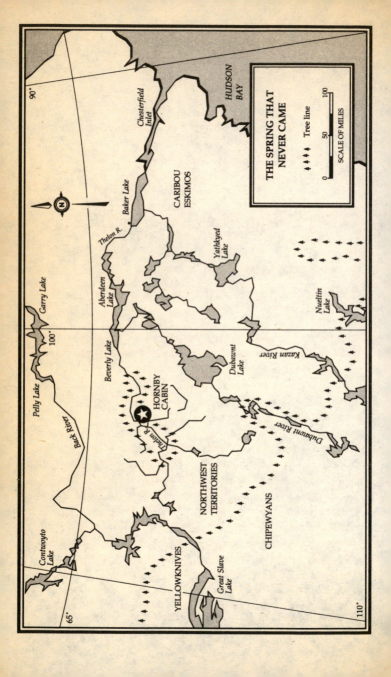

THE SPRING THAT
NEVER CAME

▲▲▲ Tree line

SCALE OF MILES

0   50   100

HUDSON
BAY

Chesterfield
Inlet

Baker Lake

Thelon R.

CARIBOU
ESKIMOS

Yathkyed
Lake

Garry Lake

Aberdeen
Lake

Nueltin
Lake

Pelly Lake

Beverly Lake

Dubawnt
Lake

Kazan River

Back River

HORNBY
CABIN

Thelon R.

Dubawnt River

Contwoyto
Lake

NORTHWEST
TERRITORIES

CHIPEWYANS

YELLOWKNIVES

Great Slave
Lake

IX

The Spring That Never Came

JOHN HORNBY AND EDGAR CHRISTIAN ON THE THELON RIVER, 1926-27

During the decade following the end of the First World War the age-old inviolability of the arctic plains began to give way before a determined invasion. White fox furs had come into fashion, and their value had sky-rocketed. The Barren Grounds were full of these small animals and they now became the lure which was to bring scores of trappers and traders into the plains from every side. These men spread quickly along the arctic coast from the mouth of the Mackenzie to King William Island. Along the west coast of Hudson Bay trappers and outpost traders pushed westward into the tundra interior. Up from the forests to the south trappers found their way northward into the Barrens around the headwaters of the Dubawnt and Kazan River systems. And from Fort Reliance at the east end of Great Slave Lake tough, solitary men paddled their canoes toward the headwaters of the Hanbury and Thelon Rivers.

The Barren-Ground trappers who went out into the open plains and wintered there were another breed apart.

Taciturn, withdrawn, motivated perhaps less by money than by the challenge of the unknown, they sometimes reacted to the isolation by losing the ability to live among their own kind. Existing precariously on the verge of starvation, often hundreds of miles from the nearest trading outpost, they lived in terrible aloneness. Since they had to carry everything they might need with them, they seldom weighed themselves down with steel traps. Strychnine was light and took up little space — and it was a deadly killer. When they had reached their chosen wintering grounds, usually in the early autumn, they made great sweeps through the surrounding plains slaughtering hundreds or even thousands of caribou. When winter came the carcasses were baited with poison, and the foxes, wolves, wolverines and many lesser beasts came to them, and died. But sometimes it was men who died — and not from strychnine. Madness lay close to those who wintered in the Barrens, and there were suicides and murders. The nature of the arctic plains had not softened during the intervening years since Hearne's time. The unwary, the incautious and the unlucky who gambled their lives for white fox furs did not always return to the shelter of the forests. Most of these silent tragedies remained unrecorded except, occasionally, for brief notations in the records of the Royal Canadian Mounted Police.[1] But one of the most poignant tragedies of all was documented, improbably enough, in the diary of an eighteen-year-old English schoolboy, Edgar Christian.

Christian was a second cousin of John Hornby, who was himself one of the oddest of the eccentric wanderers who had been drifting to the arctic plains since the turn of the century. The son of wealthy English parents, Hornby came out to Canada in 1904, at the age of twenty-three,

---

[1] As the Royal North West Mounted Police were called by then.

390

with no fixed purpose in mind except to escape from too close contact with his fellows. He drifted north, living with Indians almost as an Indian: wintered at Dease Bay on Great Slave Lake; visited the Coppermine Eskimos; spent winter in a cave dug into the side of an esker on the Barrens north-east of Great Slave Lake; and wandered so widely that he became a legend in the North before his fortieth year. Unkempt, secretive, almost always living from hand to mouth, he seemed to court disaster, and there were those who thought he was insane. But John Hornby was sane enough to emerge alive from the Barrens half a dozen times after he had been given up for dead.

Even the real Barren-Land trappers, who were among his few friends, concluded that one day he would push his luck too far. When, in the summer of 1926, he suddenly appeared in the Fort Reliance country after having been absent in England for some time, his old companions were appalled to find that he was accompanied by two complete greenhorns. One was Edgar Christian, a naive and likable young man with a boy's outlook, straight from an English public school; the other was a 27-year-old ex-Royal Air Force pilot, Harold Adlard. With these two as partners, Hornby proposed to do what not even the most intrepid of the professional Barren-Land trappers had ever considered doing—he planned to travel into the very heart of the plains and spend the winter trapping from a cabin he would build on the banks of the Thelon River.

Ignoring all attempts to dissuade him (as he had ignored every effort ever made by anyone to interfere with his moody desires), he set off with his young companions along the canoe route east and north from Great Slave; descended the Hanbury and, a few miles past its junction with the Thelon, reached the wooded oasis in the heart of the treeless tundra which Samuel Hearne had described as having been the home of a tiny group of Chipewyans who lived their lives remote even from con-

tact with their own nomadic tribe. This mysterious band has long since vanished. At the site Hornby chose for his cabin, the three men were more than three hundred miles by water route from the Hudson's Bay Company outpost at Baker Lake; and almost as far from Fort Reliance. They could hardly have placed themselves farther away from human contact, anywhere on the continent of North America.

Edgar Christian was the gently reared son of an English army officer. During a visit to the Christians in England, Hornby had talked so fascinatingly of his Great Lone Land that the boy had become hypnotized both by the man and by the world he described. Nothing would do but that he should accompany Hornby back to Canada for a first-hand look at this magnificent land of mystery. It was to have been a holiday adventure before Edgar left his childhood behind and settled down to a man's work.

Beginning in mid-October Edgar kept a diary; and this diary tells us all that we know about the events of that winter. It tells us even more, perhaps, about Edgar himself and about the shadowy figure of his hero.

Some things can be reconstructed without the diary. We know, and Hornby must have known, that the little party could not have hoped to survive without a plentiful supply of caribou meat. It was impossible for them to have transported a full winter's food supply by canoe from Fort Enterprise. Yet few if any caribou were killed and cached. Some fish were netted in the Thelon but not for human food — they were intended as trap bait. Perhaps Hornby miscalculated the timing of the autumnal caribou migration and so postponed the hunt until too late. Perhaps the deer changed their path that autumn — for, as the Chipewyans say, the caribou are like the wind, and go where the wind takes them. One thing is certain: when winter closed down upon the little oasis of time standing on the banks of the Thelon, hunger came with it.

EXCERPTS FROM *UNFLINCHING* BY EDGAR CHRISTIAN

October 15th. Jack and Harold took a short walk on [snow] shoes to get in rest of meat. I took walk upstream and set six marten traps. Returned at 2 p.m. to see weather had started to turn cold. Jack and Harold came back in the evening bringing another white fox alive, a good companion to our other little captive. 21° F. No wind but freezing slightly all day.

October 18th. This morning first thing I was obliged to sit and make moccasins before I could go out at all, so got up before light and finished sewing by breakfast time. Jack says before going out, one pelt means one bannock, so I went around yesterday's trap line. Returned at 11:15, nothing in traps except one Whisky-Jack and mice in another. Owing to snowshoes cutting, I was forced to turn home but wanted to take advantage of a fine day and have a look around for caribou. Jack returned in the evening with glad news, having seen thirty caribou on a distant ridge behind camp, so tomorrow we all go out in last effort for winter's grub.

October 19th. We all started out early to see if caribou were still grazing on ridge behind camp but were disappointed in seeing nothing for miles around; and as a strong, cold north wind was blowing and caribou in any case having no fat on, we decided to turn back and finish fixing up the house. Weather much colder all day but river still flowing.
8° F. N.E. wind.

October 23rd. At daybreak the weather looked much finer and not so windy so we all decided to take a short walk on to the Barrens and see the traps. On the way we noticed wolverine tracks towards the traps but saw nothing from a distance. On reaching cache we saw he [the wolverine] had packed away all the good bones and bits of meat. First two traps were set off and in the other traps we

393

could see nothing until we got close to them. He [the wolverine] was scratching, struggling and snarling, the voracious brute. All felt very satisfied at the fact of it being a wolverine. Returned to camp and continued with house.

12° F.

October 25th. Waking up this morning to find it snowing hard from S.E. with terrific wind. Spent day indoors fixing stretchers for fox [skins], etc. Being in all day was like Sunday in civilization. Wanting to get out to traps but can't.

23° F.

November 21st.[2] Wintry. Storming all day on Barrens so had to lay up all day which meant one day's less hunting owing to lack of grub.

November 22nd. About 8 a.m. wind dropped and made travelling possible. Walked up river on ridges till 12 a.m., then turned home. Tracks of caribou going south in front of storm. On way home wind strong and very cold. Could not keep hands and face warm at all. Returned to shelter at dusk. Sixteen miles.

November 24th. Jack took a look on the ridge for caribou but nothing as usual. Harold caught fine big trout on hook so we were able to feast for a day and rest up. We have now hunted over all country as marked ''Musk-Ox murderous''[3] but have seen none to get photographic records of in winter scenes. I rested up in house all day and did a little sewing.

November 25th. Temperature low all day and wind blowing. Jack set net in willows for ptarmigan in afternoon. I took a walk on Barrens but saw nothing although views good. Harold looked at hook but no fish.

− 15° F.

---

[2]There is a gap in the diary from October 30 to November 21.

[3]''Musk-ox *Numerous*''—a misspelling in the diary. Edgar was probably referring to a sketch map made by W.H. Hoare of the Thelon district.

November 27th. A fine day but we are all taking life easy to economize in grub. I went out to Barrens and got one fox and reset traps. Jack dug up all the fish left, sixty in all, which will last just two weeks, and then if we have no meat we will be in a bad way.

November 30th. Making an early start Jack and I set out down the river in search of meat of some kind. We walked a considerable distance and covered a large area during the day without seeing any signs or tracks beside hares.

December 2nd. Weather exactly as nice as yesterday except a little hazy on Barrens. Jack and Harold set out with about four days' grub with them and I am staying behind.[4] I cut wood in morning and put down floorboards in afternoon. Visited ptarmigan net but none at all and no fresh tracks. The place seems very desolate and I feel certainly lonely by myself, but can always find lots of odd jobs to do and keep busy to pass the time.

−37° F. No wind all day.

December 3rd. At daybreak was slight breeze from S.W. and temp. at −30°; by 9 a.m. was strong wind and temperature going up. Blew hard all day and snow drifted. This means one day's less hunting for Jack. I put in floorboards and tidied up in general about the place. In evening temperature −4° −30°. Very strong S.W.

December 4th. I had intended today to go out on Barrens to look at traps but before going, to get in some wood. While packing a log I slipped and the log hit me plump in middle of back, laying me out for the time and keeping me indoors resting. The monotonous silence was broken during the day by a flock of little American white-winged crossbills coming around. In evening went to look at ptarmigan net but again no signs. Took a last look out to see if Jack is coming home but no signs. At about

---

[4]This was a desperate attempt to find and kill some caribou.

4 p.m. Jack and Harold arrived after their fruitless journey.

December 5th. All took it easy to economize grub and rest. Now we must throw up trapping and practically den up and get hold of any grub we can without creating big appetite by hunting on short cold days.

December 6th. On counting fish see there are enough for fourteen days at two per day and then we have only a hundred lbs. of flour between us till spring when caribou ought to come again.

December 9th. The coldest day we have so far had −36° in morning and −42° as soon as snow started on the wane. I took a look around hare traps but got nothing. Jack got sticks and hole ready for net fishing [under the river ice]. Harold not feeling quite the ticket and stayed in. One ptarmigan in net, just a bite and that's all.

December 18th. Today is one which has completed many days hard work and anxiety. Have safely got the net into the river. Jack went down by moonlight and there was one fat trout in and this certainly made an evening's feasting. One ptarmigan in the net also, going to try a piece of it for bait on a hook.

December 19th. All anxiously waiting to see what was in net by daybreak and to our disappointment when we got there the floats were frozen somewhere in the middle. All day we laboured in vain digging holes in the ice but were no further ahead by dark. One trout on hooks.

December 25th. Christmas Day and although it seems hardly credible I enjoyed the feast as much as any although we had nothing in sight for tomorrow's breakfast. When we awoke today we had made up our minds to enjoy ourselves as best as the circumstances would permit. Our frugal meals of rich bannock I enjoyed as much as a turkey. During the day we put in the net successfully. Now we hope for the best. I went round martin trail and got one hare (breakfast). A wolverine had upset two traps and got away, but I reset everything and hope tomorrow he is in.

Weather much warmer by 20° F. Only −28° at dusk. I hope everyone in England has enjoyed today, and at the same time hope to God we rustle enough grub for a month from now and not wish we had not feasted today.

December 28th. We are now very shy on candles, only eighteen left and this means long nights and denning up to save grub.

January 3rd. Another mild day but at that turning slightly colder and trying to snow all day. Harold went up river and got one fox and two ptarmigan. Jack got one ptarmigan in net and in evening with him we set traps all around camp for a troublesome weasel. Under one tree I found a very welcome addition to the larder, fourteen white fish we had thrown there for bait if wanted. Jack's trap caught weasel in half an hour. During morning I went out on Barrens and only saw hare and ptarmigan tracks.

−4° F. −4° F.

January 4th. Jack's leg is paining still and has been for several days. Visited traps and got one hare in runway. No fish in net. In evening I found a cache of meat we had quite forgotten, having not eaten it before owing to not being good but right now we eat it with relish.

January 6th. Today weather has turned colder but there was sunshine which is certainly much brighter though does not feel warm and only gives a cheery appearance. Harold went for a walk up the creek. I think he saw nothing all morning before going [he did not speak?] and never spoke for some time after coming in, which makes things so unpleasant for us. I did very little all day, only visited hare trap and cut wood. Jack looked at net and trap by creek. No fish or ptarmigan.

−22° F. S.W. wind.

January 8th. Blowing from N. most of the day and −26° F. making things cold. Jack hauled out net and decided to keep it out. No fish on hook either. During day I started making stretcher.

−26° F. −30° F.

January 11th. Storm moderating considerably but still too bad to go anywhere outside. Had to keep indoors and economize in grub as best as possible.

−30° F.

January 15th. Weather turning much colder but bright sunshine which seemed to have quite a little warmth about it. Jack pounded bones which, when boiled, gave off quite a nice cup full of grease. Harold set ptarmigan net over river. I took walk over old martin trail. Could only get to first four traps and then snow too soft and deep.

January 18th. Although very cold it has been a successful day. In traps which Jack set close to house was one hare which we had for breakfast and then in the eddy was one wolverine quite fat, and a fat fox by the creek. Both had been travelling together by the tracks.

−47° F. −45° F.

January 31st. At last the end of the worst month is over and still grub on hand for ten days but damned slim at that. Harold went out and got nose frozen which means denning up more and eating less grub because impossible to go hunting if any danger of freezing. A very cold day blowing hard.

−30° F. −30° F. N. wind.

February 1st. A great day of feasting. Harold went out near house and saw caribou crossing river going north. He eventually shot one and wounded one. Jack and I then went out at dusk to bring in meat and make sure it does not get cleared up by wolves. Got back long after dark with heavy packs. Strong wind at −30° F. and bad snowdrifts. Having a great feast now and tomorrow we hope to get the wounded animal and calf.

−28° F. −30° F. North wind.

February 2nd. In morning first thing was very cold but sun shone bright and warmed up a little. Jack and I went on Barrens but saw no signs of caribou. Wind very cold at times and I began to freeze my nose and turned into

398

sun and came home while Jack walked on round a line of ridges in case the wounded caribou should be anywhere close. Now we have grub on hand things are better and gives one a chance to have a good square meal, even if we go shy a little later on.

−43° F. −40° F. North.

February 9th. Again we are out of meat and grease but Jack managed to bring in some frozen blood from Barrens where caribou was killed which makes great mixture with flour. I fixed up several traps today and expect something tomorrow.

−38° F. −26° F. West wind.

February 11th. Very stormy but mild weather and could not get out on to the Barrens and look for caribou. Took a walk up creek but got nothing in traps. Hope to God we get caribou soon as nothing seems to get in traps, and flour is nearly gone and we are grovelling round for rotten fish.

−15° F. −14° F. N. wind. Snowstorm.

February 17th. Words can hardly express what bad weather it has been today. All last night no wind and very cold and at sunrise today a terrific wind got up and blew all day, at low temperature. Could not get out to traps or hunt ptarmigan, so spent day in scraping hides and fishskins to eat.

−50° F. −42° F. North.

February 20th. At last something good has turned up. Mild weather and Jack got wolverine and hare, both fat and good. Jack not feeling at all well just now and he also froze his hand which is hard lines for even I felt damned chilled today. Fixed six traps and dug up five big traps to set elsewhere for hares. I saw several ptarmigan in the creek and not very wild.

−20° F. −15° F. N. Fairly strong.

February 23rd. An exceptionally mild and nice day, but even then both Jack and I felt cold fixing traps. I brought home one fox, not fat. Harold took a walk on the

Barrens and saw a band of forty caribou but could not get near them at all. However, it is good to know they are moving around here and I hope we get them soon as this game of going short of grub is hell.

−10° F. −8° F. E. wind.

February 24th. During the night Jack decided it best to have a good breakfast this morning and plenty of sugar to make an effort to get caribou. We all set out according to plans in different directions and Jack and I returned first, feeling played out. Harold went on out into the Barrens and got one young calf so this makes things much better, if the weather is good enough for getting in all the meat.

−10° F. −5° F. No wind.

March 5th. Weather today again very mild but stormy atmosphere. Jack and Harold both set off to go to cache[5] at midday, with one pot of sugar each and whatever other grub they have or what they hunt. I am well fixed here for several days and hope to catch something in traps. I went up the creek today at 3:30. Fixed traps and shot one ptarmigan which made an excellent meal for tea.

2° F. 3° F. N.E. Slight.

March 6th. After an early breakfast and sewing moccasins this morning at 10:30 I set off out on Barrens to see to traps and hunt caribou. Walked four hours without seeing any signs of any animals at all. Jack returned just afterwards from the cache. He had had no sleep during night, not much [in the cache], for a wolverine had packed it off and broken into camp. Jack shot one hare on way home which made excellent supper. Plans are now to go back to cache as soon as everything here is fixed safe and hunt from there as we are out of grub. Harold, footsore, with five days' grub is waiting for us [at the cache].

−8° F. −13° F.

---

[5] A small food cache and shelter established in the early autumn some distance west of the cabin.

March 10th. Managed to finish packing and start up to the cache by 2:30, which meant getting in late. At the bend was a wolverine in a trap, so Jack took it on his pack which was already a heavy one. Encountering soft travelling and a strong wind, we eventually got into the cache at dark. Here we found Harold, who had only shot four ptarmigan and seen no signs of caribou. We crossed tracks on lake halfway, but saw nothing else.

3° F. 00° F. East. Strong.

March 12th. Weather much colder today in the morning. Had to wait till 12 noon before starting out, for Harold to mend snowshoes. This he could have easily done yesterday. Going west we spelled at 2 p.m. in clump of trees and had tea and a little sugar. Here we saw a raven going north so caribou must be on the move. Before leaving camp snowstorm got up and we could not see where to travel. During afternoon we walked on over a large lake hoping to strike the river. We saw caribou tracks going north but could get nothing for supper. At 5 p.m. we pulled into clump of heavy timber and made camp, then prepared some caribou hide to eat. I slept a little at night. Jack and Harold were awake all the time.

−20° F. −18° F. Wind. Snow.

March 13th. Seeing how conditions were in the morning, it was obviously foolish to carry on. All feeling tired from want of sleep and little grub, heavy packs and soft snow. After a breakfast of hide we started to make tracks for the river. Travelling very bad, making packs feel heavier. Took turns at beating trail and struck river at 2 p.m. about eight miles from camp. Here we spelled and had a cup of tea and frazzled hide with a little bit of sugar. From here we shoved on, knowing we would have a camp fixed for the night if we got to the cache, and also hide mat which we could eat and then get back home as soon as possible. On way down river saw ptarmigan but they were very wild and we could not get one. Got in late, feeling very tired and I soon feel asleep. Jack and Harold again did not sleep but sat by the fire all night.

14° F. 9° F.

March 14th. A real hurricane blowing today so we cannot move at all and spent the day preparing hide to eat, and resting up. Tomorrow we hope to make home with sleigh and everything [from the cache].

−5° F. −10° F. N.E.

March 15th. Starting about 12 noon with sleigh we found travelling very bad indeed. All feeling as weak and feeble as anything and intensely cold. Pulling hard for a long time in soft snow certainly showed we had the stuffing knocked out of this, but we have to get back home as making open camp tonight means too much work and we would all be in the next day. At about 8 p.m. we had to dump the food and pack on with bare necessities. On way home Jack fell and must have hurt himself badly. On arrival I could hardly do a thing. Jack was a marvel, lit fire, made tea and cut firewood. I fell asleep about 11:30 and woke at daybreak.

−28° F. 00° F. No wind.

March 16th. We did as little as possible today and rested through. Jack took a walk downriver and shot one ptarmigan which was excellent [boiled] with a hide and saccharine. In our absence caribou and wolverine passed close to house and traps are not in order so it shows what a mistake moving from a warm house was.

−9° F. −2° F. West wind.

March 22nd. Conditions very bad today. Strong north wind and low temperature. Rested up all day and cut hide to eat. Went down river all muffled up to look at ptarmigan net but nothing. Saw three ptarmigan near house and on going to shoot, my rifle bolt jammed. Exposed to wind, fumbled about without mitts on and froze my right hand.

−22° F. −16° F. North.

March 26th. Clear and bright during day but cold. I

visited hare trap and found hare had been caught and got out again. A great pity as we are now starting to eat fur capeau[6] and then wolverine skins. Jack at last took a rest in the house and Harold was out a short while. Nothing coming in, but time is surely passing and although we may go damned hungry, we can keep on till caribou come north and then what feasting we can have. Only a matter of patience really, but very trying mentally and physically, for we are weak and easily tired and two meals of hide per day.

$-10°$ F. $-26°$ F. North.

April 1st. This month has started in none too good. We had to eat wolverine hide for supper. Stormed hard all day and we could do nothing much. Jack took a walk to creek, located hare trail and set a trap which I hope to visit tomorrow. Jack is suffering agonies in left leg which must make life absolute hell under the present conditions. Harold getting wood and water and says he feels rotten. So do we!

$-20°$ F. $-11°$ F. S.W. Strong.

April 4th. I now write today's diary as far as it goes to make sure of it. Jack during night decided that as the weather seemed milder he should make an attempt to get in caribou guts from Barrens[7] as his leg is getting worse and he feels it is the last day he can move on no more grub than we have without eating wolverine [skins]. Harold dug up fish scraps and bones from bait pile and cooked them up. Meanwhile I rested and Jack kept on saying he would be all in and absolutely crocked when he eventually got home again and that we would have to carry on. What a mental strain it was. I felt homesick as never before and hope to God they know not what Jack is suffering. I rubbed his leg amidst tears and he had saved a little fox meat for

---

[6] "Capote" — their caribou-skin coats.
[7] The offal from caribou killed in the autumn.

me to eat. This cheered me up. I suppose I was crumbling up because of no grub but still, by midday Jack started, all muffled up, looking as cold as charity and could hardly walk. I wish I could buck the cold more and share his hardships, but he has a mind and will of his own which no one else has got. I now sit here with Harold frying up bits of fish to eat and wait for Jack, who by now must be icy cold in the Barrens.

5 p.m. At last Jack is safely home again. Got very cold digging in the snow and could not find the grub. Tonight we sit around the fire and have fish scraps for supper and will get more for breakfast. Jack feels content to have got back and done as he did and this makes us all feel better and more optimistic as there must be a burst in weather soon. During day saw a raven twice. In evening clouded over and turned milder. Whether to stay or not?

 $-8°$ F. $-3°$ F. N.E. and ½ S.W.

April 6th. Affairs none too good today. Harold woke up complaining of bad weather to get out and dig in snow for scraps. He said he felt rotten and miserable, etc., etc. This is an awful selfish way for him to go on when Jack is suffering and takes long walks when possible. Jack had to curse Harold eventually to stop his carrying on and it was like water on a duck's back. He is very queer at times now and one must keep an eye on him at all times till we get grub. Poor devil must be feeling bad but we are all feeling just the same and I find it hell to move around at all. Jack took a walk and looked for ptarmigan but got nothing. We have found scraps for tomorrow and bones for next day which keeps us a-going.

 $-8°$ F. $-4°$ F.

April 11th. 9 a.m. Situation is now very serious. Jack last night told both Harold and myself that he felt he was sinking fast and might pass away at any moment, so he talked to us as to what should be done. I promised him I can carry on for five days on wolverine hide, doing heavy work and hunting. Harold took a walk after ptarmigan last evening which proved he can walk, so Jack has told him he must get on to the Barrens and dig up the caribou paunch. I am myself capable but do not know even where they are and Jack says I must keep my energy in case caribou come on the river in a day or so. Last night Jack said he could last a week if I would, but he had a bad night, legs paining and now he says that two days is the most. Harold kept fire all night while in vain I tried to rest, but how can I now under such worry?

April 13th. Jack this morning asked me to take a walk before breakfast to see if there was a hare in the trap. I got Harold a meal ready and then started off. On way home was taken bad on the river and had job to get home. Harold in same state and also Jack. The whole trouble being [we are] bound up from bones which we must have eaten ten days ago. Harold eventually got away to hunt but came home all in and played out in short while. Jack and I so far had no meal at all and had eventually to share it with H. as well, then wood to cut, etc., and all time to see to Jack who is very weak, but says by clearing his system of bones will be O.K. Very mild weather, raining at night, house drenching.

April 14th. Jack is still bound up and so am I and feeling awful to stay up with Jack who is fighting on wonderfully well. Harold at daybreak absolutely unhinged. I eventually got rid of some bones but feel weak.

April 16th. After a very restless night and Harold and I both played out and weeping at times to see poor Jack in such a way, at 4:30 a.m. heard ptarmigan calling. Harold went out and shot one after about an hour. Simply wonderful of him really, but alas, Jack is too far gone now to enjoy such a meal.

4:30 p.m. Between us have managed to prepare a meal of hide and rest a little. Jack still breathing but unconscious. Have got some broth from ptarmigan in case he can take it at any time. Must now get out and cut wood for tonight and get water.

April 17th. One o'clock. At 6:45 last evening poor Jack passed peacefully away. Until that minute I think I remained the same but then I was a wreck. Harold good pal was a marvel in helping me and putting things a little straight for the night. I managed to cut some wood by dark, Harold promised to do the rest. He talked to me so wonderfully and realized my condition, I am sure. I lay on my bed and listened to him talk and occasionally I dozed off feeling so worn out, and he kept fire during night and brought me tea and aspirin to help along, which was a relief as I was able to sleep. Today Harold and I do just the essentials and I am looking over certain things as well. We both are very weak but more cheery, and determined to pull through and go out to let the world know of the last days of the finest man I have ever known and one who has made a foundation to build my life upon. Snowstorm all day.

20°. N.E.

April 18th. Snowstorm terrific all day, as bad as any we have ever had in winter. Lots of odds and ends to be done but even that is too much for us both now. Cutting wood is an effort which seems incredible. Harold after doing so well in helping me yesterday fixing up is simply played out, and both of us are in a bad way of being bound up by bones which have now been in our systems for weeks. Harold fixed up syringe and performed on me, which was successful, so if we can clear ourselves like that we can get out and hunt when weather is fine again.

−4° F. 00° F. N.E.

April 20th. From bad to worse conditions go on. Harold is very weak indeed today and can hardly swallow his food. What is the matter I simply cannot make out, for I am able to keep on my legs and get wood on the same food of boiled wolverine hide. We remembered a fox that died had been thrown under the snow, so I went out and dug it up to cook for supper. I hope this will do some good. I have not been able to relieve myself normally today, so

406

will use syringe before night. Tonight I make a boil of spruce needles as a tonic to see if it does good. I seem to remain cool and collected now, but if anything might happen to Harold, God only knows what state I will be in, but of course hardships and worries have been so tremendous for so long now that I am prepared for the worst or best.

– 15° F. – 10° F. N.E.

April 23rd. A very worrying day for both Harold and myself, especially poor Harold who had an uncomfortable night, through leaving me to sleep when I felt played out last night. Harold managed to relieve himself in the evening, and I was not able to at all. We still both have an abundance of hair in our systems. In the afternoon the wind which was bad dropped, and the sun came out. I was able to gather in scrap pile near house enough fish-skins for supper, which were excellent, and this left a boil of bones for breakfast tomorrow. I feel very weak today to cut wood and water, and hope I am no worse tomorrow.

April 26th. Weather seems to be much nicer in morning, though there is a lack of sunshine which makes life more miserable. Slept till 9 o'clock after turning in at midnight, and fixed up breakfast and a boil of bones. Endeavoured to relieve myself but without success. Harold too weak to make the attempt, and I was too weak and played out to assist properly. During the day I got in enough scraps to make a couple of meals, but I got so wet and chilled in so doing that I could hardly cut wood after it. All this time Harold should get much more attention. He is suffering, but grub and wood are important also.

May 4th. Now I start in writing my diary again, from here. At present can only state that since I last wrote I have not had as much as a moment's time to do such a thing, for Harold's condition grew worse and so did mine. That night Dear Harold passed away after a bad relapse the previous night. During the day he seemed to get better and wanted to relieve himself. This was managed as usual each day except the previous one, and the result was pounded bones again, proving I think that bones have been the trouble all along. After this he was able to move around in bed much more and said he felt much better, and had shaken off the illness but felt weak, so I went out to cut wood and get water. When I came back he said he felt very queer and knew not what to do, although not painful. By 10:05 he had gone unconscious and slept. As for myself, now I am played out after no sleep and food for a long time so have managed to make up some soup from bones and have a cup of tea and rest. Today I must fix things up as best as possible, cut wood, dig in snow for scraps of fish which we are surviving on still and rest as best I can and trust for a good day tomorrow. I cannot hunt, as walking around in soft snow is beyond my powers now, and the weather is bad.

May 6th. Woke up at 4 a.m. and put on fire. Made some tea and had a little snack I had cached from last night's supper. Prepared my breakfast of fish, to which I added a little gut fat. Not feeling very fit during morning, chiefly due to [being] run down and bound up for last few days, I suppose. Weather cold and blowing hard from Barrens. Did odd jobs in house till 12 noon, then went out, got water and dug for scraps. Managed to get in one more day's food consisting of scrapings of bones and little bits of meat and caribou skin. Being so cold outside I came in at 2 p.m. to work in house and keep warm. Sorted out clothing and suitcases to try to get the place a little bit straight, then cleaned up scraps which had been thawing out and got my supper ready, which is wolverine heart and a little lights boiled and gut fat added.

$-2°$ F. 00° F. N.E. Strong drift. 20° in sun.

May 7th. 10 a.m. I write my thoughts down just now while I think about it all, and explain my day's actions and reasons for such. Last night I went to bed eventually at 9:30 having relished my supper. I awoke at 8 a.m. having slept well. I felt much better, but to my surprise I was as thin as a rake about my rump, and my joints seemed to jerk in and out of position instead of smoothly. I have now used syringe on myself, and only freed myself of two small hard lumps of excreta, chiefly bones. These bones have been eaten at least a month ago, and other food has passed by. I write all this down as I think it is of importance seeing how suddenly Harold and Jack went ill, but I must stick to my guns and endeavour to cure myself now. Going out to look for grub, get wood and water now. 12 noon.

3 p.m. Having no one to talk to, I must relieve the desire by writing my thoughts. I have three days' food on hand, but want to keep on getting in an extra day every day at least from the scrap pile while the weather is too bad to get game; therefore I cannot risk denning up and being too bad to get more in three days. However, I think I managed to scrape up a meal today at least in the way of scraps. When I came in I had a little bit of wolverine lights, and tea. Just little snacks like this during the day keep off the aching pangs of hunger and must do good.

8:30 p.m. Just looking out for last time and saw four ptarmigan feeding in front of the house. Had to hurriedly go out and took little rifle being the lightest. Birds were wild and I could not get close; one shot and they went; however, hope more come around, for they are the first things I have seen for a long time now.

00° F. 10° F.

May 9th. I have today not done any digging in the wet snow for scraps as it seems to give me such a chill which gets no better, and at the same time I am trying to clear my system of bones with syringe every day. I can only just cut wood and get water, but have such pains in my back that walking is difficult, and to get out and hunt for fresh food in a day or two I must at least be able to walk. Just now there are no very good signs of caribou, for the ridges are hard and covered with snow and cannot be thawing out. I have three more days' food on hand, so by getting in none today I hope I have done no harm. Kept warm in the house as much as possible and had success with relieving myself, but my back aches and moving around seems to be a wobbly process.

Cold S.E. wind. 10° F. 10° F.

May 11th. A very cold and dull day, blowing from the north. Felt as if I don't know what to do with myself, having a cold, being bound up and short of grub, yet have not got a healthy appetite for what little food I have. I did not give my cold a chance to get worse today by digging in snow, but kept warm in house and decided to fix up food for tomorrow. When coming back with wood tonight, noticed quite a nice little piece of fish lodged in a tree from where the snow had thawed.

10° F. 10° F. N.

May 13th. After my breakfast of fish scraps and bouillon I used syringe with much success eventually and my system still contains bones which are the root of all the trouble, and shortage of good food does not help me to get better. What food I now eat is near the door in a heap of ice so cannot go; therefore I think it best not to dig today but try and get strength for wood cutting in the evening, have an early supper of boiled fish scraps and bones and see how things are tomorrow. Feel very tired now so will wrap up and try to sleep.

15° F. 10° F. Fairly strong sun.

May 16th. Just as yesterday only worse. Could not cut wood and seem to have a chill and can hardly move at all. Feel an awful pressure on my spine but using syringe makes no difference. Eventually got enough brush off nearby trees to cook some fish scraps for supper along with hare guts. Tomorrow I will have meat scrapings for breakfast, probably wolverine stomach for supper and hope for the best and burn up what I can of furniture.

May 17th. Another bad day, no fine weather, could not move out to get wood so eventually cut bed-pole to burn. If I cannot get grub tomorrow, must make preparations.

May 18th. Weather changed, managed to pound up bones out in sun and gathered in some scraps which make meal and some for tomorrow, I hope. Ptarmigan came near to house once but could not get. One swan flew over, one raven and three robins I saw.

May 19th. Thawing in morning. Got out again and had in few scraps, but few, and then snow in afternoon so had to den up and hope. Rest till tomorrow and then [if] sun I might get out again.

May 20th — June 1st. Have existed by walking and crawling in and out of house, finding plenty of food, — in fact, more than I could eat, — but owing to its quality did not keep me going sufficiently to get rid of it as I ate it, being insufficient in grease, I think.

On 22nd I found lots of meat under snow and four good meaty bones covered in fat and grease. These put me on my legs for three days cutting wood, etc. I cooked up enough fish for four days and then rested, thinking I could lay to and strengthen when the weather might be warmer and I would find more grub thawing out and even shoot ptarmigan if I could walk. Alas, got weaker and weather was blowing in snowstorm for four days, after that not even thawing in daytime.

Now June 1st. I have grub on hand but weaker than have ever been in my life and no migration north of birds or animals since 19th (swan).

Yesterday I was out crawling, having cut last piece of wood in house to cook me food I had which is a very fat piece of caribou hide; but while out, I found fish and meat in plenty and greasy gut fat on insides of foxes and wolverine, containing liver and hearts, kidneys and lights and one fox carcass. All this I cooked up, leaving the hide as a cache. I ate all I could and got rid of much foul food from my system, apparently been stopping me walking.

At 2 a.m. went to bed feeling content and bowl full of fish by me to eat in morning.

9 a.m. Weaker than ever. Have eaten all I can. Have

food on hand but heart petering? Sunshine is bright now. See if that does any good to me if I get out and bring in wood to make fire tonight.

Make preparations now.

Got out, too weak and all in now. Left things late.

Before autumn came in 1927 a number of people had begun to worry about the failure of Hornby's party to appear either at Baker Lake or Fort Reliance. One of them, the explorer Vihjalmur Stefansson, seems to have smelled death. He made every effort to persuade the Canadian government to send out a search party; but nothing was done. The winter passed and there was no news from the Barren Grounds.

In July of 1928 a party of four young prospectors decided to risk descending the Thelon from Great Slave Lake. As their canoes swept along the broad river below the Hanbury junction, the men noticed axe marks in the trees, and a few moments later they came in sight of a small cabin. Curious to know who might have chosen to live in such a lonely place, they landed. The diary of the leader of the party, H. S. Wilson, tells the story of their macabre discovery:

> Landed to investigate. Found cabin door closed and two corpses outside, one neatly done up in burlap and canvas, other wrapped in blanket. Broke open door and found third corpse on bed completely covered by red H. B. [Hudson's Bay] blanket. In removing blanket J. T. [John Thompson] accidentally knocked corpse off bunk to floor. Small trunk and several suitcases around bodies apparently those of J. Hornby and his two nephews. Moved some articles around but left cabin and contents much the same as found. Bodies in very bad state of decomposition and probably been dead a year at least. Death probably due to illness followed by starvation.

The mystery of what had happened to Hornby and the two young men was solved. But it was not until the following summer that the R.C.M.P. managed to get a patrol to the cabin. The police found it much as Wilson had left it; but their investigation was more thorough and on top of the stove they noticed a scrap of paper with an almost illegible message:

WHO————LOOK IN STOVE

They looked, and in the ashes of the long-dead fire they found the diary of Edgar Christian.

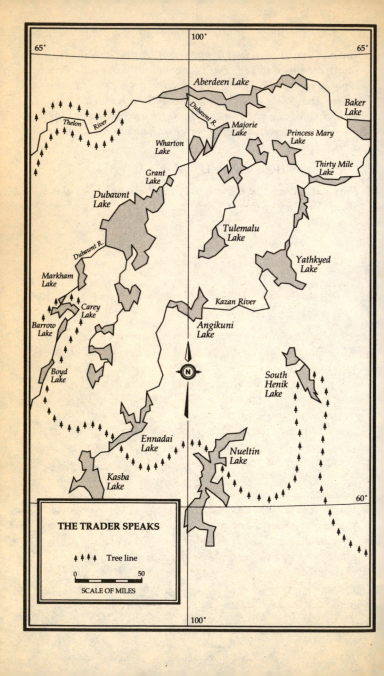

65°   100°   65°

Aberdeen Lake

Baker Lake

Thelon River

Dubawnt R.

Majorie Lake

Princess Mary Lake

Wharton Lake

Thirty Mile Lake

Grant Lake

Dubawnt Lake

Tulemalu Lake

Yathkyed Lake

Dubawnt R.

Markham Lake

Kazan River

Carey Lake

Angikuni Lake

Barrow Lake

N

Boyd Lake

South Henik Lake

Ennadai Lake

Nueltin Lake

Kasba Lake

60°

THE TRADER SPEAKS

▲▲ ▲▲▲ Tree line

0   50

SCALE OF MILES

100°

X

The Trader Speaks

THIERRY MALLET'S VIGNETTES OF A DYING LAND, 1925-29

Many of the explorers and adventurers who found their ways into the Barren Lands left written accounts to tell of what they saw and did; but there were two groups of intruders who left few records of their sojourn in the tundra. These were the trappers and the traders. Their silence is a great loss, for these men nosed their ways into almost every hidden place in the arctic plains during the decade after the First World War when white fox became white gold, and a gold pelt might fetch as much as fifty dollars. The trappers, in particular, were a taciturn and mysterious breed not given to speaking much about their doings, and mostly lacking both the ability and the desire to write of their experiences. Most of the traders also kept their peace, for reasons best known to themselves. Yet there was a time during the late twenties when the traders were following close on the heels of the white trappers, trying by every means they knew to acquire the furs that the inland people — the Caribou Eskimos — could be prevailed upon to trap.

415

The two great companies of those times — Revillon Frères and the Hudson's Bay Company — waged a bitter war against each other and against a score of independent entrepreneurs — "free traders," as they were contemptuously called.

Along the southern fringes of the Barrens the fierce competition between the traders had the effect of attracting most of the surviving population of Caribou Eskimos down to the edge of timber and into a country which was a sort of no-man's land where neither Indians nor Eskimos had ever been able to support themselves on the true substance of the land — the deer. In the end this concentration of inland Eskimos in the south-western corner of Keewatin was to prove fatal to them, for the day came when the price of white fox fell and the trading posts were abandoned, leaving the Eskimos with no source of supplies other than what a ravaged land could provide after the once innumerable caribou had been decimated.

Portents of what was to come were clearly to be seen while the white fox boom was still at its peak. And some of these portents were recorded by a trader who was also a man who saw and understood the world he lived in, and could and did write movingly of his impressions.

Thierry Mallet was an exception to the general rule of reticence observed by traders and trappers alike. In 1930 he published privately, in New York, a slim volume which he modestly called Glimpses of the Barren Lands, *and it is from his book that I have taken the concluding section for this present volume.*

Mallet joined Revillon as an apprentice trader and travelled widely in the Arctic, particularly in the Barrens where he was personally responsible for establishing a chain of posts that eventually extended northward from Reindeer Lake in Manitoba to the shores of Ennadai Lake — the headwaters of the mighty Kazan River.

In the late twenties Mallet attempted to do what no other white man had done — he tried to descend the Kazan to its mouth at Baker Lake. He failed, but during the journey he met and came to know some of the people of the interior.

GLIMPSES OF THE BARREN LANDS

I

Our camp had been pitched at the foot of a great, bleak, ragged hill, a few feet from the swirling waters of the Kazan River. The two small green tents, pegged down tight with heavy rocks, shivered and rippled under the faint touch of the northern breeze. A thin wisp of smoke rose from the embers of the fire.

Eleven o'clock, and the sun had just set under a threatening bank of clouds far away to the north-west. It was the last day of June and daylight still. But the whole country seemed bathed in grey — boulders, moss, sand, even the few willow shrubs scattered far apart in the hollows of the hills. Half a mile away, upstream, the caribou-skin *topeks* [tents] of an Eskimo settlement, fading away amid the background, were hardly visible to the eye.

Three small grey specks could be seen moving slowly above our camp. Human shapes, but so puny, so insignificant-looking against the wild rocky side of that immense hill! Bending down, then straightening up, they seemed to totter aimlessly through the chaos of stone, searching for some hidden treasure.

Curiosity, or perhaps a touch of loneliness, suddenly moved me to leave camp and join those three forlorn figures so far away above me near the skyline.

Slowly I made my way along the steep incline, following at first the bed of a dried-up stream. Little by little the river sank beneath me, while the breeze, increasing in strength, whistled past, lashing and stinging my face and hands. I had lost sight momentarily of the three diminutive figures which had lured me on to these heights. After a while a reindeer trail enabled me to leave the coulee and led me again in the right direction, through a gigantic mass of granite which the frost of thousands of years had plucked from the summit of the hill and hurled hundreds of feet below.

At last I was able to reach the other side of the avalanche of rocks and suddenly emerged comparatively in the open, on the brim of a slight depression at the bottom of which a few dead willow bushes showed their bleached branches above the stones and the grey moss. There I found the three silent figures huddled close together, gathering, one by one, the twigs of the precious wood. Two little girls, nine or ten years old, so small, so helpless, and an aged woman, so old, so frail, that my first thought was to marvel at the idea of their being able to climb so far from their camp to that lonely spot.

An Eskimo great-grandmother and her two great-granddaughters, all three contributing their share to the support of the tribe. Intent on their work, or most probably too shy to look up at the strange white man whom, until then, they had only seen at a distance, they gave me full opportunity to watch them.

All were dressed alike, in boots, trousers, and coats of caribou skin. The children wore little round leather caps reaching far over their ears, the crown decorated with bead-work designs. One of them carried on the wrist, as a bracelet, a narrow strip of bright-red flannel. Their faces were round and healthy, the skin sunburned to a dark copper colour, but their cheeks showed a tinge of blood which gave them, under the tan, a peculiar complexion like the colour of a ripe plum. Their little hands were bare and black, the scratches caused by the dead twigs showing plainly in white, while their fingers seemed cramped with the cold.

The old woman was bareheaded, quite bald at the top of the head, with long wisps of grey hair waving in the wind. The skin of her neck and face had turned black, dried up like an old piece of parchment. Her cheeks were sunken and her cheekbones protruded horribly. Her open mouth showed bare gums, for her teeth were all gone, and her throat, thin and bare as a vulture's neck, showed the muscles like cords. Her hands were as thin as the hands of a skeleton, the tip of each finger curved in like a claw. Her eyes, once black, now light grey, remained half closed, deep down in their sockets.

She was stone blind.

Squatting on her heels, she held, spread in front of her, a small reindeer skin. As soon as the children dropped a branch beside her, she felt for it gropingly; then, her hands closed on it greedily, like talons. She would break it into small pieces, a few inches long, which she carefully placed on the mat at her feet.

Both little girls, while searching diligently through the clumps of dead willows for what they could break off and carry away, kept absolutely silent. Not only did they never call to one another when one of them needed help, but they seemed to watch each other intently whenever they could. Now and then, one of them would hit the ground two or three times with the flat of her hand. If the other had her head turned away at the time, she appeared to be startled and always wheeled round to look. Then both children would make funny little motions with their hands at one another.

The little girls were deaf and dumb.

After a while they had gathered all the wood the reindeer skin could contain. Then the children went up to the old woman and conveyed to her the idea that it was time to go home. One of them took her hands in hers and guided them to two corners of the mat, while the other tapped her gently on the shoulder.

The old, old woman understood. Slowly and carefully, she tied up the four corners of the caribou skin over the twigs, silently watched by the little girls. Groaning, she rose to her feet, tottering with weakness and old age, and with a great effort swung the small bundle over her back.

Then one little girl took her by the hand, while the other, standing behind, grasped the tail of her caribou coat. Slowly, very slowly, step by step they went their way, following a reindeer trail around rocks, over stones, down, down the hill, straight toward their camp, the old woman carrying painfully for the young, the deaf and dumb leading and steering safely the blind.

II

Dawn. The sun had hardly set when once more it flashed above the horizon, for we were still at the beginning of July. From the top of a hill where I had been lying, watching the country, the Barren Lands stretched northward indefinitely. Not a tree in sight. Rocks, more rocks. Huge plateaus covered with moss, then lakes—small ones, large ones, in every direction, a hundred lakes, all blue, gleaming in the sunshine. Exactly in front of me to the north, on the other side of a deep hollow shaped like a crater, a long narrow ledge of sand ran lengthways, forming the top of another hill only a few feet lower than mine. In a straight line, barely forty yards separated the two spots. Sheltered from the north-west wind behind a cairn of stones erected there by some roaming Eskimo hunter, I was completely hidden.

Suddenly something caught the corner of my right eye as I watched the distant shores of a lake to my left. A lone wolf, a great big arctic wolf, had silently appeared on the ridge and was standing, facing me, absolutely unconscious of my presence.

Scarcely daring to breathe, rigid, motionless, I watched the huge beast in the full glory of his strength and beauty. Pure white except for a black streak running from the forehead down the neck and the middle of the back to the end of the tail, I judged him to weigh 150 pounds and to be twice the size of a very large dog. Head erect, ears pointed, his tail curved down, the brush only an inch or so from the ground, he calmly gazed around him. His eyes had a bright gold tinge in them. They rested a second on the top of the cairn above my head, then swept farther away, past me, to the right.

After that, slowly he lowered his head, the muscles playing round his neck and shoulders, and sniffed disdainfully at the sand at his feet. Raising his head again swiftly, he pointed his muzzle straight up to the sky and began to howl. First a deep, low howl coming from far down his throat, then rising and rising until it reached a shrill, haunting note, ending abruptly in a short, sharp cry. Twice again, without moving from where he stood, he sent out that long, nerve-racking call.

Then — something in me snapped. I could not stand the tension any longer. I felt that I had to show myself. I refused to be peering any more through the crack between two stones. I wanted that wolf to see me. I wanted to be face to face with him.

Without a noise, in one movement I rose to my full height, stepping away from my hiding place. The wolf flinched slightly, his legs bending a little under him. The hair on the crest of his neck rose, his ears flattened back, and he bared his teeth in a noiseless snarl. For the space of a second, perhaps two, he remained there, looking straight at me. Then with a mighty sweep of his legs, his body straightened like a bow. He flung himself backward over the ridge and disappeared like a ghost, without making a sound.

III

Noon. Our canoe swept round a sharp curve of the river, rode the last waves of the rapids, and shot into the backwater under a high rocky bank, in the lee of a hill.

A family of Eskimos watched us land. They were travelling upstream and had stopped there to "make fire" among a few willow trees.

My men started collecting sufficient firewood to boil a kettle of tea, and the natives helped them, hoping to share our meal. I strolled away, examining the Eskimos' outfit, strewn on the shore. Six Husky dogs, each tied to a rock by the chain of a fox trap, rose, cringing and snarling, as I passed them. A kayak stood upright against a boulder. An old wooden canoe was fastened to the bank by a long rope of reindeer hide. A handful of pemmican was thrown carelessly on the ground, while beside it lay a large platter made of old cast-away planking, containing a few sun-dried fish.

Forty feet away, upstream, a mass of loose rocks strewn on the bank caught my eye. But what really attracted my attention was a patch of colour amid the grey of the stones.

I approached to find, sitting in a little hollow between two boulders, a tiny little girl. She was about four years old. Dressed in caribou hide, with coat, trousers, and boots, she was bareheaded except for a thick band of native copper which encircled her forehead just above the eyes. Her mother had tied round her fat little "tummy" a wide strip of bright-red stroud, in the form of a sash. That was what I had seen from the camp. The child was busy playing with something white which she was rolling back and forth on a little flat rock between her knees. It reminded me of the movement of an Indian squaw crushing barley with a round stone. The child looked up and gazed at me thoughtfully for a few seconds. Her little round dark face was shining and her eyes were very black and serious between the slanting eyelids. Then, satisfied, she looked down again and went on with her game, crooning to herself in baby Husky which sounded very weird.

At that moment her mother called out sharply from the campfire. Obediently she rose and toddled away, leaving her toy behind her.

I stooped and picked it up. It was a human skull, a very, very old one, covered with mildew. Moss had crept into the sockets of the eyes and inside the cranium. I turned it round and round in my hands, wondering a little at the strangeness of my discovery; then I remembered the mass of loose stones. At a glance I recognized a very old grave. Eskimos bury their dead on the surface of the ground, for no one can dig down more than a foot or so without finding rock or ice. I realized that the mound of stones which had been piled so long ago over the body had fallen apart, and that the baby girl, playing about, must have seen the skull between some of the stones and picked it up.

Just as I was going to throw it away I saw something dark on the forehead. Looking closer, I found that it was a large round lead bullet which had just pierced the forehead from the inside, remaining wedged into the bone. Turning the skull once more, I also found, at the base, the hole which it had made going in. With some effort I extracted the bullet with my knife. It was a round ball, of an unknown calibre. No firearm dating as far back as half a century had ever fired it. The little girl had been playing with the skull of an Eskimo who had been shot — possibly a direct ancestor of hers, who knows? — and not only shot, but plainly murdered from behind.

IV

We had been wind-bound for two days. Twice we had attempted to get out on Yathkyed Lake; twice we had been forced to turn round, with water pouring in over the gunwales of our canoe, and to seek shelter in the river. Finally we gave it up and pitched our camp a mile or so upstream, in the lee of a rock on the edge of a small sandy cove, where the river narrowed to barely one hundred yards.

On the other side of the water the country rose slightly, and extended for miles and miles without a tree, a shrub, or a rock to relieve its appalling monotony. Just a desert of grey moss, rolling in waves away from us, as far as the eye could see.

We were sitting round a little fire which we constantly fed with small dry twigs picked up here and there on the beach, when we saw across the river, on the horizon, a small yellow streak which seemed to be moving toward us. It looked exactly like a huge caterpillar creeping on the ground. We watched it intently. The yellow streak, little by little, grew in length and width until suddenly, in a second, it spread into a large spot which, widening and widening on either side, still kept moving in our direction. It reminded me then of a swarm of locusts, such as one sees in South America, spreading over the fields after dropping to earth in a cloud from the sky.

In a few minutes the yellow patch had grown to such a size that we realized, far as we were from it, that it covered many acres. After that we began to see in the mass of yellow hundreds and thousands of tiny dots which moved individually. Then we knew what it was. It was a great herd of reindeer, the Barren-Land caribou, migrating south.

Spellbound, we remained beside our campfire, watching probably the most stupendous sight of wild game in North America since the bygone days of the buffalo.

On and on the horde came, straight for the narrows of the river where we were camped. While the flanks of the herd stretched irregularly a mile or so on each side of the head, the latter remained plainly pointed in the same direction. One felt instinctively the unswerving leadership which governed that immense multitude. For two hours we sat there, looking and looking, until the caribou were only a few yards from the water's edge, right across the river from where we were.

An old doe, nearly white, led by twenty lengths; then came three or four full-grown bucks, walking side by side. After them started a column of animals of all sizes and descriptions. That column widened like a fan until it lost itself on either side of a swarm of caribou, so closely packed together that acres and acres of grey moss were completely hidden by their moving bodies. And the noise of their hoofs and the breathing of their lungs sounded like faraway thunder.

When the old doe reached the water, she stopped. The bucks joined her on either side. Little by little, right and left, thousands of animals lined the bank for over a mile. Behind them thousands more, which could not make their way through the closed ranks in front of them, stopped. Then all their heads went up — bucks, does, yearlings, fawns — and motionless they looked at the Kazan River. Not a sound could be heard. My eyes ached under the strain. Beside me I could feel one of my Indians trembling like a leaf in his excitement. I started counting and reached three thousand. Then I gave it up. There were too many.

After what seemed to us an interminable pause, the leading doe and the big bucks moved forward. Unhesitatingly, they walked slowly down the bank, took to the water, and started to swim across, straight for our little sandy cove.

In an instant the whole herd had moved, and with a roar of clattering hoofs, rolling stones, and churning waters, all the animals were pouring down the bank and breasting the icy current until the river foamed. On and on they came, swimming madly to the nearest point of the opposite shore. Nothing could stop them. Nothing could make them swerve.

As soon as they landed they raced up the bank, giving way to the next ones behind them. We were standing up then, behind our fire. The first ones saw us from the water, but they never changed their direction until they touched bottom. Then they scattered slightly on either side, giving us room. The next ones followed suit. And for what seemed to us an eternity we were surrounded by a sea of caribou galloping madly inland.

Finally the last one went by, a very small fawn, his mouth open and his tongue hanging out. Then silence reigned supreme again. The Barren Lands resumed their aspect of utter desolation. And nothing was left to show that the great herd of caribou had passed, save countless tracks on the sand and millions of grey hairs floating down the river to the sea.

V

We were waiting for two Eskimo dog trains to haul us across Hekwa-Leekwa Lake.[1] It was the 10th of July and the ice of the lake was still solid, lying unbroken from shore to shore. Eighty miles long, twenty-five miles wide, it was still sleeping under its white winter covering. Around it, on land, it was already summer, with little flowers showing their heads between the stones, stray willow clumps waving their new green leaves in the breeze, and countless birds singing and flitting about beside their nests. Walking inland, I decided to climb the highest hill which could be seen in those parts. It rose about three miles from the river and lake and towered above the surrounding country, very much in the shape of a pyramid.

The weather was bright and clear and the heat of the sun radiated from the rocks, but every puff of wind blowing over the ice of the lake was like the frozen breath of the Arctic itself.

I toiled slowly up and up the steep incline, zigzagging among boulders and through coulees of loose stones, watching the horizon receding gradually from me, obeying unconsciously the call which comes to all white men in the wilderness and which bids them go on and on, through forests, up or down rivers, across lakes, over mountains, searching, ever searching for something new.

I reached the summit at last — just a few square feet of level ground — and there I found an Eskimo grave. Five feet high, seven feet long, it was entirely made out of loose rocks which had been brought up there by hand, one by one, and neatly piled one on top of the other, over the dead. Thus it formed a solid block on which, one would think,

---

[1] Hicoliguak — the Eskimo name for Yathkyed Lake.

neither weather nor time could make the slightest impression. Forming part of the landscape itself, that grave seemed to be there for all eternity.

At the head of it, a few feet away, a spear stood erect, stuck deep in the ground and solidly wedged in at the base between heavy rocks. The point was of native copper. From it fluttered, in rags, the remains of a deerskin coat.

At the foot lay, side by side, a kayak with its paddle and harpoon and a twenty-foot sleigh with its set of dog harness and a snow knife. Both kayak and sleigh were held down by stones carefully placed along their entire length.

On the grave itself I found a rifle, a small kettle with a handful of tea leaves inside, a little wooden box containing ten cartridges, a pipe, a plug of tobacco, matches, a knife, a small telescope, and a neatly coiled rawhide belt. One could see that everything had been lying there a few weeks only. No inscription of any sort. But the weapons showed that it was a man who had been buried in that lonely spot.

As I leaned against the grave, my eyes wandered around. I tried to picture to myself the faithful companions of the deceased hunter struggling up that hill, bearing on their shoulders the rigid body of their dead; their search for those hundreds of rocks, and the work of piling them, one by one, for hours and hours, until the mound was able to defy the efforts of the wild animals and the incessant pressure of the years to come; finally the long descent to the camp, to bring up again, one by one, the precious belongings of the deceased.

To me, there alone, leaning on that grave on the top of that immense hill, the whole undertaking seemed incredible. The more I thought, the more I marvelled, searching for the motive which had prompted those natives, not only to choose that almost inaccessible spot to lay their dead at rest, but to abandon unhesitatingly on his grave that wealth of articles which I knew represented an immense value to them, in their constant bitter struggle for mere existence.

Pagans they were—pagans they still remain. Although they have a certain code to which they are faithful, unlike the old Indians they have no form of worship. Still that grave, those weapons, those articles of daily use, of absolute necessity, carefully laid near the body from which the spirit had just flown—all these must have had a meaning, must prove that somewhere in the innermost part of their hearts there exists a hope, a belief in after life, something to look forward to when the last day comes.

And while I thought those thoughts, I pulled out my pipe and filled it slowly. It was time for me to go; the icy wind from the lake made me shudder with cold. As I turned for a last look at the grave, my eyes fell on the little wooden box. Then an impulse struck me. I opened the box, took a handful of tobacco out of my pouch, and laid it carefully inside, closing the lid securely.

VI

The long, long trail was nearly over as far as the Barren Lands were concerned. We were on Ennadai Lake, halfway across already, and our canoe ploughed its way through water as still as a mirror.

It was August, and one already felt the unmistakable touch of the fall. Long strings of duck were flying in all directions, while on land we could see small herds of caribou already migrating to the South. Everything was still. The splash of our paddles as they dipped into the clear water of the lake seemed all out of proportion to the dead silence which surrounded us, while our voices brought out long muffled echoes from the nearest hills.

Hour after hour we glided on, intent on reaching the end of the lake before dark. Little by little the sun went down behind us. Just before sunset we went through the last narrows and entered the southern bay into which the Kazan River flows. And then suddenly the first trees since we had entered the Barren Lands two months before came into view. The rays of the dying sun fell, slanting, on their green branches, and to our tired eyes the first spruces and tamaracks of the Canadian forest seemed to welcome us home.

Instinctively we stopped paddling, letting our canoe drift slowly forward, while we looked back for the last time on the bleak northern land through which we had toiled for weeks.

The sun was setting, like a huge ball of fire, and the lake far away to the north was beginning to flame. Around us the water had lost its tinge of blue, streaks of purple appearing here and there on its glassy surface. The hills glowed pink where they faced the sunset, while the other side was lost in deep shadows.

A mile away from us, on the extreme southern point of a ridge of rocks, four human figures stood motionless, silhouetted black against the crimson of the sky — the last Eskimos of the Barren Lands, watching us go south toward the unknown country of plenty, where lives the white man!

From where I sat in my canoe I sent them a mute good-bye. Those four tiny dots appeared to me very forlorn and pathetic.

There they were, at the edge of their native land, but looking south, as if straining for something which was not theirs to have. To me it looked as if they realized that they could come up to where they were but no farther, that an unwritten law forbade them to follow our footsteps, and that the gates of Paradise, the gates of the rich Country of Trees, were closed to them forever.

WHEN THE CARIBOU FAILED

I

"Crack!" went the whip. The sharp report tore the frozen stillness of the Barren Lands. A little white puff rose from the hard snow, showing where the end of the walrus-hide

429

lash had harmlessly landed. The long low sleigh quivered and plunged forward, while the team of dogs, crouching low, dug their claws frantically in the ice of the lake and strained in their harness for more speed.

Seven dogs! All pure Huskies! When I close my eyes I can see them now, after all these years.

A black and white leader. He always ran with his head turned back over his shoulder, watching the driver, when the man wasn't breaking trail ahead. Then three brindles, all brothers, silent like wolves. Behind them a little white bitch, with one yellow spot on the right cheek. She was the best dog for her size I have ever known, but she had the bad habit of whining, sharp, eager little whines, each time she had to tug a little harder at her breastplate. After that, a roan, a rare colour, like a blue fox. He was sulky and treacherous, always apt to bite the dog in front of him if he could reach him. And, last of all, an old seasoned traveller of five years, pure grey, who knew every trick of the game and always howled to the skies when he felt a blizzard coming. He was my special pet in camp.

Yes, it was a great team, the best I think I have ever had, and that day my guide and I were urging them for all they were worth.

The long, bleak frozen lake stretched due north. We could already make out the end of it, through the haze — the vague outline of rocky hills, wind-swept, desolate, snow patches in the hollows gleaming white against the grey of the stone.

It was in the dead of winter, and the cold was terrific. There was no trail. We were travelling close to the shore, on the glare ice, walking or running behind the sleigh. A light breeze was blowing from the west in uneven gusts. And when those gusts came, the little rifts of snow would curl up suddenly like wisps of white smoke, lashing our left cheek and making us turn away in an agony of pain. Meanwhile the dogs shrank also, veering toward land, until a crack of the whip straightened them out on their course.

It was noon, I remember. We were looking for a small band of inland Eskimos, led by an old man called Kakarmik. He was supposed to be trapping somewhere at the end of the lake and we had to find out if all was well with his people. He was new to the district and we wanted to meet him and tell him where he could trade in his furs next spring.

Mile after mile went by. Then a rope on the sleigh snapped, a small part of the load slipping off. While we were repairing the accident, we noticed that three of the dogs, instead of lying down and resting curled up with their backs to the wind, remained standing, looking ahead and sniffing high in the air.

Climbing on the top of the load, I searched the end of the lake with my glasses and picked out a small dark speck which was moving. It was a man, the first one we had seen since we had started travelling twenty days ago, and in the utter desolation of that frozen desert the sight of the tiny, living dot seemed to fill the horizon with colour and movement.

Half an hour later we were in plain sight of the whole band of Eskimos. The igloos were built on a rocky point, while the entire tribe seemed to be scattered a mile or so out on the ice.

"Fishing" was our thought, and at once we knew that our friends were in a bad way. No Eskimo fishes inland through the ice in winter unless he has missed the herds of caribou in the fall and has been unable to stock up with meat and fat until the next spring.

"Starving" was my guide's curt remark a few minutes later.

Then, three men who had been watching us with their small telescopes started running toward our sleigh. They still had their fish spears in their hands. We stopped our team and looked at each other thoughtfully. We were not frightened of the Eskimos, for we knew them well. But starving men in the Barren Lands are not easily handled at times, and our precious stock of food, with our seven dogs, might have proved too much of a temptation.

We had a rifle with us, but the thought of showing it never entered our minds. In the North neither white men nor red men ever use firearms except on game. The days of murder have long since gone, notwithstanding printed stories to the contrary. We simply waited, anxiously, wondering what would happen.

As soon as the first man arrived within earshot, he began calling out and waving. In a few seconds we understood his words. "Bad ice—look out—turn around—pass near the shore." With a few muttered words of relief, we slewed the excited team back in a wide circle and, obeying instructions, made our way past the igloos on the point to where all the Eskimos were standing.

Kakarmik, the old chief, was the first to greet us. Then we had to shake hands with everyone, man, woman, and child, even the babies in their mothers' hoods—a tedious job when it is forty degrees below and one must keep one's double fur mitts on. After that, as quickly as possible, my guide explained who we were, from where we came, when we had to go back, and the reason for our trip.

Kakarmik thanked us for our visit. His description of local conditions was exactly what we had guessed at first.

Being new to the district, the band had reached too late the place where the caribou cross the river in tens of thousands on their migration south, and had only been able to spear a few stragglers. After that they had spent weary weeks scouring the country in vain for smaller herds. Winter settling down in earnest, Kakarmik had finally decided to camp at the end of the lake where the water was shallow and the ice thin because of the current of the mighty river flowing from there down to the Arctic Ocean. His only solution was to fish, and, since he had no nets, to spear through holes in the ice, where the men, crouching behind a small wind-shield, watched all day long.

The fishing had been good at first. But now it was

poor, very poor. When a man caught four fish of three or four pounds every twenty-four hours, he could consider himself very lucky. They had only four spears to feed seventeen people. He didn't count the small babies at the breast. Half of them had already died and he expected the rest to go soon. They had no dogs. They had eaten them all. They were going to stay here another week, in the hope that the fishing would improve. But, if it did not, then he would leave for a certain lake he knew, twelve days' walking to the north-west. There he thought he might perhaps find musk-oxen.

Yes, they had three rifles and enough ammunition. He knew the risk he would have to take. In fact, he expected that half the band — even more — would fall on the way, but he would take the chance if the fish were going to fail entirely. And did we have food, over and above what we needed for our return trip—twenty days?

The guide and I looked at each other. There stood a band of Eskimos on the point of sheer, complete starvation. Numbering seventeen to the two of us, still they made no move to seize our food and our dogs. Obeying the eternal law of the North, they took it for granted that we had to keep our team so as to be able to travel back south to wherever we lived, and enough food, so much per man and per dog per day, to last the distance we had to cover. They simply asked us if we had, by any chance, a surplus of food. Without hesitation, we unpacked our whole outfit and laid out our complete stock on the ice.

While a woman kept our dogs quiet under the threat of the whip, we sorted out and counted the dog food, fish, then our own caribou meat. Travelling north of the trees, we had only a little gasoline stove to boil our tea. The meat we ate raw, trusting to be able to last on it until we found our cache on our way back, at the trees, where wood and fire would enable us to cook again and eat pork and beans and flour cakes.

Twenty days of travelling! Seven dogs! Three fish per

dog per day. They were very small fish. That meant 420 fish. We found that we actually had 450. We put the balance of thirty aside. Then we cut down the dog allowance to two fish a day, thus adding 140 fish to the thirty. As far as our own meat was concerned, we gave them forty pounds of it, keeping eighty for ourselves. We offered them tea, but they refused it, as they had no fat to use with moss for fuel in their little stone lamps.

Kakarmik distributed the fish and meat there and then, so much per head, and in a few minutes every Eskimo had gone to the igloos to eat.

As we turned south, after saying good-bye to the old chief, we noticed a young woman standing a few hundred yards ahead of us. When we got up to her, she beckoned and we stopped. She was very thin and very weak. She told us that she was an orphan from another tribe and having been taken up through charity and having absolutely no relations, she was not receiving her proper share of the daily catch. Therefore she was starving, and she begged us for one fish — one fish from our dog food — just one, for her alone, adding that she would eat it at once, there on the ice, before the others found her and took it away from her.

She was very pathetic, with her thin face all blackened with frostbite, and she made little pleading gestures with her hands in her anxiety to make us understand that she was dying on her feet from hunger.

We took a fish out of the bag. I chose it carefully. It was a whitefish, weighing about three pounds, very fat, and frozen, of course, as hard as a piece of granite. When I handed it to the girl I could see her trembling with excitement. One of her legs, in the big caribou trouser and boot, started shaking so badly that she nearly pitched forward on the sleigh, and the saliva began to drip from the corner of her mouth, freezing when it reached her chin.

As soon as she had the fish in her arms she tried to bite a piece out of it. But her teeth failed her. The guide gave her our little axe. Putting the fish down on the ice, she tried to chop it in pieces, but she was too weak and she missed it. The man had to cut it up for her. And then it was an awful sight to watch her gobble the chunks and swallow them whole, hardly munching. When she had eaten a large portion, she gathered the remains and hid them in her clothing against her bare skin, where they would thaw and where she could reach them easily, without attracting attention.

When we turned round to have a last look she was halfway back to the shore. She had stopped walking, and was sitting on the ice, facing us. As we waved at her she did not make a sign, but she bent her head down to her chest. I suppose she was having another mouthful of fish before getting back to the others.

And during the twenty days of our trip south, to the trees and our fur outpost, every night when my guide and I lay side by side in the same fur bag, under the little canvas tent, we both pondered over the fate of Kakarmik's tribe, while the face of the starving woman haunted our dreams as soon as we fell asleep.

II

Six months later I returned to the Barren Lands, in the same district. I was travelling by canoe with two Indians. My guide of the winter was somewhere north of me and I had arranged to meet him at the northern end of the lake where I had seen Kakarmik and his band in January.

Leisurely I proceeded on my way north. It was toward the end of July and the bleak rugged country had changed into summer garb. No more snow—a few patches of greenish moss and stunted willows scattered about between the grey rocks. No more ice—but miles and miles of sapphire-blue water. Hundreds and thousands of caribou plodding north, keeping high on the crest of the hills, seeking the wind so as to avoid the black flies. White gulls soaring aimlessly about the lake. Ducks and geese flying back and forth over their nesting grounds. White foxes — invisible — barking defiantly somewhere in the rocks. Thousands of small birds twittering and flitting about their nests on the ground. And proud piebald cock ptarmigans drumming and crowing everywhere, perched on the stones all along the shoreline.

I pitched my camp at last on the same point where I had seen the Eskimos seven months before. Not a sign of life anywhere. And there I waited a whole week before my guide arrived. My thoughts at all times were with Kakarmik and his small band of Eskimos. No one, south, had received any news of them since I had last met the tribe in the dead of winter.

Had they been able to ward off starvation where I had seen them until the first caribou had returned in the spring? Or had they risked the big adventure and faced death in their search for musk-oxen, away, far away, somewhere on the shores of the big lake unknown to all of us but Kakarmik?

For a whole week I pondered, and then suddenly, from far out on the lake, just before sunset, I saw my man coming from the north-west in a canoe manned by three Eskimos.

It was a beautiful evening, such as one sees so often in the far North during the summer. The horizon was blood-red. The canoe, silhouetted in black across the flaming background, glided through waters as still as a mirror and of all the hues of the rainbow. The regular splash of the paddles woke the echoes of the hills behind me, while the scattered drops of water fell back on the surface of the lake, around the canoe, like tongues of fire.

Silently I watched the four coming nearer and nearer until the bow of the canoe grounded softly on the sand beach and remained still.

The guide walked up the bank. So did the Eskimos. They belonged to a band from the east and I knew them well. We all shook hands, silently. Such is the way men greet one another in the wilderness.

After a few seconds, when the white man had found a flat stone to sit on, and lit his pipe carefully and slowly, I looked at him. ''Well.'' He knew what I meant. He took the pipe out of his mouth and turned the bowl slowly in his hand, gazing at it thoughtfully. Then, moving sidewise, his eyes found mine. ''All dead,'' he answered; and after that, a second or so later, as an afterthought, ''I found them all.''

Although I expected the news in a way, his few terse words stunned me and I remained silent. Meanwhile the three Eskimos, who guessed what had been said in English, remained squatting in front of me, watching my face with inscrutable half-closed eyes.

Finally I asked what had happened, and this was the story I heard.

That spring, before the ice had left the lake, my man had returned to the very spot where we had last seen Kakarmik. The camp was deserted. There were no fresh signs. One could see at a glance that the Eskimos had gone away months before. He decided to travel north-west, toward the other lake that the old chief had told us about. He took the three eastern Eskimos with him and first crossed the lake he was on. For half a day they all searched for tracks on the shore, as they had to find out exactly where Kakarmik and his band had started their walk inland. Then they found sure signs. First a bunch of traps, then a skin bundle of extra caribou blankets, finally a grave — just a few small stones scattered over the body of a very small child.

From the lay of the land it was easy after that to guess that the band of Eskimos must have taken a sort of coulee, like a small valley, winding its way more or less north-west. My guide took a chance and started walking up that trail. There were no tracks on the ground, as the thin snow had been swept away by the wind or had melted under the first rays of the sun. For a whole day the four men did not see anything that could make them believe they were on the right trail. Then, all at once they began finding things —a fish spear, a telescope, an axe, a snow knife, two pairs of boots.

Not only did they know then that they were on the right track, but they soon guessed what had happened. The weak, straggling band of starving natives had begun there to discard all extra weight. A little later they came across, in a hollow, a half-melted screen, like a portion of an igloo wall. There the Eskimos must have huddled together and slept during the first night. A mile farther the white man, walking ahead, found the body of a woman, still half frozen, untouched by any preying animal. The three Eskimos recognized her and named her at once. It was the girl to whom we had given one fish.

From there on the trail was strewn with every loose article the band had been carrying. It was easy to see that the pace had begun to tell and that the dying natives had decided to throw away everything they had except the rifles. After that, during seven weary days, my man followed the trail by the dead bodies. Generally one alone; sometimes two, side by side; once three, sitting in a group, close to one another behind a rock.

They counted the dead carefully. The band consisted of seventeen souls originally, not including the babies. Kakarmik seven months ago had told us seventeen, meaning from the youngest child who could walk, without being carried at any time, up to himself.

Well, they finally found the old man. He seemed to have been the last to fall. He was lying on his face, halfway up a little slope, but he had no rifle beside him. They searched around for a long time, but did not find it, although the two other firearms had been accounted for with the last two bodies.

It was then that the three Eskimos told my man that Kakarmik's body was the sixteenth and that someone was still missing. The guide checked up carefully and came to the conclusion that they were right; but although the Eskimos knew each one of Kakarmik's band, they did not seem to be able to name the seventeenth.

The four men decided to go on toward the lake. For five hours they walked without finding anything — and then, just as they were going to give up, they came across the last body.

It was a girl — a little girl of twelve or thereabouts. The three Eskimos remembered her name. And right alongside of her body there lay the third rifle, with a small bag of cartridges.

III

That is the story my man told me. The sun had gone down before he stopped talking and it was past midnight. There wasn't a breath of wind on the lake. Right above, the northern lights shimmered and danced in the sky.

I left the four men without a word and went to my tent. I was tired, suddenly, so tired that I could hardly lift my feet from the ground. I lay down in my blankets and closed my eyes. But I couldn't sleep. I never slept during the whole night. I just lay there, opening my eyes now and then to stare at the grey silk roof over my head.

I expected a tragedy. Starvation, after all, is a common occurrence in the Far North. I was prepared for it, in a way, the very minute I said good-bye to Kakarmik during the winter.

My man's report was no more tragic than many stories I had heard before. My thoughts, in fact, did not even dwell on Kakarmik himself, nor on the young woman whom we had saved seven months before with the one fish from our dog food.

What haunted me was the thought of the little girl, the last one to survive — then to die, all alone.

The little girl of twelve, who managed to keep up until

the very end because her mother probably had fed her with hidden scraps before she herself fell dead on the trail.

The little girl who saw the other members of the tribe sink one by one and die on the frozen land.

The little girl left all alone, hundreds of miles from anywhere, in a strange desert of ice and snow, with nothing but a sense of direction inherited from the old chief.

The little girl who never thought of giving in, even then, but who grasped the last rifle and went on and on, blindly, in the deathly Arctic winter — on and on — true to the right direction followed by her elders — on and on — with the unfailing courage of her race, until death, at last, mercifully struck her down.

Epilogue

When Samuel Hearne walked into the tundra he found a world of life in many forms. In his day the Northern Indians occupied vast areas of the southern and western arctic plains, while the northern reaches were home to the many bands of Caribou Eskimos. The tundra was not empty then, for it knew the comings and goings of many men—of men who were able to live there, and who did live there, because the land was bountiful.

It was a manifold bounty, including the fishes in the innumerable lakes, the tremendous flocks of ducks and geese, the hare, ptarmigan, musk-ox, Barren-Land grizzly and, what was all important, the seemingly limitless herds of caribou.

But it was a bounty that was not destined to survive the rapacity of European man. In a world where all creatures — both beasts and men — had been in balance, the arrival of the intruders from across the eastern ocean brought chaos and destruction. Hearne, the first of the intruders to penetrate deeply into this hidden world, sensed the shape of things to come. Yet even he could hardly have guessed that within two centuries that vast land with its wealth of life would truly come to deserve the name he knew it by: the Barren Grounds.

A few of those who followed him also had intimations of the inevitable end, but neither they nor anyone else in the world of modern men acted to avert the destruction of a living land. Life in the arctic plains was systematically given over to desolation.

When I first visited the edge of the Barrens in 1935 it still retained at least the illusion of being a living land. I visited it again in 1947, 1948 and 1953, and during those years I saw life failing fast. Then in 1966 I few across the entire breadth and depth of the tundra plains, retracing the routes of Hearne, Tyrrell, Franklin, Back and others. The aircraft flew low over the open face of the country and little was hidden from our eyes. Where, *during my own lifetime*, there had been as many as a million caribou, there were now only pathetic and scattered remnants of a species that biologists now fear may be doomed to extinction. Where, *during my own lifetime*, scores of places had harboured many hundreds of human beings, now there were only crumbling cabins and abandoned camps. The circles of stones that marked the vanished tents of Indians and Eskimos stared eyeless and void beside the mute symbolic piles of stones raised by a vanished people who called them *inukok*—semblance of a man.

Eastward from Great Slave Lake five hundred miles to the coast of Hudson Bay, southward from the arctic coast six hundred miles across the plains into the thin forests almost to Reindeer Lake, *there were no human beings living in the land*. Nearly three hundred thousand square miles lay drained of human life and, to a great extent, of caribou, wolves and other beasts who, like the people of the arctic plains, had been dependent on the caribou for their survival. Truly this seemed to be the Barren Grounds.

As we flew over that endless desolation I wondered if

the great plains were doomed to remain no more than a monument to the terrible destructiveness of modern man. I wondered if we had turned our backs forever upon the *terre stérile* we had created.

In 1967 Canada entered her second century. Her first was a hundred years of despoilment of a new and virgin world, and nowhere is this more bleakly demonstrated than in the North. The entire Arctic, once pregnant with life, has now become a hungry desert where not even the surviving Eskimos can take sustenance solely from the land and from the sea. Having destroyed the natural life-environment of this gigantic region, men can now survive there only as aliens, dependent for food and clothing, fuel and shelter, on what is brought in from the world outside. So we have inevitably come to *be* aliens in that same Arctic where the men whose stories are told in the volumes of this trilogy once lived and worked.

In Canada's second century we have the chance to undo some of the brutal, tragic errors of the past. If we turn northward again in imagination and in reality we can bring a dead world back to life, and we can share that life and be the richer for it.

All across the sweep of Asiatic tundra the beginnings of such a restoration have already been accomplished. Aboriginal arctic peoples, now numbering more than six hundred thousand, "farm" the Soviet tundra where the first cousins of the caribou, the reindeer, now graze the arctic prairies and provide protein-hungry peoples with millions of pounds of good meat every year. The Asian tundra, once as despoiled as ours, and very nearly as moribund, is again a place of life for men and beasts. It can be done. In Canada's North, the remnant populations of Indians and Eskimos, who are almost without exception dependent for survival on relief and welfare as a result of the destruction of their old world, could reoccupy that world; could find new, vigorous lives for themselves;

could re-colonize what is now one of the largest deserted regions on the planet. Musk-ox, caribou perhaps, but reindeer certainly, could bring life out of death; and the arctic seas could, with care, and under the hands of reason, also regain their vitality and provide a useful and modern way of life for the seal and walrus hunters who now cluster in abject poverty in the handful of remaining settlements along our arctic coasts.

In Canada's second century we could restore to life a portion of our country amounting to nearly a quarter of its total area, if we so willed. With ordinary human courage, endurance and hardihood, and tempered by compassion for and understanding of the natural world of the North, we may still reclaim the wasteland we have created in the Arctic.

The vital word is *reclaim*: to restore a ravaged land which is of such fragility that even the most minor blunders we have perpetrated on it in the past brought great disasters. However—and mark this well—*we will not reclaim the Arctic by waging a new war of greedy exploitation against it!* We will not restore it to life by turning from the rape of its living elements to the rape of its essential guts. If there is one immutable fact about the Arctic's future it is that our present view of that vast land as little more than a grab bag of oil, minerals, chemicals and hydroelectric power will be absolutely fatal to it. If it is to become nothing more than one further sacrifice to the bitch goddess of technical progress, then it is irrevocably doomed.

I have my own vision of the high North. I envision it being transformed—restored—into a symbol of sanity in a world where madness is becoming the accepted mode of action. I see it being rigidly protected as one vast sanctuary—a world inviolate—where men will walk softly and wield no big technological bludgeons. I see it as one of the few remaining regions of the earth where life, both human and non-human, can still be lived within the framework of the timeless harmonies which have existed since life began.

I have heard an oracle: If we who have brought such massive discord and such wasting sickness to this planet cannot bring an end to our blind orgy of destruction, then, most surely, shall we perish from the earth.

Across the northern reaches of this continent there lies a mighty wedge of treeless plain scarred by the primordial ice, inundated beneath a myriad of lakes, cross-checked by innumerable rivers, and riven by the rock bones of an elder earth. They are cold bones into which an eternal frost strikes downward five hundred feet beaneath the thin skin of tundra, bog and lichens which alone feel warmth under the long summer sun; and for many months of the year this skin itself is wrinkled by the frosts and becomes part of the cold stone below.

It is a naked land, bearing the deep excoriations which are the legacy of a glacial incubus two miles in thickness which once exerted its colossal pressures on the yielding rock. Implacable and irresistible the ice flowed outward, crushing mountains, filling lakes and valleys with the mountains' broken bones, and lacerating the tilted planes of the land's face with great gouges, some of them fifty miles in length. The scars made by the ice are still open: the wounds have never healed.

It is a land uncircumscribed, for it has no limits that the eye can find. It seems to reach beyond the finite boundaries of this earth. Brooding, immutable, it showed so harsh a face to the first white men who came upon its verges that they named it, in awe and fear, the Barren Grounds.

Yet it was not barren.

It was a place where curlews circled in a white sky above the calling waterfowl on icily transparent lakes. It was a place where gaudy ground squirrels whistled from the sandy casts of vanished glacial rivers; where dun-coloured arctic foxes denned, and lemmings dawdled fatly in the sedges by the bogs. It was a place where minute flowers blazed in microcosmic revelry and where the thrumming of insect wings assailed the greater beasts and set them fleeing to the bald ridge tops in search of a wind to drive the unseen enemy away. It was a place where the black musk-ox stood foursquare to the cautious feints of the white wolves, and where the shambling giant of the land, the massive Barren-Land grizzly, moved solitary and untouchable. But mainly it was a place where the caribou in their unnumbered hordes inundated the land in a hot flow of life that rose below one far horizon and stretched unbroken to the opposite one.

In all its apparent harshness, it was not barren; nor had it been since the first crawling lichens spread like a multi-coloured stain over the scoured rocks. Through the cold millennia after the passage of the ice, life in ten thousand forms prospered on the plain, where the caribou became a living pulse, fleshed by the lesser beasts and waiting for the day when man would come, bringing sentience to a new and waiting world.

The world is sentient no more.

The living pulse which was the caribou flutters with the almost imperceptible beat that speaks of certain dissolution.

And the great plains roll to the white horizons under the unseeing eyes of the stone *inukok* who have inherited an empty land.

Sources and Acknowledgements

The original sources from which the material in this book has been taken are shown below, with acknowledgements for permission to make use of the material.

Samuel Hearne
A Journey From Prince of Wales's Fort to the Northern Ocean, by Samuel Hearne, as edited by Farley Mowat in *Coppermine Journey*. Toronto, McClelland and Stewart Ltd., 1958. By kind permission of McClelland and Stewart Ltd.

Alexander Mackenzie
Voyages from Montreal to the Frozen and Pacific Oceans, by A. Mackenzie. London, 1801.

John Franklin
Narrative of a Journey to the Shores of the Polar Sea, by Capt. J. Franklin. London, J. Murray, 1823.

George Back
Narrative of the Arctic Land Expedition to the Mouth of the Great Fish River, by Capt. G. Back. London, J. Murray, 1836.

Frank Russell
Explorations in the Far North, by Frank Russell. University of Iowa, 1898.

J. B. and J. W. Tyrrell
Across the Sub-Arctics of Canada, by James Tyrrell. Toronto, William Briggs, 1897.

Royal North West Mounted Police
Report of the Royal North West Mounted Police for 1916. Ottawa, The King's Printer, 1917.
Report of the Bathurst Inlet Patrol, 1917-18. Ottawa, The King's Printer, 1918.

Vilhjalmur Stefansson
The Friendly Arctic, by Vilhjalmur Stefansson. New York, Macmillan, 1921, copyright renewed 1949. By kind permission of Evelyn Stefansson Nef.

John Hornby and Edgar Christian
Unflinching, by Edgar Christian. London, J. Murray, 1937. By kind permission of John Murray (Publishers) Ltd.

Thierry Mallet
Glimpses of the Barren Lands, by Thierry Mallet. New York, privately published, 1930. By kind permission of the Atlantic Monthly and Revillon Frères, Paris.

Picture Credits

Front jacket illustration by Fred Bruemmer

XI National Portrait Gallery, London

XII Metropolitan Toronto Library Board (from *Back: Narrative of the Land Expedition*)

XIII Metropolitan Toronto Library Board (from *Back: Narrative of the Land Expedition*)

XIV Farley Mowat

XV Alberta Archives (Ernest Brown Collection)

XVI Metropolitan Toronto Library Board (from *Whitney: On Snowshoes to the Barrengrounds*)

XVII Fred Bruemmer

XVIII Metropolitan Toronto Library Board (from *Tyrrell: Across the Sub-Arctics of Canada*)

XIX University of Toronto Library

XX University of Toronto Library

XXI Dan Thomas

XXII Sergeants' Mess, "O" Division, R.C.M.P.

XXIII Public Archives of Canada

XXIV Metropolitan Toronto Library Board (from *MacBeth: Policing the Plains*)

XXV Metropolitan Toronto Library Board (from *Noice: With Stefansson in the Arctic*)

XXVI Metropolitan Toronto Library Board (from *Stefansson: The Friendly Arctic*)

XXVII Metropolitan Toronto Library Board (from *Whalley: The Legend of John Hornby*)

XXVIII Metropolitan Toronto Library Board (from *Whalley: The Legend of John Hornby*)

XXIX Metropolitan Toronto Library Board (from *Whalley: The Legend of John Hornby*)

XXX Glenbow-Alberta Archives

XXXI Farley Mowat

XXXII Fred Bruemmer

All illustrations appear in a 32-page section following page 216.

Index

464